To dear El

with love and gratitude
for all her support
and encouragement.

Much love and blessings

Danny Devoy.

SCARLETT

Darwin's secret

Danny Devoy

authorHOUSE®

AuthorHouse™ UK Ltd.
500 Avebury Boulevard
Central Milton Keynes, MK9 2BE
www.authorhouse.co.uk
Phone: 08001974150

© 2010 Danny Devoy. All rights reserved.

No part of this book may be reproduced, stored in a retrieval system, or transmitted by any means without the written permission of the author.

First published by AuthorHouse 10/20/2010

ISBN: 978-1-4520-3224-5 (sc)

This book is printed on acid-free paper.

To my dearly loved children
Helen Clare Martin and Emma

'I cannot bear the thoughts of you leaving the country without seeing you once again; the past is often in my memory, and I feel that I owe to you much bygone enjoyment and the whole destiny of my life…'

Charles Darwin

The Ordinary Life

Have you ever wondered what it would be like to take your last breath?

This was the question that occupied Harry's mind as he sucked in the last gulp of air, went down into the water and watched the bubbles ripple to the surface. He tried to put the thought out of his mind. As time passed the urge to breathe grew stronger every second. Harry fought it. He told himself to focus, to hold on, to keep going. He tried to concentrate on the stillness. He clenched his fist and looked up at the surface of the water.

'Hold on,' he repeated over and over to himself but the urge, the one primeval human instinct, the need, the desperate desire to breathe filled his mind. His lungs burned until he could stand it no longer. He pushed hard to the surface of the pool. Frantically he sucked the air into his lungs and hit the stop watch. Out of the corner of his eye he saw Bloom approach with the phone. He pulled himself up onto the white stone edge of the pool and dried his hands on a towel.

'Good time today, Harry?'

'Not bad. Thirty seconds better than yesterday, but not my best.'

'It's your brother.'

'Thank you Bloom.'

'George how are you? I'm great thanks. Really? And you think it may be genuine? Very well. Give me the address.'

Bloom handed him a notepad and pen. Harry scribbled down the address.

'Yes I know where it is. Thank you George. No I really meant it, thank you.'

Harry hung up and handed the phone back to Bloom.

'Better luck with your time tomorrow sir.'

'A modicum of encouragement rather than sarcasm might go a long way during your employment with me you know.'

'Well I haven't needed it during the last five years, Harry and I don't suppose I'll need it in the next five either.'

'You know, I'm not beyond finding a new assistant.'

'Good luck with that sir.'

'Yea, you're right. There aren't many people that would put up with me Bloom. By the way, George said he's found something that might just make life around here a little more interesting.'

'I'm thrilled sir! I really am!'

The following afternoon Harry set out for Chelmsford. He stopped the Rolls Royce Ghost at the end of the drive and let his eyes wander over the pale green marshes around the river Arun. He looked at St. Michael's church and the ruins of Amberley Castle.

Shades of his mortality entered his thoughts, and gloom began to swallow up his usual joie de vivre. The sadness slowly melted away as he observed a group of sandpipers rise simultaneously from the marsh and fly westward. Then in a balletic movement they turned as one towards the sea.

Harry took the exit to Chelmsford on the M25 and then turned towards Writtle. He parked the car on the green and walked towards the pub called the Knotted Oak. He went inside and ordered a beer. The barman was young, so young Harry wondered if he was even old enough to drink himself.

'Do you know a Mr. Parsons?'

'Yes. He's here' the barman pointed to a group of three men standing at the far end of the bar.

'Would you ask Mr. Parsons to join me over there?' Harry indicated a corner table near a window that overlooked the green. The boy looked at him as if to say 'ask him yourself' but he dutifully followed out Harry's request.

Harry took his beer and sat down. As he saw Parsons approaching with the parcel he stood up.

'How do you do Mr. Parsons? I believe you spoke to my brother George.'

Parsons held out a huge hand and began to laugh,

'I met him yes, but to tell you the truth I doubted whether you would turn up.'

'Why is that?'

'Well...I have to be honest with you, it is such a long shot, and I don't know what to make of the find myself.'

'Well if you will allow me to have a look perhaps I can make a judgement. I am only an amateur of course.'

'Right. Here you are.'

Parsons put the box on the table and removed the brown paper. It was a very old oblong box made of rosewood. Harry drew it towards him and looked intently at the initials in faded gold leaf beside the small key.

'You say you found it in Church Road Upper Norwood?'

'Yes. I'm doing renovation work there and it was pushed in-between the eaves.'

'What about the owner of the house, is it not rightfully his property?'

'Well he is selling the house on. I told him I found an old box and he said he wasn't interested.'

'What is the number of the house?'

'Number 140.'

Harry's heart began to race as he ran his fingers over the initials and then turned the key. As he opened it a fragrance wafted through the air, a dank old aroma with just a hint of sweet rose. The contents of the box were scattered with dried faded rose petals and what looked like the leaves from an acacia plant. Harry looked in silence at the box and its contents. He reached for the first thing that caught his eye, an old book. He picked it up carefully. It was a miniature book cut down from an old ship's logbook The writing was exquisite, but it was not a log. Harry sighed and felt a faint twinge of disappointment. It seemed to contain romantic poems and essays. He read on for a few moments, and then he put it aside and carefully lifted out the next item.

It was a thicker book that looked like a diary. As he picked it up he saw underneath it a tiny red shoe, the sort of shoe you would find in Asia or South America, a soft silk embroidered slipper-like shoe. He put the book aside and lifted out the shoe. It had something inside it. Harry opened it gently. A blue ribbon was folded around a faded gold chain with a single pearl and beside it a tarnished old coin.

Harry returned to the second book. It was smaller, thicker, and more fragile than the first. There were loose pages with pencil drawings mostly of ports… yes they looked like South American seaports. There was one small sketch of a very beautiful woman and… and…those initials again. The writing was in the same accomplished hand. Harry began to read. His heart missed a beat when he looked at the first date of entry… December 1831.

'Are you thinking of selling this material?'
'Do you think it is genuine?'
'I don't know.' Harry said.
'Well make me an offer.'
'Very well, I'll give you five hundred pounds for it.'
'Make it a grand.'
'Very well.' Harry took out the notes and put them on the table. He took a sheet of writing paper from his inside pocket with his address on it, Lyndhurst House, Amberley, Sussex. He wrote a few words on it and passed it to Parsons with the pen. Parsons signed, picked up his money, said goodbye and left.

Harry left the pub without finishing his beer and walked towards the car. He opened the passenger door and put the box carefully on the seat. He sat into the driver seat and fired up the engine. Harry knew he had probably wasted a grand, and yet he felt happier than he had done for a long time.

Just before he pulled out into the traffic he saw a Silver Cloud Rolls Royce pull up outside the pub. Harry waited, and who should have stepped out but Sir Ronald Reed. Harry had not seen him since his days in the City. He wondered what the dishonest rogue was up to. He pulled out into the traffic and didn't think of it again. In fact all Harry could think about now… was the contents of the box and the diary in particular.

There were many delicate feelings touching my heart, and many new events that I wanted to keep in my mind and never forget. During the second week of January I picked up a pen and began to write. I started with the first thing I could remember.

Tuesday 27th December 1831

My heart jumped and with a supreme effort, I opened my eyes. I was looking into the eyes of a man in uniform. His face was full of kindness and my heart melted as I gazed into those kind dark eyes.

My head ached and every part of my body felt sore and bruised. I tried to ask where I was but no words came out of my mouth. My eyes refused to stay open. I felt drops of water pass over my dried lips and trickle down my parched throat. Then I began to lapse back into sleep, a sleep so peaceful that I could not resist returning to it.

In a flash, I felt strong arms lift me and hold me close. I could feel a breath close to my forehead. I tried to ask,

'Have I fallen off the horse father? Are you carrying me home?'

No words came and I felt the darkness creeping over me again, slowly this time like the way the evening sky gives way to night. I sank down, down into the bliss of oblivion.

Wednesday 28th December 1831

Sometime later, I began to wake. Some sound – a horrible sound, had made me jump. I felt cold water flow over my face again but my eyes refused to open. I wanted to go back to that quiet soundless place of peace.

There it was again! I listened. Then I knew it was a scream and another scream. They were horrible screams of someone in pain. Why could I not care if someone was in pain? I tried to care and felt cold beads of perspiration stand out on my forehead.

There was not anything, not even the screams of someone in pain that could make me abandon this sleep. It knitted everything together and flowed over me like gentle water. Fragments of poems came and went in my mind and I kept seeing a ploughman…

'The ploughman homeward plods his weary way,
And leaves the world to darkness and to me.'
I sank down again into a protective space, a darkness.

Monday 2nd January 1832

I woke again with a quick beat of my heart. A sound woke me. I listened. I tried to open my eyes but my eyelids would not move. There was a voice humming a strange tune. I groaned. The voice stopped and then I felt a trickle of water flow over my eyelids and down my face. A soft towel patted my face dry. After blinking a few times I managed to open my eyes.

I was lying on a bed and a young girl with satin dark skin and dark hair was sitting by the bed smiling a beautiful happy smile. I had so many questions but my throat was very dry. As if reading my thoughts the girl brought a glass of water. I sat up took it and drank. It tasted peculiar. I looked around the room It was small and strange.

"Where…where am I?'

'You are on a ship.' The girl beamed,

She straightened the blankets. Then she tried to tidy my tangled hair.

The girl looked intently at me and said,

'Now, the Captain tell me to find him when you wake up, so you sit quiet and I go for him.'

She left.

'How did I come to be on a ship? Where is it going?'

My thoughts were racing, and my body was agitated. I forced myself to stay absolutely still. Lines of songs, rhymes, fragments of poems, Keats perhaps, continued to race through my mind and come intermittently into my head.

'My heart aches, and a drowsy numbness pains

My sense…'

A knock at the door,

'Come in'

A tall man in uniform came in and stood before me. I looked into his eyes. It was those eyes again. They radiated gentleness, confidence and a total alertness that nothing deceitful would ever get past. My heart beat faster and faster and then he bent down over the bed and spoke.

'I am delighted to see you are recovering. For a while we nearly lost you: and for a few days you were delirious. How do you feel now?'

'I am feeling much better and I am very grateful to you Captain.'

'My privilege Miss.'

There was a silence now and the Captain just stared into my eyes and I into his. In my mind, there were many questions but my heart held them back to prolong this exquisite moment.

'You must be very hungry,' he said breaking the silence and moving away.

'I am sorry to say we will probably not have on board any of the delicate food you are use to, however we can provide fresh fish, rice, peas, meat and tea.'

'Captain, I don't like meat, and a small amount of whatever else you have will be very acceptable. Thank you sir.'

Another silence followed.

'Could you tell me sir how I came to be aboard this ship?'

'Indeed, indeed. As we left Plymouth, and making our way through the Channel towards the Atlantic, the watch spotted a small rowing boat. There had been a dreadful storm, and I must admit that the small boat looked very precarious. The crew was sure that it was empty, nevertheless I gave the order for us to pull alongside and there you were lying unconscious. McCormick, our ship's surgeon, was called and he treated your injuries. I assigned Fuegia Basket to look after you and McCormick gave her instructions.'

'Thank you sir, I am most grateful. And this room I am in… is it a kind of emergency room for…people like me?'

For the first time he smiled,

'No, this is my cabin.'

'Oh Captain!' I immediately tried to sit up,

'I can't take your cabin.'

He moved closer to me and said,

'It is my prerogative to give up my cabin to a most

charming…'

He gave a little cough and started again,

'I willingly give up my cabin in the interest of such a deserving person as yourself. When we found you, you were covered in bruises and blisters, and your head was bleeding badly. You needed care and it was my privilege to provide it for you. Now tell me about yourself.'

'Well sir I can remember nothing that happened before. In fact I have no recollection whatever…I have no memory of anything before waking up in your…in your cabin sir.'

He went across the room and picked up a bag.

'I had your bag sent up.'

'Thank you sir.'

He handed me a leather bag. I opened it. There were two books in it. I opened one and there on the first page was a name, I looked intently at the neat writing, and sighed. I did not think it was my name…it meant nothing to me.

'Scarlett O'Mara' I whispered.

'I seem to remember that Scarlett may have been my name sir…but O'Mara I certainly do not recall.'

Another silence followed. I thought of what he said about my injuries.

'I must have been a dreadful sight sir.'

With the hint of a smile he said,

'No Miss O'Mara you were not. I…'

'Sir please, may I ask a favour of you? '

'Certainly'

'Please call me Scarlett; it is a name I like. Can we dispose of convention sir? I know it is quite outrageous, and I hope you do not think me impertinent.'

He smiled.

'I don't think that such familiarity is polite or indeed

appropriate.'

A short silence followed. Then he said,

'Well...Scarlett!' My cheeks reddened as I heard the word fall from his lips.

'In private...strictly in private mind you, I will call you by your Christian name. On the other hand this kind of familiarity is quite improper, and I am not even sure it is prudent for me to give in to such a whim of yours, however we must never forget to use full titles in public and keep the proprieties.'

I held out my hand and said,

'It is a bargain sir.'

He ignored my hand, and then just gazed into my eyes until the colour rose in my cheeks again. Then he leaned forward and said in a hushed tone,

'Scarlett, you are not to worry about anything. Think about the situation like this: this ship is my home and you are a guest in my home; I take full responsibility for you. Fuegia will stay with you during the day. If there is anything you need, tell her. I will check on your state of health each morning after my inspection and Stebbing and I must check the chronometers at noon. Then after dinner I must come to my desk here to write up my journal and the ship's log. The rest of the time, you will not be disturbed. Now, I must go...I must be about my duties...goodbye.'

He was gone...but I felt a real joy break in upon my being. Although I could not remember being in the rowing boat, in my mind and heart I now felt a great relief. What a kind-hearted Captain. His good looks enthralled me and I found it difficult not to continually gaze at him.

I wanted to dream now and think about the scene that had taken place, but my reverie was cut short. There was a knock on the cabin door. The girl with the beautiful smile came in with a basin of water and a towel.

'I wash you now?'

It was a question. I nodded.

'What is you called?'

'I don't know my name. I have forgotten everything. In the book it says Scarlett O'Mara'

'Miss O'Mara...'

'No, always call me Scarlett please.'

'Is that a colour Miss Scarlett?'

'I suppose so, in a way, and what is your name?'

'Fuegia Basket' she said with another beaming smile.

'Fuegia, what does that mean?'

' I will tell you another time, later.'

Wednesday 4th January

The days passed pleasantly and I recovered slowly. Soon I was able to get up for a short time each day. Fuegia was kind and took care of me. She washed my clothes and brought some of her own garments for me to wear.

The Captain came to the cabin thrice daily as arranged. I began to read the books that were in the bag. One was an anthology of poetry and the other was...

'A Vindication of the Rights of Women' by Mary Wollstonecraft (1792). I looked at the books and tried to remember my life before drifting out to sea – no answers came.

I told Fuegia,

'It's like having a blank piece of paper inside my head where my memory should be.'

I picked up the poetry book and began to read.

There was Milton, Wordsworth, Keats, James Thomson,

and many other excellent poets. Some of these beautiful poems I knew by rote. During the long evenings I read, or said them aloud to Fuegia. She stopped me often to ask the meaning and that ruined the rhythm and the flow.

I think the ship is slowing down but I am unable to discern very much, for so far I have only seen the inside of the Captain's cabin. At times I can hear the waves rippling against the stern and the sails flapping against the masts.

I improved a little each day and Fuegia told fascinating stories about her life and experiences in England and tales about her own country, Tierra del Fuego in South America. The ship, I gathered was on its way to South America. What was going to happen to me? Would I be put off at some port and try to find a ship for England? It was all too much to think about so I put these thoughts aside until I felt strong enough to work it all out.

We kept to the routine the Captain had set, nevertheless I have only a brief recollection of some days. The weather was bad at one point and there was a good deal of swell on the sea. I woke often with pain in my head and then listened to the piped orders and the shouts of the officers, but I could never keep my eyes open for long and had to give in to the sleep that enfolded me.

I wondered if Fuegia was on deck the night of my rescue.

'Did you see what happened the night they took me out of the rowing boat Fuegia?'

'Yes, Capen Fitzroy lift you up like a doll.'

We both laughed.

'I remember he...'

'He what?'

'Later' When Fuegia did not want to tell she always

said, 'later'.

'No, now Fuegia.'

'Well...Mr. McCormick look after you and say take you to sickbay. The Captain say no, and lift you up in his arms. He held you very close to him...your skin very white. He tell me walk with him and I follow him to his cabin. He put you down softly in his bed, and covered you with blanket. Then he look at you and say,

'Dear God, I hope she does not die. You stay with her Fuegia.'

'Yes Captain' I say, and I see that look in his eye Miss Scarlett.'

'What look Fuegia?'

'I don't know how explain... a look that say...he know who you are.'

'How could he know who I am Fuegia?'

'I don't know, Fuegia silly girl!'

I loved hearing this account of my rescue and I asked Fuegia to repeat it for me many times. My heart thrilled each time with the thought of being in the Captain's arms.

Before the Captain came, each day after breakfast and his inspection, Fuegia came and helped me wash and dress. Then I sat back on the bed, and Fuegia sat on the floor. The Captain knocked; when he heard my voice he entered and asked if I was feeling better. Then at noon he came with Stebbing to check the chronometers. After dinner we waited for the Captain. He came punctually to write up the ship's log, arrange his papers, and make the entries in his journal.

The days continued to pass quietly in this way and Fuegia began to tell me about her life. Then one day I said,

'You like the Captain don't you Fuegia.'

'Yes, he very good man, he teach me many things. He very kind, if I want anything and he can give me then he give. He pay for me to go to school near London, in Wal... Walth... Walthamstow.'

'He sent you to school?'

'Yes, he sent York and Jemmy too.'

'York and Jemmy?'

'Yes York my friend and Jemmy boy form Woollya.'

'There are three of you on the ship?'

'Yes, three.'

'When I tried to wake up Fuegia I heard screaming. Was I dreaming? I was dreaming, I am sure of it.'

'No Miss Scarlett some crewmen were flogged.'

'No. That cannot be true. The Captain would never allow anyone to be flogged.'

'Yes Miss Scarlett, many men punished, but only four men flogged because go and drink much on Christmas day, make ship very dirty then leave and not stay on duty. The Captain mad with them, they start flogging when we out to sea.'

I put my head in my hands.

'The screams I heard were real.'

'Yes Miss, them men did scream real loud.'

I could not work it out. How could this kind altruistic Captain flog the men? There must be some other answer.

On the first day the Captain came to the cabin I sat in silence almost afraid to move. Fuegia sat on the floor and played with pieces of coloured cloth. Some days Mr. Hellyer or Mr. Usborne assisted the Captain then Fuegia left. In this way the proprieties were upheld... now that my health was improving I was never left alone with the Captain.

As the days passed, I relaxed and as the Captain

concentrated on his writing, I read poetry and tried to understand 'The Vindication of Women'. It was an engaging essay and I did remember some parts of it, so I knew that I had studied it before. Mary Wollstonecraft's ideas appealed to me and showed the way forward for women, a way that would lift us out of the dire position we are in now, especially with regard to the law of rights, inheritance and above all education.

Sometimes I looked up and saw the Captain staring at me. As our eyes met, he directed his gaze back to his papers. I often gazed at him too while he concentrated on his work.

His countenance was daunting. His presence was awesome, demanding respect, devotion, almost homage. When he looked up and saw me looking at him I looked away as he did. His features were sharp, his face slim and his dark eyes were burning with energy.

His eyes seemed to look straight through me right to my inmost soul, not in a harsh or demeaning way but in a way that seeks out truth relentlessly. There was a gentleness there too that spoke of compassion, understanding and empathy. His lips held a full and perfect elliptic shape and when he spoke his voice was kind and fresh like a soft spring breeze. It was also harsh as tree bark when he was annoyed.

His attire was impeccable. The blues and gold of his uniform looked perfect on him, as on no other officer and this added to the distinctive power of his presence. His whole life was directed by self-discipline, and strength of mind. He was assertive and wholly impatient with imperfection in any form.

Over the days I had assimilated this portrait of him, and held these details of his features in a special place in my mind, and in my heart, so that I could conjure up this image when he was not in close proximity to me.

I longed to be alone with him and converse with him and see what he thought about the world. Did he like poetry; did he read the Bible? Did he worry about slavery, about the affects of the industrial revolution? Did he care about the long hours children worked?

Did he believe that women had rights, especially to education? Did he even ever think about the position of women? It was so strange that I could remember all these details about the world yet about myself I could remember nothing.

When I felt well again, I asked the Captain to allow me go to another part of the ship to sleep, but he dismissed the request in a way that said,

'I have more important things to think about.'

Thursday 5th January 1832

It was a bright warm morning and the Captain said that I could take a walk on the deck with Fuegia each day around noon. This was the time the Captain and Mr. Stebbing checked the chronometers.

'My clothes sir, they are not very presentable.'

'Oh...borrow some from Fuegia.' he said.

I looked at Fuegia and she threw her eyes upward and shrugged.

'At our first civilized port of call Miss O'Mara, you will go ashore and buy a new wardrobe. I will draw the funds myself.'

'Thank you sir, but that would not be correct sir...I...' but he was gone.

'Why does he ignore what I say when he feels like it?' My eyes were blazing. Fuegia laughed.

'Why he think my clothes fit you?'

Then we both laughed. Fuegia ran off and came back with an armful of clothes. For the next half hour, we laughed and laughed as I, with my slim figure tried on the large capes and dresses of the very robust Fuegia.

At last, we managed to tie up a blue satin dress around my body and I put on my shabby black cape over it.

'Good' Fuegia said with her usual beaming smile. Fuegia began to brush my hair.

'So much hair Miss Scarlett…beautiful, what colour you call this hair Miss Scarlett?

'The colour… auburn I think, no a dark brown, I don't really know.'

She brushed and brushed until I said,

'Enough, please.'

'Beautiful, so beautiful.' Fuegia whispered.

Then she parted the hair and tied a blue ribbon around it and we were ready to go. Fuegia gave me her arm and we edged up the companionway out onto the main deck. The fresh sea air felt delightful and I stopped to breathe it in. The officers at the wheel fell silent. Then one of them came forward.

'Delighted to see you are feeling better Miss O'Mara. Welcome on board His Majesty's Brig' he said with a smile and slight bow.

'Thank you.'

'Fuegia maybe Miss O'Mara could sit by the gunroom sky light.'

'Yes Mr. Wickham.'

'First' I said firmly, 'I'd like to look at the sea.'

We moved slowly towards the rail. I inhaled and felt the fresh salty air fill my lungs. I stood still and admired the blueness of the sky. A faint warm, gentle wind brushed against my face, like an English summer breeze. Then a strong gust of wind blew through my hair, loosening the ribbon and whirling it and my hair all over my face. The amused officers smiled and Fuegia just laughed and laughed.

'*You must wear bonnet Miss Scarlett you must wear bonnet.*'

'*I will not wear a bonnet.*' *I said.*

The officers smiled. If they had not known my Christian name before they certainly knew it now.

The ship ran to clockwork and the routine was strictly kept. During the following days, I walked on the deck and began to recognize the officers, and they saluted me politely whenever our paths crossed. I longed to talk to them but felt it would be inappropriate, after all, we had not been formally introduced, and in any case, they, like the Captain, were always busy.

Today when Fuegia and I went on the deck for our walk, Fuegia introduced me to the other Indian boy called Jemmy Button. Like Fuegia, he laughed a lot.

'*You have much brown shinny hair Miss, but you very thin*' *he said.*

Jemmy started to ask questions, normal questions like where did I live in England, I was about to tell him about my memory when Fuegia said,

'*Captain say you ask Miss Scarlett no questions Jemmy, and he mean, no questions.*'

'*Very well, very well*' *he said and went off the deck muttering.*

'*You did not tell me the Captain said that Fuegia.*'

'*Yes he say that Miss.*'

At that moment, I turned and there was the Captain. He approached.

'Good afternoon ladies.'

'Captain' I said with a curtsey and in a low tone. I looked intently at him. He was tall, ramrod straight, and his dark, abundant hair was shining. It waved and rippled as if, allowed to grow, it would be a mass of curls. The thin line of a moustache covered his upper lip and his side-whiskers framed all his features into a most agreeable harmonious silhouette.

'Would you like to know more about the ship Miss O'Mara?'

'I would, if it is convenient sir.'

'Indeed, indeed.'

'Come and meet some of my officers.' We moved towards the wheel. Fuegia followed. 'Lieutenant Wickham, first lieutenant,'

'How do you do Miss'

'Very well thank you Mr. Wickham.' I looked at his clear eyes and black wavy hair.

'Mr. Sulivan, second lieutenant, Mr. Chaffers, Mr. Stokes and Mr. Bennett'

I said 'how do you do,' and noticed that none of them apart from Mr. Sulivan were at ease. Spread out on the poop deck skylight was a map of the boat drawn by King. The Captain explained the details,

'Besides myself, there are 74 people on board, 75 including you.'

'No, impossible it is such a small ship.' I put my hand over my mouth. I was about to apologize when he said,

'No, not impossible Miss O'Mara' to my great relief he smiled.

'Thirty four crew members keep the ship sailing, raise and lower sails, as you see climb the rigging, clean the decks, cook and keep lookout. I, with my officers plot the ship's course and give the orders.'

He looked into my eyes and then quickly looked back at the map.

'There are also on board sail makers, ship's doctor, marines, eight trainee sailors and three Native Americans, Fuegia is one of them. Then there is the ship's artist Mr. Earle, and Mr. Darwin our natural philosopher.'

'Like… Locke or Hume do you mean sir?'

'No Miss O'Mara not like John Locke or David Hume, a natural philosopher looks into the workings of natural history, geology, plant and animal life and the like.'

He sounded so severe,

'Oh I'm sorry sir.'

He smiled again. I was so relieved I blurted out,

'I made you smile twice Captain. Forgive me for being so bold sir, but you should smile more often sir.'

'You will not take the liberty of addressing a Captain in His Majesty's Navy in such a manner… Madam'

He raised his voice. The words flew out at me through his teeth like a frustrated teacher to an inattentive pupil.

'I am very sorry sir.' I said and held back the tears flowing into my eyes.

I saw him blush. I had embarrassed him in front of his officers and somehow even then I knew he would not forgive me easily. The officers were all busy pretending they had not heard. I could see the mounting tension in their faces. This interview was not going well. I wanted the deck to open and swallow me nevertheless; I took courage and said,

'Forgive me sir for unintentionally offending you. I am

most grateful to you for all you have told me about the ship. Will the Captain please excuse me now, as I feel tired?'

He looked at me for a second and then lowered his eyes back to the map. I made a curtsey.

'Mr. Bennet escort Miss O'Mara from the deck.'

His words flew through the air like crystal and they pierced right into my heart. He dismissed me as he would any member of the crew. Mr. Bennett came forward.

'Yes sir, this way please.'

'Thank you once again Captain.' I curtsied again; he did not look up or answer.

Mr. Bennett escorted Fuegia and me to the Captain's cabin. Fuegia went off to her friends. I lay on his bed and pondered.

I had not behaved correctly, speaking to the Captain in that familiar way. I hoped he would forgive me. However, did he have to be so stern with me? It was only a comment… nothing rude or derogatory. I must be careful how I approached him in future and never ever allow my true feelings for him to show.

After a beautiful day there was a bright moonlight night, and I found it difficult to sleep. The faux pas of the morning's encounter with the Captain troubled me and I could not sleep.

Friday 6th January

As the days past, I became more uncomfortable taking up the Captain's cabin. Whenever I suggested moving he refused to listen. I began to think he did not know where else I could stay. During my daily walks on the deck, I had become friendly with Mr. Sulivan, the second Lieutenant. I have to admit that I was delighted when he was on duty.

He was so easy to talk to and so full of life and vitality that my eyes lit up when I saw him. One day I explained the problem to him about taking up the Captain's cabin.

'What do you say Miss O'Mara to taking over my small cabin? It has a cramped wooden cot, but then you are of a very slight stature, and I can use a hammock elsewhere.'

'Are you sure Mr. Sulivan?'
'My pleasure Miss.'
'Shall I suggest it to the Captain then?'
'No…eh…no Miss, I think you should leave that to me.'
'I will not forget this act of kindness Mr. Sulivan.'
'My pleasure Miss.'

Fuegia and I continued the strict routine of the ship. Some evenings the Captain allowed me to have supper with the officers, but mostly I ate alone. Then before bed, Fuegia came again and we laughed, talked and read poetry, and at eight o'clock Fuegia left.

I often took to wondering then what was going to happen to me. Perhaps I could begin a new life somewhere. The question of what was to become of me began to dominate my waking thoughts and agitate my soul. What kind of life had I had before my rescue? Where was I born? Who were my parents? I tried to feel hopeful but most nights I twisted and turned until sleep took over and lulled away my anxiety. The fear never totally went away…I often sobbed myself to sleep wondering what exactly would happen to… an orphan of the storm.

It was a full two days before Mr. Sulivan spoke to the Captain and I had been almost two weeks on the ship when the Captain agreed for me to move into Mr. Sulivan's cabin. I was so relieved to have my own space that I thanked Mr. Sulivan profusely. I collected my few belongings and tidied the bed. I thought of the Captain lying there. I lifted the cover to my lips for a brief moment and left. When Fuegia came to visit me now we could talk and laugh at our leisure and we became good friends.

I had not been formally introduced to Mr. Darwin, the ship's natural philosopher. Sometimes he dined with the officers and we nodded politely to each other. The officers had great fun teasing us both. The way they teased Mr. Darwin was different from the way they teased me.

Although new to seafaring, Mr. Darwin had learnt most of the nautical terms and took a prodigious interest in the everyday sailing and mechanical workings of the ship. He would allow the officers to proceed with their trickery and then at the last moment call their bluff.

I knew that the officers called him 'Philosopher' or 'Philos' for short. I also knew that at times they called him 'The Flycatcher', especially Mr. Wickham. I longed to ask him what a ship's Natural Philosopher did, and what it meant exactly. I was always a little afraid of annoying him. However, when I heard him talking to the officers it seemed to me that he was a very amiable man. After Mr. Wickham had formally introduced us I began to exchange a few words with him on different subjects.

When I heard he was about to become a vicar I asked him questions about the Bible, the Creation and the Flood. I wondered how I knew the Bible so well. I was told that for a time he studied medicine, so one evening I approached the subject of my loss of memory with him.

'Mr. Darwin, sir, I believe you studied medicine for a while is that so?'

'Yes indeed at Edinburgh.'

'I wondered if then you knew anything about memory loss, and do you think I will ever remember again sir where I was, or what kind of life I had before I was rescued?'

'Yes, I think so, just when you least expect it. Perhaps

some trivial thing, something you see or hear may just open the floodgates and you will remember everything.'

He smiled,

'On the other hand, you may just remember little by little. The human brain is a complicated organ Miss O'Mara and my knowledge of it, to say the least, is minimal.'

'Ever since I regained consciousness sir, I have tried each day, and each night to remember, but it is all a blank.'

'Ah…well…now perhaps therein lies the problem Why do you not go about your daily life as if your memory was intact. Cease every effort to recover it. Maybe your effort is the one barrier in the way of its recovery.'

'I will try your method Mr. Darwin.'

'Now do not expect miracles. It is only a thought.'

'Yes, thank you sir, I am much obliged to you.'

'My pleasure Miss'

'By the way, if I may be so bold sir…how are you feeling? I understand the motion of the ship causes you to feel ill?'

'Very well indeed, thank you.'

Darwin stood, excused himself and left. There was a snigger from some of the officers.

'Did I say something wrong gentlemen, was I unknowingly impolite?'

The officers laughed aloud then.

'I am sure you meant well Miss, but you see Mr. Darwin has had to put up with a lot of teasing about his illness from us officers. To mention it in front of us was hardly appropriate.' Mr. Sulivan said.

'But…I had no idea… will he forgive me?'

The officers laughed again.

'He will not even remember what happened.' said Mr.

Bynoe.

Nevertheless I thought, I would apologize to him, for it seemed to me that he was the kind of person who would never forget anything.

From the moment I moved into Mr. Sulivan's cabin strange things started to happen. For weeks, I had twisted, turned and screamed in my sleep. I only knew this because the officers on the watch told me. When I was in Captain Fitzroy's cabin I never made a sound... what was happening to me? Sometimes the officers on the watch came and knocked on the door. I woke up then and said,

'Sorry, I am perfectly well thank you.' Then I stayed awake for hours afraid that the dreadful dream would come back and I would begin screaming in my sleep again. Sometimes Captain Fitzroy heard my screams and came to me himself.

'Miss O'Mara what is the matter?'

'Sir I am awake now. Kindly accept my apologies for disturbing you.'

I longed to tell him to open the door...my heart was aching to speak to him. However I knew too well how fastidious he was about such things.

One night during a rough sea, Mr. Stokes heard me screaming intermittently all night. At 3.45 am the screams were continuous and Mr. Stokes, knocking loudly on the door, and calling my name, received no reply. He entered the cabin and found me writhing on the floor. He tried in vain to calm and console me. He sent Usborne to fetch the Captain. Captain Fitzroy and Darwin both came and squeezed in filling the tiny cabin. My head was aching and I felt agitated. I could hear everything they said although their voices seemed far away.

'Thank you Mr. Stokes for alerting us, please return to your duties.'

'Yes sir…shall I fetch Mr. McCormick sir?'

'No, we will attend to this.'

I felt a damp towel placed on my forehead.

'No…no…go away' I shouted.

Then I felt a very cold hand lift up my wrist as if to take my pulse. From that moment I felt safe again. A feeling of serene calm came over me instantly. Although I could not open my eyes or speak I could hear the Captain speaking, but he sounded far away. The Captain said,

'I am almost sure all this is the result of trauma. It must have been dreadful in that small boat all through the storm. What was she doing in the boat in the first place? Did you notice Darwin how she reacted when I held her hand?'

'Remarkable…perhaps all those hours alone in the storm…she may be reliving them in her dreams. Then a human touch reassures her she is not alone.'

'Yes, perhaps.'

'Look at all these notes, she certainly seems to write a lot.'

'Yes, and they seem to me to be ill organized and in a very disordered array.'

The Captain let go of my hand and lifted me into the cot. He covered me with a blanket. Almost immediately, I came to myself again and opened my eyes. The shock of seeing the two gentlemen so close to me in the cabin astounded me, I pulled the blankets up around my throat,

'Oh, Captain Fitzroy…Mr. Darwin…what is happening?'

'Nothing my dear…you were having a bad dream I think.' Fitzroy spoke quietly.

'A bad dream…is it night…or day? What time is it?'

27

Fitzroy consulted his watch.

'Just after four in the morning'

I covered my face with my hands.

'Please forgive me gentlemen…what a trouble I am to everyone.'

'No that is not true, is it Darwin?'

'No, but we would like to help you. Can you remember anything…were you dreaming?'

'Yes. It is always the same dream sir. I see the cabin filling with water and I can't move to get out. The water keeps coming, first over my legs and when it gets to my mouth I panic and try to hold my breath.'

'I see.' Fitzroy looked anxious.

'Do you remember anything before being found in the boat?'

'No sir '

'Did you follow my instructions in the matter?'

'Yes Mr. Darwin I did. I put every effort aside as you instructed.'

'Well we must talk about this again at a more civilized hour Miss O'Mara. I hope you are comfortable now.' Fitzroy said with a sigh.

'Yes sir, I am much obliged to you both gentlemen.'

The gentlemen ducked out of the small cabin and then I called out,

'Captain Fitzroy'

'Yes… go ahead Darwin I will be along shortly.'

'Oh certainly.' said Darwin.

Captain Fitzroy ducked back into the tiny cabin.

'Are you sure you feel better?' He asked.

'Yes sir, forgive me for saying this sir but tonight I have discovered a wonderful thing, a feeling of relief such as I

never knew before in my life...that is...that you will always be there when I am in need of help. I have not known that feeling of security since my parents d...died. My goodness, I have just remembered my parents are dead.'

Fitzroy bent down towards me,

'I am so sorry to hear that. Can you remember them... what they looked like I mean?'

'Yes...yes...I can. They were exceptional parents and I don't know how they died.'

For some strange reason I was not sad. I felt no hint of sadness.

'You are not to worry Miss O'Mara. You have come onto this ship and are now under my patronage. Be assured I will look after you.' Fitzroy whispered.

I nodded and looked into his dark tired eyes. He looked into my eyes and for a moment, I knew heaven existed. I did not dare speak. My head felt light and my heart pounded. I was afraid to utter a sound, afraid to think lest anything might end the consummate joy I was feeling.

'Sir may I ask you a question?'

'Of course, what is it?'

'Do you think we have met before sir?'

He smiled.

'When I lifted you out of the boat that night and you opened your eyes and looked at me, I felt sure I had seen those eyes before...they are not the kind of eyes one would ever forget Miss O'Mara. However, when I could not remember I put the matter out of my head.'

'Do you remember Christmas time 1817?

'What! When I was twelve years old!'

'Yes, my family were the guests of the Marquess of Northampton at Castle Ashby House...you knew the

family, their name was Compton.'

'Yes of course'

'We were out in the carriage for a drive and stopped near your home, Wakefield Lodge. My half brother James and I were playing in the meadow when you came up to us and insisted we go with you to the house for tea'.

'Was that you? But you said your name was Charlotte.'

'No you thought I said Charlotte, but I said, Scarlett.'

'I see.'

'There was a beautiful lady...do you remember what she said?'

'Yes... she said, what an exquisite, beautiful little girl. I hope you always have such good taste Robert.'

I smiled,

'You remembered.'

'Yes'

Then I lifted my hand and put it gently against his hand. For a moment I thought I saw a soft tenderness shine through the strict features, but in a second it was gone. He now looked astonished, stood up and back from the cot.

'Goodnight dear child.'

I whispered back,

'Goodnight'

I sat quietly in the bed. How did I remember that incident when it is almost impossible for me to remember anything about the past? I remained very still because I was experiencing such feelings as I had never felt before. Feelings that let me rise on eagle's wings; my heart was full in a way words can never say. My body felt light as if I could just stretch out my arms and soar upwards, gravity having no control over me.

I knew now that this is what was called falling in

love. Words and lines from all the love poems I had ever read began to stream into my consciousness. I went over words of Wordsworth, Keats, and Shelly. However it was the words of the Bard I kept repeating,

> *'For thy sweet love rembere'd such wealth brings*
> *That then I scorn to change my state with kings,'*

I repeated these words like a prayer. These new thoughts and feelings had ignited my entire being with a new energy; it was a long time before I fell asleep. From that night onwards, I never screamed in my sleep again. By contrast, my memory did not return whether I tried to remember the past or not.

A Forgery

While Harry read the diary he kept all the pencil drawings in place, now he noted the pages and placed them in a line on the table with the sketch marked Scarlett. There were six sketches altogether. He looked at the drawings intently under the magnifying glass; they were ports along the east coast of South America. They had the old names. The first one which read, 'Porto Praya C.V' must mean Cape Verde Islands. Then 'The rocks at St. Paul' and by far the most detailed sketch was 'Bahia' or San Salvador, and smaller sketches of Rio de Janeiro and Montevideo.

He looked at them for a long time and then turned them over. On the back were small flowers and sea creatures so faint you could barely see them. On the back of the one marked Montevideo there was a sketch of a man…not a very good one, she was better at drawing flowers and ports than people. He gazed at the minute sketches for a long time and then replaced them within the diary.

'Well Bloom, what do you think?'

Bloom and Harry looked at each other trying to read each other's thoughts.

'It is obvious that the diary tells about some events

on board ship, and the log book is a work of fiction written by the same person.'

'Yes' Harry whispered. He concentrated on the quality of the writing, the aging of the paper, the slight fragrance as he absentmindedly drew his fingers through his thick dark hair. Bloom began to speak and then stopped. After a few moments, Harry stood up and walked to the window. It was a glorious day. He turned and said,

'Is it possible that the diary is genuine?'

'It may be or…of course it could be a forgery'

Harry resumed his seat.

'But the drawings, the initials, the quality of the paper, the box, it all looks real. All the clues are there'

'That is true sir…but…a good forger would always leave clues.'

A long silence followed while Harry turned the tiny red shoe over in his hands.

'So what do we do now?'

Harry put the small shoe down, stood up and walked back to the window. He looked through the Georgian window out over the rose beds to the line of poplars. Harry was well aware that he had a romantic streak, especially about marine artefacts. However, it was time to make a rational decision.

'We leave it be Bloom. I will continue to browse through the diary and add it to my collection as a curiosity.'

'Very well sir, a good decision I think.'

Harry looked down the drive and across the vivid green fields towards Amberley. He was well known in the village. He made generous contributions to many local causes. Three times a year he gave extravagant parties. He invited the local M.P., friends in government and in the business world, and a few celebrities. He knew that anyone looking at his life from the outside would see that it looked good, clean, happy and fulfilling. His life was not like that. There were irritating problems that kept him awake at night.

He had never found anyone he felt he could ask to marry him, and not a single member of his own family ever came to see him. There was a rift, a long time ago, trouble concerning his eldest brother Billy. His family would not forgive him and George was the only one who spoke to him.

There was the loneliness of course. He had been attracted to several women over the years. They were mostly quiet unobtrusive women. He had never met that special woman, a woman he could call a soul mate, one who would be a friend, one who would share his enthusiasm for ships, for nature, for books, antiques, no, that one he had never met.

There was something else, a strange thing, a secret he had kept since his youth. When it happened he never told anyone. It affected him badly. He developed a stutter and had to attend a speech therapist for a year. While he applied himself to making a fortune it had passed out of his consciousness. Now, in his mid thirties it had come back to haunt him. This ghost from his teenage years woke him up at night in a feverish heat and the whole scene loomed up before his eyes as if it were happening again.

Apart from his underwater prowess, Harry had two passions, one was naval history and the other was fencing. The only addition he had made to the house when he bought it was to build a west wing containing a gym, a Jacuzzi and a salle d'armes.

Bloom and Harry, being roughly the same build, made excellent sparing partners, and they spent the latter part of this glorious summer's day locked in a duel. They moved energetically through the streaks of light and shade that speckled the room from the waning sun. It lit up the shining blades of their epees and turned them sapphire blue as the last rays of the setting sun flickered through the stained glass window.

'Has it occurred to you Bloom what kind of adventure we might embark upon if the diary is genuine?'

Bloom noticed the intensity in Harry's deep blue eyes and said,

'Indeed it has sir.'

The following day Harry pulled into the car park at Kew and made his way to the archives. He stepped towards a computer station, inserted his card and ordered the documents he wished to read. While he waited he sat down and opened the diary. Sitting near him was a very attractive woman, who looked at him and said, pointing to the diary,

'That looks interesting'

'Yes, I'm hoping to check out the dates.'

She stretched out her hand and asked,

'May I?'

'Certainly' Harry said. He passed the diary.

She looked at it carefully and after a few minutes said,

'Don't be too disappointed but I would say almost

without a doubt, that it is a forgery.'

She seemed to observe the look on Harry's face and added,

'Forgive me' she opened her handbag, took out a card and passed it to Harry.

It read,

'Lucy Harrington, archivist...'

'How do you do' Harry stretched out his hand, and Lucy shook it and said,

'I'm sorry to have said that so abruptly, you obviously were hoping it was genuine.'

Harry took a card from his inner pocket and handed it to Lucy.

'Well I'm exploring the possibility.' He smiled and asked how she could have made such an instant judgement.

She looked at Harry's card,

'Well, when you are looking at old documents everyday you get a feeling about them.'

'And you feel this is a fake.'

'Yes...that is on an instinctive level, but of course I could be wrong.'

'To tell you the truth, it was the place where the diary was found that really set me thinking seriously about it.'

'Where was that?'

'140, Church Road, Upper Norwood.'

'Oh! The last residence of Admiral Robert Fitzroy.'

'Yes. Goodbye Miss Harrington.'

'Goodbye.'

He looked at the computer and saw that the documents were ready. He checked through to the reading room. Not for the first time in his life did Harry allowed his eyes to delight in the scrupulous log and meticulous handwriting of the Captain of the Beagle.

Sunday 8th January 1832

Apart from speaking to Fuegia during the day, I sometimes spoke with the officers when I walked on deck if they were not busy. From time to time I had the pleasure of their lively conversation when the Captain allowed me to have supper with them.

However, he only gave his permission now and then, and I often thought he gave it reluctantly.

I had a deep admiration for Captain Fitzroy that could never be openly expressed. My love of literature, poetry, nature and my interest in the life on board kept me occupied but the only fun and enjoyment in my life was when I sat with the officers at supper.

Sunday was kept as a special day on board with the Divine Service and Hymn Singing. It was a time of relaxation, for the crew of course...not for the Captain. My heart softened and my spirit ascended as I listened to the Captain's pure voice and perfect diction ring through the clear air as he read from the Book of Common Prayer. The hymns rang out over the deep blue sea and became associated in my mind with the harmony of the young choristers of King's Chapel Cambridge and rose like incense on the evening air.

Sometimes Mr. Darwin was in the gunroom. Mr. Earle, the ship's artist was often there too. He looked at me in a strange way. He made me blush. From the beginning, I had a strong dislike of Mr. Earle and avoided him as much as possible. I was aware that he was a great artist and the Captain thought highly of him. Mr. Darwin seemed amazed at the stories he told of his life in Australia and New Zealand, but if I came upon them while they were speaking they inevitably stopped talking or changed the subject.

Sometimes Mr. Matthews, a preacher from the Missionary Society came in. He was hoping to set up a mission station in Tierra del Fuego, where Fuegia was born. Although I enjoyed talking about Christianity and the Bible, I found Mr. Matthews a very quiet person. No matter what views I expressed he simply nodded. I wondered how he could possibly communicate with the native people if this was the extent of his communicating abilities.

The language of ships and sea faring was new to me so the officers set up traps for me, asked me impossible questions and teased me.

'What do you think 'Scrub the mud off the dead man's face' means Miss O' Mara?'

'I don't think I know exactly. Is it about taking a template from a dead man's face?'

They all roared with laughter and Mr. Darwin smiled.

'What does it mean then?'

'It is a song the crew sings, and 'the dead man's face' is a triangular piece of metal with three holes in it used to connect the two anchor chains when the ship is moored. It is often covered in mud.' Mr Sulivan replied with a smile.

'I see. Well may I put a question now to you Mr. Wickham?'

'Please do.'

'Are you familiar with these lines?'
'Now the black Tempest strikes the astonished Eyes;
Now down the Steep the flashing Torrent flies;
The trembling Sun now plays o'er ocean blue,
And now rude Mountains frown amid the Skies;'
'I'm afraid I don't know Miss.' said Wickham.
'What about you Mr. Sulivan?'
'Is it…Milton?'
'No not Milton' said Mr. Darwin.
'Tell us who wrote it, please, Miss O'Mara.'
'It is a poet you should all know. Very well, shall I give you a hint?'
'Yes please do' said Mr. Bynoe.
'What can you say about 'Rule Britannia?'
'James Thomson' said Mr. Sulivan.
'Well done Mr. Sulivan…and the name of the poem?'
'That I do not know.'
'It is from 'The Castle of Indolence' his last poem if I remember correctly gentlemen'.
'We are all quite sure you remember correctly Miss O'Mara.'
Wickham shot a smile across the table at me.
'You were careful not to give a quote from 'The Seasons' Miss O'Mara…because you knew right well we might have recognized that.' Sulivan raised his eyebrows.
'Well I would say the score is even now Miss O'Mara.' said Wickham.
'Oh! Indeed I do not think so Mr. Wickham. You officers are well ahead on points for making a fool of me. At least I only test your poetic knowledge.'
I looked hesitantly at Mr. Darwin.
'What do you say for a philosophical question? Mr.

Darwin perhaps you would set one for us.'

'Do you not consider that you have shown up our ignorance sufficiently for one night Miss O'Mara…how about we save it for the next time,' said Wickham.

'Very well gentlemen, but remember it may be a long while before the Captain gives me permission to dine with you again.'

A kind of weighty silence fell on the company, and I wondered if I had said something wrong.

'Did I say something wrong gentlemen?'

No one answered my question and then Mr. Darwin said,

'I must say Miss O'Mara you take all this jesting in the very best way.'

'Thank you sir.'

'Will you sing for us Miss?' a voice asked from another part of the room.

'Very well…how about 'Amazing Grace' gentlemen?'

'Thank you Miss O'Mara.' said Darwin.

I stood up, paused to find the note and take a deep breath. Then Covington, who played the fiddle and I think helped Mr. Darwin, gave me a very squeaky 'D' and accompanied me very quietly.

'Amazing grace how sweet the sound
That saved a wretch like me.
I once was lost but now I'm found
Was blind but now I see.'

When I finished all the verses, the entire company clapped and shouted for an encore.

I sat down.

'Encore' another shout went up.

I then stood to take my leave. The officers stood.

'I will sing again another evening if the Captain

allows it gentlemen.'

'Goodnight Miss, thank you Miss'

'Goodnight gentlemen, Mr. Sulivan, Mr Darwin, Mr. Wickham.'

Tuesday 10th January

I began to take every opportunity to observe Mr. Darwin's work. It was pitiful to see how the motion of the ship disturbed him and made him ill. He fought it off in such a manly way, he never complained and yet the ashen colour of his skin revealed the true nature of his constitution.

I became fascinated with the overwhelming interest he had in the natural world. He had made a kind of bag on a trailing net tied with bunting. He hung it out astern at night. Each morning he drew it on deck and examined what he had found. I decided to go on deck early this morning. I took off my shoes and walked among the wet and slimy creatures. There were innumerable tiny coloured spiny animals, a selection of small sea urchins, starfish, sea cucumbers and many other strange looking living things. I picked up a starfish and noticed how it seemed to operate on tube like feet.

'Mr. Darwin, forgive me if I interrupt you, but would I be able to help you?'

Darwin smiled,

'In what way?'

'Could I make lists, or write up descriptions of these creatures?' Darwin smiled again.

'Thank you Miss, but that is not necessary.'

'Mr. Darwin, please think of a way...I think your work is a most intriguing and worthwhile project.'

Darwin's eyes lit up, he smiled although his discomfort

was obvious,

'I will think about it Miss O'Mara but a lot of the work is tedious and dirty and...unbecoming to a lady.'

'There I disagree with you Mr. Darwin. A lady will always make observations about things that differ from those made by a gentleman.'

His eyes opened wide as if shocked by my frankness.

'Oh! Forgive my outspokenness please Mr. Darwin. It has always been my worst fault.'

'Indeed, I admire your spirit of adventure...and I will think about it Miss O'Mara.'

'For instance Mr. Darwin look at this starfish...it looks as if it may have the power of regeneration...can you see...that looks like a new arm, yes, I think it is growing a new arm! How full of surprises, how full of joy is nature Mr. Darwin.'

Darwin looked intently at me and then took the starfish and said,

'Yes I believe there are creatures such as this that... Fitzroy...'

I turned to see Captain Fitzroy frowning, eyes blazing and his temper visibly rising.

'Captain Fitzroy' I said quietly, with a slight curtsy.

'Miss O'Mara you will kindly return to your cabin and refrain in future from keeping Mr. Darwin from his work.'

His voice was ice in the morning air, and authoritative. Darwin opened his mouth to speak, but seemed to think the better of it and said nothing.

'My apologies sir, and to you Mr. Darwin.' I picked up my shoes, left the deck, and went back to my cabin. Fuegia was there.

'You sad Miss Scarlett?'

'Oh! Fuegia.' I paced the few steps each way the cabin allowed.

'There is not an officer on board who would have thought it was wrong of me to speak to Mr. Darwin. We have spoken often in the gunroom, yet the Captain was furious. Why Fuegia, why can I never please him? Everything I do is a cause of annoyance to him.'

Fuegia smiled. I sat on the cot.

'I know Miss Scarlett…you want get off the ship.'

Then she burst out laughing. I laughed now at the way my life had turned into an endless cycle of displeasing the Captain and wanting to get off the ship.

Soon afterwards, Fuegia left and I opened the poetry book and began to read Thomson, 'The Seasons' until I forgot where I was. A knock on the door startled me and I opened it to see Mr. Musters with my dinner. I looked at the rice and peas and felt like feeding it to the seagulls. I was not hungry…just sad…because there was one man on board… and everyday he seemed to find new faults in me. Yet, when I was with him I could not think straight nor express my feelings in an acceptable manner.

In his presence I was completely overwhelmed. His striking good looks, his manners, his goodness, his daily striving for perfection and all his other qualities had a profound effect on me.

Yet, I was keenly aware of the dark side to his nature. When you are the one in a position of power the slightest flaw in your character is noticed and becomes open to criticism. When seventy-four pairs of eyes are looking upon you day after day it is not easy, or even human to be calm and benevolent at all times. When he was perturbed and volatile he found fault with anything that did not achieve absolute perfection.

Often when I thought he would be in a good mood that would be the very time he would glare at me.

That dark side of his nature I feel sure he has little or no control over, and it was surely that other person who stood on the deck and read out the punishment log on the day of the floggings. How did such a man allow flogging? I knew from experience that he would always help any sick or distressed person.

In the afternoon Fuegia and I were playing a memory game when a knock came to the door. Fuegia went to open it.

'Please tell Miss O'Mara the Captain wishes to speak to her.'

'Very well, thank you.' I called out.

'My pleasure Miss.'

I was tempted to keep him waiting. Fuegia set about brushing my hair and handing me the blue ribbon she knew I liked. I put a cream shawl, belonging to Fuegia, over my shoulders, gave Fuegia a little kiss on the cheek and left. Walking slowly towards the cabin, I tried to breathe steadily and collect my thoughts. I knocked.

'Enter'

As usual, his voice pierced the warm evening air. I entered. He was sitting at his table. He stood and indicated the chair opposite him. I sat. I could see the anger still flirting around the edge of his mouth and in his eyes.

'Miss O'Mara what am I to do with you?'

'The answer is simple sir…put me off at the next port.'

'In South America…in the middle of nowhere?'

'Why not if I am such a burden?'

He looked down at his papers. I knew, and he knew that no one ever dared to speak to the Captain this way. There was an ancient coin on his desk. He picked it up and turned it quickly over and under the fingers of his right hand with the dexterity of a conjuror. He repeated this procedure as we spoke.

'Be sensible, you must stay on the voyage until I find some way of returning you to England.'

'No I must not sir. I could not endure it.'

I read the shock in his eyes. He was taken aback. He thinks all the endurance is on his part, I thought.

'I have done my best to make you comfortable.'

'No one could have done more sir, nevertheless I am not a member of his Majesty's Navy, and therefore I believe that gives me a certain amount of autonomy.'

Fitzroy stared into my eyes again. He put the coin down.

'Has anyone upset you, why this sudden determination to leave the ship?'

I looked down at my thin fingers, if only I had the courage to tell him how I missed talking to him, and that the pain I felt at his indifference was unbearable.

'Well?'

'It is not sudden, and everyone has been kind to me… especially…' *His eyes darkened.*

'Especially you Captain.'

'My privilege Miss O'Mara.'

My heart pounded… the way he said my name. I looked into his dark eyes and at his stern features and yet he was so handsome. He must surely hear the pounding of my heart, I thought. A long silence followed. It felt like the only sound in the cabin was my pounding heart and it seemed to me that it sounded louder and louder.

'Miss O'Mara what on earth were you doing on deck this morning disturbing Mr. Darwin?'

'Indeed sir, I was not disturbing Mr. Darwin.'

Now I began to feel angry, here we go again I thought. No sooner had I felt a real affection for him than he began to accuse me. The anger flared in my eyes.

'I was inquiring of Mr. Darwin if I could be of some assistance to him.'

'Assistance' *Fitzroy smiled.*

'Really Miss O'Mara you are outrageous.'

'No sir, I am not and I do not believe Mr. Darwin thought me so. I am a person with a mind, a heart and a spirit. I am as capable as any man of making catalogues and writing up descriptive details, and I do not like being bored.'

Fitzroy's mouth dropped. He held a startled expression, one I had never seen on his face before. Then he smiled.

'I have never met a young lady like you, that is for certain Miss O'Mara.'

Before he could go on, I said,

'And I have never met anyone like you…sir.'

Fitzroy looked at me for what seemed an age. Then he said,

'You are bored.'

'Yes sir.' *Another long silence while he again looked at his papers.*

I took the initiative and spoke,

'I am fascinated by Mr. Darwin's work. I am quite capable of helping with his notes and handling slimy creatures.'

'Indeed' *he smiled*

'I suppose you will tell me next that you are quite capable of helping me check the chronometers'

'Why not?'

'Really Scarlett… you take liberties.'

My name slipped from his lips and I could see the embarrassment he felt. His manners were always impeccable and it was obvious that he had high social skills and connections. Indeed it was clear that he was a member of the aristocracy, but for all that, he was a very shy man.

'Why sir? Do you think that a woman cannot do the tasks men do?'

Fitzroy laughed aloud now. I began to feel angry again.

'Let me ask you another question then, am I the least intelligent person on board the ship?'

'No'

'Am I as intelligent as any of your officers?'

'Yes- the difference is that they have spent many years of their lives training to carry out their duties.'

I was at an impasse now.

'If I had the training they have had I would do what they do.' I said in low whisper.

'Indeed, how is your map-reading?'

'Is not map-reading part of the training?'

He looked down at his papers. I could tell he was getting impatient now and as usual; I had failed to make my point. I waited for the tone of dismissal in his voice and in anticipation the pain began in my heart. So, I took courage and said:

'I am sorry Captain Fitzroy I have done it again…I have annoyed you…when it is the last thing I ever want to do.'

He looked relieved and I knew then, at that moment that he had little or no control over his irritation. That was an amazing fact in a man who was so disciplined in every other aspect of his life. A gloomy mood seemed to seize upon him and he had no way of stopping it. He picked up his pen and wrote something.

'Miss O' Mara here is a note to our librarian, Mr. Stebbing. Find some books in our library and do not be bored.'

I looked over at his bookcase and wondered why he did not offer me a book from there.

'May I also mention to be careful at which time you enter the library for, as you know it is also Mr. Darwin's cabin. Ask one of the officers to escort you and…'

'Thank you Captain Fitzroy… and have you forgiven me for the trouble I cause you? I can endure anything except being on this ship with you and not being on friendly terms with you, sir.'

There, I had said it! A light came into his eyes. He said nothing.

I stood up and took the note. He seemed startled. He stood up.

'Miss O'Mara before you leave would you accept this box.'

He handed me a wooden box. I noticed his initials were on it.

'While I was in your quarters the other evening I noticed the disarray your notes were in. Perhaps this box will help you keep them in order.'

'But Captain… your initials… it must be of sentimental importance to you.'

'Well… it was a gift from my sister Fanny.'

'I can't possibly take an object that is a gift from your sister.'

'My sister Fanny would gladly bestow it on you had she seen the confusion in which you keep your writing.'

'Are you sure?'

'Yes'

'Very well...and ...do you forgive me?'

'Scarlett' now he meant to say my name,

'I could never be cross with you for very long. You are like a wayward child in need of my guidance.'

'Thank you sir'

I curtsied and left. I held back the tears until I got inside the cabin. Fuegia looked at me,

'Captain cross with you again Miss Scarlett?'

'No Fuegia he is always kind to me...like a father is kind.'

I put the box on my table and began to put my notes in order. I stopped and ran my fingers over the gold leaf of those letters, those initials, R. F. They stood for the most important person in my life, the person who held my life so precariously in his hands and whose initials were indelibly printed on my heart.

Friday 13th January

I continued to enjoy my daily walks on deck with Fuegia. Today we met Mr. Sulivan, he smiled at Fuegia and said,

'Good day ladies'

'Mr. Sullivan I feel so bad that I have taken your cabin.'

'Think nothing of it Miss...it is my privilege.'

'It is not much of a privilege Mr. Sulivan when you must sleep in a hammock.'

'A hammock Miss O' Mara is the sailor's best friend' he said with a rye smile. Fuegia laughed.

'You have kissed the Blarney Stone Mr. Sulivan.'

'You have a fair pleasing gift with words yourself Miss…I recall you singing at The Divine Service on Sunday… and you were in good voice if I may say so Miss.'

Mr. Sulivan had no idea how much I loved the Sunday services when the ship's company assembled and Captain Fitzroy's voice swept across the deck and out to sea and the hymns rang out in the clear air.

'Shame, Mr. Sulivan, you flatter me!' Fuegia laughed again.

'What date is it Mr. Sulivan? Fuegia asked.

'It is the 13th of January.'

'It seems to me I have been on this ship much longer than that.' I said

'Indeed Miss, did you notice that we were unable to land at Tenerife?'

'I did notice something was happening.'

'We were told to wait for twelve days owing to an outbreak of cholera in England.

Then, after a short tense time the Captain said, 'Up Jibb' and a great cheer went up and we were on our way.'

'The Captain would never wait twelve days for anything would he Mr. Sulivan?'

'You might know that Miss O'Mara, the officers might know that but on board ship we wait for orders.'

'Yes indeed, I am beginning to know all about orders.'

Without warning Fitzroy appeared on deck.

'Excuse me Miss.' Sulivan bowed his head, smiled at Fuegia and within seconds, he was back at the wheel. Fitzroy approached.

'Miss O'Mara…Fuegia'

'Captain Fitzroy' I made a curtsy and Fuegia moved slightly away as if she instinctively knew he wished to speak to me. Fuegia was a clever girl. She communicated much with her body movements and eyes. She knew it would not be right to move too far away so she discreetly moved a little towards the rail as if to look out to sea.

I looked into his eyes and then at the deep blue and gold braid of his impeccable uniform. He looked so regal...my heart almost stopped.

'Have you been avoiding me over the past few days Miss O'Mara?' His voice was harsh and even hurt, I thought.

'Oh no, certainly not sir.'

Immediately I knew I had over emphasized my reply, protested too much, and he could read me like a book. From the day, he called me 'child' and started treating me as if he were my father, I decided to try and avoid all contact with him. He knew I sometimes sneaked up to the deck in the afternoons and on a few occasions he saw me there. He said 'Good afternoon' and pretended not to notice it was not my time to be there. I had memorized his daily routine and more or less knew where he was at any hour of the day. In this way it was easy to avoid him. Now I felt embarrassed.

'Would you care to take supper with the officers this evening?'

His voice, as sharp as a whistle flew at me.

'I would like that very much thank you sir.'

'Very well I will tell Mr. Wickham to take care of you.'

'Thank you sir.' I caught the note of dismissal in his tone, made a slight curtsy, touched Fuegia on the arm and we both left the deck. In the cabin, I sat on the bed. My heart was beating furiously as it always did whenever I was in contact with Captain Fitzroy.

I knew I was never in his thoughts, how could I be? He was so preoccupied with all the work he did. He could not be distracted in any way. He was so devoted to his duty, to the Navy, to the crew; to Mr. Darwin…no there was no room and no time in his life for me.

The tears rose in my eyes…and yet…he noticed I had been avoiding him. I wiped away the tears and began to read again, 'The Sonnets of Shakespeare' that I had borrowed from the ship's library.

Saturday 14th January

The weather is warm, sunny and exhilarating. I took a chance this morning and went on deck.

'Good morning Mr. Darwin.'

'Good morning…should you risk the Captain's displeasure Miss O' Mara? He clearly does not like you being on deck at this hour.'

'Oh it is not about being on deck Mr. Darwin, it's about talking to you that I risk the Captain's wrath.'

The officers at the wheel listened and then smiled. Mr. Darwin continued to release little creatures from the net. I took off my shoes and picked up a slimy plant,

'Is this what they call a sea lily with its long stem?'

I didn't wait for the answer as I was distracted by a sea cucumber expecting it to be spiny and it was…leathery.

'Oh! How interesting!'

'What is?' Darwin asked.

I explained. Darwin smiled.

'I've discovered that some of them can almost turn themselves inside out.'

He said with a smile. His complexion was dreadful. I admired his endurance and wondered how seasickness might feel.

'Do you think that when the world was made that all these creatures were created from the beginning?

Darwin did not answer.

'I do believe God created the world, Mr. Darwin, and that the whole of nature is a mystery to us. That is why your enquiries are so absorbing sir. You are trying to uncover the secrets of nature, is this not so?'

Darwin looked at me but did not answer.

'I know your investigation goes beyond animal life Mr. Darwin and that you have a prodigious interest in geology and the formation of the earth is that not so?'

'Yes indeed.'

'Do you believe the Bible word for word Mr. Darwin?'

'I do.'

'May I say that I have spoken to some of the officers and midshipmen on board who do not see the creation in the same way as it is expressed in the Book of Genesis.'

'I am aware of that now, but I must admit I was shocked when I came on board and heard them say so.'

'I was shocked too, Mr. Darwin.'

'By looking carefully at all these little creatures Mr. Darwin you are drawn into the wonder and the gifts of creation, to say nothing of the beauty of the earth, the sea and the sky; it just fills the heart and mind with awe and veneration…perhaps the way God intended, I think.'

Darwin did not answer. I picked up my shoes,

'Thank you Mr. Darwin,' I said and left the deck. I stopped at the end of the companionway to put on my shoes. I heard one of the officers speak.

'Have you ever met any woman Stokes who thinks and talks like a man?'

'No, of course not.'

'Yes you have. I tell you Miss O' Mara is a beautiful looking woman but she thinks and talks like a man.'

'Don't be so outrageous sir.'

'Whether you like it or not Stokes…it is true.'

The officers must have listened to my conversation with Mr. Darwin…now they implied that I thought and spoke like a man…maybe in their eyes that was a compliment!

Sunday 15th January

When I saw what Mr. Darwin had retrieved from the ocean each day it gave me something to think about other than my studies, and I looked forward to having supper with the officers. However, I had taken supper alone in my cabin for a number of days. I wondered if the Captain would ever allow me to dine with them again.

The days passed slowly and although I read many books and tried to write there were times when I would truly have loved to explore the ship but I was only allowed to stay in my cabin, go to the gunroom, and once a day go for a stroll on the deck.

The constant motion of the ship always calmed my restless heart and soothed my spirit. My heart and mind longed for time and conversation with the Captain and I knew now that this was never likely to happen. Then he sent me a message by Mr. Wickham to tell me I could dine with the officers if I wished.

'I hope you wish, Miss O'Mara' Wickham said with a broad smile.

'Indeed I do Mr. Wickham.'

'I will escort you if you wish.'

'No thank you Mr. Wickham, I am quite capable of getting myself to the gunroom.'

He smiled again and left.

At least on Sundays I saw the Captain at the Divine Service. I looked at him, so young, even younger than Mr. Wickham, and yet in his stature and address he held the authority of a much older man. He had the heart of a young man though, and although he sometimes looked at me, there was no way of telling where the heart of this young man might be.

I returned to my cabin. There was a knock on the door, and Fuegia came in.

'I am to dine with the officers tonight Fuegia.'

'I help you get ready.'

'Oh Fuegia you are so sweet. I could never have stayed on this ship without you. I must leave it soon.' Fuegia smiled as usual, and then laughed.

'The Captain say no…you not get off.'

'Well I will get off if I want to. He can't tell me what to do. I am not one of his loyal sailors.'

Fuegia roared laughing; when at last she stopped there was a knock on the door.

'Yes?'

'Miss O'Mara the Captain would like to see you.'

I recognized the voice of Mr. Hellyer.

'Now, Mr. Hellyer?"

'Yes Miss.'

'Very well, thank you."

'I brush your hair' Fuegia said.

'I will tell him now that I am getting off this ship.'

'You tell him, yes Miss Scarlett, but he no listen.'

Then she started that distinctive honey coated laugh as she brushed my hair. I put the blue sash on my dress and a cream shawl over my shoulders,

'Thank you Fuegia.'

I walked slowly towards the Captain's cabin and knocked.

'Enter' his sharp voice flew through the air like a whip. Slowly I opened the door and entered the cabin. He was sitting at his table. He stood up and said,

'Please sit down.'

I noticed everything about him even the slightest inflection in his voice, and if I was not mistaken this was a different tone of voice. It was a tone he had never used before when addressing me. He indicated the chair. I sat down. He said nothing. He looked at his papers. I was afraid to breathe. He picked up the coin and began moving it between his fingers. Then he looked at me and said,

'Miss O' Mara I am afraid… I have neglected you. Please accept my apologies.'

'You have done everything you could for me sir.' I tried to hide my astonishment.

'It is not easy to run the ship, do the daily surveying and perform all the extra duties the voyage entails…'

I took a chance and interrupted him even though I knew he hated to be interrupted.

'Forgive me for interrupting sir but you do it admirably.'

'I am glad you approve.'

Was there a note of sarcasm in his voice? I looked into his eyes. Did he think I was patronizing him?

'I mean that you are one of the best Captains in the fleet sir.'

Fitzroy slowly began to smile, then laugh and then laugh robustly. I smiled.

'Not my words sir, the words of the men who serve under you.'

'Is that true?'

'Yes sir.'

He looked astonished and the joy that flowed into his eyes was unmistakable. He stood up, walked a few paces behind the table and looked up at the skylight. All this, I thought was to disguise the embarrassment he felt. He returned to his chair.

'It is utter hyperbole of course; however, it could not be the opinion of all on board... for as you know I am a strict disciplinarian, and that does not always endear all the crew to me.'

'They admire and respect you sir, as I do myself. They know how meticulously you prepared for this voyage and how you have done everything possible to ensure their good health and safety. However...' I stopped.

'However' he repeated,

I could see the hurt now that flooded into his face and his countenance changed. Why had I spoken out?

'No one admires you as much as I do sir, but I could never accept flogging as a normal part of life. It is barbarous.'

'Look, I disrated as many men as was possible. The remaining four I had no alternative but to flog. You do not understand that if I had failed to do so my authority would have suffered. The crew would have thought me an easy going Captain. Now Miss O'Mara, why do you speak as if the whole ship's company had been flogged?'

I looked at him keenly but I did not speak.

'Miss O'Mara! ...What am I to do with you?'

'You can put me off at the next port.'

'Certainly not.'

There was a long pause in which we looked into each other's eyes. I could see the uncertainty creep across his face and I longed to reassure him. I was afraid to speak, I wanted to reach out hold his hand, and God forgive my boldness – I even wanted to kiss his cheek!

Then slowly, almost wistfully, he said,

'How could I possibly do without our conversations Miss O'Mara? Who would brighten my days, and give me other things to think about?'

Whatever I thought he was going to say it was not that. Without thinking I reached across the table. He looked at my hand. Quickly I drew back. As usual I had broken the protocol that I cared so little about but which he strictly observed.

'I am sorry, sir. You must forgive my impetuous behaviour.'

Now he began to smile and happiness at last shone in his eyes.

'It is your most endearing quality.'

'Thank you sir, may I go now sir?'

'Are you bored with my company already Scarlett?' He said smiling.

'Sir, I could never be bored with your company…to discuss and exchange ideas with you …yes, that would be delightful…'

He looked down at his papers.

'So are you to my thoughts as food to life'…I whispered.

He looked up quickly;

'If we were not on this ship sir, and … we could sit under the blossoming trees and I could tell you…tell you… of my true feelings.'

He frowned. He was completely taken aback.

I had indeed been far too forward, overstepped the mark, yes even impertinent to mention such things. Nobody had ever dared to speak to him like this, and I knew that above all else at that moment that he needed affection and praise. Not in a stupid way and not because he was a coxcomb, but because he was a truly diligent man, a man of integrity, trustworthiness and courage. His loyalty to his country, the Navy, Mr. Darwin, the crew, to his faith and to all things good and upright was paramount in all he did. I wondered if indeed he had ever been given the slightest recognition for his talents or praise for all his efforts.

I knew he needed affection but somehow I never managed to strike the right key with him. I either said nothing…or was too bold. The pregnant silence continued. I blushed. I stood up. He stood. He didn't take his eyes away from mine, yet he said nothing. At last I found the courage to speak.

'Apologies again Captain, for not keeping to the protocol.'

'Accepted.'

'May I say that when you are not in a temper, you give glory to God in all you do.'

'If that is intended as a compliment Miss O'Mara, thank you.'

He had reverted now to formalities, and this was always a sign that he was annoyed.

'However, I beg you think of putting me off the ship.'

A short silence followed.

'Yes, you may go ashore in Rio de Janeiro with Fuegia and Mr. Stokes to purchase clothes.'

We both smiled and I opened the cabin door.

'What they say about you is true sir. So please spill no more coffee.'

'Miss O'Mara…what do you mean?'

Fitzroy called after me, but I walked quickly away.

He did not know but I knew that when the young

officers came on duty they asked about his temper in that coded way,

'How much hot coffee was spilt this morning?'

Monday 16*th* January 1832

Today the ship arrived at Port Praya, the capital of Cape Verde Islands. We anchored about 3 o'clock. Mr. Wickham told me that we would be at anchor for some time. The weather was glorious. Never had I felt such warm sun, never had I seen such azure blue skies and clear crystal water. It was paradise. My heart beat fast as I drank in the tropical surroundings. At anchor surely I would see more of the Captain?

17*th* January

After breakfast Mr. Darwin went with the Captain to Quail Island. It was there that the observatory and the tents were to be set up.

19*th* January

Mr. Darwin went ashore today with Mr. Musters and I envied them their escape. I saw Mr. Wickham on deck and asked him,

'Mr. Wickham would the Captain allow me go ashore do you think? I know the islands don't look too inviting from here, but I would dearly love to see further a field.'

'Miss O'Mara there's not a chance in the world that the Captain will let you go ashore, and I beg you do not send him into a temper by asking him.'

'Very well Mr. Wickham, that's why I asked you first.'

'Thank you Miss, now please give me your word that you will not mention it to him.'

'Very well Mr. Wickham.'

22nd January

I had not anticipated that the Captain would be away from the ship most of the time. He has indeed set up an observation post on Quail Island and many officers and crew are there also. He only comes aboard occasionally. The ship for me is like a hollow shell without him.

I had taken three books from the library, a volume of the Britannica to look up the section on seafaring, and a book on the natural world. A book on Spanish caught my attention and I began to practice with Fuegia who was very quick at picking up languages, but we both laughed at our attempts at the pronunciation.

I read for long periods and then walked on the deck with Fuegia. We did so several times a day, as we were not restricted to our noon walk now that we were at anchor. I noticed that the officers, when off duty, relaxed and played cards. They also told jokes and laughed. When I heard them laughing I thought of the Captain. He never had time to laugh and I wondered how long any man could continue to work relentlessly as he did. The other sailors washed their hammocks and sang.

Most evenings Mr. Darwin came back and I went on deck to see the treasures he had brought on board and to ask him questions about the islands. One evening I asked him,

'Was it a profitable journey Mr. Darwin?'
'Indeed it was.'
'The islands look so forlorn and barren from here.'
'Yes indeed they do but they are the first volcanic islands I have ever experienced. You cannot imagine how it feels like to collect a number of geological specimens and animals from the sea and the pools, and to be so close to the exquisite Coral formations.'
'How wonderful!'

'To be able to stroll in the valleys under the coconut trees and walk by the thickets of banana and coffee plants, and to see masses of wild flowers this is indeed a time of great joy for me.'

'The wild flowers would be my favourites.' I said.

Mr. Darwin then produced from his pocket a beautiful wild peach and handed it to me.

'The freshness and taste is wonderful.'

'Thank you Mr. Darwin', I said.

'Could I help you Mr. Darwin?'

'Miss O' Mara however much we would both like this, we know that the Captain forbids it. I can tell you plainly I would never go against his wishes.'

'I apologise for asking but I also feel that the Captain forbids it on very flimsy and illogical grounds.'

Mr. Darwin smiled, but he said nothing. I felt he agreed with me, but I had to leave the deck and sit alone in my cabin. My great joy at this time, apart from trying to capture the beauty of the location in a pencil drawing, was to write in my other book; the one I called my journal, where there were no partings or tears.

24*th* *January*

Today the Captain, Mr. Wickham and Mr. Darwin left early. Mr. Wickham told me they were about to take the measurements of a famous Baobab tree. In the evening I continued my routine of going on deck when Mr. Darwin came back. I exchanged a few words with him about the strange creatures he caught. I was very careful never to mention anything controversial, and afterwards I went back quietly to my cabin.

25ᵗʰ *January*

Despite what Mr. Wickham said, I was tempted to ask the Captain if I could go ashore. Then I remembered I had given my word to Mr. Wickham. In future I will not give my word so easily to him.

Whenever the Captain was aboard he was either writing up the ship's log or his journal, and then he would leave again quickly, away in the cutter with other members of the crew for many days at a time. The ruthless taking of measurements went on incessantly.

I listened in my cabin every morning on the odd occasions when the Captain was on board so I could hear how his morning inspection was going. One morning when all seemed well, I decided to go on deck and ask him again about helping Mr. Darwin.

I went up to the deck slowly and thoughtfully. I knew his mood could change abruptly.

'Ah, Good morning Miss O'Mara'

'Good morning sir, what a beautiful morning.'

'Do the tropics suit you then?'

'Indeed they do sir.'

'While we are at anchor you may take supper with the officers who remain on board, Miss O'Mara.'

'That is very kind of you I am sure.'

'My pleasure' He made to leave.

'Sir?'

'Yes.'

The officers at the wheel froze, and I did not know what to say. If I mentioned Darwin he was sure to fly into a temper.

'Would you not think of relaxing yourself sir?' I paused.

'We are at anchor yet you seem to be working harder than ever.'

Fitzroy frowned, and then glared. I blushed. Then he started to laugh.

'I am busy Miss O'Mara because I have to measure the exact location of these islands. Now I realize that may seem trivial to you but in fact it involves a great deal of calculations.'

'Yes sir, I mean no; I do not think it is trivial. I had just hoped sir that at sometime you could have a chance to stop working…and…and enjoy some convivial company.'

'Miss O'Mara that is not a possible for a ship's Captain and I am quite sure you will find your convivial company with the ship's officers.'

'Yes sir' I stood still.

Fitzroy left the deck shouting some order or other to the Boatswain.

Before Mr. Wickham could reprimand me for putting the Captain in a bad temper I went back to my cabin. I did not mean that I wished to have some convivial company but that he, the Captain should have some. He turned my plea around, and I think he knew that he did. He probably did not want any officer to think that I was thinking about him, but about myself. I wondered indeed if he had succeeded. It was no use trying to tell him he was killing himself working. He never listened.

Why could he not laugh and joke like the other officers? Why did a Captain have to remain apart from all on board? There is no doubt I do not understand anything to do with life at sea.

I kept making the same mistakes. Why could I not accept that there was never ever going to be a time when I could have any kind of conversations with him? To him I was an added difficulty in a long day's work.

27ᵗʰ January

I turned my thoughts now to learning Spanish properly, in an orderly fashion. I decided to learn some new words each day. I went back to the library for books and became engrossed in learning the pronunciation. Fuegia laughed and laughed as we tried to get our tongues around the difficult sounds.

29ᵗʰ January

Sunday is a most delightful day on board the Beagle. Everyone is at peace. Some midshipmen teach those who cannot read to do so, and some study from books. Then the Divine Service takes place and all acknowledge the place of God in our lives. I began to think that sailors are constantly at the interface of the power of the elements and the fragility of life, and consequently sing out to God in praise and veneration.

2ⁿᵈ February

The days at anchor passed by slowly and the 1ˢᵗ of February came and went. I envied Mr. Darwin who was able to take many walks across the island and many riding expeditions. He went with Mr. Bynoe and Mr. Rowlett the purser, and other members of the crew. Even Mr. Musters was allowed to go ashore. Today Rowlett, Bynoe and Mr. Darwin left early. Mr. Darwin told me they were taking a riding excursion to St. Domingo.

It seems to me that all the crew have had a most enjoyable stay here. I, on the other hand cannot wait for the day that we set sail. I believe we hope to sail on the 6th February. If I could have left the ship, even once it would have made a difference. I wondered whether it would always be this way with the world and whether women would forever be excluded from every interesting activity.

8th February

Sailing on the 6th was postponed but to my great relief we left Cape Verde today. Over the following days the weather became warmer as we approached the Equator. Sometimes there was a slight swell on the sea and I think it has affected Mr. Darwin for I have not seen him for a number of days.

Everyone on board is in good humour from what I can gather on my daily excursion from my prison cell. The Captain has not seen fit to allow me to dine with the officers, and therefore am I deprived of any friendly company in the evenings.

12th February

The warm beautiful weather is delight to me and has enhanced my well-being. I have spent many hours writing, reading and learning another section from 'Paradise Lost'. While I was studying it the words of the aria 'Mi tardi quell'alma ingrata…' all my love on him I lavish, sung by Elvira in Don Giovanni came into my head and I thought I would sing it one evening for the officers…that is of course if the Captain ever allows me dine with them again.

14th February

Today I saw the Captain at noon and he told me we were one hundred and fifty miles from the Equator. We spoke about the beauty of the sky and he asked if I had noted how extraordinary were the stars and night sky in these latitudes. My heart raced as I looked into the keen intelligent eyes and wondered if in fact he was aware that I sometimes sneaked out of the cabin to observe the night sky.

16th February

Yesterday we saw the rocks of the tiny island of St. Paul and came today within three miles of the island. Two boats were lowered, one with Mr. Stokes for the surveying and one with Mr. Darwin and Mr. Wickham. There were hundreds of birds there and Mr. Wickham and Mr. Darwin brought back hats full of eggs and a boatload of dead birds, mostly boobies and terns. I looked at the poor things and was glad that I never ate dead creatures.

17th February

Today we crossed the equator, crossing-the line it was called. I did not see, I just heard the commotion and the uproar of the ceremony and the whole ship's company seemed to have been partaking in some kind of ritual. Mr. Darwin was the honoured person as it was his first time to cross the line. I wondered if in all the excitement his seasickness had abated.

20h February

We arrived at another small island, Fernando Noronha. The landing was difficult owing to the high surf. Mr. Darwin went ashore. It seemed to me a strange place with leaping crabs on the shore, and the glimmer of pink blossomed trees in the distance. As usual I kept watch for Mr. Darwin's return.

'Was your trip interesting sir?' I asked as he climbed over the rail.

'Well, I daresay Miss O'Mara you would have appreciated the natural beauty there. The whole island seems to be one large wood. The trees were all matted together with creepers. There was no chance of leaving the trodden path. One thing did capture my attention and that was the utter blueness of the foliage on the Acacias.' He smiled.

'Here, I put a bud and a few leaves in my pocket for you.'

He handed me a rather crumpled white flower with striking blue leaves.

'Mr. Darwin I will treasure it, and when it begins to fade I will dry it out…in a book.'

23rd February

Over the past few days the journey towards the coast of South America has been troublesome. Either there has been a dead calm or unfavourable wind. The evenings now are delightful and I think the Captain knows about my escapades, so I have taken to sneaking on deck after sunset. The sight of the amazing multi coloured sky, the crimson tinted clouds and clear constellations is sufficient to send me to my cabin in good spirits.

25th February

We are roughly three days from Bahia or San Salvador. I have not dined with the officers or had any company apart from Fuegia since we left the Cape Verde Islands. I set aside time to read, to study, to write and to pray each day, nevertheless there are times when I am extremely lonely.

Not a single soul on board could possibly imagine what it is like to be on a ship where everyone has their place, their duty and their identity-except me. This is too much like feeling sorry for my fate and I must banish these thoughts.

28th February

Today the ship arrived in Bahia. We pulled into the Bay of all Saints around 11am.

The view of the Bay from the ship raised my spirits. The whole town appears to be enclosed in a copious wood and on a steep hillside scattered with houses and lush vegetation.

The rhythm of the ship changes when at anchor. I saw the Captain go ashore in the cutter, and the tedious taking of measurements goes on. Mr. Darwin told me that he will go ashore each day but then return to the ship in the evenings.

1st March

After the morning inspection today I went on deck to sketch the bay. Having made a preliminary sketch I stood on deck and looked longingly at the Bay of All Saints. A shiver of sadness came over me for I knew I was never going to see any of these places. All this beauty but no one to share it with…

'And the sunlight clasps the earth,
And the moonbeams kiss the sea –
What are all these kissings worth,
If thou kiss not me?'

I whispered Shelly's words and tears began to fill my eyes. I held onto the rail.

'Miss O'Mara' I jumped, when I heard his voice.

'Yes sir' I answered quickly as if I were a member of the crew. The Captain smiled, and then frowned. Had he noticed that I had been crying?

'Are you feeling well?'

'Yes thank you sir.'

'I have decided to allow you to go ashore for a few hours. Fuegia, Mr. Bynoe and Mr. Bennett will accompany you. Would that please you Miss O'Mara?'

I wanted to jump up and kiss him on the cheek. Instead I restrained myself and said,

'It would be delightful Captain Fitzroy.'

'Only for a few hours now, those are my orders. Do not try to persuade Mr. Bennett to stay longer, and do not go wandering off looking for books.'

'I would not dream of it sir.' I smiled and he smiled. We both stood still.

'Go along then'

His eyes were smiling; he was the most handsome adorable man I had ever met. I went quickly to my cabin and Fuegia brushed my hair. I put on the cream shawl. When we arrived on deck Mr. Bennett and Mr. Bynoe were already in the dingy and Mr. Sulivan came over to help us down the ladder. Fuegia went first, and then Mr. Sulivan, who was always ready with repartee, said,

'What gifts have Mr. Bennett and Mr. Bynoe do you think Miss O'Mara that they are honoured to escort you today?'

I smiled and said, 'Thank you Mr. Sulivan, we could not manage without you.'

'My pleasure Miss.'

I stepped into the dingy, sat down and Mr. Bennett began to row.

Encouraging Words

Throughout the following days Harry continued to read the diary. One morning he sat by the fountain with it in his hand. He valued the extraordinary fountain built in the style of Piranesi by Dermot his estate manager. Harry looked up and saw Dermot approaching. He said,

'I don't wish to disturb you Mr. Harry.'

'No, you don't disturb me. Do not call me Mr. Harry.'

'I prefer to sir. I think the difference in rank should be acknowledged.'

Harry looked up and began to smile. Dermot smiled.

'Sit down Dermot I want to ask you something.'

Dermot sat down. The rhythm of the water in the fountain vibrated like a heart beat.

'Dermot look at this book and tell me what you think'

Dermot took the book. He looked at it for what seemed like an age. Then he handed the diary back and said,

'It seems like the account of a sea voyage, but not written in that boring way of daily entries, but rather written from the heart.'

'Yes'

'I seem to think you have a question about it.'

'Yes Dermot, my question is: does it warrant further investigation or is it an extravagant hoax?'

Dermot thought for a while, and then,

'You know I am not a historian Mr. Harry, but over the years of working on the land if a problem arises I follow my instinct. I trust to my inner self.'

'Do you think I should do the same?'

'I do'

'By the way would you …have time to look at the b…b…bridle path sir?'

'Yes of course.'

Harry walked in silence with Dermot towards the east wood where the dark shadows were broken by the sunlight that flickered between the hornbeams, the silver birch and the oaks.

'Do you see the way the water gathers here from the small streams…well I thought of trapping it further up and making a water fall and a small lake, a small one mind you.'

'Yes…is there a problem?'

'Well yes, I would like to turn the bridle path west, well before the bend here…for safety sake.'

'Very well…you always know better than I do about these things Dermot. What about the leaves though, and debris from the trees?'

'Yes…I thought of clearing…well cutting back a few branches to let the light in.'

'Yes very well Dermot, a splendid idea.'

'Thank you Mr. Harry'

Harry walked further into the wood. He allowed

the quiet ambiance of the old oaks to enfold him, and the solitude to enter his heart. He was setting out on a path and he didn't know where it would lead.

He walked back to the stable. Perkins had the horse ready. He mounted and set off towards the bridle path. He trotted over the meadows and galloped up to the highest point of the estate. He looked over the fertile summer plains of pleasant England. His proud heart thrilled with the natural beauty of the landscape, and the civilized, rural, peaceful life that enshrined his native countryside.

'Once again I see
These hedgerows, hardly hedgerows, little lines
Of sportive wood run wild: these pastoral farms,
Green to the very door; and wreaths of smoke
Sent up, in silence from among the trees!'

Harry smiled. His thoughts slipped back to days past. Both his parents were teachers, and his mother taught poetry with such enthusiasm that however immune you were some of it was bound to lodge in the subconscious. The words of Wordsworth echoed in his thoughts and for a brief instant he felt the sheer joy of boyhood days.

The elation faded instantly as Harry remembered the pain of rejection by his family and how the years were passing with no sign of a solution. The sky was darkening as he made his way home and he just managed to reach the stable before the rain poured down furiously.

'Well timed sir' Perkins shouted as he took the horse.

Harry walked toward the house with a new spring

in his step and a new project in his heart. Then the old energy came surging back, empowering him and he knew he would no longer hesitate.

That afternoon Harry said to Bloom,

'I have decided to investigate the diary.'

'Are you sure you are doing the right thing sir?'

'Yes Bloom, I thought we would start at the Maritime Museum at Greenwich. We could leave in say…an hour.'

'Very good sir'

At the reception desk in the Maritime Museum Harry asked to see the curator, and explained to him that he was interested in the Beagle and any letters written by Fitzroy,

'They are not kept here sir. You will probably find them at Kew or Admiralty House.'

'I 'm wondering whether there is any possibility of anything about the Beagle in your possession here or at the archives as we are about to research the voyage.'

'As far as I know we have examples of the barometers Fitzroy invented and a small box made from the wood of the Beagle, but letters sir, sorry that kind of information is not kept here.'

'Thank you'

Harry was disappointed. He and Bloom stood still by the desk. As the curator went back into the adjoining office…they heard to their astonishment a young assistant say:

'I'm sure I have seen a letter from Fitzroy in the concealed chamber.'

'Keep your voice down, don't you understand you are not even allowed to mention those documents under the Official Secrets Act.'

'Sorry.'

Harry and Bloom walked away quickly.

'Did you hear that Bloom?'

'Yes.'

Harry picked up a brochure and they walked to the first floor. They studied the site map.

'There is not much hope of finding such a room in this building; it is probably up at the Observatory.' Bloom said.

'Just a minute look here Bloom on every floor this particular space is accounted for… except the ground floor.' Harry scrutinized the map.

'Let's go and have a look.'

They reached the ground floor and walked past the stained glass windows of the old Baltic Exchange, and towards the huge doors facing the Observatory. Harry noted the doors had an alarm in place.

'It could be here;' Bloom said with his arms outstretched indicating an area between the staircase and the toilets. Harry agreed because that area was not marked on the site map.

'How do they enter it?'

'Let's walk around and see what we can find?'

Harry was looking intently at a panel in the wall, just about the size of a door.

'If it is a door sir, how does it open?'

Harry hit the light switch and the panel slid back revealing a small door marked 'Private'.

'How about the lock?' Harry asked. Bloom scrutinized it for a few moments and said,

'Looks an ordinary lock, but it isn't.'

'Can you manage it?'

'Yes.'

As Bloom studied the lock Harry walked half way up the staircase and soon realized that the room probably spread over two floors. He then returned to find that Bloom had just succeeded in unlocking the door.

'Bloom you keep watch here. The room is probably hardly ever used, so nobody will come. However if anyone does come you will have to find an excuse to way-lay them and knock twice on the door.'

'Very well.'

'Oh! Has the room an alarm?'

'This door doesn't have an alarm, I don't know about the room. It may have heat detectors.'

'I'll have to take that risk,' Harry said firmly.

Harry quickly opened the door. No alarms went off. He stepped into the room and looked around. He gasped; it was like a treasure cave of models of old ships, sextants, barometers, paintings, and all kinds of instruments. There were three filing cabinets. It was a veritable paradise for Harry who would gladly have spent weeks exploring the contents. He looked around for a place to hide if the need arose. Then he opened the first cabinet. It seemed to be full of details and plans of ships. He opened the next cabinet. Yes this one had an alphabetical system.

'I'll look under 'F' for Fitzroy' he whispered.

'No, nothing, I'll look under 'B' for Beagle'

'No nothing'

'I'll look under 'S''

'Yes here we are a letter dated….

Harry spread the letter out on the top of the cabinet, took a small digital camera out of his pocket and clicked.' He quickly put the letter back.

'Ah! I'll look under 'G' for Graham, Sir James Robert, George Graham.'

Harry's fingers moved like lighting.

'Yes here we are…a letter to Fitzroy'

He made the photo quickly but as he did so the knocks came as Bloom kicked the door gently twice. Harry put the letter back, and closed the drawer. He squeezed in and crouched down behind a row of models of ships. The door opened. He could not see who entered the room, but remained perfectly still, afraid almost to breathe. The footsteps approached, cabinet doors opened. Harry's mind was racing and he felt sure now he would be detected. He would say that…

A buzzer on a walkie-talkie went off and a crackled voice spoke some undecipherable babble.

'Ok, on my way' A man's voice answered, so close to him it was unbelievable that he did not see him. The footsteps receded and moved towards the door. The door opened and closed. Within seconds Harry was out.

'Did you find anything sir?'

'Maybe.'

Back at Lyndhurst House Harry downloaded the two letters from the camera.

1st March 1832

While Mr. Bennett rowed the dinghy across the Bay of All Saints my heart beat fast as I could not wait to see the city of San Salvador. Then Fuegia asked,

'What date is it Mr. Bynoe?'

'It is the first day of March 1832.'

'I am sure she knew the year Mr. Bynoe.'

Fuegia laughed.

'You get off ship at last Miss Scarlett'

'Were you anxious to get off the ship Miss?' Bennett asked.

'Well, yes Mr. Bennett I have never known anyone in my life as kind as Captain Fitzroy but he never lets me get off the ship.'

'He fears for your safety Miss.'

'I know Mr. Bennett, but I have been on the ship over sixty days, and that's a long time for someone who is not a seafaring person. Besides I know I am at fault, I am a very impatient person, full of curiosity about people and places.'

'Yes, we all know that about you Miss.'

I looked at him. How could he or any of the officers know what I am like? On the other hand I did know most of the characteristics of the officers. Being at sea was strange, living in such close proximity you began to know more than you realized about people. Soon Mr. Bennett was pulling in to the slipway.

'Oh Mr. Bennett, I have never seen anything quite so beautiful! Have you been here before?'

'Yes Miss.'

I climbed the steep hill to the town running in front of Bennett, Bynoe and Fuegia. My legs felt a bit strange at first but soon I could jump and skip. I felt such relief in the terra firma that I wanted to sing. I breathed in the scented air and began speaking rapturously about the trees and plants.

'The New World agrees with you then Miss?' asked Bennett quite bemused at my attitude.

At the top of the hill, I stood still and looked back over the Bay of Saints, the deep blue water, the translucent blue sky, the sailing ships, white sails, and scattered boats. My eyes were drawn to the little barque they called a brig... 'The Beagle' my very home over the last months was swaying gently in the warm sunshine. Wherever I was in the world I knew my heart would always be back there with a man who hardly knew that I was alive.

'The wood and trees Mr. Bynoe, they seem to enclose this beautiful old town.'

I looked around now at the narrow streets, the white towering houses with long narrow windows and the classically built public buildings. I breathed in the scent from the blossoming trees, shrubs and brightly coloured flowers.

'Fuegia, look at the elegant lady getting out of that carriage.'

'Beautiful clothes Miss Scarlett, yes.'

'Yes beautiful...I feel very poorly dressed now.' We both laughed.

'Mr. Bynoe did the Captain tell you buy clothes for Miss Scarlett?'

'No.'

'Oh Fuegia...how could you...don't ask Mr. Bynoe.'

'Well he say he buy clothes and the Captain always do what he say.'

'He probably meant in Rio de Janeiro Miss Scar... I mean Miss O'Mara.'

'Mr. Bynoe I would never expect the Captain to buy clothes for me, please excuse Fuegia.'

'You may not expect it Miss, but if the Captain says he is going to do it I can assure you he will.'

'See I tell you.' Fuegia said with her usual smile.

I looked all around and the beautiful white houses appealed to me, and the evergreen trees and extraordinary plants that filled the air with exotic aromas.

'May we walk towards the trees Mr. Bennett?'

'Yes certainly Miss.'

We walked under palm trees; marvelled at the banana trees and the coconut groves.

'The scent, the humming of the insects, the song of the birds, and the glorious sunshine…oh Mr.Bynoe this place is paradise.'

Fuegia laughed.

I walked ahead and sat on a bench just absorbing the sheer beauty of the place. How could I ever thank Captain Fitzroy? Not only had he saved my life, put up with all my foibles, and now he let me see a town and a forest in the New World.

'Would you like to walk through the street market Miss? You might like to buy a souvenir.' asked Mr. Bennett

'I might, but I have no money Mr. Bennett.'

'It would be my pleasure to buy whatever you need to purchase Miss O'Mara.'

'That is very kind of you Mr. Bennett, but what I wish no money can buy.'

'And what is that?' asked Mr.Bynoe

'Never mind that now. Come Fuegia let us see what the shops have to offer.'

We walked and laughed among the stalls in the market place. Fuegia bought sweets and a bracelet. Mr. Bennet said,

'Miss O'Mara may I be so bold as to buy you a bracelet.'

'Thank you Mr. Bennet, that would not be appropriate, thank you again nevertheless for the thought.'

'My pleasure, Miss'

Mr Bynoe pointed out the flower stall and we both went to look at the incredible range of flowers in bright vibrant colours and extravagant scents.

'Miss O'Mara, if you wish to purchase some flowers may I offer you the money to do so?' Mr. Bynoe asked.

'I appreciate your kind thought, Mr. Bynoe but it would not be proper.'

Mr. Bynoe nodded. While we were engaged looking at the flower stall Fuegia took Mr. Bennett aside. She showed him a single pearl on a gold chain that I liked and he bought it.

'I bought this for you, Miss,' he said, handing me a small box.

'No, Mr. Bennet, this is not an acceptable way for me to behave. Perhaps you will be able to return it and retrieve your money?'

'Please Miss Scarlett I tell him you like it.'

'Oh Fuegia, what am I to do with you? What am I to do with you both?'

'You could just accept it Miss, it is only a small gift.'

'No sir, you should not have purchased it. Keep it for someone else Mr. Bennett.'

'Miss Scarlett this not good, I tell him buy it for you.'

I looked at Mr. Bennett and he seemed upset.

'Very well Mr. Bennett, thank you for your kindness.'

'My pleasure, Miss.'

I took the lovely little box and put it in the pocket of my dress.

We walked around the town, and I did look at books, but soon I heard Mr. Bynoe say,

'Now it is time ladies to make our way back to the slipway.'

I looked all around and wondered whether I would

ever see this beautiful town again. The question that really tugged at my heartstrings though was... would I ever be able to visit this town with the man I loved?

Soon we were back at the quayside. The little dinghy pulled out and before long we were pulling up beside the Beagle.

'Thank you Mr Bynoe, Mr. Bennett for your protection and kindness.'

'My pleasure, I am sure Miss.' said Mr. Bynoe.

'Our pleasure Miss' said Mr. Bennett.

Mr. Wickham approached the ladder and extended his hand.

'Why, thank you Mr. Wickham.'

I stepped aboard followed by Fuegia. I noticed that the Captain was by the wheel. I hesitated for a moment, and then walked towards my cabin.

As I reached the end of the companion way,
'Miss O'Mara'
'Yes sir.'
Fitzroy smiled,
'Did you regain your land legs?'
'I did sir, and I wish to thank you.'

2nd March

During the day I met the Captain on deck and he asked,

'Miss O'Mara, this evening after supper would you like to join me and Mr. Darwin in my cabin to tell us what you thought of the town.'

'Oh! Are you sure sir?'
'Miss O' Mara!' he said reproachfully.
I always forgot his word was law on board.

'Sorry sir, I will'

I went directly to my cabin and sat on the bed. Never before had he asked me to converse with him and Mr. Darwin. Had I suddenly gone up in his estimation? I stood up and looked at my warm cheeks in the tiny mirror; my eyes were sparkling because of the Captain's invitation. I placed my hands over my cheeks. A knock at the door drew me away from my romantic thoughts.

'Come in.'

'Oh you look so happy Miss Scarlett' Fuegia beamed.

'I am Fuegia. Can I ask you a favour?'

'Yes Miss Scarlett'

'May I borrow a dress for this evening?'

'Yes Miss Scarlett…but…all too big.'

She looked at me keenly and then,

'Oh Miss Scarlett!' Fuegia's eyes filled with joy as if she had understood all the time how I felt about the Captain. She joined her hands and said,

'Good, good'

I had never confided in her, yet she was perceptive and deep down she understood.

'I bring my green velvet Miss Scarlett; it is the smallest and long.'

'Oh thank you Fuegia.'

Fuegia ran off and came back quickly with the dress, a large scissors and needles and thread.

'Fuegia, I am not cutting your dress.'

'Yes Miss Scarlett, I never ware. You put on I cut, you sew.'

'Oh Fuegia are you sure? It is such beautiful velvet.'

'Quickly Miss Scarlett put on.'

I put on the dress. Fuegia put in the pins drawing it in

to fit my slim frame.

'Take off quickly Miss Scarlett'

I obeyed and Fuegia spread out the dress on the floor and began to cut the velvet into a new shape. Fuegia worked quickly and precisely like a professional.

'Fuegia were you taught to sew?'

'Yes I learn some at the school.'

Fuegia pinned the dress while I threaded several needles with dark green thread. While I sewed Fuegia made a sash from the left over material. We two friends sewed and laughed and I sang the ballads Fuegia liked so much. After three hours, the dress and sash were ready. I put them on.

'Oh Miss Scarlett…your eyes…dress same colour as eyes.'

'Thank you Fuegia, you are a real treasure.'

We attended the Divine Service and then I returned to my cabin with Fuegia.

'You wash now Miss Scarlett and I come back to brush your hair.'

'Will you? Very well, thank you Fuegia.'

Fuegia left and I began my toilet in the tiny cabin. I washed with the freesia soap that Fuegia had given me. I washed and dried my hair. Then I put on the green velvet dress. I looked in the mirror and felt I looked 'good'.

Fuegia came in and said,

'Beautiful, very beautiful.'

'Fuegia began to brush, and then out of her pocket she took a green ribbon and a hair clip.'

'Oh Fuegia…'

'Yes, tonight, Miss Scarlett, you look as beautiful as the moon.'

I began to laugh,

'This is not right thing to say?'

'Yes I am sure it is Fuegia.'

I lifted some of my hair up into the clip and Fuegia tied on the ribbon.'

We both stood still. Then Fuegia said,

'Now Miss Scarlett you put on necklace, quickly while I shine your shoes.'

Then at last I was ready. A knock came on the door and my dinner was delivered. I could not even look at it. Fuegia knew exactly how I felt about food and said nothing. Then she said,

'Now Miss Scarlett you look proper lady, and please... be happy tonight...and'

'And... what Fuegia?'

'And you say nothing to make the Captain angry, please, you promise Miss Scarlett.'

'I promise Fuegia.'

I took the little pearl and gold chain from the box, and Fuegia closed it at the back of my neck. I put on my shoes.

'Good. I see you tomorrow.'

'Thank you again Fuegia' I called out but she was gone.

I looked in the mirror and pinched my cheeks.

'Good' I said aloud.

I know now that I secretly hoped that I would return to my cabin happy and not out of favour with the Captain again. I seemed to irritate him sometimes without any reason. I decided I would let nothing trouble me this evening and hoped and prayed that this might be the beginning of many nights of enjoyable conversation, and even song, on board the Beagle.

Maybe I knew I looked 'good' or maybe I just wanted to show off, or maybe I just wanted to be admired, for one or all of these reasons before I went to the Captain's cabin I went on deck. The officers stood still.

'Good evening Miss O'Mara'

'Good evening gentlemen, what a splendid evening it is.'

'May I be so bold as to say how beautiful you look Miss O'Mara?'

'No you may not Mr. Sulivan, 'beauty is in the eye of the beholder' remember?'

'Yes Miss.'

Then I approached the Captain's cabin, and knocked.

'Come in' the Captain's happy voice rang out.

I opened the door slowly; the Captain was sitting at his table. Mr. Darwin had drawn his chair away from the table as far as the cramped cabin would allow. The gentlemen stood. Captain Fitzroy looked at me and I could see he was taken aback by my appearance. He hesitated and then said,

'Oh good evening Miss O'Mara, Darwin, I have asked Miss O'Mara to join us as she went ashore yesterday for the first time.'

Darwin said 'I am delighted Miss O' Mara. Please be seated.'

He pointed to the only other chair in the cabin. The Captain moved quickly and held the chair. I sat down. A silence ensued and then Darwin said,

'Did the town suit your spirit of adventure Miss O'Mara?'

'Indeed it did Mr. Darwin. Never would I have believed that such beauty existed. The trees, the flowers, the scents, the droning of the insects, all beyond my wildest imaginings… all so different from the green fields of England.'

'What of the buildings?' Fitzroy asked.

'With such natural beauty around I hardly noticed them sir...except to say that the strange long narrow windows puzzled me until I remembered how hot it was, and how the inhabitants probably long for shade. The classical public buildings were impressive, but we had no time to explore the churches.'

A short silence followed. Darwin continued to look at me. I was never embarrassed with Mr. Darwin; he always saw me as a fellow traveller and rejoiced in my small achievements as I rejoiced in his vast accomplishments. Then he said,

'May I say Miss O'Mara how different you look this evening, pray do forgive me for passing such a personal comment?'

'Well Mr. Darwin, I thank you.'

I glanced over at Fitzroy who was frowning and not at all amused at what he considered forward behaviour.

'There is a long story behind my attire Mr. Darwin. You know already how I was brought aboard and my life saved by Captain Fitzroy,' I smiled at him,

'Well, the truth is I had no finery of any kind to make myself look personable. Today Fuegia very kindly cut one of her dresses to fit me, and so, perhaps I look different.'

'I would say you look a picture Miss O'Mara.'

'Thank you sir, but more than most people you know that it is what is in the heart, the mind and the soul that makes a person what they are, and certainly not clothes.'

'Ah but we must not neglect to mention the beauty that the clothes adorn.'

I looked at Mr. Darwin. He sounded slightly inebriated, but that could not be as there was never any alcohol on board the Beagle as far as I knew. He always chose his words so carefully when the Captain was present yet tonight he seemed not to care what the Captain thought.

I looked at Captain Fitzroy and saw anger rising in his eyes. I felt fear and panic rise inside me that I had done it again… made him angry.

'Captain have I said something wrong? Have I offended you?'

'No Miss O' Mara save to remind me that as yet I have not provided a wardrobe for you as I promised.'

'Captain Fitzroy, sir, I do not expect you to buy clothes for me.'

He sat silent glaring at Darwin who seemed quite oblivious to his humour.

'Did you go to the market, Miss O' Mara and perhaps purchase that rather becoming necklace?'

'Yes, we went to the market, Mr. Darwin and I am afraid to say that Fuegia, unknown to me, told Mr. Bennet that I liked this necklace. He purchased it. I told him he should not have done so, and that it was quite improper for me to accept it. He seemed so upset I had to relent and after all it was kind of him.'

'Indeed and it becomes you Miss O' Mara.'

'Thank you again Mr. Darwin.'

'Tell me how are your studies going?'

'Studies?' Fitzroy tried to sound indifferent, but I saw that look in his eyes.

I wondered how we could get to a safe subject.

'Yes sir, I am trying to acquire a working knowledge of Spanish.'

'Indeed' Fitzroy's shoulders rose in tension as he frowned. He spoke Spanish fluently.

'Miss O'Mara's knowledge of poetry, song and Scripture

are good Fitzroy, as we know from our conversations in the gun room, now she wishes to become a linguist.'

'Oh not so Mr. Darwin, you flatter me. I am not very good at any of those subjects and even less so at languages. No, it is just that I know a little more than the officers about poetry and it is my way of retaliating.'

'Retaliating for what may I ask?' Fitzroy's voice was cold as ice.

'Well sir, they know that my knowledge of sea faring is practically nil, so they ask me impossible questions and set traps for me. I generally oblige by falling straight into them.'

At last Darwin sat up straight and became alert. He looked alarmed now, knowing how the Captain reprimanded the men for any slight offence.

'It is all done in a very respectful way, and in no way compromises your dignity. Is that not so, Miss O' Mara?'

'Oh that is correct Mr. Darwin. I thoroughly enjoy ever moment of the charade.'

A long weighty silence followed. Fitzroy looked at Darwin, Darwin looked at me. Then Darwin said,

'Will you sing for us Miss O'Mara?'

'If you wish and the Captain approves.'

'Of course I approve' the words shot from his lips like an order.

'Is this yet another one of your hidden talents Miss O'Mara?' He asked in a quieter voice. He looked at me coldly and sounded annoyed. I wondered if I should make some excuse not to sing.

'Indeed it is not hidden Fitzroy. Miss O'Mara often recites and sings for us in the gunroom. What will you sing for us tonight?'

'Well, let me think…how about 'La ci darem…'

'Do your linguistic abilities extend to the Italian Miss O'Mara and Don Giovanni?'

'Indeed not Captain, and to tell you the truth I have no idea how I know or remember these arias, ballads and poems that I recite, but I know your own knowledge of the Italian is substantial.'

'Prey begin, then' he said enthusiastically.

'Please remain seated gentlemen. I will stand.'

I took a deep breath and mentally tried to find the key, and then I began,

'La ci darem la mano…'

This was the first time I was able to sing for the Captain and to say the least I felt embarrassed, as I never did in the gunroom. I sang quietly, however my voice seemed too loud for the small cabin. My embarrassment soared and I have no idea how I managed to sing to the end with all these distractions.

When I finished Mr. Darwin began to clap,

'Bravo, beautiful, thank you Miss O'Mara.'

'My pleasure sir.'

I looked at the Captain. He just stared at me, and I did not know whether he was astonished or further annoyed.

Mr. Darwin stood up,

'Will you excuse me Miss O'Mara, Fitzroy, I have my journal to write up and the night draws on.'

'Indeed, goodnight Darwin.' Fitzroy said immediately.

'Good night, Mr. Darwin.'

Then I looked at Fitzroy's countenance, stood up and said,

'I am sure you have work to do also Captain.'

'Well…please wait a moment Miss O'Mara' he said standing up.

Darwin smiled at me, left and closed the door.

'Please sit down.'

I sat down and waited to hear how I had displeased him as usual. I braced myself and after a few minutes silence Fitzroy said in a soft voice,

'To say the least I am upset. There are two things in particular that have upset me this evening.'

'Why sir…have I done something, said something? I would never ever do anything to upset you.'

A new light came into his eyes. He stood up.

'Allow me to move your chair close to the table.'

I stood and sat down again opposite the Captain. He went back to his chair.

'Firstly, Scarlett I find that Mr. Darwin knows far more about you than I do. Also that he thinks he can converse with you and compliment you at will, and I am furious that he should feel he can be so free and familiar with you.'

'But sir…'

I knew I was not meant to speak to Mr. Darwin.

'Sir you must admit that he is a very interesting man, the enterprise he pursues is fascinating and his enthusiasm is inspiring and…'

I stopped as I saw Fitzroy's mouth harden and his shoulders stiffen.

'Yes, yes, yes and …' he snarled.

'And you have to admit that apart from all that he is a very amiable person.'

I said in a whisper.

'Am I not an amiable person?'

'I don't know'

'You are sure about Mr. Darwin but not about me?'

'What I am trying to say sir... is that I can be no judge of what you are because my affection for you does not allow me to judge without prejudice.'

A long silence followed

'It seems to me Miss O'Mara that as far as you think about me at all, it is with an irrational fascination, whereas you think of Mr. Darwin as a hero in a very rational manner.'

I did not answer; I knew that this was not true. I also now knew that once he had arrived at this way of thinking I could never make him understand. No one could ever tell the Captain of one of His Majesty's ships that he was wrong anyway.

'Dare I ask you – something very personal?'

'Yes. Please ask me anything.'

'Do you think perhaps... you find yourself in an irrational way, to be in love with me?'

'I don't think, I' know' sir, that I love you with all my heart...and it is not irrational.'

There I had said it and come what may I felt relieved to have spoken the words that had been hidden in my heart for so long. I knew also that in a certain way it was irrational, but not in the way the Captain meant.

Fitzroy stared at me now and I knew from his eyes that I had made a dreadful mistake. To say such a thing aloud and so boldly was not ladylike, but...but he had asked the question. Then his eyes took on an incredible sadness. He stood up and started to walk. He walked three paces forward, three paces back, repeatedly until I thought that maybe I should just leave. He seemed unable to regain his composure. At last I could stand it no longer,

'Was it wrong of me to say what I did so boldly sir? It was rude of me. I apologise.'

The silence persisted apart from the sound of his footsteps, and I thought they must have been echoing throughout the ship by now.

'Are you betrothed to another sir?'

'Do you know what you are saying Miss O'Mara? '

'Yes sir.'

'You say that, even though you are well acquainted with my changeable temperament, at times my …ill humour… my long silences… I fear you know too little about me to make such a declaration of love.'

'I know more about you than you think sir. I always listen if your name is mentioned and I am well aware…'

I stopped, too often had I said too much to him. I was about to say that I knew about what happened on the Thetis when he was Flag Lieutenant, and what happened when the whaleboat was taken. On both of these occasions he had acted unreasonably.

Instead I said,

'…that I constantly displease you and do not conform to the decorum of the genteel ladies of your acquaintance.'

For the first time he stopped pacing and he began to smile.

'Indeed, that may be so, but what, I wonder, has the very astute Miss O'Mara to say of my failings?'

'I have nothing to say sir. I only know that whatever happens my love for you will never change nor will it die…
'it is an ever-fixed mark that looks on tempests and is never shaken;'

I looked at him and smiled. He sat down. Another silence followed and then to my amazement tears began to flow from his eyes and drip down his cheeks. .

'Why are you crying sir?'

'Because, Miss O'Mara,'

He took a handkerchief and wiped his face,

'…there is not a man on this ship, or anywhere in the world perhaps, who would not be completely overwhelmed by…by your beauty, and if you told any man… you loved him he would no doubt, celebrate his good fortune, shout aloud for joy, drink champagne and consider himself the luckiest man upon the earth.'

He stood up again and walked away from the table, came back and sat down again. He looked into my eyes and said, 'Alas, in my position as a Captain in His Majesty's Navy, all these reactions would be inappropriate. Bankrupt as I am of all these possibilities, I can only weep. Indeed the fascination you feel for me at this moment in time will soon pass. It has come about no doubt because I rescued you from the storm.'

He looked so intently into my eyes now that I felt faint.

'Does that mean sir that it is impossible for you to feel any affection for me…or love me?'

'There is no question of love here Miss O'Mara.'

I felt an arrow of sadness cut across my heart as if a grave wound had entered my body and the pain began instantly. Tears began welling up in my eyes.

'Do you not believe that I love you sir?'

'No of course you do not love me.'

His tears had passed and he was back to the Captain… in charge.

'You are enchanted with the life at sea; for some reason you are infatuated with me.

In fact you hold this fascination probably because you continue to see me as your rescuer. You harbour these romantic notions, you are not your self in this regard, and if you will forgive me saying so, from what I have observed this evening you have a far more firmly based friendship with Mr. Darwin.'

I looked at him intently. I put my hands over my face. I wanted to say I would not forgive him for that outrageous statement. It was impossible to try to tell this man anything. Whatever he made of any situation that was what it was. He was never challenged, that was what a Captain's life was like.

I took my hands away from my face. He was looking at his papers. He looked up and for the first time that evening, I sensed the old agitation coming over him. He looked at me so coldly that I thought I would die. I longed for that look to change into the one he had when the tears fell down his cheeks. I tried to collect my thoughts and act with dignity. I must be realistic. He had no time for me. For the rest of my life the words he uttered would ring in my ears,

'There is no question of love here Miss O'Mara.'

Yes, these words would haunt me forever. Then I stood up. He shot to his feet.

'I will go now Captain Fitzroy. It has indeed been an informative evening. Thank you sir.'

'There is no need to leave yet. You... will not comment then on what I have said Miss O'Mara.'

'No sir, I am sure you are right in everything you say.'

'But...' he stopped

I thought this was the only way to speak to him. He looked at me. Then I noticed the sadness lingering about his eyes. Had he hoped I would contradict him? While these thoughts were running though my mind, he said,

'Good evening Miss O'Mara.'

I walked towards the door.

'By the way sir, you said there were two things you were not pleased about this evening. What was the second?

'Oh! It concerned the necklace you are wearing Miss O' Mara. Wearing it may give Mr. Bennett or other members of the crew the wrong impression about you. It may be as well to wait until you leave the ship before you wear it.'

'Be assured sir, I will never wear it on board again.'

'Thank you Miss O' Mara.'

'Good night sir.'

I could not remember walking back to the cabin. When I became conscious of things again I was on my knees by the bunk. I tried to pray. Then I began to sob. Scenes of my childhood that I had tried so hard to remember and could not, now came floating into my conscientiousness.

I remembered how my mother read from the poetry books. She read the sonnets of Shakespeare, the poetry of Donne, Wordsworth and Blake. I could hear her soft lilting voice, her perfect diction and the beautiful poetic words lifting me into dreamlands where I met fascinating people.

I closed my eyes and tried to think until my head fell exhausted on the bed. I stood up and carefully took off the dress and folded it across the chair. My thoughts kept flitting away into other years. I tried to think only of the scenes that had just passed in the Captain's cabin. I wanted to go over them again because however remote the possibility I might be able to find an explanation for the Captain's words, and that would ease the pain. Otherwise that pain would throb away in my heart for the rest of my life.

I wanted to see how I could have avoided hearing the words spoken frankly from his lips. He had no interest whatever in me as a woman. I was looking for a word, a gesture, an inflection on a word, anything that might give me hope. I tried in vain and my mind began to play tricks on me. No matter how hard I tried the scenes of my childhood kept looming up before my eyes, then back to the Captain again.

He thought my friendship with Mr. Darwin had a sounder footing. How absurd! I have no friendship with Mr. Darwin. However the Captain had no interest in what he called 'my infatuation with him' or 'my romantic notions'.

If I had not been so frank in declaring my love for him perhaps, I would not have known for a long time how he felt. However hard it is, it is better to know. It is better to embrace the pain now and try to let go of it forever.

Never before had I been interested in any gentleman, as far as I could remember. But then I had never met a gentleman like the Captain. I could not think of a single day in the rest of my life when I would not long to spend it with Robert Fitzroy. This incredible man who saved me from the howling ocean and a sad early grave, I loved with all my heart.

I got into bed and tried to lie still. I knew I would never sleep, well not for many a long hour anyway. My heart was still throbbing. My body continued to quiver as I felt cold then hot consecutively. I shivered uncontrollably and all these feelings raced through my body and mind for hours.

Even if he finds me attractive in any way, which he does not, he will never even think of me as a ...bride. He looks upon me as a duty...a duty... he has to return me to England...that is his only concern about me. Surely it would not break the protocol for him to praise something about me, but he never dose so. Now I know my heart must truly break.

'Break, break, break then…and let it be over.'
Yet I know it is never over. Love is never over.

4th March

Over the last few days I have felt dead inside. I hardly ate or drank. Today I went on deck when Fuegia had dressed me and made me walk up the companionway to embrace the fresh air.

'All this is not good Miss Scarlett'
'I know' I whispered.

Mr. Wickham saluted me but I could not bring myself to respond. Mr. Sulivan said something, but I could not understand what he said, and I was back in the cabin within the quarter hour. I attended the Divine Service but the Captain didn't even look in my direction.

7th March

During these lonely days I did not even have the pleasure of seeing Mr. Darwin, with whom I longed to exchange a few words. He was confined to his cabin with a knee infection. I longed to go to the poop cabin and read to him. However that would not be acceptable in this very silly world in which we live where women are barred from so many situations. I thought of gaining access under the pretence of borrowing a book from the library. Indeed the cabin was used as the library and chart room and to store some gear or other whose name I can never remember.

10th March

There seemed to be a grand dinner on the quarterdeck today as a Captain Paget has come aboard. The Captain and all the officers seem to be enjoying the festivities, and I envy the conviviality and cordiality these young men have together.

12th March

Then one evening, because of my deep sadness I fear I have lost track of the correct date – Mr. Darwin returned to the ship. Without any warning I heard voices raised in anger. First Mr. Darwin, then the Captain's voice rang out even louder. I couldn't hear the words properly. There was silence and then another exchange.

'My God' I whispered,

'The Captain and Mr. Darwin are in the heat of an argument.'

I knew not to move from the cabin. All the crew knew about the Captain's temper, but Mr. Darwin was a passenger and not given to raising his voice. Then I heard Mr. Wickham summoned to the Captain's cabin. I heard Mr. Sulivan going to the poop cabin. An hour passed; whatever happened seemed to have been resolved.

Over the previous days I had lost all interest in what was happening on the ship. This incident brought me back to reality with trepidation. As the evening drew on I put on my shoes and went on deck.

'Good evening gentlemen.' I looked at the dark faces of the officers.

'Good evening Miss.' they answered.

I went to the rail and held on to it. It was a beautiful evening:

'…From the altar of dark ocean
To the sapphire-tinted skies'

I wondered if even Shelley ever experienced the stark colours of this dark blue ocean and the immense glow in the southern skies.

I felt a touch on my arm and jumped.

'Miss O'Mara…how good to see you! Excuse me if I startled you…you were a long way from the Beagle in your thoughts were you not?'

'I was contemplating the beauty of the evening Mr. Darwin'

He nodded.

'Tell me did you have any good discoveries while ashore?'

'I did.' Darwin hesitated.

'You think me incapable of understanding their significance?'

'No…no certainly not, to tell you the truth I feel exhausted and …'

I wondered if he was about to mention his quarrel with the Captain.

'And…I am not looking forward to the open sea.'

'Oh Mr. Darwin I wish there was something that could be done to help you.'

'Oh there you are Miss O'Mara. I have been looking for you.'

'Yes Mr. Sulivan.'

'The Captain wishes to speak to you Miss.'

'Thank you Mr. Sulivan' I said and he left.

I looked at Mr. Darwin who knew well that the Captain was now going to involve me in their quarrel. I think we both knew in our hearts about the occasional irrational malfunction in the Captain's thinking and emotions. We knew that neither of us would mention it at this time. We both had a deep admiration and affection for the Captain despite this frailty. I looked again at him, and regardless of good conduct, I put my hand on his arm,

'Mr. Darwin, I hope you have a good night's sleep, who knows we may have a very calm sea ahead.'

'Thank you Miss O'Mara' he managed a faint smile, 'I hope so.'

I made my way to the Captain's cabin and knocked.

'Come in.'

He stood as I entered.

'Scarlett, where have you been? I sent for you a long time ago.'

He said this as if we had spoken everyday since the 2nd March. What about the last ten days? Had it slipped his memory that in all that time he hadn't spoken to me?'

'I am sorry sir. I went for a walk.'

'Sit down please.'

Then the usual melancholic silence began. I waited and waited. Eventually I ventured a question,

'Why did you send for me sir?'

'Because Scarlett I am very upset.'

'What hast upset you sir?'

'Mr. Darwin accused me of supporting the slave trade.'
He picked up the coin.

'Do you think I uphold the slave trade?'

'No sir, I do not.'

He was silent then.

'There must have been a misunderstanding somehow.'

'No Scarlett, I am a Tory. He is a Whig. Why is it assumed because one is a Tory one automatically agrees with slavery? Or why would anyone think that because of my upbringing that I think the Feudal System acceptable?'

I did not answer. Then I said,

'The slave trade is innately wrong is it not?'

'Yes of course it is, but in the real world it exists, and whenever it is finally abolished it will be a process over time and not the action of a day or two,' he said with contempt.

'And… it does not follow that all slave owners are cruel.'

'By chance did you inadvertently sound as if you supported it, sir?'

He did not answer.

'If I happened to mention that as far as I could see some slaves were content with their lot…well he had the effrontery to insinuate that I am a liar.'

'To be honest sir nothing whatsoever in my opinion could justify the use of slaves, and maybe that was what Mr. Darwin was thinking.'

'Whatever he was thinking Miss O'Mara, he did not have the right to raise his voice to a Captain in his Majesty's Navy.'

'No sir it did not.' I hesitated.

'However, he respects you more than anyone I know, sir. Perhaps at times he does not show gratitude for all you have done for him but, he is an outstanding geologist. You are two outstanding men. Please do not allow this matter to come between you. Do remain good friends, as that is invaluable to both of you on this voyage.'

'Indeed. So why would he imagine that I would endorse the slavery?'

'There must have been a misunderstanding. Captain, you know how important your friendship is. You both thoroughly respect each other.'

However hard I tried I could not find the words to

change his mood. The darkness hovered over his eyes as the black dog of depression pursued him relentlessly.

'Captain the officers and crew have the utmost respect for you, that is what matters.'

He did not answer.

Then I leaned towards him and whispered,

'You know how highly I value your friendship, in fact you are everything to me, and…I have loved you from the first moment I saw you.'

He looked up astonished, put down the coin and stood up. My heart almost stopped. Was he about to dismiss me? I knew he considered bringing sentiment into any argument was quite inappropriate and so I held my breath.

Then he sat down and looked directly at me. He had become bogged down in the argument, in anger, and in despair. I was trying anything to move his mind away from the subject. He stretched out his hand, and placed it over mine.

'Scarlett' he whispered. I was astounded. A minute ago…

'Promise me sir you will let go of this trivia.'

'Trivia' he raised his voice and drew his hand away,

'This matter is not trivial'

'I know it is not, in the big picture of the life of the world, but in the everyday life of the Beagle yes it is. What counts is the voyage. You are a courageous and upright gentleman and you will not allow an insignificant argument, where, I may say, you both lost your tempers, come between you. You are both too important for that. I have heard Mr. Darwin say that he has never met anyone whom he would think of as an Napoleon, or a Nelson except you.'

'He said that?'

'Yes sir. He admires your character immensely.'

At last I saw the beginning of a light come back into the dark eyes, and then the silence continued as he looked at his papers.

'Promise me before I leave sir that you will rise above this incident.'

He looked up,
'Yes' he said abruptly.
'Promise.'
He smiled at last.
'I promise.'
'I understand how you brood over this kind of thing. Now you can't because you have promised.'

He smiled again.
'Very well. You win.'
We looked at each other and very quietly he whispered,
'There has never been anyone who understands me like you Scarlett.'

I was on the verge of crying. It was the most difficult thing for him to say…but he had said it.

'At last!' I whispered as I realized his thoughts had moved on.

Now he began to smile and then laugh aloud. At last the tension left his face and eyes.

'Will you sleep tonight?'
'Yes Scarlett you are my …'
I leaned across the table and put my finger on his lips. Then I stood up.
'Good night Captain.'
He stood,
'Good night Miss O'Mara.'
Some time later Mr. Sulivan told me that even before

I ever went to speak to the Captain that night he had already sent an apology to Mr. Darwin. It was one of the most endearing aspects of his character that he never held a grudge whether he was in the wrong or not.

18th March

The Beagle left Bahia today and the frantic life of the ship began again. Everyone is in good spirits except me. I languish away in my cabin and even Mr. Darwin has noticed that I have lost weight.

The heat is oppressive but I like the tropics. Indeed it is not the heat that bothers me. I felt sure Captain Fitzroy would have sent for me but he has not done so. How stupid of me to think after that night of the quarrel with Mr. Darwin that we were good friends again. I have hardly spoken to him since then and my heart is breaking. In my unease I long for the presence of my dead parents.

I took my last glimpse at All Saints Bay as the voyage resumed and all seemed well with the crew in the little brig. The following days passed quietly. Then a few nights later the old dream came back again. I did not wake up screaming but it's horror pursued me persistently, intent on my destruction.

21st March

One night the dream seemed more vivid and frightening than ever before. The pattern was always the same. I saw the cabin filling up with water...water everywhere. I tried to tell myself that it was not happening in reality, but the water continued to rise. I felt a sharp pain in my chest and perspiration streamed down my face. The water had *reached my lips and I was finding it difficult to breathe. I knew that I had to get out.*

I jumped out of bed, put on my clothes, pulled on my shoes and put a shawl around my shoulders. I made my way cautiously up the companionway through the darkness to the deck. I had just begun to breathe when the watch bell rang out and startled me. I drew back into the shadows… without warning a strong arm grabbed me from behind. I tried to scream when a filthy hand went over my mouth. I could feel the cold steel of a blade next to my throat. In a lightening flash my arms were held and I was turned to face my attacker. A trembling seized me when I saw the anger in his eyes.

'One sound out of you and you are dead' he said

'You are not going to cause any more trouble on this ship. You may be able to fool the Captain and the officers, but you don't fool me.'

'Know why me lady?' He made a mocking bow of his head.

'You see my home is near the Lizard and I did see you there with a man who was no gentleman – no, nor a tradesman neither. He was what us common folk call a vagrant. You were talking to him. Do you deny it?' I shivered,

'No. I… can't remember.'

'Very convenient like.'

He drew the knife into my skin and the blood began to drip down slowly onto my dress.

'You have brought bad luck on this ship. I am going to change that. You have bewitched our Captain; I am going to change that.'

'Drop the knife Russell.' Mr. Stewart's voice was strong and firm.

'No sir, she is a fraud sir. She is no lady sir.'

'For the last time drop the knife Russell.'

Russell scowled, dug the knife a little further into my skin and then threw it down so that the blade struck the deck and wobbled.

'Mr. Johnson, Mr. Mellersh take him below and put him in irons. May God have mercy on you Russell when I report this to the Captain.'

My eyes began to close, my knees buckled and I fell back. Mr. Stewart held me before I reached the deck. Everything went black. When I opened my eyes I saw several versions of Stewart go round and round in the darkness. I closed my eyes and the night closed in on me as if there would never be another dawn.

Some time later I felt a stinging on my throat and fresh water on my face and the delicate touch of Fuegia's hands dabbing a soft towel on my cheeks. I opened my eyes...it was not Fuegia it was the Captain. Before I could speak he said,

'Miss O' Mara Mr. McCormick is here.' He gestured behind him, and then stood aside. McCormick stood there looking distinctly annoyed.

'He says the cut is only superficial' the Captain said.

'I think that is all I can do for now,' said McCormick in an impatient tone.

'Yes thank you.' said Fitzroy.

He collected his medical box and left.

'Sir, you must put me off at the very next port.'

'Certainly not, where would you go? What could you do?'

'You must, you must.' I could not hold back the tears any longer.

'You must, I have brought bad luck, I must get off this ship.'

'You have brought the best of luck to us all Miss O'Mara. Every officer and seaman on board has acknowledged the elegance and brightness you bring to our days.'

'That is not what Russell said.'

'Oh! Russell…well…he was suffering from some fever or other.'

'No he was not.' Fitzroy looked startled.

'Well, if he was not, I will add another dozen lashes to his punishment.'

'No, no, no, no lashes please, please I beg you sir.'

He looked intently at me.

'I think I am the person in charge of this ship Miss O'Mara.'

He looked irritated, and I felt that if I had not been ill he would have said a lot more about my insolence.

'You concentrate on your health and your reading. I must go now.'

Then he was gone. Here I was again back in his cabin in the middle of the night. Russell was right. I had to get off this ship.

DISCOVERY

HARRY AND BLOOM SAT SILENTLY in the study and read the first letter they had retrieved from the Maritime Museum. It was from Captain Fitzroy to Beaufort, the head hydrographer at the Admiralty.

Dear Captain Beaufort,

Upon leaving the English Channel on December 27th 1831 we came across a small boat and drew alongside. In it was a young lady that on first sight we took to be dead. Considering the severity of the storm it was indeed difficult to perceive that she was alive. As well as suffering the affects of the storm she had sustained severe injuries to her head and person. You will readily understand that we had no alternative but to take her on board and treat her injuries. The ship's surgeon was called and treatment was given. Eventually she recovered save for her loss of memory.

She has two books with her, and from these she is given to believe that her name is Scarlett O'Mara. Personally, I do not believe this is her name for indeed she seems to me to be a very genteel, well read English lady of the aristocratic class. She has conducted herself on board to the highest standard of behaviour, with dignity and decorum, and gained the respect and honour of the entire ship's company.

I have, Sir, reported this incident to you at my earliest

convenience, and urgently await your instructions in the matter.

I have the honour of being
Sir,
Your very obedient,
humble servant
Robert Fitzroy Commander.

'Well this is surely our proof…she was on board the Beagle' Harry sounded elated.

'Yes, that is amazing, but what about the letter from the Admiralty?' Bloom asked

They both read in silence.

Dear Captain Fitzroy,

Captain Beaufort has passed your letter to me. It is of great vexation to me and to his Majesty's Navy that you took upon yourself to rescue this young lady and not return her immediately to the English shore. Therefore I caution you that the following instructions in her regard are to be followed to the letter.

Upon your arrival in Rio de Janeiro two agents, sent out by Sir William Knighton, previously Secretary to his late Majesty, King George IV, will board your vessel. You will hand this young lady, known as Scarlett O'Mara over to them, and to them alone. They will identify themselves with a letter to you containing the seal of Sir William Knighton. I caution you once more to follow these instructions to the letter and to inform the Lords of the Admiralty immediately this occurrence is complete.

I furthermore instruct you to obtain an oath from the entire ship's company, and all on board, that they will never disclose the presence of the said young lady upon his Majesty's ship 'Beagle' or upon oath ever to identify her person.

Sir James, Robert, George Graham,
First Lord of the Admiralty.

After a few minutes Harry asked,

'Why was Knighton sending out his agents to take Scarlett from the ship?

'I don't know.' Bloom said.

'The only information we have about Knighton is that he was secretary to King George IV who died in 1830.'

'That was before Scarlett was found in the rowing boat.'

'I think I could begin by looking into what Knighton was up to…say around 1830 to 1831.'

'Very well.'

'Bloom you take the Naval aspect of the research, see if you can find a link between Sir James Graham and Sir William Knighton.'

'I would guess that Sir James had no idea what Knighton was up to.'

'Probably not. In the mean time I must read on in the diary and look for a clue there.'

There was a knock on the door and Miss Pierce, the housekeeper entered and said,

'There is a Mr. Goldberg on the phone for you sir.'

23rd March 1831

The following day, after the attack, I moved back to Sulivan's cabin. I stayed there and did not come out for three days. I wondered if in fact there would be a scar on my throat. Fuegia said she thought it was healing very well. During the day we talked and read and today Captain Fitzroy sent for me.

I knocked on his cabin door and waited.
'Come in.'
'Fitzroy and Hellyer stood up. Hellyer moved from his chair and indicated for me to sit down.

'Are you well Miss O' Mara?'

'Yes thank you Captain.'

'Good. We have all missed your presence on the deck. It is not healthy for you to entirely confine yourself to your cabin.'

'I think it best if I keep to my cabin, or rather Mr. Sulivan's cabin sir.'

'Miss O'Mara I order…I request… you please to take your daily exercise. We all look forward to your company, is that not so Mr. Hellyer?'

'Indeed we do sir.'

'There you are. Besides your countenance is woefully pale, will you therefore please resume your previous routine.'

'Very well sir…if you are sure.'

'I am sure Miss O'Mara.'

'And Russell sir, what is to become of him?'

'He will be punished for threatening your life.'

'I wish to plead for him sir. He seemed to think he saw me near the Lizard and I am in no position to deny what he said because I can't remember anything.'

'Whatever he said Miss O' Mara did not give him the right to threaten the life of one of my passengers'

'You do not understand sir. He felt he was doing his duty, protecting you and the ship.'

'From what may I ask?'

'From me, sir'

Fitzroy burst out laughing and Hellyer sniggered.

'Miss O' Mara kindly leave the running of the ship to me. That will be all. Thank you.'

He stood to indicate the interview was over. I stood and said,

'You are an extremely intelligent man Captain Fitzroy; however in this instance you are wrong. Flogging is, and always will be, barbaric.'

I saw the shock register on his face, and the anger rise in his eyes that I should dare to speak to him like that in the presence of a member of the crew. Before he had time to reply I left.

25th March

Eventually Fuegia and I did resume our walks on the deck and when invited by the Captain I joined the officers for supper. However he never invited me to join him or Mr. Darwin again. He dined mostly with Darwin or alone. Sometimes Mr. Darwin dined with the officers.

Perhaps he thought me not intelligent enough or sufficiently well read to talk in such exalted company. Perhaps deep down he despised my behaviour because at times he believed I allowed my emotions to rule. Whatever it was it hurt me profoundly, but whatever the situation my admiration for Captain Fitzroy from the beginning of the voyage remained resolute and indeed, the love I felt for him grew stronger.

Monday 26th March

Yesterday the Captain spoke to Fuegia and me and told us to take our walk today after dinner. He offered no explanation.

This morning I heard Boatswain Sorrell pipe for ships company to assemble. I brushed my hair and but on my black velvet cloak over my shabby green dress. I edged up near the companionway and listened.

Russell was brought up from the hold in chains. I peeped around and saw that he looked pale, unshaven, and emaciated. His eyes were the eyes of a dead man, a man who had lost all hope. His skin was dark and he had a frozen look, as if held in a time span.

Fitzroy stood on the poopdeck with his officers and the ships company had assembled. He spoke clearly and distinctly,

'David Russell, for threatening the life of a civilian passenger you are sentenced to twenty-four lashes and to be kept in irons until the end of the voyage. Thereafter to be brought before the Lords of the Admiralty to be sentenced at their pleasure'…or something to that effect.

I gathered all the courage I could and moved quickly towards the poopdeck. I stood in front of Captain Fitzroy.

'Captain Fitzroy, sir, I beg mercy for the prisoner.'

Fitzroy's eyes flared and he almost exploded with anger.

'Leave the bridge at once Miss O'Mara' He said in a firm deliberate voice.

'No Captain, he was driven to what he did by…

'Mr. Sulivan'

'Yes sir'

'Kindly escort Miss O'Mara to her cabin.'

I flung myself to the floor on my knees before Fitzroy and held unto his legs with my cheek against his boots.

'Please sir, listen to me…have mercy on the prisoner…'

Fitzroy, and the whole ships company were so taken aback that nobody moved a muscle. Even the breeze and the sails seemed to be still. The silence was awesome.

'Mr. Sulivan.'

'Yes sir.'

'I gave an order.'

'Yes sir'

Sulivan stepped forward lifted me up into his arms and walked smartly towards the companionway. On the deck the silence continued. Loud and clear I stated,

'Put me down Mr. Sulivan.'

Then I entered the door of my cabin and banged it shut. I could not see but I could hear Fitzroy's infuriated voice,

'Mr. Wickham'

'Yes sir'

'Take over the punishment log.'

'Yes sir'

I went on my knees as the lashes rang out on deck. Only once did I hear Russell whimper. I lay on the bunk. I refused to cry. This man, this Captain was like a god on the ship. Surely he could have decided not to punish Russell? Was not keeping him in irons and in the hold sufficient punishment? He looked as if he did not wish to live and had the pallor of death about him.

I began to wonder what might be the outcome of such and incident, so I crept out of the cabin and listened. The Captain stormed off the deck and went to the poopcabin.

I could hear him walking back and forth in nervous agitation. After a few minutes Darwin followed him and sat at the table. There was a long awful silence. Then at last the Captain spoke,

'The sheer audacity of the woman…to say 'no' to a Captain of his Majesty's Fleet… I had so much respect for her, and then she makes a complete fool of herself before the entire ship's company.'

He continued to pace the few paces accessible behind the

chart table. Then he banged his fist on the chart table and scattered everything…

'What an appalling display of emotional indulgence.'

At last Darwin spoke,

'I think you underestimate her Fitzroy. She knows, and we all know that flogging is barbaric. The fight she put up to save that…that man …well…it took courage and she did not recoil from it.'

'I observed that you were not well disposed towards her Darwin. Perhaps you had already noticed this defect in her nature…a total disregard for authority.'

'You are misled sir, I have always admired Miss O'Mara.'

'Well why has she made such a fool of herself before the ship's company?'

'Come, come Fitzroy there is not a man on board who will not admire her for what she did.'

'Admire her…surely you are wrong. They will despise her lack of decorum and unrestrained emotional outburst.'

'If you think what she did was just an emotional outburst I fear you are wrong again. She was put to the test as to whether she would make a stand against flogging and she did, because it was on her account the man was being flogged.'

'It seems to me…I must say…that…that you seem to think a deuce of a lot about how she thinks!'

Another deathly silence followed. Then Darwin burst out laughing. Then the Captain joined in.

'If you had seen the faces on deck, and especially Russell's, the admiration was dripping from him.'

'After he tried to kill her, don't forget' the Captain said.

'He would not try to kill her now. He underestimated his victim I tell you.'

I had heard enough and sneaked back into the cabin. I stayed there for the rest of the day and as night approached I went on deck to look for Mr. Sulivan.

'Mr. Sulivan would you be able to tell me what the outcome of the flogging was?'

'Yes Miss, but firstly may I say Miss O'Mara I'm sorry for lifting you up like that, please do not be embarrassed, but being aware of your stubborn nature I was afraid an unbecoming scuffle might ensue, so I lifted you up to avoid such an incident.'

'Indeed.' I looked away. Then I asked,

'Is the Captain still angry Mr. Sulivan?'

'Well, earlier this evening when Captain Fitzroy had fully regained his composure he came on deck. We officers at the wheel stood still. The Captain joined us and stood still. Nobody spoke and the tension was increasing by the second. At last he said,

'An awful incident gentlemen.'

Nobody had the courage to speak and so we nodded. Then Sorrell said,

'It was out of hand indeed sir, but I am sure a flogging seems very cruel to a young lady sir.'

The Captain nodded.

'Most young ladies would not have had her courage sir.' I said.

'Is that what you think gentlemen?' The Captain's voice was strong and clear now, as usual.

'We do sir,' said Wickham.

'Yes sir, yes sir,' the other officers agreed. We noted the relief in his face, and then he said as he left the deck,

'Keep a straight course Mr. Sorrell.'
'Aye, aye sir'
'Thank you Mr. Sulivan.'

I quickly went back to the cabin. I pondered on all that had happened during the day and wondered if the Captain would ever forgive me.

27*th* March

The following day the Captain sent for me after dinner. Fuegia brushed my hair and I left the cabin ready for the usual reproaches and reprimands.

'Good afternoon Miss O' Mara. Please sit down.'

'Good afternoon sir.' I could see that the anger had passed out of his eyes.

The usual long silence ensued.

'Your insolence to me, a Captain in his Majesty's Navy, your emotional display, and your verbal outburst before the entire ship's company I might add, was quite outrageous.'

'I apologise if I was rude to you sir. I was trying to save the lad, as well as make a point.'

'Indeed. I feel you did not achieve either, and only succeeded in displaying a feminine emotional lack of control.'

'Yes, I thought you might see it like that, because you are so severe when you judge me and you judge me often. Perhaps there are some among the ship's company who would not agree with you.'

'That is hardly the point.'

'However you know and I know that flogging is barbaric, and for a man who in his intelligence, scientific enquiry, talent, affection and compassion is in every essence ahead of his time, I fail to see how you can allow it.'

Fitzroy was taken aback. Then he smiled, I realized at that moment that the confidence he displayed was not very deep; it was like an outer shell and I could see that he was thrilled that I thought so highly of him.

'You think so?'

'Yes sir.'

'Tell me how do you find Mr. Darwin?'

Silently I wondered why he was always comparing himself to Darwin.

'He is an exceptional man sir. In fact, I have never met his equal in purpose and enquiry, ever seeking to elucidate the secrets of nature. It is, in my opinion, his ability to collate these regions of knowledge, synchronize them effortlessly...'

Too late had I realized I was saying too much.

' eh...inside his head, and then speak with such ease and clarity about complicated matters.'

'I see.'

Straight away I saw his disappointment and bit my lip. As usual I had said too much but after the last encounter with him, and his indifference towards me, there was no point anymore in trying to shield him or protect him...or love him.

'Do you agree sir?'

'Yes, indeed, indeed.'

A long silence followed while Fitzroy stared at me, picked up the coin and moved it through his fingers. Eventually he looked at his papers. I sat still.

'Will that be all sir?'

'Oh yes. Thank you.' *I stood up. He stood.*

As usual I could not go and leave him feeling sad.

'If I may be so bold Captain Fitzroy, as much as I

admire your human and intellectual qualities I am unable to speak of you in a similar way, or make observations of this kind about you, or comment on where your own particular intellectual interests lie. I know of course that your knowledge of engineering, science, maritime subjects, travel, languages are vastly beyond anything Mr. Darwin comprehends in these areas of knowledge. However I have never had the pleasure of any conversation with you and therefore can not speak about you in the same way.'

'Yes Scarlett…' He waited.

'My duties do not give me the same freedom as Mr. Darwin, surely you understand that.'

'Yes sir, I do.'

'Here is a man, as you say intellectual and vastly talented, but he is on this voyage at his leisure, at his leisure Scarlett. I do not infer by this that he ever wastes time, however he only has himself to please. Whereas I have a heavy schedule every single day to complete.'

This utterance sounded ironic even envious, but I knew that was not his way.

'I would like you to know sir that my admiration for Mr. Darwin is insignificant compared with my admiration for you.'

He looked up quickly as if he had not expected me to say anything further.

'The qualities I see in you sir far outweigh anything I have seen in any other person I know. Forgive me sir for speaking boldly, but you know me well enough… you know I speak my mind. I am sorry if it offends you. It makes me very sad indeed that in doing so you think I am not gentile and do not conform to the rules of etiquette you admire so much in other ladies of your acquaintance.'

A long silence followed. At last Fitzroy smiled.

'You are very genteel Miss O'Mara as much as your forward-looking ideas may seem otherwise. It is true that you do not conform in any way to the behaviour of other ladies of my acquaintance. However, of all the ladies I do know Miss O'Mara not one of them would have dared to defend a man like Russell. What you did was wrong, and driven by an underlying error of premise, however, I admit that you have a strong sense of justice and do not shirk from defending it.'

'Thank you sir, good afternoon.'

'I must make time for conversation Miss O'Mara.'

'That would be delightful sir.'

Our eyes met and I thought I could read in them his willing me to stay, but he said nothing and I left. Had he forgotten that not so long ago I told him that I loved him? Was this his way of dealing with life…pretending certain things have not happened? Was this his way of saying,

'I know in a rash moment you professed love for me… but we all know that that was a delusion you had from being at sea and being rescued, so the best way forward is to ignore that such words ever passed between us.'

When I reached the deck I held unto the rail, pulled the ribbon from my hair and let the sea breeze blow on my face and through my hair. At last a feeling of freedom swept through me, for some reason it filled me with delight, and made me smile.

3rd April

This afternoon Mr. Darwin came on deck. He asked,

'What have you been doing Miss O'Mara?'

'To tell the truth Mr. Darwin…nothing…I am trying to read and learn of course…'

'Of course'

I looked at him keenly. Was he making fun of me?

'You see Mr. Darwin when you go ashore and I wait to see what you have found, and in the mornings when I wait to see what is in the trawling net that…'

'That…Miss O'Mara?'

'I have just realized how silly I must sound Mr. Darwin. I was going to say that those moments were some of the highlights of my day.'

'I would never describe you as silly Miss O'Mara, intense, liberal and courageous, yes, silly…no.'

'Thank you Mr. Darwin, you always make me feel better about myself. Thank you sir'

I moved away to go to my cabin,

'Miss O'Mara, I hope to go for supper to the gunroom tonight.' He smiled,

'Is there any chance you would honour us with your company?'

'Why certainly Mr. Darwin if the Captain agrees, it will be a pleasure.'

'Very well I will speak to him.'

As I walked towards the companionway, Mr. Wickham called out,

'Miss O' Mara would it be fair to say that you have shown deliberate favouritism in your choice today?'

'Stop teasing Mr. Wickham and the answer is… yes.'

A broad smile appeared on Wickham's face.

I went to the gunroom that night and enjoyed the company and conversation.

Sometimes there was a little tension between Mr. Wickham and Mr. Darwin, especially when the bones, clay, dead animals and birds Mr. Darwin brought on board

littered the decks. Under Mr. Wickham's eye the decks were kept in pristine condition. Then there were often raised voices when Mr. Darwin's boxed artefacts were taken from the deck and boarded onto ships heading for England. Despite these differences, they were good friends.

4th April 1832

We lay to during the night and then entered the glorious harbour at Rio on the 5th April. I heard later that the Captain didn't wish to enter at night but waited until morning so that everyone could enjoy the sheer beauty of the Bay as he had done on his first approach. I also heard that for some reason it failed to live up to his expectations this time. I wondered why, was the strain of command beginning to weigh heavily on his young shoulders?

I stood on deck enthralled. I looked at the mountain slopes covered in evergreens with palm trees towards the summit, the lush forests and coconut groves. The city is tucked in under the hills and sparkled in the morning sun. I jumped as Mr. Wickham touched my arm.

'Miss O' Mara would you kindly go below as we will soon be alongside the Admiral's ship and we will be ...'

I interrupted,

'Forgive me Mr. Wickham I was carried away with the view of Rio. I know I have no right to be on deck at this time.'

'It is important today Miss Scarlett that you stay in your cabin.' He looked keenly at me. He had not even noticed that he had used my Christian name.

'Let me assure you Miss that I will make certain you see Rio de Janeiro.'

'Why thank you Mr. Wickham.'

I went quickly to my cabin, and only just in time. Within a few minutes I heard Fitzroy's voice on deck and the officers calling the orders. Then I heard every officer and seaman getting in place for a manoeuvre.

I listened to the orders as the crew took in every inch of sail and then let it out again. I could hear the cheers from the other ships. Then I think all sails were taken in again. The Beagle had displayed a well-disciplined and co-operative crew. The crew did indeed do honour to the Captain, and he no doubt was proud of them. Then a gun fired, I think to salute the little brig now a long way from home. I set to draw a sketch of the bay while the scene was fresh in my memory.

5th April

Today Mr. Darwin went ashore. I went on deck to say goodbye to him. He could see how lonely I was, and I could read in his eyes that he understood.

'Miss O' Mara when I return I will relate my adventures and my findings to you and you in return shall sing for us at supper.'

I smiled and Darwin smiled back. I waved goodbye to him in the cutter and whispered quietly to myself,

'My pleasure sir. Until you return I will probably not speak a word nor be spoken to by another soul except Fuegia.'

7th April

The following days at anchor passed quietly. One morning I woke up and an incident that had happened near the Lizard blazed in my brain and frightened me. It was sparked off by what Russell had said when he had the knife to my throat. For many hours I pondered about it. I waited for a day when the Captain was on board and then after dinner, when I knew the Captain would be writing up his log, I did what I had never done before…I went to his cabin and knocked on the door.

'Come in'

I opened the door slowly. At first he did not look up, then he stood up quickly

'Miss O' Mara is anything amiss?'

'No sir, please forgive the intrusion …I needed to speak to you.'

Without a word he arranged the chair opposite him at the table. I sat down. He sat. His eyes were bright with enquiry.

'It may seem trivial sir, but now I remember being near the Lizard.'

'Good…does this mean your memory is coming back?'

'It is far from good sir, I mean …Russell said he saw me with an uncouth man near the Lizard.'

'Surely Miss O'Mara you have paid no attention to that scoundrel's talk.'

'I beg you sir, please listen. I remember that I was walking through the little hamlet of Poltesco on my way to the church at Ruan Minor when a vagrant approached me and asked me for help. I reached into my bag to find something for him when he fainted away in a dead faint… from hunger no doubt.'

'Quite so.' He sounded bored.

'I knelt down beside him and when he recovered he asked me if I was the person the two toffs were looking for around Cadgwith. I said no, but he said,

'They were describing what you looked like Miss, and I tell you in all my days roaming these parts, there is not one that ever I did see with such colouring.'

'Did they say why were they looking for me?' I asked.

'They said they were on business for Sir William Knighton, and it was the King's business.'

'Scarlett you have heard the name, that's all.'

'Forgive me sir, I have never heard the name before or since.'

'Let me tell you immediately Scarlett that the said Sir William Knighton is a renowned doctor and was secretary to his majesty King George the IV, so you see he could have no connection whatsoever with some vagrant loitering near the Lizard.'

'I am sorry sir, I should not have bothered you.'

'No Scarlett, you must always come to me if you are frightened or you remember something from your past... even if it has no basis in reality.'

'Thank you sir'

I stood, he stood.

'Good afternoon Miss O'Mara.'

I curtsied and left. He had returned to formalities, but I wondered if he even noticed that during our conversation on three occasions, he had called me Scarlett.

I rarely saw Captain Fitzroy again during the following days and weeks. Most days he was away from the ship doing the surveying. He did not send for me the way he used to in the past. If by chance he met me on deck he simply said,

'Good morning Miss O' Mara' or 'Good evening Miss O'Mara' and passed on. He never once looked directly into my eyes when he spoke.

Why was he behaving in this way? Yes, I know now that it had been very foolish of me to have told him how I felt about him. I had made a fool of myself, but did the punishment have to be so severe that we could no longer even speak to each other? It seemed that he would never forgive the antics of this strange girl with the green eyes. For the rest of my life I will regret the dreadful mistake I made the second day of March 1832.

For the present he was making sure I knew my place. I was an uninvited passenger on his ship. Yes, he took me from the sea half dead and brought me back to life. Yes, he would have done that for any young lady. However, I was an unfortunate extra burden aboard the already crowded ship. I was the seventy-fifth or sixth person on board the Beagle. I could not believe that such a small ship could hold so many, and although I never saw other parts of the ship there must have been places that were very crowded.

Captain Fitzroy made sure all areas were kept clean and tidy. He also made sure that I never had access to any other parts of the ship. I asked Mr. Sulivan,

'Why can I not roam freely about the ship as Fuegia is allowed to do?'

'The Captain knows that you would be upset Miss if you saw or heard the crude way that some sailors spoke and lived.'

'Why does he always want to protect me Mr. Sulivan, I am made of sterner stuff than he thinks.'

'I agree with him Miss, and you are more fragile than you are willing to admit.'

'Mr. Sulivan do not imagine that I am ungrateful, indeed I count myself very lucky to have two such courageous gentlemen as yourself and Captain Fitzroy concerned for my honour.'

'My pleasure Miss'

The Captain's dismissive behaviour was very hard to endure. I tried to pretend it was not happening. This was my way of soothing the pain because it was there in my heart from the moment I awoke each day. He had sent for me so often during the first weeks of the voyage. I waited everyday and every evening in fervent anticipation and heart uplifted for a knock on my door and a voice saying,

'The Captain wishes to speak to you Miss O' Mara'.

That day or evening never came. He was probably thinking of scandal, and that would never had entered his head until I told him I was in love with him. I knew that he was right. There could be no contact between us ever again. He thought I was a silly young girl, and I must be left alone until this ridiculous infatuation passed. I could almost hear his cold reasoning mind working it out. Honesty for him was the highest virtue.

'This nonsense that Miss O'Mara was saying is all an illusion. Things like that happened at sea. One must to be on one's guard. It is probably for the best to have no more contact with her.'

This was the hardest thing in my life that I ever had to face because I loved him more than life itself. I knew I had lost my reasoning powers, for reason would have asked the question,

'Why would a Commander such as he be interested in a little insignificant orphan of the storm?'

No reason. I also knew from all that I had read that love was no respecter of reason. I was ashamed now of what I said that night. I regretted it with all my heart. Now I am a thorn in his side…a problem…a nuisance.

9th April

I was aware that Mr. Darwin knew Fitzroy better than anyone else on board the Beagle. For this reason I longed to talk to him and see if I could detect anything the Captain might have said recently that would give me an indication where his thoughts and emotions were these days, but Darwin seemed to be off the ship most days or just too busy to spend time with me.

12th April

Early this morning there was a knock on the door,
  'Come in'
  'Oh! Hello Fuegia.'
  'You sad Miss Scarlett?'
  'Not really…no.' I tried to hide my frustration.
  'You look sad Miss Scarlett, and Fuegia always know when you are sad.'
  I said nothing.
  'We walk on deck? You spend all time in cabin now, why?'
  I did not reply.
  'Is quiet on deck now you come for walk…yes?'
  'Very well' I reluctantly agreed.
  When we appeared on the deck the officers at the wheel looked up.
  Mr. Peterson left the wheel and said,
  'Fuegia, Miss O' Mara,'
  'Good morning Mr. Peterson.' I spoke quietly
  'Miss O'Mara would you do us the honour of dining with us this evening?'
  He asked loudly.

'Is it a special occasion?'

'No Mam It is just...' he hesitated,

'It is just that we do not see you in the officer's mess... these days. I wondered if in fact we had been too rowdy for your genteel nature Miss O'Mara.'

I began to laugh.

'Not at all Mr. Peterson, indeed I enjoy taking meals with the officers. And my 'genteel nature' as you call it, is perhaps a lot more robust than you imagine.'

'Shall I ask the Captain if you may join us then Miss?'

I began to laugh again.

'Indeed Mr. Peterson while we are at anchor the Captain has given me permission whenever I wish.'

'Will you please wish this evening then Miss?' I laughed again.

'Do Miss Scarlett, please do' Fuegia begged.

'Oh! Very well I will' I said, giving in to the pleas.

'Thank you Miss O'Mara, and may I say Mam how good it is to see you laugh.'

'Thank you Miss O'Mara' Wickham echoed from the wheel. I looked over at him and he gave me a most disarming smile. I could not help but smile back at him.

For the rest of the day Fuegia fussed about getting my clothes ready and doing my hair until I was almost sorry I said that I would go. However I kept my word and went along at suppertime.

I missed Mr. Darwin, and began to realize how much I relied on him for a few moments of interesting conversation and genial company.

After the meal Mr. Wickham asked,

'Will you sing or recite for us Miss O'Mara?'

'Oh, very well'

Wickham called for silence as I stood up. I noticed that Mr. Earle was not there and that was a relief. I always felt he did not like me and was very critical of any performance I gave, although he said nothing. Mr. Darwin was not there. Then I looked up and saw that while I was having this reverie everyone was waiting.

'Oh. I beg you pardon gentlemen. I do miss Mr. Darwin's company, as I know we all do.'

I began,

The Cloud by Percy Bysshe Shelley

'I bring fresh showers for the thirsty flowers,
From the seas and from the streams;
I bear light shade for the leaves when laid
In their noonday dreams....'

When I finished, the officers responded with spontaneous applause.

'You are in a very sombre mood this evening Miss O'Mara are you not?' Wickham asked.

'Perhaps it is good to be sombre from time to time Mr. Wickham.'

'Indeed' Wickham agreed.

'Miss O'Mara how do you remember all the lines?' asked Mr. Sulivan.

'I don't know Mr. Sulivan...is it perhaps because my mind is not burdened with any recollection of my past life.'

'Or just that you have a prodigious memory for poetry.'

'Miss O'Mara may I ask you if by any chance you know the 'Skye boat song?'

'I do indeed Mr. Wickham, and would you care to hear it?'

'It would give us all great pleasure, I am sure Miss.'

I stood up and sang,
'Speed bonny boat like a bird on the wing,
Onward the sailors cry.
Carry the lad that's born to be king
Over the sea to Skye…'
When I finished a great cheer went up and Mr. Wickham said
'Sung like a true Celt Miss O'Mara.'
'Thank you Mr. Wickham.'
The officers stood and clapped.
'Good night gentlemen' I said. Then I saw Mr Sulivan move to open the door for me.
'Thank you Miss O'Mara.' He said.
As I walked out I heard Mr. Wickham say to Mr. Stokes,
'Miss O' Mara has changed you know. She is different tonight.'
I walked up to the deck and stood by the rail. The crew on duty greeted me with
'Good evening Miss' I smiled at them. Two midshipmen were sitting out on the boom. I heard them whispering and joking about asking me to come and sit with them. The air was warm the sea was glass. It was a glorious night. I did not know why but a deep happiness filled my being. Then I remembered the harbour in Greystones. The harbour I grew up by and loved so well nestled in between the Wicklow Hills and Bray Head. Why could I only recall some places and never all the details of my youth?

I remembered only certain times and episodes. My Mother and I were walking under the star filled October skies and she was pointing out many of the constellations to me. I looked at the stars now. They seemed so near as if you could reach out and touch them. I wished my mother were alive to take me in her arms and tell me everything would be all right.

Why had I chosen that poem tonight? I had wanted to say, 'Batter my heart three- personed God' a sonnet by John Donne. The lines of that sonnet I had repeated inside my head many times recently. Alas, far from addressing them to the Blessed Trinity, as John Donne had intended, I addressed them to Captain Robert Fitzroy.

'Batter my heart, three-personed God,...
Take me to you, imprison me, for I,
Except you enthrall me, never shall be free...'

I knew without his love I would never be free. Was I doomed to this heartache then? For indeed there was no hope that he would ever love me. He was the man who ignored me, the man who despised me...the man who battered my heart.

I went to my cabin and lay on the bed and thought for a long time about my life from the time I became conscious that I was on a ship. It all seemed like a dream. I thought about Mr. Wickham. Previously he had constantly reprimanded me for putting the Captain in a bad temper. He must surely notice now how the Captain never even speaks to me. What indeed does Mr. Wickham think of that?

15th April

I visited the gunroom one more time but after that I didn't go again although many of the officers begged me to do so. I spent most of the day alone, walking on deck or writing in my journal, or trying to read the books I took from the library.

I thought of Mr. Stebbing, the librarian, and how he

looked amazed at me when he saw the books I borrowed. One day I asked him about the Captain and he said,

'He is an exceptional man Miss and never ceases to amaze me both in the knowledge he has attained and his thirst to learn still more.'

'Do you think it is because of his background Mr. Stebbing? I believe he comes from an aristocratic family devoted to service of country.'

Mr. Stebbing smiled,

'Aristocratic you say…well let me tell you that the Captain is the fourth great grandchild of Charles II, his grandfather was the 3rd Duke of Grafton and his father was General, Lord Charles Fitzroy. That is more than aristocratic Miss.'

I had no idea the Captain was so highly connected. I went back to my cabin and tried to forget the pain in my heart and made an effort to improve my Spanish vocabulary but without much success.

23rd April

The days were lonely now and I began to feel tired all the time. I took to sleeping in the afternoons lying on my bed. Mr. Darwin had found lodgings and stayed ashore and now there was no one to converse with. So far Mr. Wickham had not attempted to keep his word and make sure I saw the city.

25th April

Mr. Darwin moved all his belongings from the ship today. I said goodbye to him, and wondered when I would see him again. When Fuegia came to my cabin recently I had continued to read and had not spoken much to her. Since then she had not come to visit me very often.

27*th* April

Stebbing and Bennett go ashore regularly…why could I never go anywhere? One day the Captain went ashore to see Mr. Darwin. In the misery of my solitude I began to cry. If I were a man no doubt I could have gone too.

2*nd* May

Mr. Henderson knocked on my door.
'Would you come and speak to Mr. Wickham Miss?'
I followed him unto the deck.
'Miss O'Mara I have to apologize to you that I have been unable to arrange a trip ashore for you.'
'That is a sad thing for me Mr. Wickham but I know you have been very busy.'
'The Captain wishes me to inform you Miss O' Mara…'
My eyes lit up and my heart missed a beat, and no doubt Wickham noticed that,
'He wishes me to say Miss that we have to return to Bahia.'
My heart sank.
'Did he mention the reason Mr. Wickham?'
'Yes Miss, we have a discrepancy in the measurements and we must return to measure the distance again.'
'Thank you Mr. Wickham for telling me.'
I turned to go.
'Miss O'Mara kindly allow me to finish the message.'
'Certainly Mr. Wickham.' My eyes lit up again.

'The Captain has arranged for Fuegia to stay for a month or two ashore with some friends of his. He wishes to know if you would like to stay ashore with her Miss.'

My heart froze. He wanted me off the ship. I was stunned. I stood there. Everyone knew how much I wanted to get off the ship and how many times I had asked him. He always said no. Now I was being asked if I wished to leave the ship. I did not move, Henderson and Wickham looked at each other.

'You may tell the Captain Mr. Wickham that I will think about it.'

'Yes Miss.'

I turned to go back to the cabin. Henderson called after me,

'Would it be too bold of me to ask you to join us some evenings Miss? We miss your company.'

'You can ask Mr. Henderson, but the answer is no.'

I continued down to the cabin. The anger I felt was uncontrollable. Not only did he not address me, not even at the Sunday services, now he sent Wickham to tell me what was happening on board. I fumed and raged for a long time. I wanted to go ashore yes, but only to see these places in the New World. The thoughts of not seeing the Captain for a month or more I could not bring myself to accept. He of course had no such feelings.

I decided that I would leave the ship when I wanted to and not when he told me to go.

Then I went back on deck.

'Mr. Wickham'

'Yes Miss'

'I would like to go ashore. Could you please arrange it for me.'

'I could not do that without the Captain's permission Miss.'

'Kindly obtain the Captain's permission as soon as possible Mr. Wickham. I wish to leave the ship.'

Mr. Wickham looked sternly at me and said,

'It would be impossible for the Captain to give you permission Miss. You have nowhere to stay as far as I know.'

I raised my voice,

'Mr. Wickham I will remind you that I am not a member of his Majesty's Navy. I wish to leave this ship. Is that clear?'

'Yes Miss I will ask the Captain as soon as he returns.'

'Thank you Mr. Wickham, kindly tell the Captain Mr. Wickham, do not ask him.'

'Very well Miss.'

I think, by the look in Mr. Wickham's eye he realized that I was very angry and might do something irrational. I went back to the cabin and began to gather my few belongings and put them in a bag. Two hours went by, since I had told Mr. Wickham to obtain permission for me to leave the ship. Then a knock on the door,

'Yes'

'May I speak to you Miss?' It was Wickham's voice. I opened the door.

'The Captain would like to speak to you Miss.'

'Would he indeed Mr. Wickham? Well I do not wish to speak to him. Kindly inform me when you have arranged my transport into Rio de Janeiro. As you can see I am ready to go, or will I be forced to swim ashore Mr. Wickham?'

Wickham's mouth fell open. I moved back inside the cabin and closed the door. Another twenty minutes or so went by. I had not calmed down and if I had been a good swimmer I would have been gone by now. Another knock at the door,

'What now, Mr. Wickham?' I raised my voice as I opened the door. Standing there was Captain Fitzroy. I was taken aback but tried not to show it.

'Yes' I said in a very abrupt manner.

'May I speak with you privately Miss O'Mara?'

'There is nothing to be said private or otherwise, I wish to be put ashore.'

'Yes of course. But I would appreciate a private word with you.'

I looked at him. My heart was melting, but I would not allow it to melt. I stepped into the cabin and he came in and closed the door. I was shocked at finding myself so close to him. I sat back on the small chair. He did not speak. The silence was palpable.

'Well, what is it you have to say?' I asked curtly.

'I am sorry Miss O'Mara that you feel like this. Can you not see the impossible position I am in?'

'No I cannot. It is a simple request. Transport to the shore. You have boats going ashore every day. Why I did not just get into one of them before now I don't know.'

'Because you know very well Miss O'Mara there is not a man on board who would take you ashore without my permission.'

'So you keep me captive here. Very well, I can see now that I will have to swim ashore. Rest assured I will do that.'

I lied. Another silence. I looked at Fitzroy and for the first time saw that he was deathly pale.

'Will you please reconsider? Rio de Janeiro is not a city

a young lady can be alone in. I have a particular reason for asking you to stay, and why I have not arranged for you to go ashore. However, if you can wait another day I will try to arrange secure accommodation for you with Fuegia. You can both be escorted safely to the house of a trusted friend. Can you please trust me that I have your interest and care at heart?'

'And since when did you care?'

'I do care…we all care.'

He corrected himself at once for fear he should infer that his care was anything other than that of a Captain for a passenger.

'You do not care sir.'

He looked at me as if to say, 'If you were a man I would strike you.'

'There is not a word or a syllable you could utter to tell me you care. You have treated me over the last month with total contempt. If I were a tramp or a vagabond you could not have treated me worse. I ended up on this ship not by design. I made a dreadful mistake not taking leave of it sooner. You will forgive me now if we consider this interview terminated.

Thank you for all your kindness and for saving my life. However I now feel it would have been better by far had you left me in the rowing boat to my inevitable demise. This is goodbye to you Captain Fitzroy. I hope that in the rest of my life I am lucky enough never to see you again.'

I jumped up and opened the door. Fitzroy looked exasperated. He walked out smartly, and I closed the door quickly and then collapsed on the bed. For the first time for months I felt alive and better about myself. This feeling of satisfaction at last made me relax and before long I fell asleep. This was a real sleep not the fitful sleep I had experienced over the past month.

A knock on the cabin door made me jump.

'Yes'

'May I speak with you please Miss O'Mara?'

I got out of bed and opened the door.

'The Captain asks if you would do him the honour of visiting him in his cabin.'

Sulivan looked at me as if I were a young chid he had to plead with.

'Mr. Sulivan you have come aboard recently?'

'Yes Miss, with the Captain.'

'I'm sure you should be off duty then.'

'Yes, but I willingly stay if I can be of any help to you… in any way.'

I thought for a few moments.

'Tell the Captain I will be with him shortly…please.'

'Oh thank you Miss.' Sulivan could not disguise the relief on his face.

'I will tell him.'

I closed the door and fell on my knees.

'Dear God please forgive me for what I am about to do. You know all things. You know I cannot live another moment in this turmoil. You know how my heart is breaking. You know how the one and only man I will ever love has rejected me.

He has looked upon my love with scorn. Then I tried to remember the words of the act of contrition I used to say when I went to confession.

'I detest my sins above every other evil…and I resolve…'

I stumbled through it, stood up and took off my shawl.

I looked into the small scratched mirror. My big sad eyes gazed back at me as I took one last glimpse of myself. I left the cabin and closed the door.

On deck Mr. Sorrell and Mr. Bennett were by the wheel with Mr. Stokes. They spoke to me, but I ignored their salutations. I moved towards the rail and looked over at Rio. It was a city I was never going to see. For some unknown reason streaming in on the breeze of my thoughts I was back in Ireland. I was coming home from school with Maeve and De. I whispered,

'Happy, happy days, happy moment in time, my mind and heart wish to go back to it always.'

I stood still until the officers and crew hands had forgotten I was there. Then, swiftly I climbed up upon the rail and flung myself into the sea. I felt the warm water rush past me. I felt my lungs filling with water. I was pushed back up to the surface, I tried not to breathe but could not stop my self. Down I went again, first came the horror, then the pain, and then relief and peace passed over me like a deep unfettered wave…then the euphoria.

That peace that I had felt once before began to come over me…then I felt someone near me trying to grab hold of my body. I half opened my eyes. It was Mr. Sulivan. I fought him with all the strength I had as he forced my body to the surface. I tried to say, 'No, no leave me be' but no words came out. I fought like a tiger and dragged Sulivan down several times until I was exhausted and could not see or hear anything.

The next thing I remember I was lying on the deck and someone was trying to get the sea water out of my lungs.

Then I began to vomit the sea water and to cough continuously. I turned and saw the crew gathered round looking at me. Mr. Sulivan, soaking wet was trying to lift me up. The last thing I saw was Mr. Bynoe putting a blanket over me. The crew must have been uncommonly silent for I heard nothing.

The taste of the salt water made me feel sick and my whole body felt frozen and still. Then I heard Mr. Bynoe's voice,

'Will I take Miss O' Mara to the sick bay sir?'
'No Mr. Bynoe. Take her to my cabin.'
'Yes sir.'
'No Mr. Bynoe' I croaked.

After that I could only half hear words, and broken sentences. Then strong arms lifted me up and I remembered no more.

When I opened my eyes Mr. Sulivan was placing me on a bed. It was not my own bed, yet, it was a familiar bed. Then slowly I remembered jumping into the water. Mr. Sulivan looked at me as I lay soaking wet on the Captain's bed. I began to groan as every part of my body was aching. Mr. Bynoe approached and tentatively lifted my wrist to take my pulse.

'Leave me be, Mr. Bynoe.'
Mr. Bynoe stepped back and withdrew.
I looked intently at Mr. Sulivan dripping wet.
'Mr. Sulivan why did you do that?
The panic in my voice startled even me.
'I wanted to die.' I screamed.
'I think I wanted to die when I was in the rowing boat. Why will you people not let me die?'

I fell back on the bed and began to cry. My wet clothes clung to my body and my wet tangled hair stuck to my face like paste. I moaned more because of the circumstances of my life than with the pain, and after all that nothing had changed.

Sulivan covered me with the blanket and walked towards the door.

'Mr. Sullivan' my voice was panic stricken again,
Sulivan turned back to the bed in alarm.

'Yes Miss, I am here Miss.'

'Mr. Sulivan, kindly forgive the impertinence of this request, and kindly place no meaning whatsoever to it other than the cry of a helpless creature struggling to feel human. Promise me Mr. Sulivan'

'I promise' he said, not knowing what he was promising.

'Would it be very bold and indeed improper of me to request you to put your arms around my shoulders sir? In no way to show affection Mr. Sulivan, understand that, nor to compromise your own integrity, but for another reason.'

I took a long breath.

'I have suffered such loneliness over the last months that I do not even feel human Mr. Sulivan, please say that you understand, please say…'

I was crying then.

'Please say you understand Mr. Sulivan and know that your actions will in no way be misconstrued nor considered compromising to either of us, but rather will be a gesture of human kindness.'

Mr. Sulivan stuttered… 'I understand'

'If you are willing to do so Mr. Sulivan it will surely help to overcome the despair and deprivation I feel at this moment. For indeed Mr. Sulivan I fear for my sanity. Therefore I ask you sir, I ask you humbly to place your arms about me so that I may at least know one thing…that I am human person.'

Mr. Sulivan, always so confident, looked utterly confused, an expression I had never seen on his features before. Then he said in a stuttering way,

'Permission…to…to…to hold…Miss O'Mara sir.'

The sharp voice of Fitzroy answered,

'Permission granted.'

I had not seen Fitzroy, but he could not disguise the irritation in his voice. Up until this moment I did not even know the Captain was in the cabin. I looked up and there he was, pale as death. Furious it seemed at yet another irrational act of this incredibly tiresome woman. I looked into his eyes and tried to imagine what he was thinking.

'If only I had let that rowing boat drift…I would not be having all this trouble now.'

Was that what he was thinking?

Mr. Sulivan dripping wet moved forward and very carefully placed his arms around my shoulders and held me. I closed my eyes and let go now of all the lonely pain of the past months. I sighed and in that moment, I felt as if my human heart began to beat again. The tears began to flow down my cheeks.

I opened my eyes and over Sulivan's shoulder, I was looking straight into the eyes of Captain Fitzroy. There were tears in his eyes. He swallowed hard and walked away. Sulivan turned his head and looked at me.

'It's all right Miss O'Mara. You are safe now, we will never let anything happen to you.'

I pushed him away. He moved quickly back from me an astonished look in his eyes.

'Forgive me Mr. Sullivan, I am not myself. I know that your kind heart is trying to comfort me, and thank you again for your patience. However, don't think for one

moment that I need you to utter sympathetic words to me. In fact note this, I will never rely on any man again as long as I live.'

'Apologies Miss O'Mara if I accidentally seemed to overrule your independent nature…it was said in all good faith and with good intention.'

'Oh! Mr. Sullivan I am aware of the privilege it is, and how fortunate I am to have such a gentleman as yourself for a friend. Thank you Mr. Sulivan, and although I certainly wanted to die…I know you have been my saviour this day in more ways than one.'

Sullivan stepped back and said,

'My privilege Miss.'

'Permission to go and change sir?'

'Granted.' Fitzroy barked.

Sulivan left and I tried to get out of the bed, before Fitzroy began to record yet another list of my indiscretions. As I lifted up my head the cabin began to swirl around and around and I fell back into a dead faint.

FRIENDS AND FOES

Harry sat impatiently in the Black Swan near Soho. He was meticulous about time and Mr. Goldberg was late. At that moment his eyes fell on three men entering the Club. Harry stared, and his mouth felt dry. There, standing in front of him was a huge man with red hair and red speckled skin. He was wearing a tweed sports jacket, huge jodhpurs and a check shirt. Harry's imagination went into overdrive and he could hear
 Shirley Bassey belting out the theme song ... 'Goldfinger'
Goldberg walked up to Harry and said,
'How do you do, Mr. Harry' and pushed a large speckled hand towards him.
Harry shook hands and wondered how this man, whom he had never seen before, recognized him. He saw the two weighty assistants dressed in black suits fall in behind Goldberg. He also observed how they scrutinized the bar and Harry felt they were probably ex Secret Service.
'Do have another drink, Mr. Harry'
'No thank you, you wanted to discuss something with me…something of a secret nature you said.'
'Oh! Mr. Harry, I see you are a man who gets

straight down to business.'

'Yes I am.'

'Well…I have heard that recently you have come into the possession of a diary.'

'Yes.'

'Well I am willing to make you a substantial offer for it.'

'Substantial?'

'Yes…say in the region of one hundred thousand pounds.'

'Why such a large sum…it may be a forgery?'

'I am willing to take that chance. Do we have a deal, Mr. Harry?'

'No, I'm afraid not, you see I have become quite attached to the diary.'

'I will double the offer.'

'No again Mr. Goldberg. The diary is not for sale.'

As Harry uttered these words the two assistants moved in on either side of Goldberg encircling Harry, pinning him against the bar. He looked into the three pairs of eyes. All had evil intent.

'You see, Mr. Harry, you will find I never fail to get what I really want.'

'Well I think you will find that I have a habit of holding on with a passion to what is mine Mr. Goldberg.'

Harry looked around the bar and saw a young woman in a long red evening dress leaning against a table with a drink in one hand and a cigarette in the other. He raised his voice,

'Hi there, babe…how are you?'

The woman looked up with a puzzled expression.

'I guess I'll see you later guys,' he said as he pushed past the bodyguards.

He walked over to the young woman and took her by the arm,

'Where have you been lately?' he asked and without a pause kissed her passionately. The woman did not resist. After a brief moment Harry let her go and walked out.

The woman stared after him.

Harry thought that Goldberg was not the kind of man who took no for an answer, but he was unaware of the full extent of the forces working against him. He walked quickly across Soho Square and into Greek Street. The odour of chips and sausages from the stalls of the street vendors hung thickly in the air and the hub of city noise filled his ears. He wondered why Goldberg was so keen to buy the diary, and then he remembered seeing Sir Ronald Reed that day in Writtle when he bought the box. Yes there was more to this diary than… his mobile phone rang,

'Hello'

'Is that you Harry?'

'Yes who's speaking?'

'My name is Lucy Harrington. Do you remember meeting me?'

'Yes I do.'

'Harry I have come across something that may interest you. Could you meet me in London?'

'Yes, I'll be at the Savoy in about twenty minutes. Can you meet me there?'

'Yes…but it is going to take me a little more than twenty minutes Harry. Let's say about an hour. Is that ok with you?'

'Yes certainly, see you then.

Harry waited in the foyer of the Savoy Hotel for Lucy. When he saw her coming his heart gave an extra flutter. She was wearing a blue designer suit and a cream silk shirt. He looked at his watch. She was right on time. Harry gazed into the cornflower blue eyes and said,

'Miss Harrington.'

'Harry I hope I am not intruding.'

'No, I am delighted to see you.' He smiled.

'Would you care for a drink or a coffee?'

'Coffee would be fine Harry thank you, and please call me Lucy.'

Harry indicated the way; they walked into the cafe, sat down and ordered. Lucy took some papers from her bag and said,

'Harry I was looking at some of Fitzroy's letters to his sister. In one of them, dated April 1832 I saw a strange reference. Here have a look, I've highlighted the section.' She passed the letter.

'The voyage is going reasonably well but I am still worried about that particular problem I mentioned in my last letter, and *'ignotum per ignotius'* is a good summary of the present situation.'

'Do you think he was referring to Scarlett here?'

'Scarlett is that her name?'

'Yes'

'Fitzroy never waffled Harry; I think the reason his books did not sell was because they were too specialized, but he was an excellent writer. When I saw that sentence about the problem he had mentioned in his previous letter I knew whatever he was talking about was a coded message to his sister.'

'You think 'the problem' he referred to was Scarlett?'
'Yes indeed, well…that would make sense.'
'The Latin I think means, 'the unknown explained by the still more unknown' in other words he is making no progress whatsoever in finding out who Scarlett is.'

Harry picked up a spoon and in an absent-minded way turned over lumps of sugar in the bowl.

'If she was on the ship Harry, why was her identity hidden?'

'I don't know'

Harry took out the copies of the letters he had retrieved from the Maritime Museum.

'Have a look at these and tell me what you think.'

Lucy took the letters and read them. She looked at Harry and asked,

'Why was Knighton looking for her?'

'I don't know. In the diary Scarlett remembers about a vagrant speaking to her near the Lizard and telling her that he heard two men talking and saying they were looking for a young lady that looked like her. They were on the King's business and also on Knighton's business he said.'

'Did Captain Fitzroy know that Knighton was looking for her?'

'Yes, he did.'

'Did he tell Scarlett?'

'No he told her that what the vagrant said meant nothing.'

'Why did he do that?'

'Because Lucy he was always trying to protect her. I think he did not want to frighten her.'

'Would you like me to look into that aspect of the research about Knighton?'

'If you have time that would be excellent, I will of course reimburse you for your time.'

'No, I'd like to make recompense.'

'For what?'

'For the look that came over your face when I said I thought the diary was a fake.'

Harry smiled.

'By tomorrow afternoon I should at least have some kind of lead on Knighton. My contention is Harry that when all avenues lead to a mystery then look to finance, and I would think that 'money' will be found at the base of this mystery somewhere. I will see you here about four thirty if that is suitable.'

'Thank you, I look forward to it'

Harry walked to the door with Lucy and they said goodbye.

Harry drove home from London concentrating on the driving and trying to keep his mind free of two major problems. One, why was Knighton looking for Scarlett; the other was more subtle… how he could stop himself thinking about Lucy Harrington.

As he approached the house the electric gates were open. Police cars on the forecourt were flashing. As he drove up the driveway he had to pull over abruptly as an ambulance passed him at speed on the way out. He parked the car and stepped out. A police constable approached him and said,

'There has been a break-in sir.'

5*th* May 1832

I woke up and didn't know where I was. I tried to open my eyes. I could hear a very strange squeaking noise. Then

I remembered I was in the Captain's cabin, after throwing myself into the sea. I could taste the salty water in my mouth and I felt sick. I moved my hand to my throat, felt a rough material next to my skin, and ran my fingers along my arms and chest. It…was…a…nightshirt.

'Oh! My goodness!' I shouted and sat bolt upright.

'You are safe Miss O'Mara.' Mr. Bynoe put down his pen.

'You are safe…'

'This nightsh…garment, this garment I have on Mr. Bynoe how did I…how was it…'

'Oh that' said Bynoe as if it was the least of his worries.

'Fuegia came and took your wet clothes.'

'It doesn't belong to me Mr. Bynoe, nor to Fuegia if I recollect correctly.'

'It belongs to the Captain Miss. Fuegia took it from his clean laundry bag. I am sorry Miss. It was probably all she could find at the time.'

I was silent. I didn't want to think about being in the captain's nightshirt, in the captain's bed and in the captain's cabin.

'Why am I here Mr. Bynoe? I am perfectly able to go to my own cabin.'

'Well, you have been here for two days Miss.'

'Two days?'

'Yes Miss.'

'You drugged me Mr. Bynoe.'

'I did no such thing Miss. It was total exhaustion.' He waited,

'The Captain said you were not to be disturbed.'

'While he took the Beagle back to Bahia no doubt.'

'No Miss, we are at anchor in Rio.'

'Where is the Captain?'

'He has gone ashore to see if it is possible for you to stay with a family he knows, that is until we return from Bahia.'

'Do you know where?'

'Yes, just outside the city Miss, in Botofogo, where Mr. Darwin is.'

A long silence followed. I thought of the Captain, his sad eyes, and how he could never understand that I would not comply with his orders.

'He wants me to vacate the ship, Mr. Bynoe.'

'The Captain is very distressed about you Miss. He thinks that if he can arrange some time off the ship for you it might be good for you.'

'If he cares about me, Mr. Bynoe, why for over a month, did he not speak even one word to me? He did not even acknowledge me as a fellow human being.'

'You don't understand him Miss.'

'Try to tell me, Mr. Bynoe. Try to make me understand. I am listening Mr. Bynoe, please try to explain it to me.'

Bynoe went back to the Captain's table and sat down.

'I don't know how to tell you, and what if I say something out of place and upset you? The Captain will take it out on me I assure you.'

'Please Mr. Bynoe'

'Well Miss, the Captain knows that one day you will return to England. You will have your own life Miss. The Captain wants to make sure that you get off the Beagle with your reputation intact Miss. He will preserve your dignity and keep you safe whatever it takes.'

Bynoe looked at the papers on the desk. Then he looked up,

'You will forgive me for saying this Miss, but Mr. Wickham says…he says Miss that the Captain is aware, and we all are, that you are no ordinary young lady Miss O'Mara. You are very beautiful, forgive my boldness. That is why Miss, the Captain worries that if you go ashore something might happen to you.'

He sighed. I put my hands over my face. Why would anyone think I was beautiful, I certainly don't feel beautiful.

'Mr. Wickham, who knows him well has said to me more than once: 'If anything ever happens to Miss O'Mara God help us all. There will be no living with the Captain.'

A long silence followed. Bynoe picked up his pen and continued with the paper- work.

'Mr.Bynoe why do you think he did not speak to me? Surely…'

'You don't know him Miss. Probably he wanted to speak to you…but thought of your reputation.'

'I don't believe it Mr.Bynoe.'

'Well believe this Miss, both Wickham and Sulivan have been given a dreadful telling off by the Captain… especially Sulivan.'

'Why?'

'Because they failed to tell the Captain that you were not eating, were loosing weight, not sleeping…by the look of you, and not going to the gun room for suppers.'

'Why should Mr. Sulivan be to blame for that? He saved my life.'

'Yes Miss, and he has expressed affection for you. However the Captain said that if only he had curtailed his raptures and spoke more plainly about your health it would have been better done.'

'Does the Captain think that I return Mr. Sulivan's affection?'

'Yes'

I felt a cold wave come over me and again I wanted to die.

'Oh! I am sorry Miss.' *Bynoe came over to the bed.*

'I have said too much. If I upset you, Miss, the Captain will…'

I closed my eyes but I felt as if I were on a carousel. After a few moments the feeling subsided and I cautiously opened my eyes.

'May I ask you one last question? Does the Captain approve of Mr. Sulivan's affection for me?'

'Yes I think so, but Mr. Wickham says anyone expressing affection for you is bound to bring about the Captain's displeasure.'

'Why Mr. Bynoe?'

'Because Miss O'Mara at the bottom of all this trouble is the fact that the Captain will not allow anyone to trifle with you or your feelings, and…and…dare I say it Miss…the Captain's own…feelings for you.'

'The Captain's feelings for me?'

'Yes Miss.'

'I assure you Mr. Bynoe the Captain has no feelings for me. He has told me so to my face.'

'The Captain is an honest man, Miss. If he did not like you we would all know that.'

'He may like me Mr. Bynoe but in no way does he love me.'

'Ah well, who knows about love, Miss? Only the man himself can know that.'

'Yes, and the Captain has made it clear to me that he has no feelings of any kind for me.'

I threw myself back on the pillow. The room began to spin again. I closed my eyes.

'Oh Miss O'Mara you have gone deathly pale again.'

Bynoe shot to his feet to take my pulse.

I felt his cool hand on my wrist, and then I took it away.

'You are so kind Mr. Bynoe to tell me things you think I long to hear and that will help to steady my mind. Would you kindly leave me now as I would like to sleep?'

'I will send for Fuegia, Miss. The Captain says you are not to be left alone while he is off the ship.'

I closed my eyes and even though I had heard nothing that could give me any hope, for some reason the heaviness in my heart began to lighten. Maybe it was because there was the slightest chance… maybe…just maybe he did have some affection for me after all.

The officers thought so. Mr. Darwin thought so too and had tried to console me as he was leaving the ship, and poor Mr. Sulivan, the most noble of men, found himself drawn into this confusion.

Mr. Bynoe sent for Fuegia. When she came he gathered his papers.

'Try to get Miss O'Mara to drink some of the water I have put here for her, Fuegia.'

'Yes sir,' Fuegia answered. Full of concern he looked at me and said,

'Try to get some sleep, Miss.'

'Mr. Bynoe, thank you for being so frank with me. You have no idea how much better I feel. You are a good doctor, sir.'

'Why, thank you Miss O'Mara,' he said and left.

'How you feel Miss Scarlett? You no want speak with Fuegia any more?'

'Poor Fuegia…I am sorry Fuegia…how selfish I have been.'

'You no selfish Miss Scarlett, you is sick.' I stretched over and took Fuegia's hand.

'My heart Fuegia, my heart is breaking. I do want to die.'

I began to cry and the tears flowed down my cheeks.

'You no die Miss Scarlett you get better. You drink water then sleep.'

'Thank you Fuegia, you are my good friend.' I drank the water.

I hated the stale taste of the ship's water. I longed for the cool clear water that came flowing down from the Wicklow hills. I closed my eyes.

Then I sat up quickly,

'Oh! No…' I exclaimed.

I had just remembered how I had asked Mr. Sulivan to hold me in his arms. My goodness, what a dreadful spectacle I had made of myself! I covered my face with my hands and began to sob.

'You upset Miss Scarlet?' Fuegia asked.

'No Fuegia, I must be calm now. Thank you for looking after me all these months.'

'You very good friend Miss Scarlett, but you go to sleep now.'

'Yes, Fuegia'

I closed my eyes and must have fallen asleep almost immediately.

6th May

When I woke up it was dark in the cabin. I was alone. I sat up slowly but the spinning began in my head. Quietly I lay down again. I thought about Mr. Bynoe and the things he had said to try to please and comfort me. True or false, for the rest of my life I would think about the words Mr. Bynoe had said.

'The Captain's own feelings for you…'

I thought about Mr. Wickham and Mr. Sulivan. Why had they not told the Captain I looked ill? There is something in all of this to do with being at sea, to do with being a sailor. Why was it up to Mr. Sulivan to tell the Captain I looked ill? He had never treated me any differently from the other officers. He is a naturally gregarious gentleman and finds it easy to converse with all sorts of different people.

However it seems that if he didn't report it, the other officers felt it was not their place to do so. Was it some kind of sailors' code I could not understand? Then I heard voices outside the door. It was Fuegia and Mr. Bynoe.

'I let her sleep sir. She look very tired.' Fuegia said.

'Thank you, Fuegia, you may go now.'

A light knock on the door,

'Come in, Mr. Bynoe. I am awake.'

The door opened slowly and the Captain ducked into the cabin. He was holding a lantern. I shielded my eyes from the unexpected light.

'My apologies, Miss O' Mara,' *the Captain said and took the lantern to its place over his table. Mr. Bynoe followed him into the cabin.*

'Ah! At last a little colour back in your cheeks, Miss O'Mara. May I take your pulse?'

I handed up my wrist like a child.

'Almost back to normal, Miss.'

'That, Mr. Bynoe, is because you are a good doctor and I am lucky to have you as a confidant.'

'Will there be anything else sir?'

'Would you like us to call anyone to speak to you Miss O'Mara?'

'Good heavens sir! Who do you think I would like to speak to?'

I looked inquiringly at him. He looked away. Then I said,

'I would like to return to my own cabin.'

'You are not strong enough to walk Miss O'Mara.' Bynoe said quietly.

An awkward silence followed. The idea of being carried to Mr. Sulivan's cabin flashed across my mind.

'That will be all Mr. Bynoe. Thank you.'

'My pleasure, sir. Goodnight Miss O'Mara, I hope you sleep well.'

Bynoe shot a pleasant smile at me and was gone.

Fitzroy went to his table and sat down. I sat up and began to stiffen with anxiety. Was it going to be his deathly silence mode? Not a word of apology, not a word of comfort…not a word. The minutes rolled by. Then,

'Would you like to read Miss O'Mara? Shall I light another lantern for you? Shall I send for your books?'

I decided not to answer. If this was his way of making conversation he could make it to himself. Half an hour must have passed in silence. Fitzroy was looking at his papers but I knew very well that his agitated mind probably prevented him from concentrating properly, although he continued to write. Then he got up from his chair and came towards the bed. He looked at me. I looked at him and when I saw his sad face I wanted to jump into his arms and say,

'Everything is all right, I forgive you'

Instead I stayed very still. Then I remembered I had on

his nightshirt. I began to blush. I felt mortified and became acutely embarrassed as he stood there looking at me.

'I understand what has happened Miss O'Mara. There is no need to be embarrassed. I know now that you have formed an affection for Mr. Sulivan.'

'What? What did you say? Oh for goodness sake! Did I say I had?'

'No, but your request to have him take you in his arms left me in no doubt. I knew then there were deep feelings between you both.'

'You astonish me, sir. You apparently did not listen to one word of all that I said before I asked him to embrace me. Did you not hear how carefully I asked him so as not to compromise either my dignity or his honour? In any case, you think that a simple embrace from another person, a person who at the very least acknowledges me, and honours me as a fellow human person, who has been as kind to me as a brother since I came aboard… you think this is love? Well I am very sorry for what you call love… sir.'

Another silence followed.

'You mean your affections are not with Mr. Sulivan… but with another.'

'Yes, sir.'

Fitzroy walked back to the table and sat down. Another silence, then he approached the bed again.

'Could your affections by any chance be with…?'

I interrupted him knowing he hated it.

'No sir, they are not, and are we about to play this little game all night? Could you not just ask me one simple question …why do you complicate matters so? Just say, may I ask where your affections lie?'

Fitzroy's anger began to rise and he clenched his fists as he parroted the question, 'May I ask where your affections lie?'

I waited for a while. Then I looked coldly at him and said,

'My affections sir, do not jump around the crew like a wallaby. My affections remain steadfast…broken with pain…yes but they do not alter…

'Kind is my love today, tomorrow kind,
Still constant in a wondrous excellence; …'

This speech exhausted me and I began to sob. I lay down slowly and turned my head away from the light and from Fitzroy. He said nothing. He went back to the table and sat down. After a while I turned towards him too quickly and the room began to spin.

I closed my eyes until the motion stopped. Then I sat up slowly.

'May I now ask you a question?' His eyes opened wide.

'Why did you treat me with such distain? How could you treat me so badly? Why did you ignore me?'

'You are a passenger on this ship Miss O'Mara and I am not used to such talk or attitude from any passenger, officer or member of the crew. You seem constantly to forget that I am the Captain of this ship. I do not answer to you or to anyone else on this ship, nor do I form close relationships with any members of the crew or passengers. In fact I keep a good distance from the private lives of my crew and passengers.'

His tone was deathly, his eyes were fastened fiercely on mine and if I had not known him better I would have been frightened. Nevertheless, it was not in my nature to be afraid and I ruthlessly held his gaze until he looked away.

After another long silence I thought he would leave.

Then he stood up walked towards me and said in a much quieter tone,

'Besides there was one particular item on my mind over the past month… It was… evident to me that you and Mr. Sulivan had formed a friendship, and although I was not aware of the extent of that friendship I did think there was a distinct possibility that Mr. Sulivan might approach me as to the prospect of your being married on board. In which case, as part of my duty I should have had to perform the marriage ceremony over you both.'

He looked away. Then he walked behind the table. He said quietly

'Indeed I was quite sure that was about to happen.'

My heart broke for him now, even though I had vowed my heart would never break again for him.

'My dear Captain, forgive me, did you think that I would have no say in such an act?'

'I had no doubt but that it was your wish too.'

'Nevertheless…why did you not send for me?'

'Miss O'Mara, may I remind you again that I am not in the habit of questioning the affections of a member of my crew or a passenger.'

A long silence followed.

'As far as Mr. Sulivan is concerned sir, did he ever in all sincerity tell you he had great affection for me?'

He sat down, rested his head on his hands and I could not see his eyes.

'No.'

'Nor did he ever express such sentiment to me sir, so you see you were operating under an illusion or false premise. I now know that at sea illusions, and such things seem to be quite common.'

He lifted his head and looked into my eyes.

'In this instance Miss O'Mara, am I to believe that you do not wish to marry Mr. Sulivan?'

'No sir, I certainly do not wish to marry Mr. Sulivan, and what's more I am quite sure he has no wish whatsoever to marry me.'

I began to sob again.

'Please do not distress yourself Scarlett. It pains me to see you cry in this way, and kindly forgive me for not directing the question to you previously.'

He walked towards me and in the half-light I could see the sadness in his eyes.

'As you well know the difficulties on this voyage occupy my mind night and day and I have little time to think about such trivial matters. However the situation is resolved now. Will you be able to sleep tonight?'

'I am grieved sir that you have been upset and felt unable to ask me that simple question. Yes, I will be able to sleep sir. Thank you.'

He walked towards the door.

'Goodnight.'

He was gone. I did not answer.

A trivial matter he called it. However, I knew that deep in my heart there would never be another man like Captain Robert Fitzroy. What is it about this kind of affection that insists on staying alive against all odds, against all reason, even against common sense?

7th May

The following morning after inspection he knocked on the door of his own cabin.

'Come in,' I answered.

Before me I saw a changed man. He was bright and dare I say cheerful.

He stood close to the bed and said.

'Are you feeling better, Miss O'Mara?'

'A little sir.'

'I forgot to tell you last night that I went ashore to ask an honourable gentlemen of my acquaintance if you might board with the family. Fuegia will be boarding with them also, that is until the Beagle returns from Bahia. How do you feel about such a plan?'

I waited.

'What do you think, sir?'

'If you wish to go Scarlett I will do everything I can…' he hesitated.

'Well, on my part I would prefer you not to enter Rio at this time.'

'May I know the reason sir?'

'It is a matter I'd rather to keep to myself.'

'I see.'

'There is of course the matter of your health…are you well enough? This latest …episode I fear has greatly affected your well being. I am anxious to take care of you and see you return to your former beau…healthy state.'

He paused and looked at me. I said nothing, trying to work out what he wanted me to do.

'The sea has a strange effect on us all Miss O'Mara, and a young lady such as your self may indeed begin to …get things out of proportion. So, in some ways, a time ashore may restore your equilibrium.'

'Do you think, sir, I have some things out of proportion?'

'Perhaps…I hesitate to make any judgement…because whenever I do in your regard I am usually wrong.'

He smiled.

'Come now, Captain Robert Fitzroy, has not the most profound lesson since I came aboard this ship been to know that you can never ever possibly be wrong?'

He smiled again.

'Be serious, Scarlett' I thought for a few moments.

'Captain Fitzroy, I want only to do whatever pleases you. However, if I do not wish to go would that upset your plans sir?'

'No... not in the least, I would be delighted, for although you may not be aware of it, and I in my position as Captain am unable to express it openly, nevertheless everyone on board benefits from your presence. So... are you sure now you wish to stay on board?'

'Yes, Captain'

'In that case, Miss O'Mara, I feel sure we should take the advice of Mr. Bynoe. He says you are not well enough to go ashore.'

'I feel Mr. Bynoe is right, sir.'

'Indeed so do I.' He smiled again.

He reached over, took my hand, and held it to his lips.

I almost fainted with the shock. He released my hand and said,.

'If this is your decision, Scarlett, I ask you please to suspend any fanciful thoughts you may have about any members of the crew. Try to remain quiet and composed for your health's sake. You are indeed woefully thin and pale.'

'That is not fair, sir, I have fanciful thoughts and feelings for only one person and he is certainly not crew, in the strict sense that is... and you are very thin and pale yourself sir.'

He smiled and then raised his eyebrows in a slight

reprimand. I knew that whatever feelings might be between us I was not allowed to speak to the Captain that way.

He moved towards the door.

'I would like to go back to my cabin, sir.'

Fitzroy hesitated,

'Oh well…I must inform you, Miss O'Mara that Mr. Sulivan has returned to his cabin.'

After a short reflection, I said,

'In view of the misunderstanding regarding Mr. Sulivan sir, could you find me other accommodation?'

Fitzroy looked serious, and moved back to the bed.

'Miss O'Mara'

I understood now he was back again to his official Captaincy.

'In view of the circumstances I would consider it better by far that you return to Mr. Sulivan's cabin.'

'No.' I said with a sigh,

'I will never understand you sailors. However if it is your wish sir, then it is mine.'

'I thank you, Miss O'Mara, we will make a fine sailor of you yet!'

'You should say that to Mr. Darwin.'

'Indeed, poor man he suffers greatly.'

'Is he suitably settled in Botofogo?'

'Yes indeed, I see you are well informed of his whereabouts.'

'An accident, I assure you sir.'

'It will take Mr. Sulivan a few days to vacate his cabin.'

'A few hours you mean… oh! I am sorry sir, a few days of course.'

'I will ask Fuegia to come to you each day after nine until she departs for Botofogo herself. Is that acceptable?'

'Very acceptable sir, thank you.'

He looked at me now as he did in the past as if he was taking a picture of me to take with him. Of course, I had no proof of this, only my own instinctive fanciful thoughts which he had warned me to suspend.

'Before you go, sir, dare I ask you a question?'

'If I say yes Scarlett I will be here for an hour debating the ...very well.'

'Will you mind if it is embarrassing?'

He threw his eyes upward and said,

'For goodness sake get on with it'.

'When Mr. Sulivan put his arms around my shoulders, I saw over his shoulder that there were tears in your eyes. Why sir?'

'Against my better judgement I allowed the question.'

He began to smile.

I was so glad that he was smiling, but then he stood still and just looked at me. Again I remembered the nightshirt and began to blush.

'But will you not answer, sir?'

'Yes, I will answer. You looked so beautiful, so vulnerable like a child in his arms...a child I had failed to look after properly.'

'I absolutely refuse to allow you to talk to me or about me as if I am a child. I am possibly two years younger than you are yourself.'

Then he laughed.

'Scarlett I know roughly how old you are. I was not referring to your chronological age. I was talking about the innocence you carry with you, that illusive quality blended with a deep love of the arts, literature and music, that openness, that thirst for knowledge, surely you know what I mean.'

'You are not to call me a child whatever you mean by it...sir.'

'Very well, Miss O'Mara, I will never again refer to you as a child for you seem totally incapable of understanding what a compliment it is.'

He smiled. I returned his smile, and then he was gone.

Why did he say I looked beautiful when I had just been dragged out of the sea? What must I look like now in a striped rough nightshirt, tangled hair and pale as death?

10*th* May

Today the Beagle set out to return to Bahia. The Captain had advised me to stay in his cabin until he spoke to Mr. Sulivan. While I was there I delighted in the fact that at least he saw me and I saw him three times a day. Nevertheless, I knew right well those thoughts were only for my journal, and for the imaginary world I lived in, inside my head.

Either Mr. Hellyer, Mr. Bynoe or Mr. Stebbing always accompanied the Captain. Sometimes he was able to dismiss them early and he spoke to me for a few moments. I longed for these brief interludes although they only lasted seconds.

The days passed quietly and I knew the time had come to leave the Captain's cabin. Sulivan's cabin was vacant now. I knew I had to face the separation. One afternoon

I said ,'It's time for me to leave your cabin, Captain.'

'Yes indeed, I hope you will be able to sleep properly in Mr. Sulivan's cabin.'

'Yes I will thank you, Captain.'

'Sir, I have no wish to bother you but could I ask you a question?'

'Certainly.'

'I know you will think me very childish, but can you begin to understand how important to me are the few interviews I have with you? I know you are a very busy man and I have no right to make further demands on your time, but if you knew how much it meant to my life I'm sure you would be willing to see me from time to time.'

He hesitated.

'You flatter me, Miss O'Mara. You may spend as much time as you like with the officers who have more time on their hands to entertain you. If I may say so they are nearer your age. Do these not provide all the society you need?'

I looked into his eyes, and at that moment my heart almost stopped beating. How could anyone fathom this man? One day he seemed almost ready to declare his love, and the next he dismissed me as if he hardly knew me.

'You do not answer Miss O'Mara.'

'Oh forgive me Captain Fitzroy, you are right of course. Thank you.'

He nodded. I hesitated. He looked at me and smiled, he was waiting for me to go. I knew that... yet I was wondering if I could try one more time.

'You seem to want to say something to me, Miss O'Mara.'

'Well I hesitate, Captain, for fear of annoying you.'

'Come, come, Miss O'Mara, do we not understand each other in a more civilized way now?'

'Yes sir, I hope so, sir. I was thinking of making a study of the History of the Royal Navy. If so, sir, would I be allowed to consult you from time to time?'

'You think the officers incapable of helping you in this regard?'

'Forgive me, sir, I am sure they can.'

'However, Miss O'Mara if there is any point of detail you feel you would like to talk over with me please feel free to do so.'

'Thank you sir…if I study the subject sir, who better to help me than the man, the first in the history of the service to pass his lieutenant's exam with full numbers?'

'Is there anything you do not know about me, Miss O'Mara?'

'Nothing sir.' I smiled.

He smiled in return. His sharp features at that moment seemed to blend entirely into a loving harmonious whole.

'Very well, let us try your plan.'

I held out my hand to say goodbye. He looked astonished and then he took it and held it for a brief second before releasing it.

'Remember sir; I will fade away if I do not talk to you and see you alone from time to time. I don't mind if it is only to be reprimanded.'

'I understand, Scarlett.'

He gave a slight bow.

I looked at him, curtsied, went out and closed the door.

I moved back into Mr. Sulivan's cabin. The Beagle had set out to return to Bahia. I resumed my old routine. Fuegia was gone and I walked on deck alone. In my utter loneliness I often sneaked up to the deck and marvelled at the colourful evening sky.

11th May

Today as I took my walk at noon Mr. Wickham came near to me at the rail and said,

'God afternoon Miss.'

'Travelling north for a change Mr. Wickham.'

'Are you homesick Miss?'

'Well...not as much as I was.'

'I am glad to hear it Miss. Does that mean we might see you in the gunroom Miss...or ...perhaps...'

'Perhaps, Mr. Wickham?'

'I was going to say perhaps you wish to wait for Mr. Darwin's return.'

I began to laugh. Wickham looked shocked,

'It is very good to hear you laugh again Miss O' Mara.' he said.

'I'll come to the gunroom Mr. Wickham as soon as I can alter a dress belonging to Fuegia. Indeed I don't know what I would do without Fuegia's kindness. She has given me several dresses.'

'Miss O'Mara, how are you? The Captain's voice, I turned to face him.

'I feel as if I have been given a new life, sir.' I curtsied and smiled.

'I am delighted to see you in such good spirits Miss O'Mara. What are your occupations to be today?'

'Well today Captain I must try to make some of Fuegia's dresses fit me.'

'Oh! Miss O'Mara! How I have neglected to send you ashore to purchase a new wardrobe. Mr. Wickham,'

'Yes, sir.'

'Kindly do not let me forget when we return to Rio to send Mr. Sul...' He hesitated, but he had started so he continued,

'Send Mr. Sulivan ashore with Fuegia and Miss O' Mara to purchase clothes.'

'Yes, sir'

'Thank you Captain Fitzroy you are most kind.'

'My pleasure' He looked at me for half a second and was gone. There was no doubt he looked at me in a different manner now. Perhaps we had been through our baptism of fire together and now we were sure of each other's affection. Now I knew that nothing, neither God nor man, sea, nor storm, light, nor darkness, life nor death would come between us…or was this my overactive imagination at work again?

During the following days the Captain resumed his distant manner. I tried to remember what Mr. Bynoe had said. He was the Captain. He had to keep his distance. He was concerned about my good name.

There was great peace and harmony on board and the little ship fell back into the rhythm of daily tasks and recreations. I felt happier than I had been for a long time. Then a dreadful thing happened, a terrible incident. It threw the crew in a dark foreboding and shrouded the Captain with anxiety and pain.

Taken

The following day Lucy did not keep her appointment with Harry at the Savoy Hotel.

He failed to reach her on her cell phone, went to the reception, and spoke to the desk clerk,

'I had an appointment to meet a Miss Harrington. She is not here I wonder if she has left a message.'

'No sir…but I think I saw a young lady waiting… yes she went into the coffee room with three gentlemen and then they all left about fifteen minutes ago, sir.'

'Did Miss Harrington say anything…give any indication where they were going?'

'No sir.'

'Thank you.'

Harry walked into the coffee lounge and approached the waiter,

'Do you remember four people who were here earlier, three gentlemen and a lady?'

'Eh…yes, sir, I do.'

'Where were they sitting?'

'Over here, sir.'

Harry moved into the booth.

'Will you have coffee, sir?'

'Espresso please.'

'Very well, sir.'

'Did you notice anything distinctive about the people who were here earlier?'

'Eh…no sir.'

The waiter left. Harry got out his phone and dialled Lucy's number. 'Unobtainable.' Harry began to feel a pang of anxiety. He made a thorough search of the table, chairs and sofa. There was nothing unusual anywhere. While he was sitting at the table he was trying to work out what to do, the coffee was served. He picked up the spoon and began in an absentminded way moving the sugar around in the bowl. The spoon hit something hard. He lifted it out. It was Lucy's gold ring. A ring with her name engraved on the inside. His brain sprang into action. What could it mean? Then it hit him like a bolt…Goldberg…of course.

Harry opened his phone and dialled,

'Bloom, come up to the Savoy as quickly as you can.'

'Yes sir. Do I need to bring anything special?'

'Just your usual bag of tricks, Bloom'

'Very good, sir'

Harry booked into the suite he kept at the Savoy. He switched on the laptop and tried to find out what he could about Goldberg. Apart from a few business references his search was in vain. He had to find another way. He began to pace up and down the room. Then out of the blue he said, 'Finch'.

Yes, Finch knew everything about everybody. The trouble was he was as discrete as he was knowledgeable. Harry decided he would tell him the truth and hope for the best. He went downstairs and walked out of the hotel and down the street. It was a beautiful day with warm sunshine and a slight breeze but Harry's mind was filled with other anxieties. He entered an antique shop and spoke to the tall distinguished looking man standing by a very old circular table.

'Good morning Finch' Harry tried to sound cheerful.

'Good morning Harry, how can I help you today?'

Harry explained the situation to him. There was a long silence.

'You think Miss Harrington may be in danger?'

'Yes I do.'

Another long silence followed. For a few moments Harry thought he would say nothing and then he picked up a pen and wrote down an address in Mayfair. He handed the paper to Harry.

'I won't forget this Finch.'

Harry walked back to the hotel and waited for Bloom. When he arrived Harry said,

'Call a taxi Bloom. We are going to Mayfair.'

12th May 1832

The ship was going north now back to Bahia, and all seemed well. Then without warning the atmosphere changed. A tense foreboding hung over the crew and gloom seemed to permeate the decks and reach into the crevasses of every person's heart.

Three of the crew were ill before we left Rio, but two days after sailing, Mr. Morgan became very seriously ill indeed. Then the condition of the other two sailors deteriorated. It was malaria and everyone on board seemed to know that despite Mr. Bynoe's best efforts to save them, in reality there was nothing anyone could do.

I understand that when the ship was docked at Rio a

party of young sailors and officers had gone snipe shooting, around the estuary of the River Macacu. The party included the three sailors who were ill.

Sunday 13^h May

Mr. Morgan has died and was buried today after the Divine Service. He was a very strong and powerful man and the last person one would have expected to succumb to illness. He was also brave and courageous and is greatly missed by all.

18th May

I have spent many days alone. The Captain visits the sick bay several times per day.
Sometimes I see him and we exchange a few words. His heart is heavy and his eyes incredibly sad. He seems to find it difficult to speak.

19th May

The ship has reached Bahia and Mr. Jones and Mr. Musters remain seriously ill. The Captain continues to visit them in the sick bay and is greatly troubled by all that is now happening. I met the Captain on the deck today and told him of my sorrow and assured him of my prayers. As usual his countenance was distraught, and he could hardly speak. He bowed his head and went back to his cabin.

23rd May

Mr. Jones died two days after our arrival in Bahia and Mr. Musters died today. Poor young Mr. Musters who often brought my supper. His family were friends with the Captain, and news of his mother's death had come only a few days before. I felt desolate and knew that Captain Fitzroy would be blaming himself for the incident. I prayed for their souls. I said the De Profundis off without any hesitation, even though I had not said it for many years. Then I went on deck.

'Mr. Wickham may I speak with you?'

'Yes, Miss.' He approached the rail where I stood.

'No doubt the Captain is distressed, Mr. Wickham, at the deaths of these young sailors.'

'As we all are, Miss, not least Mr. Bynoe who tried his best to save their lives.'

'Indeed. Should I go to talk to the Captain, Mr. Wickham, or is it your judgment that he is best left alone?'

'Best left alone, Miss…that is apart from your good self. I am sure he would appreciate your kind words. I also know that he will be blaming himself.'

'Thank you, Mr. Wickham, would this be a good time?'

'Yes I think so, Miss.'

'Very well, Mr. Wickham.'

I went back to the cabin and freshened my face and hands. I brushed my hair and put on the one respectable dress I had managed to alter. I put the cream shawl around my shoulders. Then I made my way to the Captain's cabin and knocked.

'Come in.'

I opened the door cautiously. Fitzroy sprang to his feet, as did Mr. Hellyer.

'Miss O'Mara' Fitzroy said quietly.

'Mr. Hellyer, if you don't mind, I would like to speak to the Captain privately for a moment.'

'Certainly, Miss' Hellyer looked relived to be able to leave. I knew that he had probably endured one of the Captain's long melancholic silences.

'Please sit down' Fitzroy said. I could see the pain in his eyes and that far-away look. This is how he tried to deal with the hideousness of the horror. He tried to distance himself from the reality of it.

'My heartfelt sympathy is with you Captain.' I whispered.

'Oh Scarlett! Mr. Musters…I promised his father he would come back safely. Why the deuce did I let him go? Forgive me!'

I stood up slowly and walked around to the other side of the table. I put my hand on his shoulder.

'It was an accident, sir. Nobody blames you.'

'I blame myself.'

'It is wrong to blame yourself…you who trust in God so much.'

Fitzroy shot a glance at me.

'Are you mocking my faith?'

'No, no, I am trying to say that your strong faith must be your consolation.'

He put his elbows on the table and his head in his hands.

'Sir, you would have given your life for the boy. I know that, the crew knows that, and most of all, God knows that.'

He did not answer.

'I know you have made exhaustive inquiries as to why these three sailors became ill and other members of the party did not, and how you are trying to work out why and where and how the malaria strikes.'

A long silence began and continued. I walked back to the chair and sat down.

I began to speak quietly,
'But the fair Guerdon when we hope to find,
And think to burst out into sudden blaze,
Comes the blind Fury with th'abhorred shears,
And slits the thin spun life.'

He lifted his head slowly and spoke as if his thoughts were far away...

'Lycidas,' he murmured.

'Please do not blame yourself. He is with God. He is happier than ever he could have been here on earth.'

'Do you truly believe that Scarlett?'

'Yes I was brought up... well... what you would probably call a Papist, but I believe in God and in the afterlife.'

There was another long silence; then tears began to flow down the Captain's cheeks.

I sat still. The tears came down my cheeks now. I took out my handkerchief and dried my face. The Captain did likewise.

'We need to let our feelings out. We all need to cry sometimes. These tears are tears of 'fever and fret' of deep sorrow for the tragic deaths of such young men. Why do we, and especially men, sir, associate tears with weakness? They are an involuntary expression of emotion. They show our human side.'

After a few moments he said,

'You always understand Scarlett. No condemnation... rather the reverse. You always understand me.'

'I don't sir. I just love you.'

He said nothing. For a moment I thought he was going to reprimand me for such language. Then he reached out, drew my hand across the table turned it over and kissed the palm. He looked at my hand for a moment and then put it back. I tried not to show the joy I felt that he trusted me enough to make such a gesture.

'I know it is very difficult for you to bear this sadness because you go to such lengths to ensure the safety of the crew.'

He sat in silence.

'I realised how difficult the funeral service for Mr. Morgan was for you sir.'

'Yes.'

'The service for Mr. Musters and Mr. Jones will be equally difficult for you, even more trying for you perhaps, but remember I am with you in spirit, heart and mind.'

'Thank you.'

'The officers and crew will accompany you into Bahia for the internment sir?'

'Yes.'

'Remember, please, my thoughts and prayers are with you sir.'

I stood up. He stood. Was it my imagination or did he look as if he had made the leap back to reality?

I reached the door, opened it, looked back at him, and then closed the door. Out by the companionway I saw Mr. Hellyer.

'I think the Captain may need you in a few minutes.'

'Yes, Miss. Thank you, Miss.'

I went back to my cabin and fell on my knees praying for the immortal souls of the dead. I sobbed then for all three but especially for poor Mr. Musters and his family. I prayed also for the man I loved, that he, one day might enter the kingdom. I prayed that I also, might one day be worthy to enter the kingdom of God.

When the bodies of the dead had been interned in

Bahia, the calm of the ship's routine was restored and we set out on the journey back to Rio, but the black cloud of the deaths hung steadily in the air and everyone was in low spirits. Each day the Captain and Stebbing dutifully took the measurements and although the air of gloom persisted on board there were no more incidents and soon we were back in Rio de Janeiro.

3rd June 1832

We arrived late in the evening and I heard Mr. Wickham saying that the previous chart was four miles out, and they had confirmed their own correct measurement. I was glad to be back in Rio. I looked out over the bay wondering whether I would ever see it other than from the brow of the Beagle.

4th June

There was a knock at the door.
'Come in.'
Fuegia opened the door. I jumped up and hugged her.
'O Fuegia, it so good to see you'
I stepped back and looked at her.
'You better, Miss Scarlett, you don't want leave the ship and come stay with me?'
'No Fuegia I was not very well. Then the Captain was very upset when the three young sailors died.'
'Yes Mr. Darwin tell me.'
'Have you had a good time, Fuegia? Tell me what it was like in Botofogo.'
'I no like it Miss Scarlett. I prefer stay on ship. But the Captain think it better for me go there.'

'But everyone was kind to you…yes?'

'Yes very kind, but look after children teach them speak English and learn some Portuguese. I look too at the nice clothes of the ladies, but no Miss Scarlett have fun with.'

'Well you are back now, Fuegia and I am very glad to see you.'

'I come back later Miss Scarlett.'

'Yes please do. You rest now, you look very tired.'

Fuegia left and I opened my book. This was my third time to read 'A Vindication of the Rights of Woman'. I wondered then if there was a single man on the planet who would listen to Mary Wollstonecraft. Then inside my head I rephrased the question. I wondered if there were any women on the planet who would listen to Mary Wollstonecraft!

6th June

Mr. Darwin came aboard early and had breakfast with the Captain. I managed to have a few words with him before he left, although he left and came back several times during the day. He said his time in Botofogo had been inspirational, and not just because of his discoveries in Natural History but because of the number of people he had met and who had befriended him.

21st June

Today Mr. Sulivan appeared to have a little free time and I asked him about the Captain.

'Do you know anything about the Captain's time at the Naval College Mr. Sulivan?'

'Well, I know he completed the three-year course in half the time allotted. He also won the first medal for mathematics.'

'I think he must have been very happy there.'

'I am sure he was. It was perhaps the place where his talents were nurtured and he was allowed to prove his true ability.'

'You greatly admire him, do you not Mr. Sulivan?'

'I do, because he always wishes to share any knowledge he has gained for the good of the Service and he has helped me with valuable advice and perhaps most of all by his example.'

'Indeed.'

'I gather you think very highly of him yourself, Miss O'Mara, despite the fact that he is often severe with you.'

'I do, Mr. Sullivan, and he is severe with me because I often give him trouble and I know I am an added burden to his already heavy schedule.'

Mr. Sulivan began to laugh.

'Why do you laugh Mr. Sulivan, am I not right?'

'Indeed not, and I am laughing because no one would be more amused than the Captain to hear you describe yourself as a burden.'

28*th* June

Mr. Darwin came aboard today and has taken up his place in the poopcabin.

'Mr. Darwin, it is good to see you back on board.'

'Thank you, Miss O'Mara, and have you enjoyed our stay here in Rio?'

'I have indeed sir. It is of course of great pain to me that the Captain did not see fit to allow me to go ashore. Yet I am sure he has his own good reasons for doing so.'

'Yes indeed.'

'Will I be able to see some of the treasures you have found Mr. Darwin?'

'Of course.'

'May we celebrate your return, Mr. Darwin in the gunroom this evening?'

'That would be delightful. Thank you, Miss O'Mara.'

During the evening I went to the gunroom and enjoyed the company of the officers and the account Mr. Darwin gave of his adventures.

Sunday 1st July

The Divine Service is always uplifting. It takes our hearts to another plane, and gives respite from the earthly daily toil on board. These days are enjoyable and I often take supper with the officers. We have spent many pleasant evenings testing each other's knowledge and although I can say off by rote the answers to many questions about seafaring, alas, I mostly have no idea what the words mean. This causes waves of laughter among the young officers.

3rd July

This evening while I was on deck I saw Mr. Darwin coming onto the boat and decided to wait and speak to him.

'Miss O' Mara,' Fitzroy was standing beside me, sounding barely civil.

'Captain…I see Mr. Darwin returns…and…' He looked at me with a question in his eyes but he did not speak.

'And, I am going to my cabin now, sir.'

'Yes indeed, I think that appropriate.'

I left the deck. I knew then certainly that he resented Mr. Darwin's regard for me. This did not alarm me as I think I knew it for a long time. Tears came into my eyes as I remembered the words of Paul to the Corinthians:

'Love is patient and kind; love is not jealous…'

A tear trickled down my face.

I wondered if it is ever possible fully to understand another person. As I was reflecting on these things there came a knock on the door and I was amazed to see Mr. King.

'Mr. King, why do you bring my dinner?'

'I wanted to ask you a question, Miss. Would you like some fresh snipe Miss?'

'Mr. King, how kind of you, but I never eat meat of any kind, not even game birds.'

'But…that's what I want to ask you, Miss. Why Miss? It tastes very good.'

'I'm sure it does, Mr. King.'

'Will I fetch some for you, Miss?'

'No thank you.'

'Could you tell me why Miss…or is it uncouth of me to ask?'

'No Mr. King, I don't like the taste of meat, therefore I do not eat it. Also, Mr. King, I don't like the look of dead creatures.'

Mr. King looked at me with such pity I could not help but laugh.

'There is no need to worry about it, Mr. King. There are so many other foods that I can assure you I will never be hungry.'

King looked puzzled.

'Go along, Mr. King, and enjoy your dinner.'

'I don't understand, Miss.'

'No, I am sure you don't. But go along now Mr. King, go along.'

I smiled, took the dinner and began to close the door of the cabin. Mr. King went off looking more confused than ever and I didn't have a chance to ask him about Botofogo. I knew he had gone to see Mr. Darwin almost as soon as the ship arrived.

I looked at the dinner of rice and peas. I had no appetite for food. I put it to one side and took out my journal. I began to write and lost myself inside my fantasy world.

5th July

We left Rio in the early morning, the little ship was given an exciting send-off by the other ships in the port. Sailors manned the rigging of the 'Warspite' and three cheers sounded across the bay. To my amazement a band struck up and played 'To Glory you steer'.

I will be glad to be on the high seas again as I must admit that some of the days at anchor were very tedious. I had to suffer never being allowed to go ashore but I had enjoyed the company of the officers. This was company of a kind, but not the company I truly desired. The Captain often went ashore and kept his distance again. I longed for the ship to be in full sail again and for the routine to return, because when he was on board there was the possibility he would send for me. As we set sail I heard that Mr. McCormick, the ship's surgeon, had left the ship.

6th July 1832

The days at sea towards Buenos Aires were tedious. Everyone on board seemed to be busy most of the day. The weather was colder and the sea was either too calm or very rough. I was cold. Fuegia was back on board, but she had very few warm clothes. She gave me a woollen walking dress. I didn't want to take it but Fuegia did not seem to feel the cold. It was too wide, too short, and the loudest crimson red I had ever seen. However, as the weather changed I was forced by the cold to wear it.

9th July

Over the last few days Mr. Darwin has suffered greatly as the Beagle rolled and pitched over the rough sea. After a day's calm, just when he had begun to recover the rough seas would set him back again. He confined himself then to the poop cabin. After sitting at the chart table for a while he often had to stretch out on it. 'Going on the horizontal,' he called it. At this time, Mr. Darwin grew a beard, as did most of the officers.

13th July

Today the weather is fine and the sea calm. When I went on deck with Fuegia Mr. Sulivan told me we had made good progress and we were roughly just over one hundred and fifty miles from Rio.

18th July

While taking our walk at midday Fuegia and I had sometimes seen whales break the surface and spout alongside the ship, but today we saw hundreds of dolphins. They leaped clear out of the sea and criss-crossed the bow. Fuegia shrieked with delight and I wanted to do likewise. Mr. Sulivan told me we were travelling at nine knots and yet the dolphins were faster.

21st July

Today I met the Captain on deck. He asked if I was feeling well. I told him how thrilling it was to see the dolphins. He nodded, excused himself and left the deck. I felt something other than the death of the young sailors was preoccupying him. It was probably the responsibility of the voyage on such young shoulders. Yet he thrived on his role of leadership, but no doubt felt the weight of it also.

23rd July

Mr. Darwin was on deck today and we spoke about the dolphins. He told me he was thinking a lot about 'migration' particularly of birds. He said,

'Everyone knows how strong the maternal instinct is; nevertheless the migratory instinct is so powerful…Fitzroy' I turned and curtsied,

'Captain'

'How do these latitudes suit you Miss O'Mara?'

'Very well thank you Captain.'

'Good.' He gave a nod of his head and walked away.

Mr. Darwin and I exchanged looks. Had the Captain decided at last it was acceptable for me to speak to Mr. Darwin?

'Kindly excuse me Mr. Darwin.'

I left the deck with Fuegia, and went back to my cabin.

26th July

Today the Beagle entered the River Plate. We called at Monte Video and then set out for Buenos Aires. Over the following days many strange events seemed to be happening and I kept to my cabin for most of the time.

2nd August

Today while I was reading in the cabin I heard a shot fired, followed by another that passed over the rigging. I looked out of the porthole. I didn't have a clear view but in the distance I could see a very large ship, an Argentinean ship.

The Beagle continued towards the anchorage at Buenos Aires. I heard the Coxswain, on the Captain's orders, dispatch two boats to shore demanding an explanation of the shots fired. Before the boats reached the shore, a Customs Officer came out and ordered them back saying they must submit to a quarantine inspection. 'Submit.' That was never a good word to use when speaking to Captain Fitzroy.

The Captain ordered the ship put about. I heard the orders to prepare the guns and the men jumped to their stations. Then I heard the order:

'Mr. Sorrell, back the fore topsail' I wondered what that meant and I heard the sailors jump again to carry out the order. The Beagle came to a stop alongside the Argentinean ship. The Captain stood on the rail and bellowed,

'If you attempt to fire another shot we shall send our whole broadside into your rotten hulk. Is that understood?'

He repeated it in Spanish so that there could be no doubt as to his threat. The men and guns on the Argentinean ship stood down. Then there was silence and the Beagle moved out into open water.

By sundown, the Beagle had come down the north side of the river to Monte Video. I heard the cutter lowered into the water. I crept out of the cabin and could see the British Frigate lying at the mouth of the river and guessed that Captain Fitzroy had gone across to speak to the Captain. I went back to my cabin, waited an hour, and then went on deck.

'What a day of activity, Mr. Wickham, is all well?'

'Yes Miss.' Wickham seemed in a bad mood and said no more. I walked towards the rail. Mr. Sulivan came up beside me.

'Were you frightened Miss?'

'No, should I have been?'

'No.' he smiled.

'When I saw the size of the other ship...'

'Guardship'

'Guardship, why did they not fire again?'

'If they had we would have been done for.'

'Exactly, so why did they not fire again?'

'The Captain's judgment, Miss, is always correct.'

'You mean he knew they would not fire.'

'Yes, his naval expertise is amazing. You see why I tell you he is one of the best Captains in the Royal Navy.'

'I agree with you there Mr. Sulivan. He is forever certain and fearless.'

'Sulivan' Wickham called Sulivan back to his duties.

'Excuse me Miss' Sulivan said and was gone. I looked at the dark brown colour of the water and began to laugh.

'It's the colour of mud.' I whispered, and felt the soft breeze on my face and looked over at the town of Monte Video sitting on a peninsula of land. I could see the Mole and the Customs House. I looked around and there was Mr. Darwin coming towards me.

'Mr. Darwin, I thought you had left on the cutter with the Captain.'

'No, he has gone to speak to the Captain of the Druid.'

'It was an eventful day was it not Mr. Darwin?'

'Indeed. The Captain is a fearless man, I have never met a man so brave and fearless and so shrewd and *intuitive that he rarely permits violence and then only as a last resort.'*

'You think very highly of him...despite his ...flaws. Forgive me'

'I know exactly what you mean, Miss O'Mara and forgive me for pointing out that both of us have felt the sting of his wrath. Yet he is the most remarkable character I have ever come across.'

'Let us say, Mr. Darwin that we both admire him exceedingly and know very well that his virtues far outweigh any blemish in his nature.'

'Could not have expressed it better myself.'

Darwin was looking very sad. His shoulders were bent and he reached out for the rail with both hands.

'You are downcast, Mr. Darwin. Is it the old complaint?'

'No.' He glanced quickly at me and I could see there were tears in his eyes.

'Bad news from home.' He moved closer.

'I have heard in a letter from home today that my cousin Fanny Wedgewood, only twenty six years old, has died of the cholera.'

'Oh, Mr. Darwin'

I placed my hand on his outstretched arm.

'Please accept my deepest sympathy. Was she a favourite with you, sir?'

'She was a beautiful intelligent young lady Miss O'Mara. She encouraged me to come on this voyage, and prayed constantly for my safety...she was also full of fun.'

Darwin took out his handkerchief and wiped his face.

'How can we accept such tragedies Mr. Darwin? There is no point in talking about God's will at a time like this. It could not be anyone's will, God's or another's for such a beautiful young lady to die.'

'Indeed, my sentiments exactly, Miss O' Mara.'

'I will pray for you Mr. Darwin…'

'Miss O'Mara' Wickham's voice rang out across the deck.

'I will pray that God will give you grace to bear the pain, and take the young lady's soul to heaven.'

'Thank you.'

'Excuse me, Mr. Darwin.'

I walked towards the wheel where Mr. Wickham was looking thunderous.

'Yes, Mr. Wickham.'

'You might care to leave the deck Miss O'Mara.' He smiled.

'I have just spotted the cutter returning.'

'Thank you, Mr. Wickham.'

'Indeed, good night gentlemen, Mr. Darwin.'

Mr. Sulivan bowed, and Darwin nodded towards me as I made my way back to the cabin. I went in and looked at my papers, open books and logbook scattered across the table. I took off the dreaded crimson coat and sat down.

Everyday Mr. Wickham astonished me. He did not know that the Captain seemed to have found it acceptable now for me to talk to Mr. Darwin. However he was right to warn me about the approach of the cutter for if by any chance the Captain was in a bad mood he might not be at all pleased with me talking to Mr. Darwin.

I heard the Captain come aboard. He was in good spirits by the sound of his voice and he had brought someone with him. I wondered if on the morrow I might suggest something to Mr. Wickham – that I go into Monte Video to buy clothes.

5th August 1832

The next morning the British Consul and Chief of Police of Monte Video came aboard to speak to the Captain. It was to give notice of a mutiny. It seemed that while the President was away the Commander of the troops attempted to seize power. The prison was opened and the prisoners armed. They had taken over the Citadel, the seat of the government.

All this did not particularly interest Captain Fitzroy I am sure. He was used to news of innumerable revolutions in this part of the world and was very wary of getting involved in politics. When he understood however that the lives and property of British families were at risk he lost no time in taking action.

The orders were given and long and complicated they were. I understood very little of what was happening and the noise was thunderous. I heard the Captain tell Sulivan to organize a platoon of fifty men, Mr. Chaffers to take control of the ship and the Mr. Boatswain to open the armoury.

The Captain left the ship and when he reached the Mole, he signalled the sailors to proceed to shore, and within minutes all fifty-two men armed with cutlasses, muskets and pistols manned the boats. They seemed to do these manoeuvres remarkably quickly and then silence.

I wondered if it were safe to go on deck and where I could find Fuegia. It was notable that Fuegia could go on deck regardless of what was happening and no one, including the Captain ever said one word of reproach to her. Yet, if I so much as put my toe out of the cabin I was in trouble.

It was a dull day with hazy sunshine. I took courage, reached for the crimson coat and went on deck. Mr. Chaffers was at the wheel.

'Good morning, Mr. Chaffers. May I ask you is the ship empty… no I mean…'

'You mean vacated Miss. No there are some twenty of us here.'

'Could you tell me what is happening, Mr. Chaffers?'

'Yes Miss.' He explained to me then about the mutiny and how the Captain and fifty-two men had gone ashore to fight and restore order. I felt a chill come over me, the Captain could be killed or injured. I looked at all the guns in place facing the shore. I must have turned deathly pale because Mr. Chaffers said,

'Miss O'Mara, there is no need to be afraid. The Captain will do anything rather than fire these guns.'

'The chronometers!' I exclaimed.

'You begin to understand him Miss.'

'Maybe, but is he in danger Mr. Chaffers?'

'They are all in danger Miss, but I can tell you this, the Captain will not shed blood unless every other possible solution has been attempted and has failed.'

'Yes I do know he hates violence, and yet…'

'Where's Mr. Darwin?'

'He too has gone with his pistols and cutlass.'

'Oh! No'

'What do you mean, Miss? He is a strong man.'

'Yes Mr. Chaffers but he is in no way as fit as our Captain, or as experienced.'

Chaffers began to laugh.

'Miss O'Mara the Captain will not allow Mr. Darwin to act as if he is a member of His Majesty's Navy. Be at ease.'

'Very well Mr. Chaffers, until I see the Captain return, my heart…'

I had not meant to say anything about my heart and the Captain in the same breath.

'...will not be at ease.'

I tried to cover over my mistake.

Chaffers looked at me and smiled. I blushed. It was a fact; all the officers knew about my regard for the Captain. In their eyes I probably seemed very silly.

'As soon as I receive a signal, Miss, I will let you know. May I respectfully ask you to go below now please, we have to be cautious.'

'Yes of course Mr. Chaffers. Thank you.'

I knew the Beagle might be fired at from the shore if the rebels were in control. I wondered though if it was not for another reason that Chaffers had asked me to leave the deck. The Captain, from wherever he was, might have turned the spyglass onto the deck and, if he saw me there, Chaffers would have 'hell to pay' as the sailors put it.

I went below to my cabin. I sat at the table, found a clean sheet of paper, picked up a pen and wondered if I could compose a love poem, maybe a sonnet, and write it out and give it to the Captain upon his safe return. Of course, he might think it sentimental. If it is he will dismiss it. I wondered how a love poem could not be sentimental. On the other hand he might just appreciate it. That was probably what made him so interesting. You never knew exactly how he was going to react to anything. I began,

To Captain Robert Fitzroy,
I love you through the length of each new day,
Through sunrise, heat of noon and evening sky.
I love you when you stand aloft and speak,
And in those quiet moments of self- doubt.
I love you as you face disaster bravely,
And try all ways so that no blood is shed.
I love you in wind and storm and tempest,

*In deep silence and glow of candlelight.
I love you when your spirit fails within,
And you wrestle with the darkness to find light.
I love you with the innocence of my youth,
With silent tears, laughter and rational truth.
I love you all the days that I may live,
May God decree I love thee – eternally.*

I thought in my innocent youth that one day I would marry a poet who would sweep me off my feet and I would love him until the day I died. How extraordinary life is! Just imagine if anyone had said to me when I was at school that one day I would be aboard the Beagle in the New World and that there would be a person on board who would steal my heart away…

Then I prayed that all the sailors would come back safe and well. Would it be inappropriate to put in a special plea for the Captain?

I spent the rest of the day researching the history of the Royal Navy. I tried to concentrate, but my thoughts were never far from the dangers facing my beloved Fitzroy. As evening approached there came a knock on the door

'Come in.'

'Mr. Chaffers would like to speak to you on the bridge Miss.'

I grabbed my shawl and ran past the midshipman, and Fuegia whom I had not seen all day. When I reached the bridge I held my breath and looked keenly at Mr. Chaffers wondering if there was bad news.

'I have had a signal, Miss, to stand down.'

'Does that mean all is well Mr. Chaffers?'

'It means, Miss that the rebels have fled and the whole company are enjoying beefsteaks at the Fort.'

'Oh thank God. Oh, forgive my expression Mr. Chaffers.'

'No Miss, I thank God also. Will you be able to rest easy now as you know there is no danger to the Captain…and of course Mr. Darwin and the crew?'

'I will Mr. Chaffers, and I thank you for your consideration.'

I looked at the inscription on the wheel as I had often done. I repeated it aloud,

'England Expects Every Man To Do His Duty'

'No doubt all the crew have done their duty today Mr. Chaffers.'

'Yes Miss.'

I turned to leave. I wanted to be alone; to rejoice with all my being that Robert was safe. I returned to the cabin where Fuegia was looking at my open books. There was no chance of being alone so I said,

'Come Fuegia let us breathe in the air before the night falls.'

We went on deck and walked to the rail. I looked over towards the Mole and the Fort. I wondered how the Captain was. I was quite certain about one thing- wherever he was, and whether or not he was eating beefsteak, he was not thinking about me.

The boats returned in the evening to collect all that was required for the night at the Fort. Mr. Darwin came with them and stayed on board. However he seemed in no mood to speak about what had happened.

6th *August*

Today the crew returned. The Captain had a friend with him when he came on board. I heard the cheers as the Captain stepped aboard. I wondered how the mutiny was resolved and thought I would ask Mr. Wickham whenever I saw him again. I washed and then brushed my hair. I put on the beautiful green velvet dress that I had made with Fuegia from one of her dresses. I put on the sash and looked at myself in the tiny mirror. I pinned the emerald comb Fuegia gave me into my hair.

The dress was so extravagant looking that I put it on only for special occasions. Even now, I thought it far too lavish to wear during the day. It was more suited for a ball. I waited… maybe, just maybe the Captain would send for me.

The hours passed. I went back to my poetry studies. Dinnertime came and went. I was about to take off the dress, put on another and go for a walk on deck when a knock came to the door.

'Oh Mr. Chaffers surely you are not all this time on duty.'

'I am just going off duty now Miss. The Captain would like to see you Miss and he says to tell you that he has Mr. Darwin and Mr. Hamond with him.'

'Very well, thank you Mr. Chaffers.'

I tried to be calm but I could not keep the light of joy out of my eyes and I knew that Mr. Chaffers noticed it. Chaffers left and I took one last look in the mirror, pinched my cheeks, and straightened my dress. I went slowly to the Captain's cabin and knocked on the door.

'Come' his voice sounded happy.

I opened the door and there, squashed into the space were three gentlemen who rose to their feet blocking out the light. I looked into the eyes of the Captain. He looked well and happy.

'Ah! Miss O'Mara kindly come and join us. May I introduce Mr. Robert Hamond?'

'He joins us from the Druid.'

'How do you do Mr. Hamond? Good evening Mr. Darwin, Captain.'

Mr. Hamond opened his eyes wide and looked intently at me. His mouth opened and then he stepped forward, took my hand, and raised it towards his lips. Gentlemen of course made no contact between hand and lips.

'Miss O' Mara, a pleasure indeed, please take my seat Miss.'

'Thank you' I said sitting down on his chair. I glanced over at the Captain and could see already that the storm clouds were gathering. Then I looked at M. Darwin and knew immediately he was ill. It was best to say nothing.

'Mr. Hamond and I sailed together on the Thetis,' the Captain said.

'However today we are to celebrate a good day's work gentlemen.'

'Indeed, you know it amazes me Fitzroy how you returned to the ship without striking a blow.' said Mr. Darwin.

'I wish it were always that way.' The Captain replied.

He looked keenly at Mr. Hamond who never took his eyes for one second away from me. Without taking his eyes away, he said,

'There is no better Captain in his Majesty's Navy, Darwin.'

'I raise my glass to that sentiment, Hamond.'

Hamond at last withdrew his scrutiny and said,

'Except, Darwin, you have no glass.'

'And what of your thoughts about the incident Miss O'Mara?'

Fitzroy smiled at me and I returned his smile. Before I could speak, Mr. Darwin said,

'Indeed, Miss O' Mara, forgive my boldness… may I say how well you look this evening.'

I looked at Darwin again. His words were slurring and he was certainly out of sorts.

I thought that there was no alcohol aboard, and yet he sounded distinctly inebriated. Perhaps the euphoria of the battle was affecting him.

'You make no answer Miss O'Mara.' Fitzroy's voice was cold as ice. It brought me back from my reverie.

'Thank you Mr. Darwin.'

I looked back at Fitzroy's darkening eyes, smiled at him and then looked at Mr. Hamond and asked,

'Will you be staying aboard, Mr. Hamond, or is this a fleeting visit?'

'No I will be staying aboard, Miss.'

I followed his eyes to the Captain, who was glaring at him,

'Kindly excuse me, Miss, gentlemen, I must be about my duties.'

He made an extravagant bow towards me, and left. I put my fingers to my lips to cover my smiles, and then Darwin stood up.

'Excuse me Miss O'Mara…I feel…I feel, I must go on the horizontal…excuse me Fitzroy.'

Darwin left and Fitzroy stood up. For a moment I wondered if he was going to ask me to leave. Instead he put a chair by his table and said,

'Please sit here, Scarlett.'

I moved to the chair and sat. He went back to his place. He looked at his papers. Then he asked,

'Will you remember these days on the Beagle with joy or with sorrow, Scarlett?'

'I assure you, sir, with joy.'
'Will you forget the times I have been very severe with you?'
'I will always remember you with affection, sir.'
'Thank you Scarlett.'
He stood and said 'Goodnight'.
'Goodnight sir.

10th *August*

The Captain sent for me early this morning and said,
'Scarlett, I want you to go ashore tomorrow with Fuegia to purchase some clothes. Who would you like to accompany you?'
'I leave the choice to you sir.'
'I think Mr. Bynoe in case… and Mr. Sulivan'
'Are you sure you can do without Mr. Sulivan sir?'
'Yes, I choose him because I would trust the man with my life and therefore your life.'
'Very well sir but why do you always think my life is in danger?'
'I have my reasons.'
'May I know these reasons?'
'They are not for you to worry about. They are for me to worry about.'
'That is not fair. Why should you have to worry about my life on top of all the other problems of the voyage?'
'Scarlett, do you trust me?'
'I trust you in every possible way sir.'
'Very well, first, you must promise me you will be careful and not leave the side of the officers for one single moment. Do you promise me that, Scarlett?'
I smiled.

'No Scarlett you must promise me wholeheartedly.'

'I promise you sir.'

'You are not to go off looking at paintings or books is that clear?'

'Yes sir.'

'I know you Scarlett, you are quite unaware of the dangers in these cities.' He paused.

'If you only knew how much I wish to accompany you myself, to make sure you are safe, however, that is not possible with the amount of work I must complete, and indeed it would not be appropriate…you understand that don't you?'

'I do indeed sir.'

'Would you be able to tell me what happened at the Mole sir? I prayed that you would not be hurt or injured. If you were…my heart would break.'

Fitzroy stretched out his hand across the table with the palm upturned, and I placed my hand in his.

'I don't want to waste time talking about a mutiny, Scarlett.'

'No sir'

'Talk to me. Tell me what you are thinking about these days.'

'You mean what do I think about apart from your good self sir?'

He drew my hand towards him and put his lips to my fingers for half a second. Then he let it go and started to laugh.

'Would any other person on this ship dare speak to me like that?'

'No sir…however… there are only certain times when I can speak to you like this, don't you think it is a credit to my discernment that I know when I can?'

He picked up the coin. He smiled.

'Sir, I am making a study of the history of the Royal Navy and, believe it or not, it has absorbed my mind.'

'I hope not totally.'

'At last…you jest, mon Capitaine' *He smiled again.*

'I know I must seem unbearably serious to you, Scarlett.'

'I know you are often happy, but not always with me.'

'Do you forgive me for the times when I am annoyed with you?'

'Yes of course I do. You always have your reasons.'

'And what were you saying about studying the history of the Royal Navy?'

'Well, you sir, know what nobody else knows: that there is one big distraction in my thoughts. Remember I have to content myself with the exploits of other naval captains, while a certain naval Captain has many duties to perform and has no time for me.'

He looked serious and I wondered if I had done it again- said out too boldly what ought not to be mentioned.

'Sometimes it is unbearable for me too Scarlett.' *He looked directly at me. He seemed more relaxed than I had ever known him and he found it easy to say that he found my absence sometimes unbearable. Did I hear him truly say that?*

'There is something else I need to talk to you about…I don't know how to approach the matter.'

'Why is that sir? Is it an unpleasant matter?'

'No…I think…well the President is giving a ball in the Teatro Solis in Monte Video to celebrate the favourable outcome of the mutiny.'

'How wonderful…oh Robert…sorry…I mean sir, you don't know how pleased I feel that people appreciate the part you played in solving the matter.'

'In reality I did very little.'

For a moment he looked at his papers. One of the most attractive things about him was that he never believed he did anything remarkable…only his duty. After a few minutes I said,

'Are you upset sir? Did I say something wrong?'

'No Scarlett, you are never wrong. It is always me. It is always my selfishness about you and my desire to be the only one you trust…'

'What do you mean sir?'

He stood up and walked behind the table, then he stood still for a few moments, came back to the table and sat down.

'There is nothing I would like better than to walk into that ball with you.'

'I know you can't do that, sir.'

'Yes…I know you understand that, but will you understand this…'

He hesitated. Then he frowned. He put down the coin.

'You should go to the ball with one of the officers. I think that would be the correct procedure, and no doubt the officers will expect that…but…'

'You have an objection?'

'Yes…no…I mean my heart will break Scarlett if I see these men looking at you, and I would have to watch you dancing with the officers… knowing I could not ask you to dance.'

'You could not ask me to dance. Why ever not sir?'

'It might be inappropriate. I could not be seen to pay too much attention to you Scarlett.'

I wondered what he would say if he knew that most of the officers felt that he liked me very much, and Mr. Darwin did too.

'May I ask you a question sir?'

'Yes'

'When you said 'looking at me'– what did you mean sir?'

'I was right to call you a child, for child you are when it comes to the ways of the world.'

'No I am not a child. I can understand the world as plainly as you or anyone else can...apart from my loss of memory.'

'Scarlett, your innocence is the most desirable quality any man could ever wish for in a bride.'

Bride...bride...he was confusing me now. Why was he talking about brides?

'My dear child you know I would never insult you. You have, as Darwin so aptly put it, a keen enquiring mind, I know you understand many things about the world, but about gentlemen you understand very little.'

'Why have you tears in your eyes?'

'Because...because...there is no luckier Captain in his Majesty's Navy, because the affection you have for me... breaks my heart. Oh Scarlett! Your affection for me is beyond my understanding.'

'Oh sir, why are you so complicated? Why can you not just accept my love and affection for you?

'Very well.' He looked away.

'What did you want to say to me about the ball?'

'Only this, that in my selfishness I do not wish you to go.'

'Is that all? How could you think I would want to do anything against your wishes? I have no desire whatsoever to go to the ball. In fact were you to ask me whether I would like to go to the ball or have fifteen minutes conversation

with you, the latter for me would be the choice I would make, and make willingly with all my heart.'

'Oh Scarlett! Are you sure? I know how young and beautiful you are and that by right you should go and enjoy yourself.'

'How could I enjoy myself if I were not with you sir?'

'I do not deserve the affection you have for me.' He paused.

'And …maybe…upon reflection Scarlett, tomorrow or the next day will you think me a selfish uncivil man for making such a request?'

I waited to gather my thoughts…to see how I could convince him…

'You will not think me an utterly selfish creature?'

'I could never think about you like that, so please, please do not complicate this matter. I am very content to stay on the Beagle while you go to the ball. If the next day you find time to tell me about it, well that would be delightful. There will be many beautiful ladies there. Mr. Darwin has told me how beautiful the ladies are here.'

'I assure you Scarlett all these so called beautiful ladies could never reach your standard of beauty, intelligence or empathy.'

'Thank you sir, will you remember in the days ahead that you said these things?'

He looked down at the papers on his table for a second, then he looked at me, and whispered,

'Whatever you think Scarlett, and however I may seem on various occasions, I never forget a single thing about you, or anything you have ever said to me.'

Our eyes met and I saw that for the first time since I had met him he was his true self and able to convey his true feelings. It had taken all these months for him to trust me.

Of course the dreadful possibility was always hovering inside my head that maybe… just maybe, tomorrow he would regret what he had said and revert to the austere, ice cold, distant Captain he sometimes appeared to be.

He continued speculating about the ball

'It is to be expected that some officers will ask you to go with them.'

'Well, I will say no.'

'They will wonder why, Scarlett.'

'I will tell them that I am an ordinary creature with ordinary tastes and a grand ball in Monte Video is far beyond my expectations.'

'I hope they believe that.'

I knew that the officers, to a man would not believe that and would know exactly why I was not going to the ball. I wondered if I could ask him…but…how terrible if after all this he flew into a temper…

'Tell me… am I really like a child? Do you think because of the death of my parents that I never in fact grew up?'

He looked shocked and for a dreadful moment I wished I had not asked. Then he smiled.

'Oh you have grown up Scarlett, you have grown up in the most beautiful way.'

'I am not a child then.'

'You are, in the most perfect way.'

'Oh dear, I will never understand what you mean.'

I stood up. He shot to his feet,

'Scarlett please do not go yet. I have no idea when I will be able to see you alone again.'

I sat down again. How strange that he was able to say aloud all the things I had been feeling for months but not allowed to mention.

'Do you know what I was thinking about in the Fort last night?'

'No.'

'Do you remember when you were in the grounds of Wakefield Lodge and I thought you said your name was Charlotte and I dragged you up to tea?'

'Yes.'

'Well I remembered then what you said to me that day. You said, 'how dare you hold my hand so tightly.'

'Yes I remember, even though you were twelve and I was about nine you were determined to take us to the house. When we eventually sat down James, my half brother, whispered to me,

' I think we have been stolen.'

We both laughed.

'You sent someone to the carriage to tell our relatives where we were, but you did not tell us, and all the time we were thinking we would be in a great row. You see even then, Robert, you were determined to have your own way.'

'But not for any reason other than I wanted you to enjoy...'

'Well no...but sometimes when I hear the morning inspection I am very glad I am not a sailor on board the Beagle.' His eyes darkened.

'You know you can be very stern.'

'Yes, but that is my way of keeping a pristine ship.'

'Perhaps you could do it a little more quietly. I am usually awakened by the noise of it all.'

He began to laugh.

'At last sir, at last you have relaxed. At last you can see the funny side of things.'

'Thank you Scarlett, I know I am far too sombre for

your light-hearted ways, but try to understand that it is the lot of a Captain to be so. But with you...'

He hesitated.

'My dear captain as much as I am enamoured with this conversation, I think I should go.'

'Don't go yet, Scarlett.'

'You have much to do before you can go to bed and you look very tired. So please promise me you will go to bed happy in the thought that I will never do anything that would not be keeping with your orders.'

I began to laugh and then he laughed.

'That dreaded word 'orders' again.'

I took from my sleeve the poem I had written out during the day. It was written on a small piece of folded paper.

'Before you go to bed will you read this?'

'Yes, what is it?'

'It is the way I think about you.' I whispered.

'When you read it, remember that these words are my very poor attempt to describe your character, and do not remotely do justice to the honourable and upright man that you are.'

He took the folded sheet in silence and put it on the table.

'Very well and thank you for...thinking so highly of me.'

I stood up. He stood and came around to my side of the table.

'Goodnight'

'Goodnight'

'Scarlett, before you go, may I be so bold as to say how beautiful you look tonight.'

'Why thank you Captain Fitzroy.'

He opened the door,

'Good night'

IMMANENT DANGER

Harry and Bloom raced towards Mayfair, and Harry grew anxious about Lucy. If he hadn't met her she wouldn't have become involved in this business. They got out of the taxi and stood still in Berkeley Street a short distance away from number 27.

'It's a veritable fortress, sir' Bloom said as he looked at the house. Harry handed him the satellite printout he had downloaded from the internet.

'Hold on Bloom…let's see, look…there is a spot in the hedge, next to the side gate…I think we could squeeze through there when the camera turns in the other direction. If we get through, we can sneak round the back.'

'You mean the moving surveillance camera, yes, there are a few seconds before it returns to the spot. The next time it turns lets go.'

They crossed the street, ducked down behind the hedge to watch the surveillance camera. As soon as it turned Bloom forced his way through the thick shrubbery and Harry followed. They moved quickly to the back of the house. Harry weighed up possible entry points.

'Which part of the house is the most vulnerable Bloom?' Harry whispered.

'Well...I'd say the second window on the ground floor.'

'Can you get in by it?'

'Certainly, but it will trigger the alarm.'

'How long will it take you to open it?'

'About four or five minutes.'

'No Bloom, I must know precisely.'

'Say four minutes then.'

'Ok. In four minutes exactly I will ring the bell furiously and bang on the knocker. In that time can you get in, close the window, make it look as if it was not opened and hide before anyone comes?'

'Yes.'

'Very well if Goldberg is here and he probably is, he and his bodyguards will hold me captive. You look for Lucy and if you find her you make your escape immediately. Is that clear Bloom? Above all get Lucy away from here, that is an order.'

'What about you, sir?'

'Forget about me...I'll be fine. Just get Lucy out.'

'What about the police, sir?'

'Bloom, whatever you do on no account contact the police...our friend Goldberg has all the right social connections.'

'Very well, sir'

Bloom moved towards the window.

'Are you ready?' Harry asked looking at his watch.

Bloom moved close in and gave a sign. Harry set the timer and moved cautiously back out to the street. He walked up and down impatiently. Then he slowly moved towards the front door and waited. On the exact count of four minutes he banged on the knocker incessantly, rang the bell and held it down and shouted as loud as he could,

'Open the door…open the door…I know you're in there Goldberg…open the door.'

He heard the alarm go off. He saw the door camera switch on. He turned his back only to be picked up by another surveillance camera. He continued to shout and bang on the door. The door opened. A young girl in an apron was standing there,

'God's truth, what's the matter Mister?'

'I need to see Mr. Goldberg urgently.' Harry raised his voice,

'Mr. Goldberg is not…'

'Oh yes, he is' Harry said brushing past her. As he did so two pairs of strong arms grabbed him and put him in a lock. He felt his bones would break if he tried to move. The two guards were the same ones that he'd had the pleasure of meeting at the club.

'Hey guys what's up, you put on some weight?'

One of them twisted his arm harder.

'Can't you take a joke guys? Come on, I thought ugly people had a good sense of humour!'

They dragged him across the huge circular hallway to a door at the rear of the house opened it and threw him to the floor. Goldberg was on the phone, sitting behind a huge LouisV desk. Slowly he put the phone down.

'Ah! Mr. Harry I have been expecting you…but not so soon I admit.'

He stood up and moved towards Harry. Harry stood up and looked around the room.

'I see you employ a good designer, Goldberg. I

doubt if this style bears any resemblance to your crass taste.'

'That is where you are wrong. I like beautiful things, and I always employ the best people. Sit down, sit down, have a drink.'

'No thank you. I have come for Lucy.'

'How should I know who Lucy is?'

'You abducted her.'

'Well …perhaps we did.'

'Where is she?'

Goldberg turned and sat back at his desk

'She's fine. I am not going to harm her,' he said flippantly.

'If you so much as speak to her rudely, Goldberg…'

'You'll what, Mr Harry?' Goldberg laughed.

'Where is she?'

'Let's say she is quite safe.'

'There is a possibility that what you call safe and I call safe may be entirely different.'

Goldberg lit a cigar.

'Why do you want Lucy?' Harry asked.

'I don't want Lucy…I want you, Harry.'

'Well, you have me now. Let her go'

'Well, well…always making a bargain Harry.'

A knock on the door, Goldberg growled,

'Come in'

A huge man in a black suit entered,

'Dixon?'

'All clear, sir'

'Nothing?'

'No, sir.'

'Search again' Goldberg barked.

'Yes sir.' Dixon turned and left the room.

'Where is Lucy?'

'You are beginning to bore me Harry…why are you so impatient. I will…'

There was another knock at the door.

'Come in,' Goldberg shouted.

Then into the room came the most ruthless man Harry had ever known.

'Well if it isn't Sir Ronald Reed…why am I not surprised to see you here?'

'Oh…Ronald come in, come in old boy. Meet Mr. Harry.'

'Well Harry' he placed his silver topped cane and leather gloves on a side table.

'We meet again.'

Goldberg left his desk and stood between Harry and Reed. He looked from one to the other.

'You know each other?' Goldberg asked.

'Oh we know each other.' Harry smiled.

'Not only did we come from the same district; we went to the same school. However I can't see that you have made much of your life Harry, I on the other hand am the Minister of Culture…a seat in the cabinet.'

'Imagine… do you know what we use to call you Ronnie on the stock exchange…Sir Ronald Greed.'

'Come now Harry that was a long time ago. I agree, although a little reluctantly, that… yes I did need money… and I made plenty of it.'

'Yes but not honestly.'

'Harry I am surprised at you. Are you calling a member of her Majesty's Government dishonest? I needed money to make up for all those boring hours

I spent doing public service, while at the same time climbing the tree of privilege of course. I was in charge of the National Gallery, Head of the Portrait Gallery… and the rest. Mind you I spent my time well. When I found the legacy from George IV and Fitzherbert I knew I had struck gold. With the help of a few friends, including Adolph here…'

'Adolph' Harry stood up

'You two are well matched'

'Are you saying Reed that Scarlett was the child of King George IV and Maria Fitzherbert? Because if you are you know that can't be true. They never had any children.'

'That is the official view, and to tell you the truth Harry I don't care who she was. As far as I am concerned she was left this legacy, and that is the only interest I have in her.'

'Of course.'

Harry looked closely at Reed. Until now he had no idea there was a valuable legacy in Scarlett's name. It was left to her by the king and Maria Fitzherbert. It all began to fall into place. Knighton wanted to kill Scarlett so that the legacy came to him and then to his descendants.

'The Trust stands at two hundred million Harry, that is without the cache of diamonds and jewellery.'

'Yes but it does not belong to you. How do you think you can claim it?'

'Easy…in six days time the deadline is up, and if no descendants of the said Scarlett O'Mara can be found the trust reverts to the descendants of Sir William Knighton.'

'And…' Harry asked

'My dear Harry it has taken me years to fix up my family tree…and you are looking at the direct descendant of Sir William Knighton.'

'What about his real descendants?'

'Line has faded, unaware of the trust…who knows?'

'You will be caught Reed.'

'No I will not. We propose to hold you here until after the deadline, then there is absolutely nothing you can do.'

'I can expose the fraud of your family tree.'

'No Harry, it has impeccable signatories. You would be laughed out of court.'

'Ok I give in…but let Lucy go, she knows nothing of all this.'

'I'm afraid she does. She is not the best of archivists but I'm sure her exquisite good looks made up for that Harry.'

Harry sprang at Reed, held him by the throat and threw him up against the wall. It was not just what he had said about Lucy but about a much deeper anger Harry felt towards Ronnie Reed from many years ago. Goldberg was there like a shot. He put a hand on Harry's shoulder,

'Now Harry, you know I keep several bodyguards… don't be foolish.'

Harry let go and Reed put his hand to his throat and coughed.

'I never realised you had feelings for the girl Harry. Why didn't you say? Now this makes things very interesting'.

Harry starred at the wall, and Goldberg followed his stare. There fastened to the wall was a pair of crossed epees shimmering in the sunlight.

'How about a duel Reed? You are an accomplished fencer, in fact world class.'

'Well a long time ago and this is childish.'

'I'll make a bargain. If I win, you let Lucy go.'

'And if you lose, which you most certainly will?'

'I'll stay here quietly until after the deadline.'

'Oh come on old chap this is silly. After all, why should I have to fight you? I hold all the cards.'

'Well yes I suppose you're right Reed. You do hold all the cards, but from what I remember about you, I think you could never back down from a challenge. I'm better than you, I guarantee you that.'

'You, better! Not a chance, I was unbeaten.'

'Yes, but you never had me as an opponent, did you?'

Harry began taking off his jacket, 'You know Reed I've been practising.'

'I can see you're not going to let this go, Harry. Oh very well, I could do with exercise'

11th August 1832

While the Beagle lay near to Monte Video, the Captain gave orders for me to be taken into the town to purchase clothes. Fuegia, Mr. Sullivan and Mr. Bynoe accompanied me. Mr. Bynoe rowed the dingy through the mud coloured water and Mr. Sulivan who was always jovial, smiled and said,

'You will be careful in the town Miss O'Mara, please. The Captain has instructed us not to let you out of our sight.'

'I will, Mr. Sulivan, but is not the Captain over anxious, even over protective?'

Before he could answer, Mr. Bynoe said,

'No Miss he is not. You have no idea how dangerous this part of the world is, and I beg you to stay close to Mr. Sulivan and myself at all times…you too Fuegia.'

Fuegia laughed as usual.

'Very well Mr. Bynoe, do not be alarmed, I have no intention of straying away. We are only going to buy clothes, is that not so Mr. Sulivan? So why does the Captain think I need so much protection?'

'The Captain may well have other reasons to protect you closely Miss, reasons that he is not at liberty to disclose to you or to any member of the crew.'

I knew well how highly the Captain thought of Mr. Sulivan. Although their rank separated them, they were nevertheless the best of friends. I knew in what high esteem Sulivan held the Captain and I had asked him innumerable questions about him. He had related to me an account of many events on board the ships they had served on together. Could the Captain have told Mr. Sulivan something none of the rest of us know anything about?

'Be assured, gentlemen, I will do nothing without your consent.'

'Thank you Miss' Mr. Bynoe smiled, and Sulivan looked out ahead.

The dingy pulled up to the slipway and we alighted. I looked around and thought the approach to the town flat and forlorn.

'It is very unlike 'All Saints Bay' is it not Mr. Sulivan?'

'Indeed. There are a few good plazas though.'

We walked into the town in silence. I looked with a keen eye at the cobblestone streets and around the plazas. There were museums, theatres, and to my great relief an abundance of shops. I also saw the beautiful ladies Mr. Darwin had spoken to me about. I observed their graceful posture and colourful clothes and how they seemed to cover one eye and peep out from behind their delicate veils. Fuegia walked towards a gown shop.

'This shop good Miss Scarlett?'

'Yes Fuegia, but perhaps the clothes are too expensive. We should look further on for a more moderately priced shop.'

'The Captain said Miss O'Mara that no expensive was to be spared and that we were to ignore any protests you might make on that subject.' Mr. Sulivan said decidedly.

'It seems to me Mr. Sulivan the Captain said a great deal too much about this whole excursion.'

'I beg you pardon Miss, forgive me for saying so but it is because the Captain knows you so well, that his instruction are so extensive.'

I blushed and Fuegia laughed. Mr. Sulivan did not leave more than a few feet between his tall masculine frame and my slight body. Although I was not short of stature and my height reached his shoulders, I felt he was too close to me. I said nothing, and walked over to the first gown shop I saw.

'Let us go in Fuegia, you gentlemen may wait here.'

'No Miss we are coming in with you.' said Sulivan.

'That will be too embarrassing Mr. Sulivan.'

'Sorry Miss…orders.'

We all entered the shop and the proprietress opened her eyes wide and said,

'Buenos Diaz Senoras, Senorita'

'Buenos Diaz senora we wish to purchase some gowns please.'

'Si Senorita.'

She walked towards a wardrobe in which were the most beautiful gowns I had ever seen.

'She very thin' said Fuegia before I had time to speak.

'Si' the lady said as if she had already noted that. She took out two dresses. They both looked exquisite. One was in aquamarine and the other in the most beautiful shade of sky blue. I took the aqua one and held it up to myself.

'Try on Miss Scarlett, try on.'

I looked over at Sulivan. He never took his eyes off me and yet when I looked at him he looked away, and Bynoe did likewise. They are as embarrassed as I am, I thought.

'Where may I try it on?'

The lady indicated a small room and said,

'Here Miss.'

'Just one moment Miss,' Sulivan said stepping forward. He drew back the curtain and looked into the little square room. There were no windows. He stepped back and said,

'Very well Miss.'

I took both dresses, walked in, and drew the curtain. I tried the aqua one first. It was made from a beautiful quality silk, tight at the waist and full skirted. I looked at myself in the looking glass and wondered if the colour was good for me, and I wondered what colours the Captain liked.

I walked out.

'Oh Miss Scarlett!' Fuegia squealed,

'What, Fuegia, what?' In alarm I looked over at Mr. Sulivan and Mr. Bynoe.

My God have I left buttons undone! I instinctively crossed my arms over the dress.

'You look very beautiful Miss.' said Mr. Bynoe.

'Yes Miss' the proprietress smiled.

'Don't squeal Fuegia, I thought…well…don't squeal.'

'Sorry Miss Scarlett.'

'You look charming Miss Scar...Miss O'Mara if I may say so.'

'No you may not, Mr. Bynoe.'

'I am very sorry Miss. It was... in...inappropriate to say so. Please for...forgive me Miss O'Mara.' Mr. Bynoe stuttered. Then Mr. Sulivan said,

'Forgive our enthusiasm Miss O'Mara. We mean no impertinence.'

'I am sorry Mr. Sulivan, Fuegia alarmed me I...I am very grateful for your protection.'

'My privilege Miss.'

I had just about recovered from the shock I had had when I thought I was not properly dressed in front of the gentlemen. I should have recognized Fuegia's squeal as one of delight.

'You will buy this one?' Fuegia asked.

'I will try the other one before I decide.'

I went back into the little room and tried on the blue dress. It was heavier and more like a walking dress. I checked everything; I had no need of a further scare. I stepped out.

'This is beautiful too, Miss Scarlett,' Fuegia cooed.

'Which one shall I take Fuegia? This one is more sensible.'

'Excuse me, Miss O'Mara. The Captain said you were to buy at least four gowns and four pairs of shoes.' Bynoe said firmly.

'Indeed Mr. Bynoe and who is to pay?'

'I have the money here Miss.' Sulivan said.

I sighed, 'Are you suggesting I take both Mr. Sulivan?'

'Yes Miss, and two more and shoes and...what...whatever else you need.'

I looked at Fuegia. She shrugged her shoulders.

'Very well, these two, thank you.' I looked at the lady who now had matching shoes in her hands,

'You think these right colour?' she asked in Spanish.

'How beautiful!' I said and began to try them on. They felt like velvet and caressed my feet. For over a year I had struggled to clean my old shoes, worn now to a frazzle.

In the mean time, the proprietress came from a back room with a delightful velvet red dress. I thought it was the most beautiful shade of red I had ever seen.

'This one good?' she asked in Spanish.

'Yes, but it is too small.' I smiled,

She shook her head.

'Try on, try on' Fuegia said in an excited tone.

'Would you like a dress Fuegia? Would you like anything?'

'No Miss, the Captain buy me plenty in London.'

I retreated behind the curtain with the red dress. I tried it on and liked it very much. I stepped out.

'It very beautiful' Fuegia smiled.

'You will take this one also?' The proprietress asked.

'Yes, thank you. It is my favourite.'

The lady brought out pairs of shoes to match the dresses. I tried on the little red shoes that felt like satin around my feet…they were my favourites too. I tried the blue shoes which had a higher heel and I felt the luxurious leather and lining against my feet.

I realized just how old and worn my shoes were. I said I would take the blue shoes, and red shoes. Then I asked the lady to find me a strong pair of shoes for walking. I put these on and did not take them off. Then I chose a cape and some ribbons.

The lady began to pack everything into boxes.

'Mr. Sulivan, Mr. Bynoe are you quite sure I have not been too extravagant? I do not need all these dresses, indeed one would be perfect.'

'No Miss, the Captain insists that you have a proper wardrobe.'

'Thank you gentlemen.'

Mr. Sulivan paid the bill and Mr. Bynoe picked up the boxes. We said thank you and goodbye and soon we were back out on the street.

'Now must buy under clothes' said Fuegia in a loud voice. I blushed.

'First, may we sit in that church across the street for a few moments gentlemen?'

It was agreed and we crossed the street and entered the church of Sancta Maria Magdalena'. Fuegia and I sat down and Mr. Sulivan and Mr.Bynoe sat behind us. I knelt down, made the sign of the cross, and prayed for my dead parents, the officers and crew of the Beagle and above all for the Captain, especially that this voyage would not kill him and that he would not work himself to death. I said a special prayer too for Mr. Sulivan and Mr. Bynoe, Fuegia, and Mr. Darwin.

I looked around the rich and spacious interior of the church. From the stained glass windows to the portraits of the saints, everything was gilded and shining. Despite this exotic interior, people came in and out from the street creating a kind of casual atmosphere, quite alien to the one I associated with the solemn style of English churches.

I stood up and whispered,

'Thank you gentlemen.'

We walked out into the stark light and heat of the midday sun. We strolled down the same side of the street *now and soon we came to a shop with bodices and corsets on display.*

'We are going into this shop.' I said firmly.

'We are coming in also Miss,' said Sulivan.

'Mr. Sulivan you cannot come into a ladies'…a ladies' shop.'

'Yes we can, Miss, and we must.' I glared at him.

'Is it necessary to act like a goaler Mr. Sullivan?'

'Yes Miss Scar…O'Mara. I am obeying orders.'

I opened the door and the young girl immediately smiled and said,

'Buenos Diaz' Her smile soon faded when she saw the two officers in full uniform, entering the shop also.

'Please excuse them.' I smiled.

Fuegia and I set about looking at various displays, in some cabinets and on shelves. I chose all I needed including a nightgown in soft cotton. The girl made the calculation, Mr. Sulivan paid and Mr. Bynoe picked up the box.

Back out on the street we were all tired and I asked,

'Shall we rest and find somewhere to drink some coffee?'

'Yes Miss,' said Mr. Bynoe

'No Miss' Mr. Sulivan said.

'If you have all you need Miss it is better that we return to the ship.'

I looked at Mr. Bynoe. He said nothing. Mr. Sulivan of course had the senior rank. I looked around and saw a tiny bookshop.

'May I look in this bookshop for ten minutes Mr. Sulivan?'

Before he could answer I opened the door. I had not taken one step into the shop until Mr. Sulivan was by my side. I sighed and began to look around. I found the rather limited English section and to my delight there were some poetry books. There was Milton's 'L'Allegro, Thomas Gray's Elegy, Wordsworth's 'Ode: Intimations of Immortality'.

'May I purchase these two books please, Mr. Sulivan?'

'Yes Miss' The books were wrapped and paid for. We proceeded back out to the street where Fuegia and Bynoe had found a seat in the shade.

'Back to the ship please everyone,' said Sulivan in a manner that made me want to salute and say,

'Aye, Aye sir' but I said nothing and we started to walk back towards the slipway.

Some gauchos coming along the street began to whistle and say a few flattering words in Spanish about me. One of them came close to me and said,

'How white your skin is Senorita.'

Sulivan promptly stepped between us and raised his arm in a threatening way, at the same time telling him in Spanish what he thought of him.

The man retreated and I said

'Thank you Mr. Sulivan.'

'Well I'm glad it didn't come to a brawl in front of the ladies.' said Bynoe.

'I did not intend to strike him.' Mr. Sullivan glared at Mr. Bynoe.

'Thank you gentlemen.' I said.

Upon reaching the slipway Mr.Bynoe put the boxes in the dinghy. We all stepped aboard. Mr. Bynoe began to row. I opened the parcel of books and began to read one of the poetry books. Fuegia began to laugh.

'What?'

'Mr. Sulivan very lucky get you out of bookshop so quickly.'

Fuegia said. We all laughed.

'Yes Miss, knowing your love of books Fuegia and I had resigned ourselves to a long wait.'

'You acted with great consideration Miss O'Mara.'

'Thank you Mr. Sulivan.'

'You seem to study a lot Miss O'Mara.' Bynoe said.

'Do you think gentlemen that my brain is very different to yours?'

'Yes Miss,' said Mr.Bynoe,

'Yours is infinitely more enquiring.'

'No that is not so, for indeed Mr. Sulivan did you not, like the Captain, also pass your lieutenant's exam with full numbers?'

Mr. Sullivan smiled.

The following days were the happiest of my life. The Captain sent for me five times all together. We exchanged ideas about our childhood days, that is about the few I could remember. I told the Captain that I had a vague recollection of my half brother called James who attended Trinity College Dublin and I had visited the University with him on a number of occasions.

'Robert, I saw the Book of Kells'

'Indeed, and do you remember your half brother's surname Scarlett?

'I think it was Whiteside'.

'You did not have the same surname then?'

'No, not if the name in the books is correct.'

We talked about poetry, philosophy, the Bible and even politics. At last I began to see how he perceived the world, what an alert well-informed mind he had and how he delighted in teasing me about the details of ships and seafaring, engineering and surveying, chronometers, sextants, storms and meteorology, about all of which I could see his knowledge was immense.

He knew I had spent hours memorising nautical terms so I asked him to put a question to me.

'Where is... 'No man's land'?'

'A space between the heels of the booms.'

'A Goose-wing?'

'Eh...eh... yes, one of the clews of a square sail, set in a gale when the body of the sail remains brailed to the yard.'

He smiled.

'And what does that mean?'

'I have no idea.'

Then he laughed aloud. He explored questions of science constantly. His knowledge of languages was wide-ranging. He spoke Spanish, Italian and French and deep down he had an immense love of nature. He read the Bible diligently and I now saw that his perception of the world far outweighed many another person's awareness of it.

From an early age he had set about acquiring a very wide general knowledge. He was a consummate reader, and his overall vision therefore was rounded and inclusive. His loyalty to his faith shone through it all.

He talked about his early years, how he loved Wakefield Lodge, and how his mother died only a year after they had moved there in1810. The following year, aged six, he was sent away to school at Rottingdean near the south coast.

'My dear Robert you must have been so lonely.'

'I was, but even then I knew it was no good giving in to feeling sad, and the one way to fight it was to work hard and try to enjoy the present.'

'...Heaven lies about us in our infancy!' I quoted Wordswoth in a whisper.

'Shades of the prison-house begin to close

Upon the growing Boy,' he whispered back.

'Was it better when you went to Harrow?'

'No. I did not find any real joy until I went to the Naval College.'

'That was about two months after we met at Wakefield Lodge.'

'Yes that was 1818, and may I ask you something Scarlett?'

'Of course'

'Did you ever think you would meet me again?'

'If I tell you, will you promise not to laugh? No don't answer that. I hesitate to tell you, it sounds so childish now, but you must have made an enduring impression upon me because I can remember that you were my hero. I dressed up dolls ready to marry Robert Fitzroy!'

He began to laugh.

'This was despite the fact I held your hand too tightly.'

'Well yes, and …and dare I tell you…from the little I can remember, that you were the hero in many of the stories I wrote when I was young. So that night when you lifted me out of the rowing boat and I opened my eyes and looked into your eyes…I knew I had looked into them before, but the memory loss…I could not remember for a long time whose eyes they were.'

'Well I am glad I made an impression upon you…more than I did when we met this time.'

'No, the impression this time was much the same only more intense. So you see I had grown up…a little anyway.'

He reached across the table and held my hand turned it over and kissed the palm.

On a number of occasions he asked me to recite for him. I was too embarrassed to recite any love poems so I recited from Milton, 'At a Solemn Musick' and some lines from 'Sabrina Fair',

> *'Listen where thou art sitting*
> *Under the glassie, cool, translucent wave,...'*

Once or twice he asked me to sing, and I then lost the embarrassment I had felt the first time. I became calm and sang with ease. I pressed him to tell me about his early days on the 'Owen Glendower', a ship on which he gave two and a half years service. He spoke about several weeks living ashore at Buenos Aires, where he went riding and hunting. He had sailed round Cape Horn for the first time during the month of November 1820, when he was only fifteen years old. This was the first of many such journeys.

'Did you begin to learn Spanish then?'

'Yes, I had started earlier that year to concentrate on it although I did wish to be fluent in French first.'

He said he visited Valparaiso in Chile, and had travelled in land. He described the countryside and the mountains, I knew then the heart of the man, and how the beauty of the landscape filled him with joy and the awe of the natural world had never since deserted him.

> *'To all delight of human sense expos'd*
> *In a narrow room Natures whole wealth, yea more.*
> *A heaven on Earth:...'*

The Captain opened his eyes wide and looked at me.

'How much of 'Paradise Lost' do you know by rote?'

'Oh! I tend to remember only a few lines from certain parts...like these from 'The Prospect of Eden'.

He continued to look intently at me. Then he looked away. I began to think that he found praise difficult. Not through any resentment but through sheer dread of sounding insincere. That is why he said so little in the past about any talents he thought I might possess.

'Did you look forward to going home?' I asked.

'Yes indeed and to see my father and especially Fanny. I have always been close to Fanny.'

'I know you spent the same amount of time on 'The Hind'.

'How do you know such things?'

'Ah! well, I ask Mr. Sulivan hundreds of questions about you.'

'Scarlett, that is hardly appropriate.'

'I know sir, but he admires you greatly and does not mind answering my questions. Tell me about your adventures at the Mediterranean.'

'Well I began to learn the Italian, and I visited the Bay of Naples, and went to see Pompeii and Herculaneum. One day Scarlett I hope I will be able to tell you of these adventures in detail, and also of my visits to the Greek islands of Cos and Rhodes and a visit I made to Smyrnia where we were in harbour for a long period.'

'I heard you did not care for the balls at Gibraltar when you were stationed there.'

He began to laugh.

'Is there anything you do not know about me?'

'No.'

'Well it was more to do with the status of a Midshipman that anything else. One had no chance of a partner to dance with when there were Colonels and Captains around and I was only seventeen years old.'

The more I knew about the Captain, the more I marvelled at his achievements. When I considered all he had done before he was even eighteen years old and how he had lost nothing of those experiences, I was impressed. He observed, read, and never wasted time. Since I had met him I too had come to appreciate the value of time well spent.

All on board were witnesses of his fidelity to duty and honesty of heart. That is not to say that we did not all suffer when the black mood consumed him and he was as stern as could be. But mostly he took it out upon himself with long melancholic silences and he never held a grudge. When an incident was over it was over.

Everyone on board must have seen how happy I was and I delighted in my new wardrobe. Each time I went to see the Captain I wore a different dress and found out that he indeed liked the plainest one best, the one the colour of the blue sky.

Sometimes as I left he lifted my hand to his lips. He seemed at ease and whereas in the past he would speak barely but a few sentences, now we engaged in a proper form of conversation. The time passed incredibly quickly and I was captivated in his presence. I think from time to time there were moments when the rest of the world did not exist.

These meetings never lasted more than fifteen or twenty minutes but to me time stood still and they had a meaning beyond time, beyond the present. The Captain gave me a book that Fanny had sent him. A novel by Miss Jane Austen called, 'Persuasion'. I read it very quickly and wondered if all love stories ended with the lovers being together. My heart wanted to believe that one day this would be my fate. Yet an angel of doom hovered above me, sometimes resting on my shoulder and sometimes filling my soul with fear.

Indeed I knew in my heart that these days were the most beautiful I ever experienced since my days in the Wicklow mountains. I found time to spend many happy hours in the gunroom. From the beginning of the voyage Mr Davis, the cook, had tried to please me by cooking in a special way I liked, any vegetables he had available. He now took delight in trying out many different ways of serving the 'calabaza' a green pumpkin I liked so much. Ash served it with a smile knowing it would be eaten and not just moved around the plate like other meals he had served.

I sang many ballads, recited some of Shakespeare's Sonnets, Wordsworth and Thompson. I slept each night in a fever of delight and woke with each new dawn feeling happy and free... as if my childhood innocence had returned.

16th August 1832

The Captain left a message with Mr. Wickham saying that after dining with the officers he would like me to go to his cabin. At the arranged time I knocked on the door.

'Come in'

'You wanted to see me sir?'

'Sit down, Scarlett. I need to speak to you.'

I sat down. He looked very serious and although he no longer spoke to me in that authoritative way I knew he had something difficult to say.

'The remainder of this voyage, especially the Patagonian coast and rounding the Horn will be extremely difficult.'

'Yes of course.'

'Also... Scarlett... I have to consider that when we have returned Fuegia to Tierra del Fuego you would be the only female aboard.'

'Yes I understand. That would not be appropriate would it Robert?'

'No, and I have other worries in your regard...'

A long silence followed. I tried to hold back the tears for his sake. I knew how difficult he was finding the situation.

'Are you unable to share these worries with me?'

'If you trust my judgement Scarlett...'

'I do, I do implicitly.'

'Well I choose not to tell you at this time, Scarlett, because my dearest wish is that you will be happy.'

Another long silence ensued.

'Upon hearing these reasons I would not be happy?'

'Think about it like this...I will take upon myself these worries and you remain at liberty to be the beautiful free spirit you are.'

'Thank you, Robert.'

'My pleasure.'

'I have arranged for you to stay with an English family near Monte Video.'

I did not answer.

'I know the British Consul. He has offered his residences to you. However I chose instead for you the home of the Charge d'Affair, Mr. Gore. It is more secluded, the house is run exactly as an English home should be. His town residence looked safer to me as it too is secluded...that is if you ever have any reason to stay in the town which I hope will not often be the case.'

I did not answer. We sat there looking at each other and the tears came flooding into my eyes and down my cheeks.

'Oh Scarlett, please do not cry. I don't know how I am going to do this if you cry. I will come back next year between October and December.'

'Yes but you will not be able to take me with you.'

'No, but I promise you, at the end of the voyage I will arrange transport for you to Bahia. I will collect you there and take you home.'

I said nothing.

'I give you my word, Scarlett.'

I stretched out my hands across the table and he held them.

'You know whatever happens I will come back for you.'

I said nothing.

'Do you believe me, Scarlett?'

'Of course I believe you. Never have I seen you break your word.'

In his usual way he kissed the palm of my hand. He looked at me and his eyes looked extremely sad.

'When do we leave?'

'Tomorrow.'

'Very well, let me say that you will always be in my heart wherever you are in the world, and wherever the Beagle is that is where my heart will be.'

'Oh, Scarlett'

He stood and paced in his usual manner.

'Promise me you will not lose your temper and that when you feel…'

I stopped. I had gone too far. Then I took courage.

He returned to the table and sat down. We looked attentively at each other and I said,

'When you feel the darkness consumes you, and your mind is in a fragile state, promise me that you will go to your cabin and rest. You know there is no sense in trying to fight it. The pain is too great. Then, with the grace of God, when it passes and you begin to see the light again, promise me that you will not rush back to your duties, but come out of it slowly just as the dawn comes in slowly from the east and gives way to a clear blue sky. Promise me.'

He swallowed hard and said,

'I promise.'

'When these dark times monopolize your mind and heart try to remember that out there in the world is a person…a person who loves you.'

He nodded.

'Allow me to thank you, sir, for all your kindness to me…words are so inadequate at this time.'

He stretched across the table and put his finger on my lips. I smiled.

'Please do not call me 'sir' ever again.'

'Robert'

'It is I who have to thank you. Have you any idea Scarlett what it is going to be like without you? Mr. Wickham and Mr. Sullivan have expressed to me how much your presence will be missed in the gunroom. I have noticed how all the officers have kept up appearances…that is your influence. However not one of them can imagine how much I will miss your presence.'

I smiled. Indeed they know very well I thought, and are probably dreading the following days.

'In dark days I will read the sonnet you composed for me and try to live up to the person portrayed in it, and that will not be easy.'

'That sonnet is only a very pale reflection of the amazing man you are.'

He looked away as the tears came into his eyes.

'Promise me that nevertheless you will be of good cheer for indeed the whole ship reflects your mood and you would not want to run a gloomy ship.'

'How am I to endure these spells of darkness without you Scarlett?'

'This thing of darkness I acknowledge mine'

'The Tempest' he said

'Act V Scene1' I said

'As usual your memory does you credit.'

'Indeed it has been all the lonely days and nights on the Beagle that I have to thank for that.'

'You made good use of that time.'

'Only because you are an example to everyone on board. You, who never wastes a moment.'

After a few moments, as we looked at each other, I asked,

'What time tomorrow do we depart?'

'After dinner, I have arranged for a trunk and travelling case to be put in your cabin.'

'Thank you.'

'My pleasure.'

A long silence ensued. I asked him then,

'Your box Robert?'

'No keep it and…remember me when you see it.'

'I do not need a box to remind me of you. For every moment of everyday you are here in my heart.'

I stood up. He stood

'I will be ready'

'Very well'

I looked back at him standing behind the table. It would be my last time to see him standing there. I left quickly. I did not even say goodnight. Back in my cabin the first thing I noticed was that the trunk and case were there. I sat on the bed. Why had I stupidly thought I could stay on this ship forever?

Once I gave it consideration I knew the Captain would never have taken me around the Horn into the turmoil of rough seas, inclement weather and risk to life. Then when Fuegia left…of course I could not be the only female on board…but I was once…when we returned to Bahia, but that was different.

I tried not to think of the year ahead without seeing him. I tried to think about learning Spanish properly, perhaps some Portuguese, and maybe being able to ride a pony again. I use to love horses…so long ago…will I remember how to ride? I opened the trunk and began to pack. Then there was a knock at the door. I opened it.

'Mr. Sulivan?'

'I just came to say Miss O'Mara that on behalf of the crew we wish you well and thank you for all the delightful evenings in which you honoured us with your presence.'

'Mr. Sulivan, I am the one who is grateful… you officers treated me from the start with kindness and respect, and especially your good self. I could not have asked for a brother as kind as you have been Mr. Sulivan.'

'Thank you, Miss.'

'You look sad Mr. Sulivan; please do not be…without you and the Captain I would be dead. Each of you saved my life. Do you think I could ever forget that? Most ungrateful I was to you both on many occasions. Please do forgive me Mr. Sulivan… because these last weeks I have been so glad to be alive.'

'Yes Miss.'

'You will have a glorious future Mr. Sulivan, I am sure of that, for you are handsome, gallant, clever, intelligent, and dare I say it, you have a good sense of humour. This quality in a gentleman Mr. Sulivan is, in my opinion, of great importance.'

He smiled.

'Thank you Miss, may I inform you of the transport details for tomorrow?'

'Yes please do.'

'The Captain, myself and Fuegia will go in the dinghy

with you to the slipway where a carriage will be waiting. We will then proceed to the estancia where we will…we will…

'See me settled and leave me there.'

'Yes Miss.'

'Very well I will be ready.'

'Thank you, goodnight Miss'

'Good night Mr. Sulivan.'

After packing the entire wardrobe the Captain had purchased for me, I began to pray. This was my last night on board the Beagle, my last night to sleep a few paces from the man I love.

'Dear God please do not let him forget me. Please keep him safe and all on board. Please bring him back to me, please keep him alive for me. I know this is a very selfish prayer dear Lord, forgive me…'

The next morning Fuegia came and helped me finish the packing, brush my hair and prepare my clothes.

'You wear blue dress Miss Scarlett?'

'Yes Fuegia' *I looked at her. She was crying. Never before had I seen her cry.*

'Now Fuegia this is a very difficult time for me. You must be strong. If I see you crying I will cry. I do not wish to cry Fuegia until the Captain comes back to the ship. Do you understand?'

'Yes' *I gave her a hug and we set about putting my papers away and leaving the cabin ready for Mr. Sulivan.*

'Fuegia, I am going to take one last walk on the deck.' *She nodded.*

I wanted to feel for the last time the salty air that strikes the nostrils and the lungs and the sensation of the ocean breeze lifting my hair and flowing past my face. I walked out of the cabin and stopped by the companionway.

Mr. Darwin was raising his voice. He was in the Captain's cabin and the door was open. I felt a shot of fear pass through my body. Had there been another disagreement between them? I listened.

'I object most intensely to this Fitzroy. It is a lot of fuss about nothing.'

'That may be your opinion, however I am under orders.'

'Yes, that may be so but I am not a member of his Majesty's Navy.'

'I call your attention to the letter I received today from the Admiralty. Look here… it says… 'all on board the Beagle' it could not be clearer.'

'Will you not take my word as an Englishman and a gentleman?'

'Of course I do my dear Philos, but I regret to tell you the Admiralty will not.'

'The deuce with the Admiralty…'

There was a brief silence.

'Fitzroy, if only I understood the meaning of it all. To take an oath…and what if I am ever asked the question, 'Was Miss O'Mara ever aboard the Beagle? Am I then expected to lie? That is what worries me, Fitzroy.'

'I see your point. However I can almost guarantee you Darwin that no one will ever ask you that question.'

'Yes, but there is always the possibility.'

'Yes there is.'

'What I don't understand Fitzroy is why everyone has to take an oath. What is there so important about Miss O'Mara's presence on the Beagle that we all have to be sworn to secrecy?

Fitzroy was silent.

'You must give me some explanation Fitzroy. Why is Miss

O'Mara's presence or absence on the ship so important?'

'It is a labyrinth of complications and... her life has been threatened on more than one occasion.'

'I do not understand. Why would anyone want to harm Miss O'Mara?'

'It is, my dear Darwin because of her true identity.'

'Her name is not O'Mara?

'No. It is not.'

'Do you mean Fitzroy because of her true identity I have to keep this secret for the rest of my life?'

'Yes, Darwin, as we all are obliged to do.'

'Let me tell you that, whatever the reason, I object most intensely.'

'I am sorry Philos that this matter upsets you so. Will you take the oath nevertheless for my sake?'

'Well let me tell you I am not a man for taking oaths and it upsets me greatly that I have to take an oath to conceal something. It is ridiculous Fitzroy and you are well aware that it is.'

'Nevertheless will you take it for my sake?'

There was a brief silence and then,

'Very well Fitzroy as a mark of my respect for you, but I object most profoundly.'

I quickly walked back to the cabin. My heart was beating fast and my mind was in disarray. I was not Scarlett O'Mara! Who was I then? Whoever I was, the Captain seemed to be well aware of it. He said my life was threatened.

'Everything is packed now, Miss Scarlett' Fuegia smiled as I entered the cabin.

'Thank you my dear friend. I will miss you.'

What could all of that mean? Why should anyone care

whether I was on the ship or not? Now I understand Mr. Darwin's objection...he did not wish to take the oath... and I agree with him. However I knew that this was not the time to think about all these things and so I made a great effort to concentrate on leaving the ship and on the journey ahead. Now I will never know what all of this is about because it is certain I cannot worry the Captain today by asking him about Royal Navy business.

Mr. Wickham came to the door,

'Miss O'Mara I can't begin to tell you how much we will miss you.'

'Nonsense Mr. Wickham in a few days you will not even remember I was here.'

'You know that could never happen Miss.'

'Well then, will you try to remember my few good qualities Mr. Wickham and not all my irrational and discourteous times?'

'Miss O'Mara how could you think you were ever discourteous? You are the most polite lady...the officers have remarked upon it.'

'Even Mr. Sulivan?'

'Especially Mr. Sulivan.'

'He forgives my impertinence then?'

'You were not yourself Miss.'

'Thank you Mr. Wickham will you do something for me?'

'Of course Miss.'

'Will you take care of the Captain...especially during those times of darkness...I know you suffer it too, for he does indeed often take it out upon you Mr. Wickham.'

'Yes indeed it is so, but he is the best of men Miss O'Mara...as I think you know yourself.'

'Will you promise me then that especially when these dark days seize upon him you will try to understand the pain he is in and be patient and kind to him. For indeed it does pass... eventually.'

'I promise you Miss O'Mara that I will always stand by him and honour him for the courageous and talented Captain he is.'

'Thank you Mr. Wickham. I will never forget you and all the officers who have been so kind to me. Goodbye'

'Miss, may I say that your affection and loyalty for the Captain has touched all our hearts.'

'A fact you will keep from the Captain Mr. Wickham, I am sure.'

'Yes indeed Miss. Goodbye to you and good luck in the future.'

'Thank you Mr. Wickham' He bowed and was gone. Then it was time to go. Mr. Chaffers took my trunk into the dinghy. I went on deck; Fuegia came up to me and took my arm. I tried to think that this departure was not happening. It was just a dream and in that way I could hold together my emotions and depart with dignity.

Trial

Harry tried to goad Reed into a fencing contest in order to bargain for Lucy's release.

Goldberg removed the epees from the wall with all the glee of a schoolboy. He handed one to Harry and one to Reed and led the way to the circular hall. He rang a bell and the two bodyguards removed most of the furniture.

Harry and Reed took up their positions. They began very slowly. Harry needed to assess Reed's ability and style. Before he could do so Reed had made several ferocious lunges, throwing all the rules aside.

Then they began to move cautiously around the alternative salle d'armes. There was no doubt Reed was good, very good, but Harry had the advantage of many years' practice and of keeping cool. Reed's thrusts were strong, his footwork neat and his stance perfect. He calmed down and allowed advance and retreat. His crossover steps were graceful, his dexterity and his swift lean body moved with balletic lightness. Harry knew he would only win if he could provoke him into some ill judged lunges or somehow take him off guard.

The noise was stupendous as they moved vigorously too and fro. Reed used many unorthodox moves. Harry watched his eyes. He began to realize that he was used to the foil, and here Harry had the advantage for he preferred the epee.

Harry's patient analysis paid off and soon he saw the boredom enter Reed's eyes, caught him off guard, flung the epee out of his hand, pressed him to the wall and held the epee to his throat.

At that moment Goldberg called out. The door opened and the bodyguard called Dixon rushed in. He grabbed Harry, proceeded to tie his hands behind his back, and frogmarched him back into the drawing room.

'Well, will you let Lucy go now?'

'No' Reed smirked.

'How come it does not surprise me that you did not keep your word Reed?'

'We have a surprise for you Harry' Reed grinned.

Goldberg walked slowly to his desk and hit a number of switches. A concealed screen emerged from the wall at eye level. After a few seconds the static gave way to a clear picture.

'You scoundrels' Harry screeched.

Lucy was tied up and gagged in a cellar or old building somewhere with what looked like the tide rising around her. It was up to her knees.

'What do you expect me to do?'

Harry couldn't take his eyes from the screen. He saw Lucy struggle incessantly with the thick strong ropes.

'We expect you to give us the diary Harry. It is the only piece of evidence that might prevent us from claiming the legacy.'

'Very well. Let me out and I'll bring it to you.'

Up until that point Harry had hoped that Bloom was free in the house somewhere and would soon rescue him. Then the door opened and the other bodyguard threw Bloom into the room. All Harry's hopes faded. He knew he had to give Reed and Goldberg the diary to save Lucy's life.

'Let me go and collect the diary, I can do it before the water reaches her throat if you don't delay.'

'No Harry. Dixon will go with Bloom to collect it, and when we have the diary in our possession we'll inform you of the location in which Miss Harrington is being held.'

'Bloom hurry up, any delay and Lucy is dead.'

'Very good sir'

'Dixon take the four by four, and watch him…' Goldberg grinned,

'Very good sir.'

They left.

'I assure you Reed I will take my revenge on you for this. I did nothing the last time I found you out in gross deception. Believe me Reed this time you will not escape.' Harry's voice was cold and clear.

'What is he talking about?' Goldberg's eyes opened wide.

'Nothing…it happened a long time ago when I was a teenager.'

'Tell me about it.' Goldberg smiled.

'Not now. Put him in the cellar, Watson'

'No I feel better when I can see what Mr. Harry is up to.' retorted Goldberg.

'Let us move to another room then. You can watch the screen Harry and see the water rising, and Watson keep guard at the door. Make sure he doesn't escape.'

'Very good sir.'

Harry struggled with the ropes. The tide was coming in so fast that it meant certain death for Lucy if he could not escape soon. He watched the perspiration gather on Lucy's forehead and the look of desperation in her eyes. Goldberg's agents had set up a camera so that he could watch Lucy die.

He scrutinized the screen. He saw behind Lucy the steel frame…a steel…yes the stone work was cosmetic… it was a bridge. At the edge of the picture he could just see the faint shadow of what looked to be part of a large gear wheel…yes it was…it was…

He tried energetically to free himself from the ropes. The water was almost up to Lucy's waist now and he could not understand why Goldberg and Reed had not come back into the room. Watson checked on him frequently. Harry asked,

'Why have I not seen the delightful Mr. Goldberg and the honourable Reed?'

'Because they are playing chess for a very large amount of money.'

Harry marvelled at their cynicism and then he felt the panic kick into the base of his stomach. He struggled relentlessly with the ropes and had one hand almost free. His frustration increased and a feeling of powerlessness began to consume him because it was taking him so long to untie the ropes and Lucy was in mortal danger.

The minutes ticked by, then to his great relief he heard Bloom's voice outside the door. Bloom opened the door. He held a gun on Watson, Reed and Goldberg who were issuing all kinds of threats.

'You will regret this Harry.' Reed said.

'I will hunt you down and dispose of you Harry.' Goldberg said his eyes blazing.

'Will you Goldberg? Well we'll see about that.'

Dermot then came in and removed the ropes from Harry's wrists. He proceeded to tie up Reed. Bloom gave the gun to Harry and tied up Goldberg. Bloom and Harry then took Watson away and tied him up.

'I've locked the other one…Dixon in the cellar.' Dermot said.

'Good, Dermot find a disc and record what is happening to Lucy, then take the disc and get out of here. Keep in touch with Bloom. Bloom you come with me.'

Bloom was scrutinizing Goldberg's desk and removing the gun from the middle drawer.

'Should we be interested in someone called Rice Trevor?' Bloom asked.

'Yes. Photocopy that document Dermot before you leave.'

'Anything else?' Dermot asked.

'Yes, get out of here as quickly as you can'

Bloom took his tool belt and a few other things out of the boot of the Ghost and jumped into the driving seat.

'Where to?'

'Tower Bridge Bloom as fast as you can.'

'Very good sir.' Bloom with his usual expertise, drove fast.

'What if it is the wrong bridge sir?'

'Don't even consider the thought.'

At Tower Bridge Bloom brought the car to a halt.

Harry took off his jacket. Bloom handed him goggles, the tool belt, a small torch and another belt with florescent lights.

'Put it on around your chest. It will be dark as night down there.'

'Thanks, Bloom.'

Harry got out and Bloom steered the car back into the traffic.

Harry stood and looked at the two towers of the bridge. He had no idea on which side of the Gothic structure Lucy was kept captive but he knew the north pier entrance was the one used for tours. He looked over the wall. The tide was high. He ducked under the barrier and ran down the steps. He attached the tool belt, florescent belt, and put on the goggles. He put the torch in his pocket, waded into the Thames and dived.

Harry swam around the south tower foundations that bulged out in a circular form at the base of the bridge. He swam lower and lower into the water, the florescent belt gave him a dim view of the brickwork, but nowhere could he see an entrance. He came up to breathe. His heart began to beat faster… what if he had made a mistake? He began to swim over to the north tower and although he was a very strong swimmer it seemed to take forever and he knew every minute mattered.

At last he was there. He took a deep breath and went down. He swam around going lower and lower in the grimy water and again no sign of an entrance anywhere. Harry began to feel a sharp pain in his chest. Had he made a mistake? Was this the wrong place? If it was Lucy was surely going to drown. He came to the surface again and took a deep breath. He went down, going in the opposite direction this time.

Then he saw it. Very deep and concealed very well, the rectangular marks of a small doorway. He drew near and tried to push the door open. It would not dislodge. He took a chisel from the tool belt and forced it into the side cavity. He pushed with all his strength but the door did not move an inch. Once again he had to go up for air. He had to go up three times altogether and then at last the door moved a fraction he shoved the chisel further in. He paused and then pushed with all his might. It moved slowly inward and then swung opened fully. As it did so a huge gush of water entered the camber adding to the volume of water already in there.

To his great relief he saw Lucy standing feebly on a ledge in an almost unconscious state. Her skin was blue and her eyes vacant. The water was up to her throat. When she saw Harry she seemed to recover slightly and a light came into her eyes. Then the water washed over her head, completely submerging her. Harry swam over to her, there was not a moment to spare.

He pushed himself up above water-line to breathe, took a knife from the tool pack, and went down again to cut the ropes. It took so long to cut through the wet ropes that Harry had to come up for air once again. At last he managed to free Lucy's feet, then her hands, and then he removed the gag. Lucy sank under the water and when she came up Harry put his arm around her. For a brief moment he held her in his arms. Lucy regained her breath and they swam out of the tower and up to the surface. The daylight hit their eyes, and Lucy muttered,

'I'm... I'm...all right Harry' in response to the

anxiety in Harry's eyes.

They began to swim towards the steps, and then Harry heard it… the click of a gun.

17th August 1832

It was the day of my departure from the Beagle, but that was the one thought I was trying to keep out of my mind. The officers had assembled. They all looked sad. I did not even see Mr. Darwin until he stepped forward,

'May I say, Miss O'Mara, that you have brightened all our days…and how we will miss your kind words and your songs.'

'I thank you. May I say that whatever paths our lives take in the future Mr. Darwin, we are all indebted to Captain Fitzroy for his infinite kindness.'

'Yes indeed Miss O'Mara.'

'Will you not tell your children and grandchildren, Mr. Darwin, tales of this exceptional naval Captain?'

'Indeed I will, Miss O'Mara, and may I wish you a pleasant stay in Monte Video.'

'Thank you, Mr. Darwin.'

'May I thank all you officers for your kindness and will you please convey my thanks to Davis, the cook, for all the times he made the 'calabaza' for me.'

'Yes Miss.'

The Captain came up to the deck looking very serious as usual. He stood talking to Mr. Chaffers.

'Goodbye, gentlemen'

The officers made their farewells and I walked towards the dinghy. I did not look back. Mr. Sulivan gave me his hand and I stepped into the dinghy. Fuegia was sitting there trying to look cheerful. Mr. Sulivan stood back and the Captain stepped in, then Mr. Sulivan followed.

Mr Bennett and a midshipman began to row. I looked at the mud coloured water and thought of the sparkling clear water that flowed freely down from the Wicklow hills. I looked ahead and began to think of the 'Meeting of the Waters' and Lough Dan. Then…Wordsworth…

'………………And I have felt
A presence that disturbs me with the joy
of elevated thoughts;'
Dear God take my mind away from what is happening,
'……………… a sense sublime
Of something far more deeply interfused,
Whose dwelling is the light of setting suns,
And the round ocean and the living air,
And the blue sky, and in the mind of man;'
'Good afternoon Miss O'Mara'
In my effort to keep hold of my emotions I had forgotten to speak to the Captain.
'Good afternoon Captain…what a beautiful day!'
'Indeed'
He was looking intently at me and I was trying not to look directly at him.
'This dress very beautiful on you Miss Scarlett, you like?'
'Yes thank you Fuegia.'
I wanted everyone to leave me alone, and not to speak to me. In my thoughts I am walking by the Avoca River, I can see the blue Wicklow hills and the heather blowing in the breeze on the little Sugar Loaf. Far away I can hear…
'You buy clothes just at right time Miss Scarlett.'
'Yes Fuegia'

We arrived at the slipway and alighted. The carriage was waiting. The Captain gave me his hand and I stepped into the carriage. Fuegia and I sat together. Mr. Bennett stored the luggage at the rear of the carriage. I sat opposite Mr. Sulivan and Fuegia sat opposite the Captain. I said goodbye to Mr. Bennett.

As we drove along Mr. Sulivan tried to make conversation,

'There are usually many horses and ponies on these estancias Miss O'Mara. Will you learn to ride do you think?

'Oh I am able to ride Mr. Sulivan. It just seems such a long time ago and I hope I haven't forgotten.'

'I'm sure you will remember and it will be a blessing for these pampas stretch out for miles.'

He went on to speak about the vast herds of cattle and the rough life of the gauchos.

He was a fluent Spanish speaker. I tried not to listen.

'Then sometimes, in that silence, while he hung
Listening, a gentle shock of mild surprise
Has carried far into his heart the voice
Of mountain torrents…'
Dear God let me hear the mountain torrents!

Every time I looked at the Captain he looked away. I could never remember exactly how long that journey was. I do remember what happened when we turned off the road and into the long driveway that swept through parkland and eventually came to a most beautiful French-style mansion tucked away under the pine trees.

It had graceful balconies, terraces, and wide windows. There were peaceful lawns, stylish colourful gardens and the tall pines and palms seemed majestic to me that day.

The centre entrance had a canopy, a balustrade and steps up to a magnificent door. The name said 'Estancia Dos Talas'. It was situated in the middle of pampas that stretched away into eternity...or so it seemed to me.

Mr. Sulivan stood up and stepped out. He told Fuegia to get out and took her away from the carriage. I was afraid, but I quickly took his place by the Captain put my hand on his face and kissed his cheek. For a brief second he drew me softly towards him and kissed my lips with a gentle, delicate gossamer touch. A kiss a young lady could never forget.

'Robert I will always love you' I whispered.

Then I stood up, and the Captain quickly stepped out and gave me his hand. Mr. Sulivan came back and said,

'Well what do you think Miss O'Mara? Is this not a beautiful residence?'

'It is indeed, and Mr. Sullivan... I thank you.' He smiled.

'I will always remember that you...'

I was about to say in some coded way, that you arranged those few brief seconds of privacy for me and the Captain.

'Thank you Miss O'Mara' he cut me short. The officers always strove to conceal their knowledge of my feelings for the Captain.

Mr. and Mrs. Gore came out to greet us and we all entered the colonial styled hall and expansive drawing room with views across the pampas. We were served afternoon tea in the English way. Then the Captain said,

'Mrs. Gore would you kindly show Miss O'Mara where her accommodation is?'

'Certainly. Come this way.'

We climbed the staircase to the first floor and entered a large bright bedroom beautifully furnished. Straight away

I walked to the window, and looked out over the pampas, dotted here and there with low trees, the cattle grazing under the immense sky and the little silver sparkling river flowing slowly along.

'Will you be comfortable here Miss O'Mara?'

'Mrs. Gore please forgive my lack of courtesy as I am quite distracted today. This is perfect and I am most grateful to you and your husband for offering me this beautiful room.'

'We are so happy to have you, Miss O'Mara'

'Please call me Scarlett'

'Miss Scarlett the Consul offered to accommodate you but Captain Fitzroy thought that our residence, and this location better for you.'

'How kind of him.'

'Yes…shall we join the gentleman?' We went back down the stairway.

'Is everything to your liking Miss O'Mara?'

'Yes Captain it is a beautiful room, and a perfect location, and I thank you again and Mr. and Mrs. Gore for their kindness.'

'It is our great pleasure to have you here Miss O'Mara' said Mr. Gore.

'Miss O'Mara may I take this opportunity to show you the extensive and secluded grounds?'

'Yes indeed, thank you Captain'

We walked outside and just when I thought how wonderful of him to think of a way we could be alone together for a few minutes…my heart beat fast and…

The Captain looked around at the lush vegetation and exotic flowers for a moment and then he called out,

'Antonio'

Out of nowhere a voice answered,
'Oui mon Capitaine'
'Venez ici'
'Scarlett this is Antonio; I have employed him to watch over you. If you go to town, he goes to town, if you go out to ride, he goes out to ride. He will sleep under your window. He speaks Spanish, French and sufficient English so that even a quiet call will alert him.'
'Captain...'
'Say nothing Scarlett. Just trust me.'
I looked fixedly at him. He looked away,
'I trust you.' I whispered.
'Antonio this is Miss Scarlett, you will guard her with your life.'
'Oui, mon Capitaine with my life.'
'Senorita' he bowed. He was not very tall but robust and strong.
'Gracias.' I said
'D'accord' the Captain said,
'Mercy mon Capitaine, Senorita' He bowed again walked away.
'I can see in what high regard he holds you.'
'No...no...I helped his Father once...'
He had asked me to say nothing, so I said nothing. When he had asked to show me the grounds, my heart leaped as I thought he wanted a few minutes alone with me. It was only to tell me about Antonio. His thoughts and motives were always noble and far above my own.
'Scarlett the days will pass slowly until I return. Will you write to me and tell me what you are doing and what you are thinking about?'
'Yes of course I will.'

'I beg you now, Scarlett, to go back into the house and do not to come out again until we have departed.'

'As you wish, my dear Robert'

'Say it again…say my name again'

'Robert'

The tears that I had held back all day began to come into my eyes. I held them back. I have months ahead to cry, and this was not the time I told myself.

'Robert, wherever you are, whatever is happening to you my heart and my spirit is with you. My dearest Robert wherever the Beagle is, that is where my heart is. Each new day, I am with you, morning by morning my hand is in your hand. Goodbye, may God bless you and keep you safe and all the crew until we meet again.'

I looked into his eyes. He looked into mine. Our eyes were used to conveying feelings that it was impossible for us to express any other way. We both knew how much we wanted to be in each other's arms, but that could not be.

I kissed my fingers and pointed them towards him, without taking my eyes from his, and so to keep their memory alive in my mind and heart, I curtsied. He whispered,

'Scarlett'

I turned and walked into the house as he had asked me to do. I gave Fuegia a kiss and a hug and thanked her for her kindness to me. I thanked Mr. Sullivan, and told him I would never forget him, above all for his devotion to the Captain. The tears appeared in Mr. Sullivan's eyes. Then quickly he bowed, and he and Fuegia walked away. I walked to the door and looked at Robert. He was looking towards me. Our eyes met again for a brief moment and I could see the pain in them. They entered the carriage and the horses moved forward down the drive.

I went inside and asked the family to excuse me and I went upstairs. I looked out of the window and watched the carriage move slowly down the driveway until it reached the narrow road… until it was almost out of sight. Then I said aloud,

'God bless and protect you, Mon Capitaine.'

The tears came flowing down my cheeks then. I had held them back all day.

'All days are nights to see 'till I see thee.

And nights bright days when dreams do show thee me.'

I sat on the bed and wept. However hard I tried the tears kept coming. After a while I decided that was enough self-indulgence.

'That is sufficient crying' I said aloud.

'This is a different life and I must make plans and not waste any time.'

Although I tried to be brave, deep down I knew my heart had gone in that carriage and back to the little barque that lay at the mouth of the river. The little barque that had been my home for many months. I gazed for a while out of the window at the vista over the plains. Then I looked down and there sitting under my window was Antonio.

I walked to the table and began a letter…Dear Captain Fitzroy…

The following day I gave the letter to Mr. Gore who promised me he would make sure it would reach the Beagle by the best route.

The days passed quietly and Mrs. Gore treated me like a sister. I soon adjusted to the routine and customs of the household. I liked their unpretentious and simple way of living and they respected my need to spend many hours alone. They had a good comprehensive library and Mr. Gore invited me to make use of it. I did, and was delighted to find that he had brought an extensive range of books with him from England.

The Captain, Mrs. Gore said, insisted that I have a personal maid, Maria, who was not only beautiful but as dear a young girl as ever one could meet. He had chosen her from yet another family who I assumed were also in his debt. She looked at me with wide eyes and never spoke until we were alone. After a few days she remarked,

'Your skin Miss…I never see like this…'

She quickly became used to my ways. She did not disturb me if I was reading or writing. As my Spanish improved she began to tell me about the poverty of her family and the joy she had in coming to the beautiful estancia of Signor Gore.

20th August

All my clothes were unpacked and when I opened the wardrobe there were two riding habits, both in blue, and a pair of riding boots. Mrs. Gore told me the Captain had asked her to purchase them.

'Did you know the size required?'

'Yes indeed the Captain explained.'

I would dearly love to have heard that conversation, I thought!

'Was it the Consul who asked you to accommodate me Mrs. Gore?'

'Well the Consul offered his town house and if I may say so, his very grand mansion to you. The Captain however thought this setting would suit you better. I am so glad Miss Scarlett that it turned out this way. It is a pleasure for us to have your company.'

'Thank you Mrs. Gore, and he chose it because of the isolation, the peace and quiet that he knows I love so well.'

'He also said that Antonio is never to leave your side.'

'Yes, the Captain takes all his responsibilities very seriously. He wants to make sure that I get back to England safely.'

'Well, many ships call here on their way to England. Would he not think of taking passage for you on one of these?'

'I see you do not know the Captain, Mrs. Gore. He is determined that I shall return to England on the Beagle, whenever that may be.'

'I see.'

'Will I be an encumbrance Mrs. Gore if my stay here is extended?'

'Miss Scarlett please, my husband and I are delighted to receive you. You can't imagine how pleased we are to accept you. We don't see many people from home despite my husband's position, so please stay with us as long as you wish.'

'Thank you Mrs. Gore.'

'Have you seen the horse my husband has purchased for you?'

'No.'

'Do go and see, it is a…well go and see.'

'Thank you for all your goodness, and prey excuse me.'

I walked out quickly and there was Antonio by my side.

'Have you a horse, Antonio?'

'Yes Miss'

'Do you speak English?'

'Yes Miss, a little, and French and Spanish.'

'I had forgotten.'

We walked to the stable and he brought out my horse, a beautiful strong grey with quiet eyes, and measuring just under fourteen hands.

'Who chose it?'

'The master, well he took my advice.'

'Can we ride Antonio?'

'Yes Miss'

'I will go and change if you can please prepare the horse.'

'Yes Miss Scarlett, do not say please to me,' he smiled.

'I will, if I wish to do so.' He bowed and smiled again.

I went to my room and put on the blue ridding habit and riding boots. The habit felt and looked wonderful, and I quickly went back to the stables. Antonio had the horse ready and helped me up. I rode around slowly for a few minutes.

'You ride before Miss Scarlett?'

'Yes, but a long time ago. Antonio I hate these side saddles, to me they are ridiculous.'

'Mr. Gore buy this one for you Miss. No side saddles here, his wife not ride.'

'Can I have an ordinary saddle Antonio?'

'We have no one small enough. You want me go tomorrow and buy one?'

'No that would insult and shock Mr. Gore no doubt.'

'Give him more rein.'

'Like this?'

'Yes, now slowly walk down towards the house and turn back'

I obeyed his instructions.

'Now this time walk out towards the roadway and begin a slow trot.'

Antonio mounted and followed,
'Good, very good.'
That reminded me of Fuegia, who always said 'good'.
Then we began a slow trot and I remembered the estate where I grew up in Wicklow, the horses, the sky above the little Sugar Loaf and the purple heather glowing in the sunlight.
'It is a good horse, Miss?'
'Yes, very responsive.'
'And quiet.' Antonio smiled.
'Where can we ride to today?'
'We ride down the old gaucho road.'

27th August

Today I asked Antonio where could we ride to and he said,

'A few miles south-west is a little town and there is a Monastery. Do you think that is too far?'

'No Antonio. Take me there.'

'Yes Miss.'

I could tell he was a good rider and he watched my every move. We trotted for a while and then slowly moved to a canter. The freedom I felt, the breeze in my face and the open space was like heaven after the confines of the ship.

Mr. Gore had told me that his estate was situated inland about half way between Monte Video and Colonia de Sacramento. We cantered along for a while. Jacaranda trees lined the old gaucho road and a profusion of blossoms filled the air with their extravagant fragrances. The undulating pampas stretched out on either side and a little tributary of the Rio Uruguay ran alongside the road. The herds of cattle grazed peacefully and in the distance I could see several wild horses.

We soon came to the town, Colonia del Sacramento, a sleepy little Portuguese costal town with its cobble stoned streets flanked by rows of colonial houses. Around the central plaza, Plaza Mayor, were lines of fig and palm trees and ancient buildings.

Then, to the east of the Plaza I saw the bell tower of the Monastery, and as we came upon it surrounded by trees, a sign read, 'Iglesia Matriz.'

We dismounted. Antonio tied up the horses, and we walked into the grounds.

'This is the oldest church in Uruguay Miss.'

Tucked in behind the church was the 'Convento San Bernardo' a most beautiful religious building. I could see that some parts dated back to the sixteenth century. I walked past the church and up to the convent.

The dark rococo doors carved in walnut welcomed us in. We entered the little chapel. It had lime-washed walls and was lit by high narrow windows. Around the walls there were simply carved Stations of the Cross and lamps in wrought iron fittings.

I found the statue of Mary and knelt to pray. There was a peace here, a silence that seemed filled with the presence of God. It was new and yet familiar. I remembered then the Carmelite Monastery in Delgany where I grew up. That little chapel was a replica of the one I was in now. The nuns sang the daily Office and the Magnificat. We always attended on feast days and Mother said that we needed to thank God always for the Sisters and the beautiful chapel. She called it 'a little bit of heaven'. Until I return to my native land this Monastery and this chapel will be for me my 'little bit of heaven'.

Before long the tears were flowing. I wiped my eyes, I

had promised myself I was not going to cry. Antonio came towards me and pointed towards the grill by the side of the altar. There was a curtain and just behind it the outline of a nun. I walked towards her; she drew back the veil and said in Spanish,

'If you would like to speak to a sister my child, go to the side door and into the parlour.'

'Yes Sister.'
'Do you speak English Sister?'
'I will see who is free.'
'Thank you.'
'You understand, Miss Scarlett?
'Yes I understand, Antonio.'
Antonio and I walked to the side door.

'Here I may not enter Miss Scarlett, and I am sure you are safe with the Sisters, but I stand here at this door until you return...if you call my name, then I respect no boundaries.'

'Thank you.'

I rang a little bell and the door opened. I stepped inside and the door closed silently behind me. I heard a voice say,

'Take the key and enter the parlour on the right.'

I entered the parlour and everything was just the same as with the Carmelite sisters I knew in my early life. There were plants, books and old classical furniture. I felt safe in this atmosphere of quiet repose. I knew at that moment that I was in the ambiance of a spirituality that was familiar to me...it was the spirituality of my youth.

'Are you new to the neighbourhood, my child? Come and sit down.'

I looked around, another grill behind which there was a Sister. She lifted the veil and I looked into two clear blue eyes.

'Are you Carmelites, Sister?'

'Yes we are, child.'

'Oh! how delighted I am to hear you say that.'

I sat on a chair by the grill. The nun told me that she was Mother Monica, the Prioress, and that she was English.

'You were crying child.'

'Yes mother, I am sorry. It is nothing dreadful, just that the man I love is at sea. He is a ship's Captain and he has sailed away on what I think is a dangerous mission for the Admiralty. I miss him Mother. I am trying to be polite and attend to things... but nothing has any meaning for me until I see him again. Is that very self-indulgent of me Mother?'

'My child the great love you have for this man I am sure is real... does he deserve this love?'

'Oh yes Mother and much more, he is the most courageous and upright man I have ever met.'

'When we are in love my child we do not see the faults in the other. Is this your situation?'

'Oh no, Mother I know his faults and he knows mine.'

'Despite these faults your love flows freely towards him?'

'Yes Mother.'

'Do you think this love is inspired by God?'

I thought for a while and then I replied,

'Yes... if all good things come from God, then yes.'

'Does this man believe in God?'

'More scrupulously than I do Mother for I have had many lapses of faith. I think he never doubts.'

'I see your love for him is deep and good. What is your name?'

'My name is Scarlett.'

'Scarlett, my dear child let us kneel and pray together.'

I knelt down on the prie-dieu and in silence we prayed for about fifteen to twenty minutes. Then Mother Monica stood and whispered to me warmly,

'Scarlett you must come and speak to me whenever you wish. What is your Captain's name?'

'He is Captain Robert Fitzroy.'

'This evening I will put his name upon our prayer board.'

'Thank you Mother.'

'Where are you staying?'

'At the Gore's residence.'

'The Charge d'Affaires?'

'Yes Mother.'

'Quite near, the Estancia dos Talas...yes... did you ride?'

'Yes Mother.'

'Not alone I hope.'

'No Mother. The Captain has arranged for a man to protect me.'

'Good. Promise me Scarlett you will return soon.'

'Yes Mother. I will.'

'Would it be possible for me to have confession Mother?'

'Yes if you come before Mass on Sunday the priest will be here.'

'What time is Mass Mother?'

'It is at noon, so come about eleven thirty.'

'Thank you Mother I will. Goodbye.'

'May the Lord bless and keep you Scarlett.'

'Goodbye Mother.'

I returned the key and opened the door. Standing outside was Antonio waiting patiently.

'Antonio, thank you for taking me here, you knew I was a Catholic?'

'Mon Capitaine tell me Miss.'

'Well I am so happy that this beautiful Monastery is so near to the estancia.'

'Is what Mon Capitaine say Miss.'

Antonio gave me his hand and I climbed on to the horse. We ambled along and talked.

'I will call him 'Beagle' Antonio.

'Yes, 'Beagle' is good name.'

'You feel better Miss Scarlett?'

'Yes indeed I do.'

'You love Mon Capitaine… forgive Antonio, he see it in your eyes.'

'You know him well Antonio?'

'Oh no Miss. He is far…what you say… above me.'

'This job must be very boring for you.'

'Oh no Miss, he tell me no greater purpose could any man have than to keep Miss Scarlett safe.'

'He said that? Well it is just that he wants to protect me.'

'Yes Miss…he think about you same way you think about him.'

'You might think that Antonio, but you must never ever say it again. He is a very honourable man, I would never do or say anything that would damage his well deserved reputation His good name is more important to me than anything else. Do you understand?'

'I understand Miss.'

'Forgive this question Antonio…did he remember to pay you?'

'Yes Miss, he pay me for one year, but he know, no need for payment.'

'You don't need payment?'

'No Miss, this task...mission of honour. We do anything for Mon Capitaine.'

'Why'

'Because Miss he save my Father from unjust man who take all our land, the cattle even try to take the children. Mon Capitaine call him...sco...no...'

'Scoundrel?'

'Yes Miss...A lawyer in the town tell my father, can't help him but wait for Captain Fitzroy at port and tell him. My Father see him coming, kneel and ask him for help. Captain ignore him and walk past. Then my Father weep and say,

'I have seven children.'

'Mon Capitaine turn back, listen to my Father and take papers. No small thing, study all papers two days then bring Chief of Police with him and my father and face the sco...

'Scoundrel'

'Yes Miss, make him sign papers, then put him in gaol. He save all my family. My father offer me for this job because I am strongest and best shot.'

'Oh Antonio there will be no shooting I hope.'

'No Miss, only if necessary.'

Only then did I notice the pistol he wore.

We moved into a trot. I had a lot to think about. How could the Captain know me so well? I knew he was a dedicated Christian, not just because he deemed the services on board ship of such importance, but by the way he studied the Bible and in the way he conscientiously carried out his duty, and in all he did. However I had no idea he understood my deep faith.

Soon we were back at the stable.

'Antonio, we will ride to the Monastery everyday from now on.'

'Everyday Miss?'

'Every day.'

I went into the house, took off my riding habit, bathed and put on a dress. I sat at my table. I took up a sheet of writing paper and began,

Dear Captain Fitzroy...

The following day I gave the letter to Mr. Gore before he left, and he assured me that it would get to the Beagle by the best possible route. Over the following weeks my heart was at peace. I practised my Spanish by speaking it to Antonio and my vocabulary and pronunciation improved.

As we went riding each day into the little town we frequently came across bands of friendly gauchos. I learned some of the language of the gauchos. I was captivated by the attire, the bombachas, the rastro and the bonina, and the dances, the chacarera and the carnavalito. From the cafes we could hear the rhythm of the milonga, and my heart ached for the songs of my native land.

As regards food, well, the whole population seemed to have a preference for steak cooked in the open air on an asado and called 'al cuero'. The aroma spread far out for miles and even when I sat on the balcony outside my bedroom I could detect a faint odour wafting on the air. I had to get used to it, for I, who never ate meat, was an enigma to the Gores and to Antonio.

5th September 1832

Almost three weeks passed in perfect peace and equanimity. Then early in September, a very handsome gentleman who was touring South America called to the house. The family knew him and his aristocratic family in England. I was introduced to him just before dinner.

'This is Viscount Walter Murdock, Miss O'Mara.'

'How do you do sir?'

'Are you on a visit to this country Miss?'

'In a way I suppose I am.'

I tried to listen to the conversation at dinner but to tell the truth, having conversed with Captain Fitzroy, the officers on the Beagle and Mr. Darwin over the last year, all other conversations were dull. As soon as I could I asked to be excused, and returned to my books.

After tea Mr. Gore said that the Viscount was attending an evening celebration in the town and asked if I would like to accompany him.

'Oh! No thank you sir. I would prefer to stay at home.'

'Come come Miss Scarlett, you would enjoy the change of company and the change of surroundings, surely.' said Mrs. Gore.

'No thank you Mam, the company I have in your household is delightful to me.'

'Miss Scarlett not many people visit here and this kind of opportunity may not come again?' said Mr. Gore.

'Yes, but I do not know this gentleman…I have just met him.'

'If you are worried about his credentials I assure you Miss Scarlett he comes from an excellent family.'

'And you will have the constant protection of Antonio' Mr. Gore added, with a flourish.

Reluctantly I agreed. Was I never to have any peace? Why should it mean so much to them that I go out with this man?

I found his conversation and manner boring to the point of tedium. I would not choose to spend minutes in his company, and certainly not a whole evening. However the Gores had shown me great courtesy and respect and I felt I must comply with their suggestion as they were being such attentive and good-natured hosts.

I walked out and spoke to Antonio.

'The Master has told me Miss…you will be happy?'

'Antonio how could you ask me that question?'

'I am sorry, Miss Scarlett I think you want to go out for few hours.'

I looked at him.

'No Antonio I do not wish to go out and least of all with a young gentlemen like him.'

'Sorry Miss.'

I went back to my room and found that Maria had already put out my red velvet dress. I put it away and took out another one. Each dress I wore those last weeks on the Beagle were in a kind of sacred category, and I did not want to put them on again until the Captain and the ship returned.

During the rest of the evening Maria fussed, washed and brushed my hair. At seven o'clock she helped me into my dress and gave me a necklace and earrings Mrs. Gore had put out for me.

'You look very well Miss Scarlett.'

'You may think so Maria but I can't wait to be back here.'

'Miss Scarlett everybody look at you, you be happy.'

'I don't want anyone to look at me.'

'Sorry Miss Scarlett.'

Then I remembered the Captain had said that people

would look at me. That was something he did not like… and was the reason I had not gone to the Ball in the Teatro Solis. Why would anyone want to look at me?

Threat

Goldberg's bodyguards had tied up Lucy under Tower Bridge as the tide was coming in. They had set up a camera and Harry looked on as the water rose up around her. Then Harry escaped and managed to free her.

Someone had seen Harry dive into the water and called the police. When he and Lucy came to the surface the Thames Police were waiting for them. One policeman pointed a gun straight at them.

'Thread water and do not make any sudden movements.' he said quietly

Three motor launches swirled around them and two divers were already in the water investigating the area from which they had surfaced. The Thames River Police boat pulled in alongside them and a policeman pulled them both out of the water.

'We are arresting you under the Official Secrets Act…and'

'Have you any blankets? This young lady may be suffering from hypothermia.'

Harry's voice was remarkably calm. One of the policemen passed a blanket to Lucy. Harry tried to put it around her.

'You stay very still sir,' the policeman said as he fastened the handcuffs on Harry.

Harry sat down, soaking wet and exhausted. The policeman looked at Lucy. Her clothes were soaking wet, her skin looked blue, and she was shivering and shaking from head to toe. Nevertheless he put handcuffs on her too.

'Is that necessary? You can see she needs medical attention.' Harry spoke louder now.

Before the policeman could answer, Lucy asked,

'Where…where a…are you take…taking us?'

Lucy was trying to dry her face with the edge of the blanket.

'To Scotland Yard of course.'

Lucy and Harry looked at each other and said in unison,

'Of course.'

Harry and Lucy arrived at the Yard, were separated and questioned. Harry explained how Goldberg's men had tied up Lucy under Tower Bridge and that she was on the point of drowning. Goldberg and Reed had held him captive and when he escaped he had to rescue her quickly or she would have died. He could tell none of the officers believed him. Then his lawyers arrived with Bloom, Dermot and the disc recording of Lucy's ordeal under the bridge. The police sent a delegation to Goldberg's house and found him and Reed tied up.

Eventually the officers let them go. They kept Dermot as they had to check out his story, they said. Harry instructed his lawyers to stay and do everything necessary to free him.

Bloom collected the car and drove Lucy and Harry

back to the Savoy. Lucy acquired some dry clothes on the way. In Harry's suite she showered and changed.

'Are you sure you have recovered Lucy? You look very pale.'

'So do you, Harry.' Harry smiled.

'We need to begin as soon as possible and plan our next move. Time is running out.'

They sat at the table in Harry's suite. Lucy said,

'Before I was abducted I found a Trust Fund set up in Coutts Bank and about to expire on the 9th June 2010, when the Trust is exactly one hundred and eighty years in existence. There is a clause that says if the Trust is not claimed by that date the entire amount is to be paid to the descendants of Sir William Knighton.'

'He now has a false descendant in the form of one Sir Ronald Reed.' Harry sighed.

'What do we do now, Harry?' Bloom asked.

'We have to find out what happened to Scarlett, that's what we have to do or otherwise Goldberg and Reed will be able to secure their fraudulent claim.'

'Even if we find out what happened to her, Harry, she may never have married nor have any descendants.' Lucy said.

'True'

'May I just ask you sir whether it is wise to keep pursuing this matter? So far we hardly have a case and they are ready to make their claim.'

'I understand your point Bloom. It would be easy to give up now, but whenever I think of Scarlett and Captain Fitzroy I know I will pursue this matter…yes to the edge of doom.

'Very good sir'

'In the meantime, I will continue to read the diary and search out any clues there may be there.'

5th *September 1832*

Against my wishes and I might add, against my better judgement, I agreed to go to a celebration dinner in Monte Video with the Viscount Murdock. The Gores had asked me to accompany him and I felt obliged to do so. I walked down the stairs at seven thirty as arranged. The Viscount and Mr. Gore stood up.

'Good evening... may I say how delightful you look my dear?' said Mr. Gore.

I remembered then how I chastised the officers if they made such remarks. How good and noble they were and they tolerated all my opinions. I hated anyone making such remarks because I felt sure they were not true, and I only ever wanted one man to say such things to me. Because of his position as a Captain in the fleet of His Majesty's Navy, and his aristocratic background, he was the one person who would never dream of saying them.

Eventually it was time to leave and the Viscount gave me his hand as I got into the carriage. Antonio looked at him and bowed to us both.

Mr. Gore came out with us and said,

'Do have a pleasant evening and enjoy yourselves.'

'Thank you Mr. Goer.'

Antonio took out the horses slowly and carefully. It was a beautiful evening and I thought maybe I could imagine I was with Mon Capitaine. This reverie lasted until he began to speak. The Viscount had attended a famous College and a renowned University. I felt so tempted to ask him,

'Yes, but did you learn anything, sir?'

He was well acquainted with all that was happening in the upper echelons of society, all the scandals, all the achievements and disasters in turn that are the fate of many.

I tried to listen, change the subject, and ask him if he had any particular academic interests, all to no avail.

I thought of the Captain, the officers, who kept their tongues from idle topics and who never wasted time, and how noble their lives of service were.

We reached the Embassy and Antonio jumped down and opened the door. He whispered,

'I am here by the door. You need me you call.'

I nodded.

All evening I saw Antonio coming in to see if I was safe and being asked to leave. He left, but returned every half hour. It was a high-society event and the gowns and jewellery were far beyond anything I had ever seen.

There were at least fifty tables beautifully decorated with gold cutlery, expensive china and top grade linen. Most people around the table were bilingual and slipped happily from English to Spanish.

At one point during the evening a gentlemen very close to me was talking philosophy and in particular about Kant. He said how he thought that Kant, as a person was a little too punctilious.

'Do you not think sir' I said, 'that anyone who could write 'The Critique of Pure Reason' could possibly be punctilious?

There was silence, no reply…and then many gentlemen started to laugh. Why was that remark so amusing? There was so much about the conversation that night that I did not understand. The Captain was right to call me 'child'.

As soon as it was polite to leave I stood up and thanked everyone. The Viscount had been for some time talking to some ladies at another table. I went to the door and told Antonio to bring the carriage around. Then the Viscount was by my side.

'Have you enjoyed the...the evening Miss...Miss...'

'Yes thank you, my Lord Viscount,' I lied.

'If you would prefer to stay here tonight sir I understand. There is no need for you to make the journey back as my coachman will take good care of me.'

'Oh! That...that will not do...No.. a ...gentleman must always...'

He had been drinking and was finding it hard to complete a sentence. The carriage was there and Antonio opened the door for me.

'I assure you sir there is no need...'

'Yes my dear girl...I insist.'

He entered the carriage after me and Antonio started the horses slowly, went into a canter and then to a gallop. He probably guessed that I wanted to be home as soon as possible. I sat on one side of the carriage the Viscount on the other. He came and sat beside me. I moved to the other side. He followed and this exchange of seats went on while he had on his face a repulsive grin as if it were a game. Eventually I said,

'Stay where you are sir.'

The noise of the horses and the wheels was deafening. Then like lightening he grabbed my hands, held them tight behind my back. He brought his face close to mine and the putrid breath of rancid alcohol made me feel sick. The sour suffocating smoke of his cigars filled the air as his thick lips pressed on mine. I could not breathe. I felt as if I was going to die. I kicked and kicked, I tried to scream. He lay across my body restricting my movements. He did everything with one hand while he held mine as tight as in a vice. At last I managed to give one ferocious scream with all my strength and Antonio heard.

In seconds he had pulled up the horses and was in the carriage. He looked at me and then at the Viscount. He dragged him out and punched him to the ground. Then he pulled out a concealed sword from his seat at the head of the coach and shouted,

'I will run you through.'

'No Antonio, no bloodshed.' I shouted.

He put the sword away, pulled the Viscount to his feet and hit him such a punch as sent him flying into a gully at the grass verge on the side of the road,

'Antonio…enough…take me home quickly'

He looked into the carriage and exclaimed,

'Madre de Dios!'

Then he jumped up to the driving seat and started the horses. When we reached the house Antonio carried me in and put me on a sofa. Mr. Gore had not retired as he was working on his papers and came rushing into the room. Mrs. Gore came running towards me in her night attire,

'My dear, my dear what has happened? Were you attacked by some drunken gauchos?'

'No Mam.' I sobbed,

'Who did this Miss Scarlett?' asked Mr. Gore very quietly.

'It was…it was the Viscount Murdock. I am unharmed sir. Do not upset yourself. I am only shocked and disturbed. Antonio heard my cries and threw him out of the coach.'

'This cannot be…he…surely you are hallucinating,' said Mr. Gore.

'No, it was indeed he sir.'

He knelt down by my seat.

'It is beyond my comprehension that he could do such a thing. Where is the scoundrel now?'

'He lies on the road where Antonio punched him. I had to stop Antonio running him through with a sword.'

'I fear we have failed to protect you adequately Miss Scarlett for indeed you did not wish to go.'

'It was not your fault sir. Thank God I am unharmed. Who could have guessed the sweet talking, inoffensive looking Viscount Murdock would be so deceitful?'

'I think you must rest now Miss Scarlet.' said Mrs. Gore.

'Ah, here is Maria'

Maria came close to me and whispered,

'Miss Scarlett please come to bedroom.'

'Thank you Maria.'

'Kindly excuse me sir, Mrs. Gore, may I ask a favour of you both?'

'Certainly Miss Scarlett,' Mr. Gore replied.

'Will you allow Antonio to sleep outside my bedroom door? I feel very nervous.'

'Certainly…I will have a couch put in the hallway.'

'Thank you sir.'

Later that night the Viscount arrived at the door of the house in the same drunken state shouting about Antonio. He caused a dreadful scene. Mr. Gore had one of the gauchos take out the carriage and convey him back to town. He was acutely embarrassed about the behaviour of a so-called gentleman. He apologized again to me the next morning and then the matter was never spoken of again.

Over the following weeks I recovered from the shock.

The strange feeling of having had a man come so close and force his attentions was difficult to overcome. I frequently woke up at night, jumped up in the bed crying out,
    'No…no…'
    After some time the recollection of that night passed. Life went on in the usual ordered way within the household. My Spanish improved and when Maria and I said the rosary together in the evenings we could hear Antonio quietly joining in from the passageway. Mr. Gore had a couch put there for him, but Antonio always slept on the floor by the door.

We continued our daily visits to the Monastery. The months passed and the order of the house sustained a safe protective rhythm. Late in October the Gores took their annual journey back to England. They asked me if I wished to accompany them. I declined. While my Captain is on this side of the globe this is where I wish to be.

Thursday 15th November 1832

When Mr. Mrs. Gore had gone the house was very quiet, but the routine continued and all was well. Antonio and I rode out everyday to the Monastery. I wrote many letters to the Captain and studied for long periods each day.

Throughout the remainder of September and October I made no entries in my diary as each day was a replica of the previous one. However I was happy. I continued my routine, settled down, and above all appreciated the freedom I now had after the confines of the ship. I adjusted to my new life. I was lonely yes, but I felt a quiet joy deep in my heart.

Monday 19*th* November 1832

Today while Antonio and I were riding home from the Monastery I saw, at some distance, a man on horseback riding towards us. Antonio pulled rein and looked at me. I pulled Beagle to a halt. I thought my eyes were deceiving me…but if Antonio sees him too…

'It is mon Capitaine Miss Scarlett…'

'It is indeed'

'You stay here Miss Scarlett I go to meet him…he protect you now I will go back to the estancia.'

Antonio rode away quickly. I did not stay there. I put Beagle straight away into a canter and then I saw Antonio salute the Captain. They exchanged a few words, and the Captain handed something to him. Antonio rode away. My heart was beating furiously. I brought Beagle to a halt, jumped down and began to run as fast as I could.

The Captain came galloping towards me and then he pulled rein, jumped down and we ran into each other's arms. He lifted me high and turned me round and round. I slid down into his arms and he drew me towards him and gently kissed me. I put my arms around his neck and then we kissed…a long passionate kiss. Then he declared,

'I had to come back dear Scarlett. My life was unbearable without you, I had to come back to you. The ship was like an empty shell without you'

'Oh! Robert…the joy that is my heart to see you again.'

'How could I not have known how much I loved you? How could I not have known Scarlett?'

I put my finger over his lips,

'You know now my darling, you know now.'

He put his arms around me and held me close, then he looked into my eyes and asked,

'Scarlett, is it too soon? Is it too much to ask? May I ask you...may I humbly ask you, will you do me honour of being my wife?'

At first I could not believe the words...but he had uttered them. For a moment I was incapable of speech and so I nodded. A great joy came into Robert's eyes and he drew me towards him and kissed me fervently. I melted into his arms and all the love that had been in our hearts over the past months poured out into that kiss. I, who had never been kissed in such a way before, almost lost my breath. Then he stroked my hair and my cheek.

For a moment my heart faltered, my mind seemed to go numb for I could hardly believe the words I had heard. We stared steadily into each other's eyes.

'If you are unable to answer at this time I understand Scarlett...I...'

'Oh! I do answer my beloved Captain, With all my heart I wish to be your wife.'

We kissed again with all the love that goes with the certainty that both hearts are at one and wishing the same exquisite union. We collected the horses and walked and talked in a kind of dream. We stopped, kissed, and walked again. We were together in the vast expanse of the pampas that stretch out all around us. It was in sharp contrast to the previous months and the confines of the Beagle.

Then Robert said,

'When I have seen you safely at the estancia I will ride out to the Monastery to ask the Abbe Du Bec if he will perform the ceremony, if you agree Scarlett.'

'Oh my dear Robert, nothing could be more pleasing to me...but do you mean it to take place today?'

'I do... perhaps about twelve thirty. What do you think Scarlett?'

'Yes my dear Robert I agree...but would it be possible for Antonio to ride with me into Monte Video to purchase a dress?'

'Certainly, if that is your wish.'

'It is Robert. You know how little store I put on dresses but my wedding day, Robert is special. It is the happiest day I will ever know...for this I wish to look like a bride.'

'Very well, my darling, whatever you wish. I have given Antonio a sum of money for all our needs today.'

'Thank you, and Robert...may I ask you...what about documents, birth certificates? I have never remembered who I am.'

'Do not worry about anything Scarlett. I have all my documents ready and a statement signed by the British Consul last August when you first came ashore.'

When we reached 'Dos Talas' he kissed me, gently and said farewell.

I found Antonio and asked him to come as soon as possible into the town with me as we had not time to lose.

'I must purchase a dress.'

He was ready in a few moments and we set out at a fast pace. I had only been in Monte Video once and had no idea where to begin my search.

'What kind of dress, Miss Scarlett?'

I put my finger over my lips and said,

'Wedding dress.' His eyes lit up he said something in Italian and then...

'This way.'

In a few moments I was outside a most expensive shop. Antonio handed me a wad of notes. I entered the shop and tried on several dresses. My favourite was a very plain pure white silk dress. It had a full skirt, it was high *wasted with long sleeves that came to a point on the hand in Elizabethan style.*

'I will take this one thank you' I said in Spanish. I then chose a veil and yellow roses for my hair and white very high heeled shoes. Everything was packed and the box handed to me. I paid the bill and went out.

Outside Antonio was smiling. He took the boxes and the remainder of the money. He then gave me his hand to mount the horse. He had purchased a bouquet of yellow roses for me to carry up the isle.

'Thank you, dear Antonio.'

He smiled and we were on our way back. At the estancia I took a bath, Maria washed my hair and prepared all my clothes. I noticed that she was packing a case.

'What are you doing Maria?' She answered me in Spanish.

'Before the Captain meet you he come here. He ask me do I think you Miss Scarlett will marry him. I tell him, yes... yes. He then tell me he will ask you today and to pack bag for you with riding habit. After wedding he have surprise for you. I was right to say this Miss Scarlett?'

'Yes Maria you were right'

I took my favourite poetry book from the shelf,

'Put this in the case Maria please.'

I slipped on the beautiful simple dress. Maria brushed my hair and entwined the roses into it. She placed the veil over my head and pinned it in place. I put on the shoes, picked up the bouquet and looked at myself in the mirror.

'You most beautiful bride,' said Maria.

Maria put on a blue dress and we were ready to go. We walked out of the front door where Antonio was waiting with the coach.

'Antonio…you look so smart.'

'This for fiestas' he said pointing to his colourful gaucho costume.

Then I noticed that Beagle was tethered to the back of the coach. I looked at Antonio. He shrugged his shoulders and said,

'The Captain tell me do this.'

Maria and I stepped into the coach and Antonio started the horses. This was the most wonderful day of my life and I had scarcely had time to appreciate it.

I looked out at the passing pampas. They seemed greener, the sky was the most vivid blue I had ever seen and everything was bathed in a kind of celestial light. Was I dreaming…or do dreams come true sometimes?

We arrived at the Monastery. I could see that the horse and trap belonging to the priest were already there. Antonio opened the chapel door. The priest was kneeling praying at the altar. Robert was sitting in the front seat. They both stood. Robert did not look round but as usual he looked so distinguished in his impeccable blue and gold uniform. The priest beckoned for Maria and Antonio to approach the altar. When they were in place he looked towards the convent grill and bowed his head. That was the signal for the nuns to begin singing 'O Sanctissima, O piissima'

I began to walk slowly up the isle. My heart was beating fast and then the rhythm of the hymn calmed me and the joy of that unique moment entered my soul. When I reached my place Robert looked at me with such love and adoration that for the first time in my life I felt beautiful.

We took our vows with a sincerity that comes only from a firm faith. Robert placed a wide gold filigree ring on my finger and tears of joy came into my eyes. At the Communion the sisters sang in plainchant 'Panis Angelicus' and I received the bread of Angels, as did Maria and Antonio. Robert was blessed with the sacred host. After signing the register we walked down the isle, now husband and wife to the subtle tones of the 'Magnificat'.

We never took our eyes away from each other until we were outside and Maria came over and kissed me. Antonio looked at me with great happiness in his eyes. He opened the door of the carriage. I noticed that Robert's horse was also tethered to the carriage now. We stepped in and glided into each other's arms. I felt the arms of the man I loved hold me close and all the joys of my life seemed to gather together into an immense love that not only seemed to fill the carriage but the entire world.

'What about Maria, Robert?'

He smiled,

'The Priest is taking her home. You never neglect anyone do you my darling?'

'Neither do you Robert.'

We looked into each other's eyes, the way we had done for many previous months. All the tension that had built up on the Beagle was a testing time of mind and heart. Now we were one for all eternity and nothing in this world would ever separate us again.

Then Robert whispered,

'I know that here in my arms my beloved I hold, not only my best friend and true love, but the most beautiful woman in the world, and I ask myself Scarlett what have I ever done to deserve such happiness?'

I put my finger over his lips the way I used to do in the cabin on the Beagle when we both knew that words, even poetic words could never truly express how we felt.

'I think you deserve every possible happiness Robert, and with all my heart that is what I wish to bring to your life. I imagined such a day as this Robert, but I doubted if it would ever be a reality.'

'It is real my darling, we are together. Nothing in life or death will ever separate us again.'

I cannot remember how long we were together in each other's arms but after some time Antonio brought the horses to a stop. We stepped out of the carriage. We were deep into a remote area of the pampas and before us was a hunting lodge, quaint, built of wood, surrounded by shrubs and trees, and flanked by a small stable.

'Oh Robert, how beautiful!' I exclaimed. Before I had finished the sentence Robert had lifted me up into his arms and Antonio had only just reached the door in time to open it. He walked back to the carriage.

Robert walked in and we kissed each other with a love that was natural. Neither of us had ever loved like this before, neither of us had ever given ourselves in such a way before and so this union was for both of us the first. It was thrice blest; with the innocence we each held sacred, with the truth that shone in our eyes, and enfolded into our union was a spiritual blessing, the blessing of the sacrament of marriage. We kissed with the kind of passion that is expressed only in such circumstances and in private.

After a long time Robert put me down and I looked around at the cabin. It consisted of four rooms: a kitchen, a sitting room a bedroom and water closet. It was a sanctuary of rustic charm, of scents of pine and it overlooked the pampas. An emerald lake glistened and stretched into the distance towards snow-capped mountains. It was an oasis of peace and only the song of the birds and the breeze through the trees broke the silence.

Antonio set about making fires and stocking the kitchen and then Maria arrived with the priest. He came in, gave us his blessing and left. While Robert went to collect his saddlebag Antonio whispered to me that we might take a walk while 'they put the cabin right'.

Maria helped me change my clothes and I put on my blue dress and walking shoes.

'Robert, shall we explore the immediate area?'

'On foot?'

'I think so.'

'Very well'

We walked, held hands, embraced, walked again and were in a world of our own. We arrived at a long ridge over an isolated plateau where tiny Alpine flowers grew and were interspersed with faded grass. Robert knelt down and was looking intently at the composition of the rock. I began to smile.

'What?' he asked

'Am I going to be subjected to a lecture on volcanic rock?'

However, before the last word was out of my mouth I ran and was pursued and caught, and lifted up, and caressed. We laughed together freely as we had always wished to do on the Beagle but never could.

When we returned Antonio and Maria had transformed the lodge. There were fires in the sitting room and bedroom. There were clusters of beautiful yellow roses, wild flowers and greenery everywhere. A delicious smell of spices and herbs emanating from the kitchen.

After Antonio had seen to the horses he said,

'We come tomorrow afternoon mon Capitaine.'

'Thank you Antonio' Robert said, and I echoed his

words to Maria. He left in the carriage with Maria. They were gone and we were alone together at last. The joy and beauty of that day we knew we would never forget. When evening came and we prepared the table to eat the supper Maria had prepared, Robert whispered to me,

'Would you like to put on your wedding dress?'

I put on the beautiful dress again and when I looked in the mirror I saw that my hair was in the style Maria had put it in that morning with the yellow roses in place. During the excitement of the day I had forgotten how my hair was adorned.

When I entered the room Robert had lit the candles, and we sat opposite each other and talked of the times on the ship when we had longed for such an occasion as this. We finished the meal. Robert stood in front of me and asked,

'Would Mrs. Fitzroy do me the honour of dancing the waltz with me?'

'My pleasure, sir.'

We moved the table to the side and Robert took me in his arms. I began to hum a waltz tune until my breath ran out. We danced close together quietly. The only sound was that of our feet on the wooden floor and the rustle of my silk dress. Then we danced energetically and Robert whispered,

'Can you hear the violins?'

'I can hear the entire orchestra!' I exclaimed.

Over the next three days we experienced a primeval paradise. We felt we knew each other so well and yet we discovered many amazing things about each other that only intimacy reveals. We both knew that we were the luckiest people on earth to have found each other.

When we awoke on the third morning in each other's arms, Robert said,

'Thee are two things I need to speak to you about Scarlett'

My heart missed a beat, and I looked intently into his eyes. He began to smile,

'It is nothing to be anxious about,' he held my hands,

'I have found out who you really are.'

I took my hands away and placed them over my ears, perhaps I could not bear to hear.

'Oh! Robert, tell me quickly'

He took my hands again and smiled.

'There is nothing to be upset about.'

He explained who my parents were and how I came to be born in Paris. After my birth my mother had taken me to good friends she had in Ireland, the Whiteside family. They adopted me and I grew up on their estate in Delgany, County Wicklow. It took a time for this information to sink into my mind. Some events I had already remembered but I felt incredibly sad, and although shadows and shades of my life flashed through my thoughts, nonetheless my memory did not fully return.

At first I thought there must be some mistake, this could not be... but Robert had looked into it and found... my place of birth. He passed me the birth certificate. I looked at it intently... I thought for a time. Tears came into my eyes...

'Why did my own parents not send for me? Why was I a secret never to be told?'

Robert held me tight, and over his shoulder I looked out at the pampas, and wondered how far am I from home?

'Try to understand Scarlett the kind of turmoil that was brewing in London and around the King at that time. He had already been married and was living with yet another mistress. Forgive me for saying these things. It grieves me to...'

'I understand Robert. You think it was for the best?'

'Yes I do. I can appreciate how your Mother wished to protect you from the scandal that was circulating about her relationship with the King. In fact she never told him about you until a few days before he died. She knew had she brought you back to England you would never have been allowed to follow the Catholic faith.'

It took time for me to understand this information. Robert took me in his arms again.

'Robert, the name in my books 'O'Mara' where did that come from?'

'O'Mara was Mr. Whiteside's wife's maiden name. It was another way of hiding your identity.'

'James was not even my half-brother then?'

'No.'

'Nevertheless may we visit him in Ireland Robert? For we grew up together and loved each other dearly.'

'Yes of course we will my darling.'

'Were you shocked Robert when you found out who my real parents were?'

'Yes in a certain way I was. In another way I was not. I knew that any young lady who had the manners and education you had must surely have aristocratic connections… perhaps not quite what they turned out to be.'

'Is that why I was so often scolded for my lack of genteel conduct?' I smiled.

He held me in his arms and looked into my eyes and whispered,

'Do you forgive me…not just for that but for all the times I made you sad on the Beagle?'

'You are never again to mention anything about upsetting me. I did not conform. You could not believe your eyes or your ears, admit it.'

'I admit it.' he smiled.

'My darling, will you do something for me?' Robert asked.

'Of course I will. What is it?'

'Will you promise me not to think about the past. At any rate you can't remember most of it, so please leave it that way. Just allow those odd remembrances to come and go and no longer worry about who you are my dearest Scarlett. You are Mrs Robert Fitzroy and that is all you ever need to remember, my dearest love.'

'Oh Robert! You are such a kind man.'

There was one question that had constantly annoyed me and I asked him now if he knew the answer to it.

'Robert dear, do you know what on earth I was doing all alone on the south coast of England, and walking around near the Lizard?'

'No, I'm afraid I do not know the answer to that question, but if you can look at it like this, had you not been there we would never have met.'

'Robert my darling that is so. I promise you I will not allow myself to deliberate on the past and I will think only of the present and the exquisite life that lies in the future for us both.'

We embraced for a long time, he stroked my cheek and kissed my eyelids and softly whispered,

'Never again are any tears of sorrow to flow from these beautiful eyes, only tears of joy. Whatever happens in the future to make you sad be assured I will stand between it and you and take any pain for you so that these eyes will never again be sad.'

'Oh Robert…you will for ever be not only my husband but also my hero as you were when we first met when I was nine years old.'

'And you will always be my sweetheart.'

My thoughts went back then to the day I had left the ship.

'On the day I left the ship, Robert, I overheard you talking to Mr. Darwin about an oath.'

'Well, it was a directive from the Admiralty. Darwin objected and I perfectly understand his sentiments. I think it was yet another ploy set up by Knighton. However I had no alternative but to obey orders. I think in the end Darwin took the oath for my sake.'

'Why was it so important that no one should know I was on the Beagle?'

'It wasn't important. So don't worry about it any more.'

'Very well, but Robert I wish to ask something of you that may not please you.'

'What is it?'

'I wish you to keep our marriage a secret.'

'Scarlett, how can you ask such a thing? I want to shout it aloud to everyone I meet.'

'I have my own reasons. I do not wish you to be burdened with anything until this voyage is over, and don't you think it would be better to announce our wedding to your family first when we are back in England?'

'How could you think of yourself as a burden, Scarlett?'

'When you collect me at Bahia we will be near to home and that in my opinion would be the correct time to announce our marriage.' He did not answer.

'Will you do this to humour me Robert?'

'Very well, my darling, but it will be difficult.'

I kissed him and whispered quietly,

'Thank you my darling.'

I forgot then that he had said there were two things he had to reveal to me.

Each day we took the horses and rode out over the pampas. Sometimes we walked and talked. At other times we trotted or cantered. The gentle breeze was like a fan that cooled our brows and elevated our thoughts. The purity of the air lightened our hearts and the stillness of the scenery soothed our spirits and elevated us both to a plain of existence we had never before experienced. We moved into a Utopian bliss, a Garden of Eden.

We loved the seclusion. One day as we walked along and I pondered on the vast blue sky, the wild flowers and the far off snow-capped mountains. In my immense joy I spoke out…

*'…And the light and smell divine
of all flowers that breathe and shine:
We may live so happy there,
That the Spirits of the Air,
Envying us, may even entice
To our healing paradise
The polluting multitude;…'
Robert smiled at me and said,
'Shelley'*

When we returned Antonio and Maria had cooked, cleaned, and lit the fires. They left us then after Antonio had seen to the horses. We reclined in each other's arms amid the scents of pine and roses and each day my admiration for this extraordinary man augmented.

We exchanged stories of our youth, that is to say what I could remember, and Robert expressed for the first time ever to a living soul the heartache of his mother's death and the loneliness he felt at Rottingdean, his first boarding school at the age of six. My heart took on the loneliness of those times in his life, and I could understand the undoubted effect they had had on his disposition.

We wanted these days never to end. We wanted to live like this forever. We both felt that we had touched the edge of paradise and that nothing again would ever compare to the times we were living here in this celestial union.

I tried not to think of our separation, yet I wondered how many days Robert could stay away from the ship. Each morning I dreaded that he would have to go back on board.

He asked me some evenings to recite the poems I liked best. We talked about 'The Romantics' and he asked me if I liked Coleridge.

'Very much, particularly 'Frost at Midnight.'
'................. so shalt thou see and hear
The lovely shapes and sounds intelligible
Of that eternal language, which thy God
Utters, who from eternity doth teach
Himself in all, and all things in himself.
Great universal Teacher! he shall mould
Thy spirit...'
'Tell me who your favourite poets are?' Robert asked.
'The opinion of an amateur?'
'Of course'
'Well for intellect, sublimity of thought and style, I would choose Milton and Shakespeare. Then you must forgive my preference for the Romantics: Wordsworth, for his originality of style and consummate love of nature; Keats, for verbal melody, and Shelley for his passionate love of nature and poetic spirit.'

Robert smiled and then began to laugh.

'You disagree?'
'I would not dare!' he said.

Saturday 24th November 1832

On the sixth day Robert gave me a wedding present. It was a little linnet in a cage which stood above a wooden round base. It had a winding mechanism that enabled the bird to sing.

I listened, then kissed him and thanked him. I did not tell him my innermost thoughts that in his absence I would listen, and these scenes of our cherished love would come alive again for me. Then he held me close and said he must go back to the ship.

'Must it be today Robert?'

He nodded. We kept to the routine and in the afternoon Antonio and Maria came and cleared out the lodge. Everything was put in the carriage. The horses were tethered, Maria sat up with Antonio and Robert and I sat close in each other's arms. I tried not to cry. I knew that such happiness as we had experienced was a gift beyond ordinary life and with grateful hearts we embraced and tried to face the separation bravely.

'I hope to be able to visit you once more before we leave. Then I will be back sometime around October next year.'

'But I will not be able to go with you then, will I Robert?'

'No Scarlett, but I give you my word that however long this voyage takes I will have you escorted to Bahia and we will meet there on our way home.'

I took the wedding ring from my left hand and placed it on my right hand.

'What are you doing Scarlett?'

'You have not forgotten about our secret?'

'No, but is that necessary?'

'Yes it is…a secret is a secret'

'What about Antonio, Maria, the priest and the sisters?'

'With all of these people I would trust my life.'

'Yes of course… but I will worry that you are not adequately protected.'

'Can a wedding ring protect one?'

'Yes Scarlett it can…forgive me…'

'Robert no one could do more to protect me. I rarely go anywhere and Antonio never leaves my side if I do.'

'But Antonio told me what happened with the Viscount Murdock…the scoundrel.'

'I know that was regrettable. Please Robert humour me in this instance…I have my reasons.'

'I agree reluctantly to your secret then.'

He drew me towards him and we melted into a sublime kiss, a union of lips and hearts. No words in the whole universe are sufficient to describe this state of harmony.

Too quickly we arrived at the estancia, we embraced, made our farewell kiss in the carriage, and then stepped out. Antonio untied Robert's horse and attached his saddlebags.

We held hands as we walked towards the horse. Robert drew me close into his arms and in soft tones said,

'I love you through every moment of every day until we meet again Scarlett.' Then quickly he mounted and was gone down the drive and did not look back.

The tears fell slowly down my cheeks. Then we entered the house and within the hour every routine in the house returned to normal. So much so I wondered if I had woken from a dream and that it was only an episode out of my fantasy book I had been living through. I looked down at the ring and I knew then that it was real. Although it was on the wrong finger the ring bound us together and made everything about our loving union real.

Robert managed to come back for a few hours the following day, Sunday the 25th November. My spirits soared and my heart beat faster when I saw him. We walked in the grounds; we kissed and remained close in each other's arms. I was enchanted by the sound of his beloved voice,

'Oh Robert how will I bear not hearing your voce?'

'I am feeling the same pain, my dearest Scarlett' he whispered.

He left then and my heart ached yet again as I watched him ride down the old gaucho road.

I tried to remain happy until his return and spent my time reading and writing for a set time each day. Antonio and I took the horses and went to Mass at the Monastery as part of our daily routine. I spoke to Mother Monica three times every week and without her help I could never have suffered the loneliness caused by my husband's absence, nor the changes taking place in my body, mind and soul.

Everything about Robert was meticulous. A letter from him arrived every two weeks without fail. I assumed this same method and we fell into that harmonious practice. My heart leaped when I saw his fine handwriting, and I knew how much he suffered because he could not address me as 'Mrs. Robert Fitzroy'. However, the storm clouds were gathering over me and I needed courage and forbearance, qualities I did not possess in much abundance, to endure the following months.

3rd December 1832

The month of December arrived and the Gore family

returned from their leave and I was delighted to see them. Then each morning I began to feel ill. I started being sick and this went on all through the day. Maria smiled at me and said,

'A baby'

So immature was I that I had not even thought of a baby. Over the following days I realized that I was with child. Maria assured me that the sickness would stop after three months. It felt so bad that I thought I could not endure it for three days. Nevertheless I felt very happy until I remembered that I had asked the Captain to keep our marriage a secret.

I must write to him immediately and tell him about the child. He would need to announce our marriage without delay. I sat down and wrote the letter. Then I hesitated and did not give it to Mr. Gore.

4th December

The next day I told Antonio I wanted to walk alone down the old gaucho road and I requested that he stay a distance away. I needed to be alone. I walked for a long time in the silence of the pampas. The scent of the mimosa lifted my heart and only the chirping of the birds broke in upon my thoughts.

As I walked along the pain of childbirth and the whole responsibility of having a child to care for seemed to fasten on me. I began to sob and then fell to my knees on the ground.

Antonio came running up and picked me up in his arms and carried me back to the house.

The following day as I walked along the old gaucho road again with Antonio, I told him,

'Antonio…I am with child'

In his joy he lost his usual decorum and lifted me up in his arms and said,

'Thanks be to God' in his Spanish vernacular.

Then he put me down and said contritely,

'Forgive Antonio Miss Scarlett.'

Both Maria and Antonio had continued to call me Miss Scarlett upon my instructions.

'You have told Mon Capitaine, you have told Signor?'

'No, I have told nobody but you, and…Maria told me!'

I tried to smile.

'Tomorrow we will ride to the Monastery and I will tell the nuns.'

'Yes Miss, you are very calm, Miss'

I could not hold back the tears then and I began to sob. He came forward, I held out my hand to him, he took it and dropped to his knees.'

'You love the Captain Miss, why are you sad?'

'I am not well Antonio and sick all the time. My mind is not at ease, just allow me to walk alone.'

'I will follow.'

'Very well.'

The days of December passed and no relief came from the constant nausea. Christmas passed in a haze and the New Year arrived. Robert's letters became less frequent. It was probably impossible always to find a Package ship. I wondered how Fuegia was getting on and how my beloved husband's spirits kept in Tierra del Fuego and those far off seas.

Sunday 13th January 1833

Every time I decided to tell the nuns about the baby

I changed my mind. However today I took courage and waited fro Mother Monica after Mass. I told her about the baby.

'Congratulations, my dear Scarlett, this is wonderful news.'

I began to cry and then sob.

'My dear child what is the matter?'

'First of all Mother I feel sick every moment of every day.'

'Scarlett this is difficult to bear but no doubt it will pass.'

'Yes Mother.'

'Today we will put you and your baby on the prayer board.'

'Thank you Mother.' I sobbed.

'I have such strange feelings Mother. I am overjoyed and I am very sad all at the same time. I find it impossible to attain peace in that delicate place in the mind where we try to face the future.'

'My poor child try to be still and pray and these feelings will pass.'

'Yes Mother.'

There was a long silence.

'Have you written to tell the Captain my child?'

'No Mother. You should know that I wear my wedding ring on my right hand and that I have asked the Captain to keep our marriage secret.'

'But why such a request Scarlett? Were you not both proud of your great love for each other?'

'Oh yes Mother. We wanted to shout out about our love, but consider this Mother. Robert is on a voyage, circumnavigating the globe, a hundred demands upon his time and patience, I did not want him to have to explain everything to the crew and his family.'

'But why not Scarlett?'

'Because Mother every crew member on that voyage knew that I had always loved the Captain. How could they conceal what they knew? How could they pretend to be surprised? I can tell you now that revelation would have upset him greatly.'

'Why?'

'Because, dear Mother, he was the only one on the ship who did not know that I loved him, or at least did not recognize my affection as love. If at any point any officer were to remark to him how much I had always loved him I can tell you he would be furious. He would see himself as ridiculous. In his innocence of heart he thought that he could go back to the ship, announce our wedding and that every officer to a man, and all on board would be astonished that I loved him, and be very happy for him.'

'Is this a sufficient reason to conceal your marriage now that you are carrying his child?'

'No Mother. Upon understanding my condition I wrote immediately to him…and then I thought again. The news of an unborn child, I refuse to inflict upon my beloved Robert while he is at sea and carrying such a heavy naval responsibility. I love him too much.'

Mother was silent for along time.

'Scarlett you used the word inflict…how can you possible think such news would not be accepted by the Captain with great joy?'

'Oh it would Mother to begin with…but then the practical side would begin to take up his thoughts. He, far away, worrying about my health, unable to be with me… it would break his heart.'

'Very well, if this is what you think is for the best.'

'I do Mother.'

'Be at peace then, my child.'

'Thank you dear Mother, I do have peace now.'

Wednesday 6th February 1833

Today I received a letter from my dear husband, and all goes well with the voyage. He appears in good spirits, but repeats as usual that he misses my quiet voice and gentle reasoning. He found a Package before he entered the Beagle Channel on his way to settle the Fuegians and Mr. Matthews. It has taken a long time to reach me. The voyage progresses apace he says and he is occupied unremittingly every minute of every day.

The main activity of my days was to ride with Antonio out to the Monastery. He sat beside me or behind me. We used to laugh and be so happy out on the pampas. As the weeks have gone by and the sickness never eased even for a day he began to worry. He grew thin and pale as I did myself.

As we were riding back to the estancia today, he said

'Miss Scarlett I must say something...and you no think Antonio too...too'

'Just say whatever it is Antonio.'

'Thank you Miss.'

'I think it is time you tell Signor Gore and Signora about baby...because I think you need see doctor.'

'Yes you are right Antonio and first I must tell them about our secret marriage.'

Nevertheless as the days passed I could not find the courage to tell the Gores.

However bad the nausea and sickness I was suffering, I always managed to ride out to the Monastery for Mass and to speak to Mother Monica three times a week. The ride through the pampas every day helped to keep my spirits up. The unrelenting pampas stretched out before us and I thought of my dear Robert in the confines of his cabin.

Throughout the days we had spent together after our wedding, he had arranged a unique combination of freedom and solitude, quiet and activity, love and tenderness. He did so because of the kind of person he is… an interesting, alert, discerning, intelligent and above all else–a loving man.

Under the duty of command and the confines of the ship it was difficult for him to display some of these qualities, but during the days we were together I knew the real man, the man he was in the centre of his being. I was the luckiest person in the world to have the company of such a man, the respect of such a man, the love of such a man. Nothing ever again in life or death could take away the happiness I felt deep in my heart and mind. For indeed it was for us both a unique moment in time, suffused with a radiance that would never fade.

Thursday 7th March 1833

At last I found the courage to tell Mr. and Mrs. Gore about our secret wedding and about our child. They were indeed astonished, for they had been away on leave at the time of our wedding. They promised to keep the secret and fulfil my wishes. Everything kind parents could do they did for me. Mr. Gore immediately sent for a gynaecologist.

I was very thin and no one could imagine I was with child. When we went riding Beagle was always quiet. Nothing ever startled him, so that I could ride with complete confidence. When we were out on the pampas I looked up at the snow tipped, far away mountains, the wild birds and the grazing cattle. The air was fresh and cool on my face.

I held fast to those days Robert and I were together in the remote pampas and I began to think about them constantly. I twirled my wedding ring on my finger and in the far distance I heard the faint hum of the Panis Angelicus that the sisters had sung on our wedding day. In this way I brought those idyllic days to life again.

The moments when Robert gently drew me close to him and kissed me filled me with joy. For a few exceptional days we were as one in mind, heart and spirit. Memories such as these kept me alive during these demanding days. This diaphanous, flimsy thread has held my fragile life together.

May 1833

For many weeks I have had no heart to write in the diary. The sickness continued day and night and there has been no respite from it. Antonio and I ride out each day and apart from the holy sacrament and the far off love of my dear husband these times on the pampas have kept my spirit intact and my heart, to some extent, free.

To day I was advised by Antonio not to ride again until after the birth. I demurred but I knew he was right. Now we go to visit the Monastery in the coach. I suggested to him that day that we take one last ride and he agreed. After that I missed those moments of nearness to nature, and I missed Beagle too. I visit him often in the stable, and take him walking around the rounds.

June 1833

I cried a lot, hate all food and live on apples, water and tea. The doctor came regularly and said all was well. Mr. Gore arranged for two doctors to attend the birth, one a gynaecologist. Everyone was very kind. Maria scarcely left my side and Antonio sat at the door of my room. The Carmelite Sisters gave me books to read. At night when I could not sleep I would put my light on to read and Antonio would knock and open my door, saying,

'Tea Miss Scarlett?' I nodded. Maria left several trays of tea set up in the kitchen and some nights Antonio went for tea three times. I sat up and sipped the tea. Antonio returned to the door and sat down. Often then I questioned him about his past.

'Tell me about your life before you came here.'

He spoke quietly, although there was no one to disturb in this part of the house. He told me stories of his family and of the gaucho's life, how they trained the horses with the boleadoras, how they broke in the stubborn ones.

He told me how they drank the mate, the bitter green tea, and danced to the strumming guitars and the milonga, until I fell asleep again. When I woke up the door was closed. This went on most nights and I will be forever grateful to this kind simple man who stayed with me through these long dark nights and in doing so saved my sanity.

Maria came every morning at six, and sat with me until I woke.

Monday 15th July

Today I received a long awaited letter from the Captain. I took it and walked out into the grounds to a favourite seat on the edge of the wood. Antonio followed and sat down on the grass. I opened the letter and began to read. The tears trickled down my face.

'You sad Miss Scarlett? You want to tell Antonio?'

'My beloved husband begins with the usual salutations and then he says,

'My dearest Scarlett my heart has been aching every day recently as I long to be with you, to be in your arms and looking into your beautiful eyes. Since early May I have been near Maldonado and Monte Video and have been unable to visit you. I have scarcely had time to draw breath having now purchased two schooners to help with the surveying. Many additional problems have thence ensued and my heart breaks as I have been so near and yet so far. I will set out for the Rio Negro on July 24th if all goes well. I will be back in October we will spend at least one week together then. This is a trying time for us both and I hope with all my heart, my dearest Scarlett, in the years ahead we will spend days, weeks, months and years together without any such partings.'

'I am sorry Miss Scarlett, but Mon Capitaine know you understand.'

'I don't understand,' I said through my tears.'

'You do Miss Scarlett because you love him like he love you. You know if can come to you he come. Just like you go to him if you can.'

I felt Antonio was right but it did not take the pain away, and often now, with tears in my eyes, I looked in the direction of the town and the Mole.

Monday 28th July

Today would be my last visit to the Monastery. Antonio took out the carriage and lifted me up into it. He drove very carefully. I brought with me the Captain's wooden box and I gave it to Mother Monica after Mass.

'Why do you want me to give him the box Scarlett? You may give it to him yourself surely upon his return.'

'Yes I know Mother, but will you please humour me

in this regard? When you see him will you…will you tell him…' the tears flooded into my eyes and there was such a restriction in my throat I could not speak.

'How much you love him…yes my child.'

'Thank you Mother, goodbye, pray for our child please.'

'We do so every day, dear Scarlett.'

I walked out quickly, went into the little chapel for the last time before the birth, and prayed on my knees. Antonio was behind me. I don't know how long I stayed there but when I stood up I felt very unsteady and walked out slowly.

'Pardon Senorita' said Antonio and lifted me in his arms and placed me in the carriage.

Antonio suggested that he take me for a short drive across the pampas.

'Drive slowly Antonio. I want to have the picture on 'my inward eye' to remember always…'

'Yes Miss. You look very tired Miss'

I remembered then…before our wedding on two occasions the Captain had lifted me up in his arms, once when they found me in the rowing boat, and once when I had fallen out of bed. On both occasions I was on the verge of delirium and have only a vague recollection of my feelings. After the wedding, when we arrived at the Lodge he lifted me up and carried me in, the closeness of that moment was as vivid to me now and as clear as the vast blue sky above.

Nothing of course could compare to those days together… although I could visualize every moment of them yet, sometimes they seemed far off, as if in another life. Another life is now stirring within me, a life that I hope will be happy. I came back from my reverie and looked out of the carriage at the beautiful little Monastery.

'Let me look at this place Antonio. It is where I have been closest to the Lord for a long time. It is also the place of my most precious moment...my wedding.'

'It will be all over soon Miss Scarlett, Captain return and happy days come to you again.'

'Yes, my dear Antonio, it will be over soon.'

He climbed up and started the horses.

Thursday 14th August

The first two weeks of August have passed in the same trying way. Even now there is no respite from the nausea and I have felt my spirits weaken since I have been unable to go to the Monastery nor ride through the pampas. Everyone is very kind to me but nothing can ever substitute the presence of my beloved husband at this time. To see him, his handsome features, his splendid voice...yes, that would fill me with joy.

Monday 18th August 1833

This will be my last entry I think. Everyone has been exceptionally kind to me. Over the past months I have spoken to Mother Monica for hours and without her I would not have survived mentally the ordeal of these last days of constant nausea and sickness, nor would I be able to go without the prayers of the Sisters. One thought alone sustains me, the love of my far-off husband.

Thursday 21st August 1833

It is six o'clock in the morning and Antonio has gone for the doctor. The pains have begun and they are violent and unbearable. However I feel an overwhelming desire to write to everyone, speak to everyone I have ever known. Is there some kind of fever connected with childbirth? Am I confused? Whatever the case I will write how I feel.

My hope is that if I ever did wrong by anyone they will now forgive me, and I forgive anyone who ever did anything wrong by me.

I send my heartfelt thanks to my beloved Captain Robert Fitzroy for his unconditional kindness to me always. I thank the officers of the Beagle and Mr. Darwin who were so considerate to me.

I thank the Gore family for their tireless attention to all my needs. I thank the Carmelite sisters who, through their prayer and spiritual advice have brought me through these challenging days. I thank Maria who has put up with all my whims and never left my side over these last weeks. I thank Antonio who has guarded me night and day and stayed awake with me through the lonely dark nights. My gratitude goes out to both of them who prayed with me each day.

Antonio holds a letter for my adored and treasured Captain Fitzroy. In my acute anxiety I have written a letter to Mother Monica. Please God there will be no need for Antonio to deliver it.

My dearest love always to our beloved little baby whose love and innocence I trust to God and the holy angels. May God in his mercy take care of our little darling child.

My dearest love to all who read here,
Scarlett.

TELL

Harry finished the diary and wiped the tears from his eyes. Then Lucy read the final section and cried. Harry explained what had happened to Bloom. Then he said,

'We know from the diary that Scarlett conceived a child, but that is all we know so far. Whether the child survived, or what happened to him or her later we do not know. To find out exactly what happened to Scarlett we may need to consult the records in the Carmelite Monastery in Montevideo, if it still exists. If the child survived we need to trace that genealogy through to the present day.'

'I will look on the net and see if we can find the Monastery. Do you think that you and Lucy should take a trip to Montevideo?' Bloom asked.

'Is a trip necessary Harry?' Lucy asked.

'Yes. We need to see and copy the documents there to take back to Coutts Bank.'

Bloom switched on the laptop and within a short while said he had found the monastery.

'How about you and Lucy get ready to go to Montevideo, and I will arrange the flights, take you to Heathrow and drive back to Sussex.'

'No Bloom you need to come back here and wait until Dermot is released. If we find what we are looking for in Montevideo we will need you both here.'

Bloom began to book the flights, print out the tickets and the boarding passes. Lucy rushed around the boutiques in the hotel and bought all she needed for the trip.

Harry and Lucy were ready in the foyer and decided to wait in the Coffee shop. They instinctively moved to the booth where Goldberg had taken Lucy.

'Are you sure you are up to this trip, Lucy?'

'Don't worry about me Harry, worry about Goldberg and Reed.'

'Yes, well we may have set them back for a while.'

'Harry if you had not been able to work out where I was…under Tower Bridge and if Bloom had not been able to overpower Goldberg's man, I hate to think what would have happened to me.'

'Bloom's an expert you know, ex Naval Intelligence… the best in the world.'

'You are not too bad yourself either Harry!'

Harry smiled, put his hand in his pocket and took out Lucy's ring. He handed to her.

'You remembered I invariably meddle with the sugar.'

'Yes but I wondered if you would you get the gold connection. I should have known you would Harry, and maybe one day I will be able to tell you about this ring.'

Lucy put the ring on. Bloom came in and sat down beside them. He handed Harry two copies of the document taken from Goldberg's desk that Dermot had passed to him. It was a document written by Captain Fitzroy after Scarlett's death.

'I managed to trace the estancia where Scarlett lived through the office of the Charge D'Affaires.' Bloom smiled and looked pleased with himself.

'The mansion is now a hotel, I have booked you both in, and the Monastery is there, only a few miles away.'

'Excellent'

'You are leaving in three hours for Buenos Aires, and taking a connecting flight to Montevideo. No direct flights. I have all the paper work ready except... do you have your passport Lucy?'

'Yes I do.'

Bloom stood up.

'Have you checked the weather, Bloom?'

'Yes sir, no foreseeable delays.'

For a while Lucy seemed in a trance and Harry was beginning to wonder if the ordeal under Tower Bridge had been too much for her. He should have taken her to Harley Street, made sure she had properly recovered, but there was so little time left to solve the problems. He began to speculate...perhaps they were all insane following up these events, knowing that it would be almost impossible to stop Reed...after all he was a member of the Cabinet. Then he thought of Fitzroy and Scarlett and knew he had to see it through.

Harry sat in the back of the Rolls with Lucy. Nobody spoke. There was a strange atmosphere. No one seemed to know how to react. There was the terror of what Goldberg and Reed could do, and at the same time the excitement of trying to outwit them both.

Harry was considering another matter, was he mistaken or did Lucy have feelings for him? He thought for the first time that she had. He knew that this was a flimsy hypothesis, but there nevertheless.

They pulled into the departure lane at Heathrow. Bloom went through all the documents one last time and handed them to Harry. He got out, took out the luggage, and called a porter.

'I will be at the hotel if you need me sir.'

'Thank you Bloom,' Harry said and Lucy smiled.

They checked through customs and into the VIP lounge.

'Do you need to buy anything Lucy?'

'No thanks Harry.'

They sat in silence and soon Lucy had put her head on Harry's shoulder and was fast asleep. Harry kept wondering what had happened that day that she could not tell him about. He realized that he had to wait until she was ready. He knew how impatient he was, but he would not let his impatience ruin something so precious as Lucy's affection and perhaps… the rest of his life.

Harry woke Lucy and they boarded the British Airways flight to Buenos Aires.

Soon Lucy was asleep again. Harry wanted to read Captain Fitzroy's letter carefully and slowly. He took it from his inside pocket and looked again at the exact, almost perfect, writing. He took the diary out of his briefcase and placed it on top of the letter. What prolific writers they both were!

He opened the diary and looked again at the close hand of Scarlett's writing. In a moment of turbulence the diary slipped off the table. Harry dived after it but it reached the floor before he could save it. He opened his seat belt, bent down and picked it up. He counted the pencil drawings and put them back in place and then he noticed that the inside back cover page had come away slightly. Harry ran his fingers along the back page and felt something folded underneath. How had he never noticed it before? He pulled the back page open slowly and there was a tightly folded sheet of paper. Harry's heart beat fast as he tentatively opened the page, and to his great delight he recognized Scarlett's handwriting. He felt a further surge of delight when he saw it was addressed to Fitzroy.

My beloved husband Captain Fitzroy,

It is obvious to me now my darling that I will not survive many more hours. I write in all haste to you my beloved, the joy, the raison d'être and supreme vocation of my life. My love for you goes on…on beyond the grave. You alone are my heart's desire and I long to be in your arms. Be assured that I wished to devote my entire life to you and that you and you alone have been the awe-inspiring influence on my adult life. Your gentleness and overflowing love for me is the one thought that gives me consolation at this time.

I can only imagine how sad you will be when you hear all that has happened in your absence. You, my love, who did everything humanly possible to keep me alive. Please I beg you do not set the blame at any one person's door. It was as if it was meant to be.

'Now more than ever seems it rich to die,
To cease upon the midnight with no pain,…'
I endlessly long for your presence; I wish only that you

hold me close and that I die in your arms. I do not know how I can do this without you my dear Robert. What is it like to be... no more? One conclusion I have come to, my dearest love, is that all love is filtered through the first love... the three- personed God, all love is a reflection of that first love. All love breathes life, you are every breath that I breathe, the light of my eyes, the beat of my heart, and even now I can feel new life that is yours and mine stirring within me.

Time and space keep us apart at this time but my noble and courageous Captain, if there is a chance that I will ever enter the realms of the Elysian heights, there will I pray for you and love you through eternity.

Promise me you will be happy. Promise me that you will remember me with joy not sadness. Promise me that you will never blame yourself for my death, as I know you will try to do. It is not your fault. You did everything you could to keep me alive and yet fate seems to have stepped in and outwitted us all.

We had our moment in time, we had all that life could offer, be it only for a short time, and we truly lived those idyllic days on the pampas. My dearest Robert during the suffering of recent months it was difficult to believe that they really happened,

'Was it a vision or a waking dream?

Fled is that music: - Do I wake or sleep?'

They did happen and I take them with me deep in my heart and in my spirit. Promise me that you will...

'Weep for me but one melodious tear' and then wipe the tears forever from your eyes.

With my last dying breath I will utter the Kyrie eleison, and my undying love for you.

*For ever
your beloved wife,
Scarlett.*

Harry remained for a moment or two unaware of the tears running down his cheeks. Then he reached for his handkerchief and as he did so Lucy opened her eyes,

'Oh Harry what is the matter?'

Harry said nothing. He handed her the letter. Lucy read it in silence and then tears came dripping down her cheeks. Harry handed her his handkerchief. Lucy wiped her eyes and reached out for Harry's hand. They held hands and looked into each other's eyes and for the first time they felt a marvellous union in mind and heart.

Lucy handed back the letter and Harry folded it up carefully and turned his attention to the document written by Captain Fitzroy.

27thth October 1833

Here sits the Captain of the Beagle in his cabin, broken and in deep sorrow. No matter how hard I try I cannot come to terms with your death my dearest love, my dearest Scarlett. My one duty towards you was to keep you safe, my beloved wife, so that we could both return to our native shore and live out a happy life together. In this I have failed.

When I think of the loneliness and pain you experienced in my absence my heart breaks and I am a man overwrought with pain and unable to comprehend that what began as a most exquisite union could end in such a way.

I arrived at the Estancia Dos Talas on Tuesday 22nd October 1833. My heart was happy and my spirits high. The

letters I had received from you were, as always, held on my person. Although I wondered why you had not continued to write I knew you were enjoying life. My choice of estancia for you was founded on the simple and ordered life I found in the Gore household, it's seclusion and nearness to the Carmelite Monastery.

When I entered the house that day and did not see you I assumed you were out riding…until I looked at the faces of Mr. and Mrs. Gore. My heart sank, as I imagined you were ill, but never for a second did it enter my head that something dreadful had happened to you.

They stumbled through their explanation of the events. I could not begin to understand what they were saying, and felt sure there was a mistake somehow. I asked them to excuse me while I spoke to Antonio and walked smartly out. He had seen my carriage and was waiting at the door. He looked at my face, fell on his knees and said,

'Mon Capitaine…it is true…Miss Scarlett, she is dead.'

I felt my knees weaken and I fell to the ground. I wailed,

'This cannot be, this cannot have happened…'

Antonio knelt down beside me..

'Why did you not guard her Antonio?'

'I did Mon Capitaine, even if you do not order I guard this woman with my life.'

You, Scarlett, who knows me so well, will understand when I tell you that I could not take this news in. My heart was beating so fast I felt on the verge of collapsing and the pain in my head throbbed with such severity that I thought my brain would explode. The tears ran on and on down my cheeks and my heart ached as if the pain would never cease and be there for ever. I tried to calm my spirits. I told Antonio to rise. He helped me to my feet and we walked towards a seat in the wood. I asked him to disclose the circumstances of your death, which he did, and to explain why I was not informed, which he did.

The news of these events brought me again to my knees… you had died in childbirth! Oh my beloved wife, how can I ever come to terms with these catastrophic events? How can this have happened? After some time I recovered a little and asked Antonio,

'Where is our child'
'I take the child to the Monastery.'
'Why to the Monastery?'
'Because I do what Miss Scarlett tell me.'
'Where is our child now?'
'I do not know Mon Capitaine, you must ask the sisters.'
'Is the child a boy or a girl Antonio?'
'A beautiful little girl sir.'

Oh Scarlett! Why did you not inform me about the child? I know Scarlett that you believed you had good reason for withholding this information. However I was unable to focus on the child at that time. I could not centre my mind on it because it is your death that crushes me and tears me apart body and soul.

Antonio helped me to my feet again and I sat on the seat. I stayed still for so long that no circulation of blood seemed to pass through my body and I was a dead man in everything but name.

Never once, my dear wife, did I think that you might have conceived a child and I ask myself constantly, why did I not think of leaving instructions for your treatment in the event of any indisposition. This was a grave mistake on my part and now my neglect is tearing me apart. Then Antonio handed me your letter. I opened it with much trepidation. It seemed all too short, my dearest Scarlett. I was heartbroken for at that moment I wanted reams of pages, I wanted enough pages to last the rest of my life…

Harry put the letter down for a few moments. He felt extremely sad. How did Scarlett die? Why did she die? She was only in her twenties.

He began to reflected on Fitzroy then and how Scarlett's death had devastated him. He had probably only shared this news with Darwin, or possible with Sulivan, and there again only partly for he had never disclosed his marriage to a living soul because it was Scarlett's wish.

Unable to share the whole truth with anyone, except his dear sister Fan who was thousands of miles away, he picked up a pen and wrote this letter, perhaps to keep all the events in sequence and perhaps to relieve his heavy, hurting heart. He would not then have known nor understood the therapeutic effect of such an exercise. Perhaps in some small way it did relieve the pain.

Fitzroy continued,

Oh Scarlett! Your letter broke my heart in two. Why could I not have been there for you? Why did you suffer so much? Why did you die so young, so beautiful…'

I sat there unable to move for what seemed like an age. When Antonio asked me a question I did not comprehend it. I walked back in a trance to the house and stood for a while outside looking up at the Estancia Dos Talas. For a few moments I shared your love of this house. I went in and apologized to Mr. and Mrs. Gore for my prolonged absence and said the shock was too great for me to absorb all at once.

They were full of compassion and apologies. Mr. Gore assured me that he had arranged for you to have everything you needed and had engaged the best doctor and gynaecologist for the confinement. I thanked him. I took your advice Scarlett and put the blame at no one person's door and so I told them how grateful I was for their concern. Of course it was not their fault.

'Will you visit the Monastery Captain Fitzroy?' Mr. Gore asked.

'Yes indeed.'

'May we offer you a carriage or a horse sir?'

'A horse, if you please.'

'Antonio has one ready whenever you wish to leave Captain.'

'Thank you.'

I took my leave and rode out with Antonio to the Monastery. I knew how much you loved the freedom of the wide-open spaces of the pampas. Now as my heavy heart aches I know we will never ride through them together again.

'Miss Scarlett speak Spanish very well now. She learn all the time.' Antonio blurted out.

'Did she speak about me?' I asked. He hesitated,

'You Captain, you are the only love of her life. She tell me never to speak about marriage to any person because of your rep...rep...u...'

'Reputation'

'Yes sir. She say nothing must ever taint your rep...u...ta...tion sir, because you the most honest and noble man she ever know. When many months pass she tell Mr. and Mrs. Gore and tell them to keep secret. She want you be free now in world and begin new life.'

'I can't think of any life without her Antonio.'

'Miss Scarlett she tell me when she know about baby she write long letter to you. Next day she think for long time and tell me what she want me to do.'

'What?'

'Now she ask, how could the Captain, whose marriage is a secret, then say he had a child? What kind of life could this child have?'

'Antonio I want my child. How could she think like this? There was something wrong with her thinking. She was ill, and I can tell you now I am not leaving this place without my daughter.'

'You think like this Mon Capitaine but this not Miss Scarlett's way.'

'How dare you tell me what is or is not my wife's way. It is my way and you will keep a civil tongue and obey my instructions in this matter.'

'Yes sir.'

There was a long silence and we rode on. Then Antonio ventured,

'Mon Capitaine you may wish to do something different from Miss Scarlett, but I think you know she very clever woman, and she look way, way into the future, and she tell me even when she dying not to tell you she dead, and she tell Mr. Gore the same.'

'However, I should have been informed.'

'No Mon Capitaine, Miss Scarlett say when you come here in place where you both so happy this give you courage to face her death.'

I was silent then and we rode on. When we reached the monastery I entered the little chapel, found a pew and sat. Antonio came in and sat behind me.

'Where did my wife sit?' He pointed to the seat near the statue of the virgin. I went there and sat. I remembered then our wedding day, that wonderful day. Oh my God, how you loved me Scarlett! How could you have had such love for me? I remembered then the music, the melodious voices of the sisters and the scent of the lilies filling the air. The tears came into my eyes, when I thought of how beautiful you looked and how I loved you with all my heart and soul.

Another wave of sadness came over me then as I recalled that on the ship you sang for me Mozart's 'Laudamus te' and Schubert's 'Ave Maria'. When I think of all the time I wasted reprimanding you when I was mostly the offender, expecting a young beautiful lady with a free and enquiring spirit to take orders. Forgive me. Before Antonio left he said he would take me to see Mother Monica whenever I was ready.

I sat there for a long time and, God be praised, in the silence Scarlett I felt close to you and a real calmness came over me. I began to feel thoroughly free, a freedom I had not experienced since our wedding day. I prayed, thanking God for your life and for the privilege I had of knowing you, of being your husband and of experiencing the overwhelming love you had for me, a love, as I often told you my darling that was beyond my understanding.

I felt renewed and left the little chapel in a better frame of mind, better able to endure the pain of your tragic death. Antonio was waiting. He said I could not enter the enclosure and must walk to the back door and ring the bell. This I did and Mother Monica came to speak to me.

She told me, Scarlett of her great affection for you and she said your love for me was a gift from God. I must see it *as a gift now and remember it as such; a gift that physically has gone but yet will last forever.*

She gave me the wooden box. She offered me her condolences in my grief.

'Will that grief ever leave my heart do you think?'

'Yes it will and it must. It was Scarlett's dying wish that you have a full and happy life. You would not deny her dying wish?'

'No, I will comply with her wishes in so far as I am capable.'

Then I asked about the child. She said it was a little girl and upon Scarlett's instructions she had been taken back to England and was adopted by a distinguished aristocratic family.

'This cannot be. Why would Scarlett do such a thing without my permission?'

'Because my dear sir she knew how important this voyage is to your life and your career. She knew how much it occupied your mind and heart and how you prepared and indeed even now conduct its progress as we speak.'

'All this is truth of a kind Mother but I assure you my career could never come before my own daughter.'

'My dear Captain have you any idea how much Scarlett loved you? She knew that you would not hesitate to give up the voyage and take your child back to England. But she knew that that would be fatal to all your life's work, and there is no reason why, in the future that your own daughter will not come to you.'

'No. I want my daughter now. She is all I have, and all I have left of Scarlett you might say, and what Scarlett died for.'

'Sir, may I ask you to imagine the pain Scarlett suffered knowing she would never see you or her child again? For *this reason alone could you try to comply with her wishes?'*

'Certainly not. I could never consent to such a request.'

'Captain Fitzroy I beg you. I assure you. You have my word that your daughter is safe and happy and having a very good life.'

'No.' I walked away. Why did I have to give up my child? Then my heart broke again as I knew Scarlett was right. If I left the voyage, my career in the Royal Navy would be over. I fell on my knees and prayed. I asked God why such distressing decisions had to be made. I knew even in my anguish that common sense had to prevail, and so after some time I conceded.

'Very well Mother, I very reluctantly agree. May I know now where my child is?'

'Will you allow me to write to you upon your return to England and furnish you with all the details?'

'You refuse to tell me now. Can you not imagine my concern for her everyday care?'

'Let me assure you that the child is in one of the best homes in England. She is looked after as a member of that family. You need have no anxiety Captain, on her account. As I am sure you do not know how many years this voyage will take, can you not agree to wait until your return home to know where she is living?'

'Very well, I will wait to hear from you... and thank you Mother for all you have done. Kindly forgive my incivility, I am not myself today.'

'It is a service I did very willingly, sir, for the respect and esteem I hold for you, your deceased wife, and for your child.'

She then gave me her blessing and I left carrying the wooden box. The box I had given to you a long time ago.

My belief in God has always been an important aspect of my life and I cherished it now the more, and valued the prayer and support of these contemplative women.

Antonio opened the large Iron Gate to the cemetery and pointed to the grave. He took the box from my hands and handed me a yellow rose.

'Miss Scarlett' he said with tears in his eyes, 'she love yellow roses.'

'I know.'

I took the rose and walked to the grave. I could feel a deep sadness come over me again in waves, and could not suffer for long the thought of your beautiful young body under the red, raw earth. There was a small gravestone with the date of your birth, 21st December 1807 and death 25th August 1833. Twenty-five years old Scarlett, how could this have happened? My heart was breaking when I saw the words,

'Be still my soul: when change and tears
   are past,
all safe and blessed we shall meet
   at last.'

The tears sprang into my eyes, and I recognized the words of Katharina von Schegel. I felt they were for me alone my Scarlett. I began the Pater Noster… then… I felt you were saying to me,

'Do not linger here my dearest Robert, be happy, and remember me alive not dead.'

I kissed the rose, put it down and walked slowly away. Antonio had the horses ready. We mounted and walked on.

'Were her sufferings great during the last days Antonio?'

'Yes very bad. Since this baby begin Mon Capitaine I sleep now by her door at night. How she live I know not, she only eat apples, drink tea and water. Maria come at six

and when she wake we say Rosario.'

'This is a prayer to the virgin?'

'Yes. Last days I go for doctors...they come each day... can do nothing. After three terrible days of pain the baby born. Next day, Miss Scarlett she die. She hold baby very close in her arms in bed and kiss baby on forehead. She hold hand of Maria.

Mrs. Gore she cry. Miss Scarlett tell me, in Spanish, make sure to take letter to nuns, and to kneel by end of bed, pray until she go. This I do. The Abbe come give her holy sacrament, then she die...like fall asleep. Doctor say she dead, and time just after midday. Doctor leave. Everybody very quiet nobody speak. Maria sob quietly. The Abbe say last prayers and Maria and I give answer. Everybody quiet, Abbe leave. Then Maria carry baby out of room. I go to nuns with letter. They tell me bring baby to Monastery. At three o'clock I take Maria in carriage with baby to Monastery.'

When I could speak I said,

'Thank you Antonio for all you did.'

'You no thank me Mon Capitaine I do anything for Miss Scarlett.'

We went on quickly then. When I reached the Gore's estancia I went in and thanked them for making your last days as good as possible Scarlett. I asked them if it were possible for me to see your room. I saw where you wrote your letters to me, the view from your window, where you sat on the balcony and the bed where you spent your last days on this earth.

After a few moments I walked out and said goodbye to the Gore family and to Antonio. I sent my best wishes to his father, and told him to thank Maria, and that I would not forget how both of them had been so kind to you my dearest love. I gave him two sums of money, one for his family for a year and the same amount for Maria. He reluctantly took them. I knew dear Scarlett this would be your wish as well as mine.

As I walked towards my carriage Antonio fell on his knees before me,

'Mon Capitaine I do only what she ask me, because she love you so much.'

'Yes she always knew what was best, Antonio.'

'Mon Capitaine, you all Miss Scarlett say of you…' he began to count on his fingers and repeat something he appeared to have learned by rote,

'She say, no more honourable, trustworthy, skilful man of science, and good Christian Captain ever stood on soil of South America.'

Antonio put the box in the carriage, bowed and moved away. I entered the carriage and headed back to the ship. I felt my whole life had finished. Of all the things that could have happened this was beyond what I could endure for the love of my life was dead.

Harry folded the letter. There was one more page. He would read it later. His esteem for the enigmatic captain was ignited yet again. He shared the pain and heartache Fitzroy had suffered when he found out that Scarlett was dead, and that his child had been given up for adoption. His admiration for him never faltered and he remembered again the feeling he had experienced, when for the first time, he had set eyes on the logbook of the second voyage of the Beagle.

SEARCH

THROUGHOUT THE FLIGHT TO BUENOS Aires Harry's thoughts were on Scarlett's child. He held an earnest hope in his heart that if there were any descendants they would be able to trace them. The plane landed very smoothly and Harry and Lucy alighted. The warm air of the tropics swirled about them. Harry took Lucy's hand as they walked down the steps.

He saw that the luggage was transferred to the small plane to Montevideo. It was a short flight and soon they were getting into the awaiting taxi. The driver drove fast. Harry tried to tell him to slow down, and then Lucy said,

'Disculpe, mas despacio por favor.'

'Si Senora.'

Lucy began to laugh.

'What?'

'Nothing Harry.'

'You never told me you could speak Spanish.'

'You never asked me?'

Harry looked out of the window. The cab driver was driving unbearably slowly now.

The sheer vastness of the landscape filled him with awe. The pampas spread out on every side as far as the eye could see. Harry looked out at the rolling grasslands interrupted here and there with shining blue lagoons, isolated ombu trees, and he was fascinated by the colourful birds. A sense of freedom immediately began to set into his consciousness and he felt a sense of serenity while he watched the vast cattle herds graze and move slowly in the distance under the immense blue sky.

Harry identified with Scarlett's feelings now, experiencing that sense of freedom she had described. For her it was much greater after the confines of the Beagle.

Soon they were on the old gaucho road where the jacaranda and ceibo tree blossoms were fading. They pulled off the road and into a long driveway. The parkland, cultivated for many years, was pristine, lush and mystical…just as Scarlett had described it.

The pines and palms seemed to reach to the sky, and then the house came into view. Harry's heart gave an extra beat as he tried to take in the sheer splendour of it.

The Estancia Dos Talas, a unique French-style mansion, emerged from the shade of lofty pines, shimmering in soft white bleached stone. The taxi pulled up and the driver took the luggage to the door. Harry handed him several notes. He smiled and said,

'Gracias Signor.'

Sara and Luis de Elizalde Luro, the fifth generation owners of Dos Talas greeted them on the doorstep. They were an erudite couple and as elegant as the surroundings. When he reached his room Harry immediately looked out the window, and wondered whether this had been Scarlett's room. He could see the driveway, the old gaucho road. He turned round to find Lucy at the door,

'Is your room ok Lucy? Would you prefer this one?'

'No my room is perfect, thank you. Harry shall we ride out to the Monastery now?'

'Will you be all right riding Lucy? I don't know how far it is.'

Lucy began to chat away to Sara in Spanish.

'They will have the horses ready in fifteen minutes,' Lucy smiled.

'Just time to change.'

Harry took out the third page of Captain Fitzroy's letter and read it as he waited for the horses.

You see my dear wife I was protecting you from the plotting of Sir William Knighton, about whom Lady Castlereagh had warned me. She was aware of his ambition and of his scheming treachery. I know you remembered something about this and I was not honest with you. Forgive me, for indeed I never wished your free and wholesome mind to be disturbed by the likes of Knighton.

The vagrant you spoke about had told the truth. Knighton had indeed sent two evil men to murder you. They assaulted you, and thinking you were dead, put your body in the rowing boat and pushed it out to sea in that dreadful storm. In so doing they hoped your body would never be found. By the mercy of God we found you, and you lived.

Upon reporting your presence on the ship to the Admiralty it seems that Sir James Graham, First Lord of the Admiralty, met Knighton at the Privy Council and mentioned to him the presence of a young lady on the

Beagle. Knighton, after questioning Sir Graham came to the conclusion that it was indeed you my dear Scarlett, who was on the Beagle. Having thought that you were already dead he now became very fearful. He somehow convinced Sir James Graham that it was expedient that he send two of his representatives to Rio de Janeiro to escort you back to England. He also convinced Sir James that all aboard the ship should take an oath never to reveal your identity. He sent out his murderers again, my dear Scarlett, and I was instructed to hand you over to them.

I met with them and tricked them into believing I had left you at Bahia. Only when I had seen them safely aboard a vessel for Bahia did I rest easy and feel you were safe. Even then I did not feel able to allow you to go ashore at Rio. Only for Lady Castlereagh, my aunt, and other social contacts that I have, I might have remained ignorant of all this plotting and, my dearest Scarlett, have innocently handed you over to them.

I began to think then of the many happy hours we had conversed here in my cabin. Another wave of sorrow seized upon me…knowing you would never be here again.

I sat up in deep thought all night and however hard I tried, my dear Scarlett, I could not reach a plateau of composure. I needed your quiet voice and gentle reasoning, my dearest love, to help me put the whole shocking occurrence into a proper perspective, and to calm my agitated soul.

Harry folded the letter and put it in his pocket. He walked out to the stables with Lucy and looked closely at the horse chosen for her.

'Ask him if it's a quiet horse Lucy.' Lucy asked.

'Yes Harry he is a quiet horse.'

'This gaucho's name is Eduardo, he will accompany us.'

They mounted and set out.

'How far is it?'

'About two miles, and this is too slow' Lucy said.

With that she took her reins and moved the horse in front of Eduardo. She trotted on and then broke into a canter. The two men looked at each other and moved into a canter behind her.

When they reached the town, Colonia del Sacramento Harry noticed that it was still the little sleepy town it had been when the Portuguese ruled it in the seventeenth century. Now it had become a UNESCO World Heritage Site. Soon they reached the leafy shades of the Plaza Mayor. Harry asked them to wait a moment and he dismounted. He walked over to a flower stall and bought a bouquet of yellow roses. He jumped back up on the horse and Eduardo slowly led them to the east side of the square and the Iglesia Matriz, and Harry remembered it was the oldest church in Uruguay. They all dismounted. Eduardo took the horses and said,

'The Monastery is a little far back in the grounds.'

They made their way there.

'Look Harry, the rococo walnut doors Scarlett wrote about.'

'Still intact' Harry said.

They rang the bell. Lucy asked to see the prioress. Lucy introduced herself as Miss Harrington who had telephoned from England. The sister's voice was clear, she was sorry but the gentleman could not enter the enclosure. However there was a room at the back of the building which they could use for the interview.

'If you go there, Mother will come and speak to you.'

They walked round the back. A new extension had been added to the main building. The door opened and they went in.

'You are very welcome,' an alarmingly young sister smiled at them and Harry wondered if she could be the prioress.

'Thank you' Harry said as he put the bouquet of flowers on a long oak table.

'I am mother Bernardo, and how can I help you?'

'We have come to ask if we could consult the convent archives Mother.'

'With regard to...'

'We would like to trace a Mother Monica who was in charge here around 1833.'

'Are you looking into some particular event in history?'

'Well in a way, yes Mother,' agreed Harry.

'By any chance has it anything to do with a young lady called Scarlett?'

'Yes Mother it has and can you help us?'

'Oh! Indeed we can. Scarlett's story is a kind of a legend here among us. Now Sister Veronica is in charge of the archives. I will ask her to bring along the documents. I will also accompany her as her English is a little shaky.'

'Thank you Mother' Harry stood up. He looked at Lucy,

'Did you notice her calmness Harry? And a kind of childlike happiness.'

The nuns returned and Sister Veronica set out the documents. She looked at Harry,

'What is it you like?'

'Lucy…can you tell her what we need.'

'We need a birth certificate, a baptismal certificate, and above all details of where the child was sent to in England.'

Sister Veronica laid out all the documents in front of them.

Lucy picked up the certificates, and Harry picked up the long document about the baby.

It was dated August 25th 1834 and read,

'I take up the pen on the anniversary of dear Scarlett's death to bring the archives up to date. Today I put yellow roses on her grave.

I, Mother Monica am the niece of the twelfth Duke of Norfolk. I applied to him for his help and protection for Scarlett's baby, Roberta Marie. This pledge he gave in the covering letter enclosed.

Roberta was taken to England in the spring of 1834, and entered the household of the Duke of Norfolk. He legally adopted her and she was henceforth known as Lady Roberta Howard.

January 1837

Today I have received a welcome letter from Captain Fitzroy to tell me of his return to England after his circumnavigation of the globe in the Beagle. I rejoiced for his safe return and thanked God. My poor Scarlett would have rejoiced, for she more than anyone prayed for his safety.

He asked for the name of the family with whom his daughter resided. I replied to his letter and told him the name of the household where his daughter lived. I also asked him to consider his late wife's wishes in the matter.

June 1854

Today I have received a letter from Capitan Fitzroy.

Harry asked if could see the letter. Sister Veronica took a few moments to find it.

It was dated June 1854 and read:

Dear Mother Monica,

My sincere greetings to you and to all the sisters. I trust you keep in good health and spirits. I write with great joy in my heart to tell you that at last I have seen my own beloved daughter, Roberta Marie. There is no way I can express the joy that some time ago filled my heart one Sunday afternoon when she came to visit me.

When she walked into the room I thought my mind was deceiving me, for there stood before me... Scarlett. My knees gave way and I fell back into my chair. She came immediately to me and put her arm around me and said,

'Oh! My dear Captain Fitzroy, please remain seated, you have had a shock.'

She resembled Scarlett in every way, even her voice was Scarlett's voice, and the ease with which she dispensed with protocol ... well it was the same. Here was my own daughter who had now grown into a beautiful young lady.

Roberta asked me many questions about her mother, and I gladly told of Scarlett's beauty, her love of literature and poetry, her musical talents and above all her sense of justice. Then she told me about her life. She said,

'I have been reared and have lived all my life in the household of the Duke of Norfolk. Never has anyone even hinted that I was not part of the family. Then sir, last week I brought a certain young man to meet the Duke and asked his permission to marry. This he gave gladly, but asked the

young man to leave us alone for a short while, as he needed to speak to me privately. He told me that I would need a baptismal certificate for the marriage and that this would be found in Monte Video.

He said his father had adopted me and he in turn had continued the adoption. He said it was all a very private matter, and that it could not be spoken about to anyone, with one exception…one person only, you, Captain Robert Fitzroy…I know now sir you are my father.'

'I am indeed' I said, and again she came to me and embraced me. She took from her bag a small gold locket and passed it to me.

'The Duke gave me this. It is a locket my mother had placed on me when I was a baby.'

I opened it carefully. On one side was an icon of the Virgin Mary. It read Mary of Mount Carmel. On the other side was a sketch Scarlett had made of me, and a few strands of Scarlett's own beautiful hair. The tears came into my eyes.

Roberta asked how her mother and I had met and whether we loved each other. I assured her that we loved each other dearly. I told her how amazed I was that Scarlett had chosen me. She was so beautiful she could have had her choice of aristocratic wealthy suitors.

'Did you ever see me when I was a baby Captain?' she asked.

'No. I did not have that pleasure. You had been sent back to England before my return to Monte Video.'

'Would it be possible for me to call you father sir?'

'It would fill my heart with joy Roberta if you would do so.'

She left her seat again, came and put her arms around

me in a most affectionate way. She placed her hand on my face,

'I wholeheartedly agree with my mother's choice Captain, what a wonderful man to have for my father,' she whispered.

I then knew that Scarlett was right. This young lady has had a most privileged life, one I could never have given her, and her affection for me now touched my heart.

'Should we keep our secret father, or would you prefer…'

'Your mother always knew what was best Roberta. For that reason I think it best we keep our secret.'

'Very well, as you wish father.'

I took the box Scarlett had left for me out of my desk and opened it. I then asked Roberta if she would like to keep something belonging to her mother. She looked at everything carefully. She flicked through the pages of the diary. Then she picked up the little replica linnet with the wind up mechanism that I had given to Scarlett as a wedding present. She asked if she might keep it. I gave it to her with great love and affection.

Rather shyly she asked if she might introduce her fiancé to me. She called him and a tall very handsome young man came in. She introduced him as William Johnson, an assistant master at Eton College. He was charming, polite, and indeed, in my opinion a very intellectual person. It was evident that they were devoted to each other. My dear Scarlett would have been happy for them both.

I did not see fit to tell her that over the years I had known where she was and had often longed to visit her, but that I kept to the wishes of her mother, my beloved Scarlett, in this matter.

The wedding is planned for August and no doubt in time you will hear from Lady Roberta yourself, Mother.
With every good wish,
Robert Fitzroy.

Harry looked up.

'We need to go,' said Lucy.

'You need these documents for some important reason?' Mother Bernardo asked.

'Yes we do Mother.' Harry looked at her with a question in his eyes and a doubt in his heart.

'You may take what you need and later return them to us.'

'But Mother you have only just met us?'

'I trust you Harry, and you Miss Harrington. Do you think I can not see in your eyes your honesty and your great regard for one another?'

Harry looked at Lucy and she looked at Mother Bernardo.

'We are most grateful to you Mother and I give you my word they will be returned intact.'

'Would you like to see Scarlett's grave before you go? I see Harry you have brought the yellow roses for her.'

'We could not leave without seeing it Mother.'

'Here is the key to the cemetery. Just put it at the door when you are finished. Whatever it is you are trying to do, I give you both my blessing.'

'Thank you Mother.' Harry said, and Lucy echoed.

Lucy collected up all the documents and counted them.

They made their way to the cemetery. Harry opened the gate with the big key. They found Scarlett's grave.

They stood very still for a while. Tears filled Lucy's eyes. Harry put his arm around her.

'Oh Harry!' Lucy sounded so sad. 'This beautiful woman has been in this grave all these years waiting for someone like you Harry, someone brave enough, strong enough and determined enough to tell her story.'

'Thank you Lucy. Remember you played a big part in it all too, and Bloom.'

'No Harry, no one can ever take this away from you, this is your find, your hard work, your perseverance.'

He drew Lucy close to him.

'Do you know any prayers Harry?'

'Shall we say a silent prayer, that here where my much-loved Scarlett is buried and where Captain Fitzroy stood, we too stand now and thank God for both their lives.'

They stood in silence for a long time. Then Harry kissed the roses and placed them on the grave. He looked at the words…'all safe and blessed we shall meet at last'

'Rest now in peace my dear Scarlett, rest in peace.'

They returned the key, collected the horses, and rode back to the estancia. Lucy went straight away to the laptop and within several hours had traced Roberta Marie Howard Johnson's family tree. When she had it all worked out Harry emailed it to Bloom. Bloom acknowledged receipt of the email and said that Dermot had been released. Harry replied and told him that he and Dermot should set out to collect the required items of information from the following places: Arundel Castle, the Kew Archives and to Oxford…well just outside Oxford, to the little village of Broadwell. There he was to find Doctor Robert Howard, a doctor of physics and an Oxford don. He typed in the address. He was to meet them at Heathrow at 3pm the following day and they would all go directly to Coutts Bank.

Harry and Lucy spent a delightful afternoon exploring the grounds. They had both missed so many meals over the past days they were very hungry and allowed themselves to indulge in the extravagant food served for dinner.

As the evening sun began to fade they rode the horses out again in the opposite direction to the town, down the old gaucho road and out unto the plains. They observed the clear water lagoons, the scarlet-headed blackbirds, herons, storks, toucans and in the distant sky the peach and crimson display of a flock of flamingos taking to the air. The air was clear and entrancing. The distant call of the gauchos, the slow movement of the herds combined to create an other world atmosphere. A world Harry thought he could take to very easily.

Early the following morning they set out for the airport and their flight back to London.

Return

The flight from Buenos Aires landed at Heathrow on time. Bloom waited impatiently in the arrivals hall with a very non-communicative Dr. Howard. He seemed to think that Bloom was some kind of nut who thought he had found a treasure, but as all the documents seemed in order he agreed to go with him. Nevertheless he hardly took his eyes out of a book on nuclear physics.

Harry and Lucy approached the customs desk and as the officer looked at Lucy's passport he looked over and nodded at two plainclothes policemen. Harry could tell what they were a mile off. They came forward, took Lucy's passport and said,

'A warrant has been taken out for your arrest madam for crimes committed in this country against Sir Ronald Reed and Mr. Adolph Goldberg.'

'What do you mean? They committed the crime, they tried to kill her.' Harry raised his voice.

Harry looked at the warrant, and asked to see their badges. All seemed authentic.

'Its all right Lucy, don't worry, I will call the lawyers… we will have you out in no time.'

He put his arm around her.

'Yes Harry…but…where are you taking me?' Lucy asked the thickset man standing too close to her.

'To Scotland Yard Miss'

Lucy's eyes opened wide,

'Again' she said.

Harry picked up the briefcase.

'Lucy…' he called after her,

'Don't worry…I'll be fine.' she said quietly.

They led Lucy away and Harry proceeded through customs and into the arrivals hall. Bloom came forward.

'Harry I saw them taking Lucy. She signalled to me not to approach.'

'They have arrested her over the incident at Goldberg's house. I will call the lawyers; we must not take our eyes off the ball. Whatever happens Bloom we must proceed to Coutts Bank. Have you collected Doctor Howard?'

'Yes, I suspect he thinks I am a madman…come and meet him.'

Bloom made the introductions and they walked through the exit. Bloom brought round the Rolls Ghost and they climbed in. Harry dialled his lawyers, explained in detail about Lucy's arrest and to go to Scotland Yard.

He began to explain everything in more detail to Dr. Howard. Rob, he said 'call me Rob'. He told him that they had collected all the documentation and must get to the bank now as there was a deadline.

'Are you serious? You mean there is a fortune to be retrieved in our family name?'

'Yes there is.'

'Bloom, have you all the documents?' He passed them.

'Have you your passport Rob?'

'Yes' Bloom had made sure he was carrying it.

'May I see it?' He handed it over.

Harry opened the briefcase put all the documents in order. Bloom stopped the car outside Coutts Bank in Cadogan Square. Harry and Rob got out and walked towards the impressive doors.

'Let me do the talking, if you don't mind, Rob.'

'Gladly…to tell you the truth I can't believe what is happening. I feel that any moment now I will emerge from this state of consciousness only to be told that I am involved in some crazy Tarantino film!'

Harry smiled. He asked to see the managing director of the bank on a matter of urgency concerning a considerable fortune. They were ushered upstairs and after seeing several subordinates Harry eventually saw Lord Bergin, the managing director. His office was one of opulent luxury and sophisticated technology. Harry explained why he was there, set out all the documents and then sat back.

'I must inform you Mr…Mr…'

'Please call me Harry'

'Yes…Harry…that there has been a counter claim.'

'Do you mean by Sir Ronald Reed?'

'The very person.'

'Having studied the deeds extensively may I point out that Sir Ronald's claim can only proceed if the original recipient's descendants have not made a claim by the deadline. Here sir you have evidence before you of the authentic descendant of the original person.'

'Thank you Harry. I need some time now for my staff to look into these documents.'

'Thank you, we will wait'

'Yes I'll order some refreshments for you, please make yourselves comfortable, will coffee be acceptable?

Harry looked at Rob. He seemed extremely bewildered but replied,

'Very acceptable thank you.'

They waited and waited. Rob continued to read. Harry had browsed through the magazines and could not believe the bank staff were taking so long. Three times fresh coffee was served. Still they waited. At last, after three hours Lord Bergin came back with all the documents.

'These documents are all in order Harry but we need one more. We need a confirmation from the present Duke of Norfolk that Doctor Howard is in fact the direct descendant of the said Scarlett O'Mara.'

'We have his signature on another document here' Harry moved towards the papers.

'Yes, but to be absolutely certain Harry, I do hope you understand, we would like the Duke's signature to a letter that actually approves Dr. Howard's claim.'

Harry was silent, and a few beads of perspiration appeared on his forehead.

'You have until noon tomorrow Harry.' Lord Bergin said with a smile.

'Yes I am aware of that. We will be back before noon tomorrow.'

Harry stood, collected the documents and left the office. He felt so frustrated he wanted to scream. If he had left everything until tomorrow they would have lost the legacy. He called Bloom and told him to bring round the car.

'Bloom was the Duke at home when you went to Arundel Castle?'

'Yes'

'We all need to pray that he is still there, otherwise we will not be able to make the claim.'

Harry stood on the sidewalk, found the number and dialled.

'Good afternoon, I'd like to know if the Duke is in residence?'

'Who is enquiring?'

'It is Harry, you saw a Mr. Bloom a few days ago regarding a legacy?'

'Oh yes. Yes he is in residence Mr. Harry.'

'Oh thank God. Would it be possible to see him or at least obtain his signature on a letter?'

'Hold on a moment please...yes I think you may see him.'

'We are in London, may we see him in just over two hours?'

'He will be expecting you. Goodbye.'

'I am sorry Rob but we have to go to Sussex now to collect this final signature.'

'Harry, I am expected at the University, I can't just go off to Sussex.'

'Doctor...Robert, Rob, this fortune is in the region of two hundred million pounds, and there is jewellery and I don't know what else. Surely for the sake of your family you will wait for one more day so that we can secure it for you?'

'Is this some kind of hoax Harry? If it is… fine, just say so now and I will go back to Oxford and say no more about it.'

'Rob, I have spent the last year of my life trying to secure this fortune for you.'

'Well I am very grateful.'

'There are other ruthless people trying to steal this money and if you do not cooperate they will steal it from you. I am only asking you to bear with us until noon tomorrow. That is the deadline. If we can't claim it by then they will, believe me.'

'I'm sorry if I sound ungrateful, but you must understand this is very hard to believe. However I will do as you say, I will call my wife and the University.'

'Thank you Rob, here comes the car.'

'Back to Arundel Castle please Bloom.'

They climbed in, Bloom steered the Ghost carefully through the London traffic and onto the M25. Rob made his calls. Harry composed the letter to the Duke and printed it out in the car. Harry's phone rang. He answered. It was the lawyers, to confirm Dermot's release and to say they were doing their best to have Lucy released soon.

'Sir, we have company' Bloom remarked.

Harry looked behind and there following them in a 4 x 4 was Goldberg, Reed and the two men in black suits. For a few moments Harry considered what best to do.

'Bloom speed up and then move carefully into the inside lane and take the next exit.'

'Very good sir.'

It looked at first as if Bloom had lost them, but as they made the exit Harry saw the driver of Goldberg's car scramble frantically across the lanes to the same exit amid the blowing of horns, and no doubt a few choice words from Reed. Bloom made a quick entry into the traffic and on Harry's instructions exited into a B road and pulled over. Harry took the wheel.

Goldberg and friends had followed them down the B road and they were very near when Harry flung the Ghost into gear. Very soon the Ghost was flying along when Harry slowed to pull out onto the A27. He was lucky with a break in the traffic and in no time the car had settled into a smooth speed that Harry was sure was unique to the Ghost.

'We seem to have lost them sir.'

'No, not yet Bloom'

Harry was right, within a few minutes Bloom muttered,

'I've just seen them sir, a good way back.'

Harry slowed the car and then turned it sharply into a driveway on the left. He speeded up until they were in front of an old Georgian House. Then he turned the car and waited. After a five minutes he eased the Ghost down the drive and back to the road. He steered the car out into the traffic and drove away in the opposite direction.

'Now we've lost them, Bloom.'

'Yes, but were we trespassing?'

'No Bloom. It's the house of an old friend of mine, Charlie Warner. He and I we were in the City together.'

All this time Rob had said nothing. Harry looked at him now in the mirror and asked,

'Are you all right Rob?'

'Well apart from not having a clue as to what is going on, yes.'

Soon they arrived at the little Sussex town of

Arundel. Harry's eyes followed the street of the quaint Victorian town with many buildings dating from the 18th century. The main street curved up a steep hill and there stood the Castle and the Roman Catholic Cathedral of Saint Philip Howard.

The flag of the Duke of Norfolk, Earl Marshal of England, was flying high above the turrets, and over the grounds of more than one thousand acres of parkland. They were announced and were invited to meet the Duke in his study. He was charming and said he had looked into the archives himself and had his staff trace the line down to Doctor Howard. He asked Rob about his work at the University and Rob told him how the research grants were being cut.

'Indeed' said the Duke.

'Perhaps you will be in a position now to rectify that.'

Rob looked astounded. He was in a daze; he waited every moment for someone to say it had all been a mistake.

'Would you be kind enough Your Grace to read and sign this letter for us?' Harry asked.

The Duke read through and signed.

'We are very grateful.'

'My pleasure Harry. I believe you have an estate at Amberley, a charming village which I like very much.'

'It is very appealing Your Grace.'

'Well I wish you and Dr. Howard every success.'

'Thank you again Your Grace.'

Back in the car Harry tried to call Lucy, but was told she was not allowed any calls. As they drove back to London Bloom was at the wheel again. He passed to

Harry a small photocopy of an extract from the Times dated, 10th February 1837 that he had found. It read,

'There was an incident at the Garrick Club last evening involving Captain Fitzroy, who has recently completed a circumnavigation of the globe. He challenged the Viscount Murdock to a duel, and when the Viscount refused Captain Fitzroy called him an appalling coward, and ordered him to step outside. When the Viscount refused to do so the Captain said he would strike him on the spot, which he did, knocking him down and giving him a bloody nose and a black eye.

Captain Fitzroy was asked to leave. He sent his apologises to the members, and said that never before in his life had he had the misfortune of having to deal with such a contemptible man. What the origin of the dispute was remains a mystery.'

Shock

They all spent the night at the Savoy and the following morning, 9th June 2010 at nine o'clock Bloom left the hotel with the documents in a briefcase. He was on his way to collect the car. Harry and Rob waited for him on the street. Then Harry's heart almost stopped. He saw Goldberg and his two bodyguards walking towards them. He grabbed Rob by the arm and said,

'Run, don't ask any questions, just run.'

They ran, first out into the Strand and then made for the Mall. Harry was amazed at the swiftness of Rob. He was not the kind of person Harry imagined would keep fit and yet he never faltered and ran like a professional runner.

Harry looked back. Yes they were pursuing them still. First came the two bodyguards and then he saw Goldberg a long way back getting into a car. When they reached St. James's Park Harry slowed down.

'We need a breather,' he panted.

'Who are these people?' Rob asked

'Tell you later, lets go, here they come.'

They sprinted along the grass and Harry wondered if they would ever get to Cadogan Square without being captured. Then he heard a shot. He looked back.

One of the bodyguards was shooting at them. The next shot was aimed low and almost hit Rob on the foot.

'My god, they are gangsters!' Rob shouted,

'They are going to kill us.'

'Keep running' Harry shouted.

Harry's phone rang and in a few garbled words Harry explained the situation to Bloom.

At that moment a 4 x 4 pulled into the curb and Goldberg and Dixon got out. Dixon shouted,

'Stand still, or I'll shoot '

Harry and Rob kept running and a shot flew over their heads. Out of the corner of his eye Harry saw the Ghost pull up a few yards ahead and grabbed Rob by the arm. They both jumped into the car and Bloom pulled off at speed but not before a bullet hit the back window shattering it, then it flew through the car and lodged in the back of the passenger seat where Harry was sitting.

Harry looked back and saw that Rob had gone ghastly pale.

'It's all right Rob. We've lost them.'

'Harry they could have killed us!'

He did not answer. He took out his phone and dialled 999.

At Cadogan Square Harry took the briefcase. He and Rob got out of the car and walked towards Coutts Bank. Dermot was standing outside the bank.

'Dermot what are you doing here?'

'I thought it best to be here just in case Goldberg tried any last minute tactics.'

'Yes. He has been shooting at us in St. James's Park.'

At that moment the screeching of brakes was heard

as the 4 x 4 pulled into the square, pulled up in front of the Ghost blocking it in. Goldberg and the three bodyguards stepped out.

'Here they come Harry. You two better get inside the bank quickly. Bloom and I will deal with them.'

Harry and Rob hurried into the bank. Harry looked at his watch. It was almost 10 o'clock. Only two hours remained before the deadline. He hoped nothing else would go wrong. He checked all the documents they would need including the last one signed by the Duke of Norfolk.

They were treated lavishly, but it was a long time after the noon deadline before the money was transferred into the account of Doctor Robert, who looked as though he were about to faint.

'How can I ever thank you Harry?' was all he could manage to say.

'No thanks necessary. You and your family have what is rightly yours.'

It was suggested that they go below to the vaults to open the security boxes. They took the lift down. The locker was opened. There were three boxes. The first one was marked 'K' the second marked 'F' and the third was marked 'S'. They were placed on a table and the keys were handed to Rob. The assistant left.

The first contained diamonds and pearls left to Scarlett by King George IV. They gasped, and then there was silence as they gazed at the magnificent jewels. The second contained memorabilia from the estate of Maria Fitzherbert, including a priceless ruby necklace. The door opened, and the assistant in the dark suit stood in the doorway.

'There is a Miss Harrington here sir, may I show her in?'

'This young lady is my assistant, Rob.'

'Oh certainly, come in Miss Harrington.' Rob said.

'Lucy what did they do to you? Are you all right?' Harry asked.

Harry put his arm around her. He looked into her eyes and then her perfume drifted past his nostrils and he remembered the first day they met.

'I'm fine Harry, they dropped the charges as soon as the deadline passed.'

Harry smiled and said,

'Lucy this is Doctor Robert Howard…Scarlett's direct descendant.'

'How do you do?' said Lucy.

'Very well, and you? How can I ever thank you.'

'No need sir.'

Lucy and Harry exchanged glances. They both smiled as they read each other's thoughts. They had met and that was ample reward for them both. Harry put his arm around Lucy again.

'Well sir, shall we return to the Savoy and celebrate with some Champagne?' Rob asked.

'Certainly, but you haven't opened the third box Rob,' noted Harry.

This was the box marked 'S'. Rob opened the box. They all looked at each other.

All three drew in breath as they gazed into the box.

'What do we do now Harry?' Rob asked. Before Harry could answer Rob said,

'Harry here and now I bequeath this box to you. This is a mystery beyond my powers of comprehension.'

Harry accepted. They had all three boxes returned to the vault. They went back upstairs in the lift and Rob signed over the third box to Harry.

Outside in Cadogan Square there were three police cars. Bloom and Dermot were both smiling.

'We had quite a tussle with them Harry until the police arrived.' Dermot said.

'The police arrested all of them including Goldberg.' Bloom smiled.

'I am very relieved to hear it.' Rob stated.

'What about Reed, Harry? Will he get away with what he did?' Lucy asked

'He always manages to do that. However maybe this time he will get his comeuppance.'

Back at the Savoy they drank champagne. Doctor Rob spent some time on the phone. He thanked them. He told them that they would receive a substantial reward and that there would be a gift of some jewellery for Miss Harrington. Harry assured him that nothing like that was necessary.

'I insist old chap, I insist. Would you like to be my financial advisor Harry? I don't have a clue what to do with all this money.'

'No, I'm not sure I would be your best choice. You see it is ok taking risks with your own money but a different thing when it is someone else's money.'

'Harry, I would trust you with my life.'

Harry looked at him keenly and wondered if the bubbly was kicking in. It was obvious he was not used to…the drink.

'You couldn't ask for a more honest advisor, Rob,' interjected Lucy.

'It is settled then. I will catch the train back to Oxford.'

'I think, under the circumstances Rob you can afford a taxi.'

'Well…yes of course.'

They all laughed and made their farewells.

Renew

The following day Harry drove out to Paglesham and pulled up in front of an old Victorian house at Churchend. He rang the bell and waited. He felt nervous. There was a lot of noise inside the house and he remembered then how all the family came home for Sunday lunch. The door opened and a young girl said,

'Hello, who are you?'

'I'm Harry.'

As the news spread a rapid silence fell over the house and everyone seemed to move into the wide hall. Harry looked at brothers and sisters he had not seen for years and nephews and nieces he had never seen before. They all stared back at him. Then they stood aside as Harry's mother came from the kitchen and stood in front of him. Tears came into her eyes as she put her arms around him and said,

'Harry you have come home.'

While Harry held his mother in his arms, his father came to the door. He held out his hand and said,

'Good to see you, son'

Everyone started talking at once. One young boy of about three threw himself into Harry's arms and the reunion began. He listened to all the news of his siblings. True joy now flooded into his heart and the sad separation of the intervening years seemed to evaporate. The hours flew past and when it was time to go Harry experienced the warmth and affection of his family as they embraced and hugged him and pleaded with him not to leave. He said he would return soon but he had promised to meet Lucy. He left the house with a feeling of contentment and gladness that had eluded him for a long time.

He met Lucy in the late afternoon and they drove to Upper Norwood. On the way they stopped and bought a large bouquet of yellow roses. Lucy said she felt that Admiral Fitzroy's life had been eclipsed and overshadowed by events and that he had paid the price of always trying to do the right thing.

'He never bowed to political correctness or cultivated the right connections.'

'Because Lucy he believed that to serve the country was the highest calling of any gentleman, and he did so faithfully throughout his life.'

'In the end he paid with his life though.' Lucy said.

'Yes, and what is so sad Lucy is that even in the later years of his life when he worked at the Metrological Office of the Board of Trade, he was misjudged and undervalued. He felt his one duty was to save the lives of those at sea and he invented the weather forecast, barometers and a method of storm warnings that were crucial for the safety of sailors. But the Board of Trade shut down the office and broke up the equipment.'

'How could anyone not see that the weather forecast was a good thing?'

'Well they did eventually and opened the office

again two years later in 1867. The trouble with Fitzroy was that he often extended his brief because he was ahead of his time.'

'Well at least since February 2002 a sea area is called Fitzroy after him, the one who began the gale warnings in the first place, and it is the only maritime area to be named after a person.'

'That is a small token of respect for what he did for his country.'

'Nevertheless Harry I am sure it would have pleased him.'

'What would have pleased him Lucy was that his son gained the rank of Admiral and received a knighthood. Between the two of them, father and son they served constantly for over eighty years in the Royal Navy - that would have pleased him.'

When they reached Upper Norwood Harry parked the car and they entered the churchyard of All Saints Church. They found the grave of Admiral Robert Fitzroy and stood very still. Harry stretched over the rail and placed the flowers on the simple stone surface. The silence was broken only by the hum of distant traffic and the loud call of a blackbird.

'You will always be devoted to him, Harry won't you? He will always be your hero.'

'Yes, and my inspiration.'

'Scarlett could never have imagined what fate held in store for him.'

'No, and perhaps that was for the best.'

They stood close together. Harry reached for Lucy's hand, and in that tranquil setting a serene calmness came over him. His life had changed remarkably since he had found the diary. He felt unbelievably happy. He thought about Captain Fitzroy and Scarlett and then without warning some words of Shelley came streaming into his thoughts…and tears of joy appeared in his eyes…

'Forget the past, his fate and fame shall be
An echo and a light unto eternity!'

About the Author

Danny Devoy was born in Greystones Co. Wicklow Ireland. A graduate of London and Surrey Universities, and now residing in Sussex.

Lightning Source UK Ltd.
Milton Keynes UK
28 October 2010

161990UK00001B/4/P